D1072124

Donated
To The Library by

FRIENDS OF LIBRARY

**This Large Print Book carries the
Seal of Approval of N.A.V.H.**

CARELESS CREEK

**Center Point
Large Print**

CARELESS CREEK

Stan Lynde

CENTER POINT PUBLISHING
THORNDIKE, MAINE

This Center Point Large Print edition
is published in the year 2007 by arrangement with
Cottonwood Publishing, Inc.

Cover design: Laura Wahl
Cover photograph: Careless Creek, Montana,
by Lynda Brown Lynde´
Cover illustration: Jean Giraud "Moebius"

The text of this Large Print edition is unabridged. In other
aspects, this book may vary from the original edition. Printed in
Thailand. Set in 16-point Times New Roman type.

ISBN-10: 1-58547-944-6
ISBN-13: 978-1-58547-944-3

Library of Congress Cataloging-in-Publication Data

Lynde, Stan, 1931-
   Careless Creek / Stan Lynde.--Center Point large print ed.
      p. cm.
   ISBN-13: 978-1-58547-944-3 (lib. bdg. : alk. paper)
   1. Montana--Fiction. 2. Large type books. I. Title.

PS3562.Y439C37 2007
813'.54--dc22

2006033965

CARELESS CREEK

To my sisters
Chris and Lorretta,
whose unfailing love and support
have helped me to understand
what Grace is.

Table of Contents

ONE
A Gift Horse

The first time Old Walt set foot inside the Methodist church at Dry Creek, Montana, was the seventh day of June in the year of '84. Even then, he didn't set foot exactly. Old Walt was dead, you see, and he'd been brought to the church so he could attend his funeral.

I had known Walt most all my life, but I had never heard his full name until the preacher said it from the pulpit that day, and for a minute there I had no idea who that gospel-sharp was talking about.

"O God of grace and glory," he'd rumbled, in that somber, fakey voice some folks put on when they go to praying, "we remember before you today our brother, Walter Pettigrew Finkelman." If I hadn't known "Walt" was short for "Walter" and that nobody else in Progress County had died lately I surely would have believed I was in the wrong pew—so to speak.

The little church was nearly full. Townsfolk and ranchmen, merchants and gamblers, cowpunchers and punkin rollers, proper ladies and girls of the night had all come to pay their last respects. The Bible says in the Book of Somewheres that the rain falleth pretty much the same on the just and the unjust, but that morning had dawned bright and clear as birdsong, and that particular day it was sunshine which felleth, not rain. Sunbeams slanted in through the stained-glass

11

windows and lit up saint and sinner alike. I had to grin, thinking about Old Walt. He'd have been pleased by the turn-out, and plumb tickled by the democracy of it all.

Walt was an old-timer around Dry Creek, and he'd owned the Livery Stable and Wagon Yard since the town was just a pup. He'd been a good old boy with a world of friends, and even though I wasn't but a younker of twenty I counted myself among the foremost of them.

Two years previous, my Pa had got himself killed in a horse wreck over on our home place, and Walt had gave me a job at the Livery. I worked there nearly a month before I moved on, and later I came back and worked for him again off and on through most of '83. He'd been good to me, and I had liked the old gent a lot. Hell, I had more than liked him.

The day Walt died, I was breaking colts for Tom Gladstone at his place on the Little Porcupine, and soon as I heard the news I drew my time and lit a shuck for Dry Creek. By the time I hit town, Walt had been laid out over at the funeral parlor; and Ambrose, the undertaker, had combed, curried, and painted him up to where I hardly recognized him. Doc Taggart told me Walt had passed away "as a result of influenza and complications," but I reckon the old feller had just wore out and perished from living too much and too long.

Anyway, I set there in that crowded church and remembered Walt while the circuit preacher droned on about a man he never knew and about a place he'd never been—Heaven, I mean.

We buried Walt up on cemetery hill in a grave that offered a fine view of the valley and the snow-capped mountains beyond. I was glad about the gravesite; Walt had always enjoyed looking at mountains. Afterward, we all walked soft and cat-footed back down the hill like we was afraid we'd wake him up. Some of the boys headed over to the Oasis Saloon to lift a parting glass, and I was just fixing to join them when a stranger in a sack suit and derby hat crossed my path.

"Merlin Fanshaw?," he said, "I'm Lucius Sawyer, attorney at law. Can you spare me a moment of your time?"

I sized him up. He was a slim-built jasper, somewhere in his forties, with a tight smile and careful eyes. He sported gold-rimmed spectacles and a front tooth to match, and he held a leather briefcase in his left hand.

"Sawyer the *lawyer,* huh?," says I, "Sure, I'll give you my time, if you won't charge me for *yours.*" I was no stranger to the ways of lawyers, you see.

His laugh was a slim chuckle, short and polite. "Oh, my, no, Mr. Fanshaw, there's no cost to you," he said, "quite the opposite, in fact. I'm here to advise you of a bequest."

There was something in the way he looked at me that said he didn't figure I knew what a bequest was, and I took offense some because I didn't. The dude had called me mister, though, and I had never been mistered before, so I felt both offended and flattered at the same time.

"Well, then, *Mister* Sawyer," says I, returning the compliment, "why don't we go inside and discuss the matter over a beer? A man don't deal with one of them bee-kwists—beak-wests—what you said—every day, I reckon."

I led the way in through the swing doors and ambled over to where Boogles the bartender watched sleepy-eyed and sullen from the sober side of the bar. I put my elbows on the hardwood and laid down a dime. "Two beers," says I, "and where, can I ask, have you hid the free lunch?"

Boogles drawed the beers and cut the foam off each one with a flat stick. "You get no damn free lunch with two nickel beers," he said, "You know that, Merlin."

"What I know is you're so tight you squeak, but I hoped maybe you had reformed," I told him.

Sawyer and me took our beers to a table near the front window and set down. "Here's how," I said, and we clicked our steins and drank. The brew was cold, and I swallered nearly half of mine before I came up for air. Lawyer Sawyer took a dainty sip of his, covered his mouth, and stifled a genteel belch.

"As I said, Mr. Fanshaw, I'm here to advise you of a bequest. My client, the late Mr. Finkelman, has named you one of his legatees."

This Sawyer bird was commencing to irritate me some. He was flinging words at me aplenty, and while I was catching maybe one out of three, most of them

14

was flying over my head like geese going south. It seemed to me he druther talk fancy than straight, and I couldn't decide if he was trying to make me feel ignorant or if I merely was. Anyway, I ran his chin music through my mind, studying on it and trying to pick the nuggets out of the gravel, and slow but sure I began to pan out some color.

"Now hold on, pardner," I said, "are you sayin' Old Walt left me somethin' in his will before he took the big jump?"

"Yes, Mr. Fanshaw, I am. Are you familiar with a horse called Quicksilver?"

Well, of course I was. Quicksilver had been Old Walt's pride and joy, a five-year-old blood bay thoroughbred, pretty as a sunrise and fast as a random thought. Walt had set a world of store by that stud, and I confess I had coveted the horse some myself. "Yes, sir," I told him, "I know, and admire, the animal."

Sawyer moved his beer aside and set his briefcase on the table. "Then," he said, "I'm sure you'll be pleased to know that my client, the late Walter Finkelman, has bequeathed the horse to you."

Well, I ain't often speechless, Lord knows, but I surely was right then. Old Walt had long since hung up his saddle, but he had trusted me to ride and care for Quicksilver, and it had always been a pure-dee pleasure. I had rode the big bay in a half-dozen local races that spring, and no other horse even came close to matching his speed. While it lasted, Walt and me made some good money, but it didn't take long for

15

word to get around that if having too much cash was your burden the way to lighten your load was to bet some of it against Quicksilver.

I closed my eyes, remembering, and felt again the sudden surge of power as the big horse made his drive for the finish. I felt like I'd been shot from a cannon, and I could taste the wind and feel my eyes water from the speed. I could hear the crowd holler as we thundered across the finish line, and I could see Walt slap his skinny old thigh and flash me a gap-toothed grin of pure delight.

As I saw the old man in memory, my throat got tight and my vision went blurry on me, but it wasn't from the wind this time. After a bit, when I figured I could trust my voice, I lifted my stein and looked lawyer Sawyer in the eye. "Well, I'll be," I finally said, "Here's to Old Walt."

By the time I left the Oasis I had put away two more beers and had growed more sentimental with each one. I'd signed my name to all the legal paper Sawyer had stuck in front of me, and for his part the lawyer had gave me a bona fide bill of sale and title clear to the horse called Quicksilver.

I shook Sawyer's hand and high-heeled it up the boardwalk to the Livery, where I'd left my saddle-horse, Little Buck. Five minutes later, I was mounted and riding west on the road that led to Rolly Kincaid's ranch, the place Walt pastured Quicksilver.

I had no real plan at the time, but as Little Buck single-footed through the low hills a notion commenced to take shape in my mind. The singular nature of my windfall had by no means escaped me. I had just turned twenty, and of course pretty much figured I knew everything. I *didn't,* of course, but I was too green in them days even to know how ignorant I was.

All the same, I did know a thing or two about horse-flesh, even then. I knew Quicksilver was more than just another good-looking thoroughbred. The big stud was a racehorse, and a good one.

I had a little money put aside, maybe sixty dollars, plus another thirty I'd picked up breaking Gladstone's colts. It occurred to me that with a ninety-dollar stake and Quicksilver's long legs and mighty heart I could be well on the way to the making of my fortune. All I'd need would be a few well-heeled sporting gents with more cash than sense, and I knew from experience there were plenty of that breed. I also knew I wasn't likely to find them around Dry Creek. Walt and me had burnt the local horse-players pretty bad that spring. I figured the chances of getting a local bet against Quicksilver, even at long odds, would be somewheres between unlikely and impossible.

I decided I'd fetch the animal back to Dry Creek and work with him there until I judged him ready. Then Quicksilver and me would go out into the world and see if we could maybe find us a horse race.

Daydreams may not be good for much else, but they do have a way of making the time pass. When I got through building castles in the clouds and counting

17

my unborn poultry I had imagined myself richer than old King Midas, with a sixty-room mansion, servants and flunkies galore, and a stable of race-horses that was the envy of every high-roller and nabob in the nation. Fact is, I got so caught up in my wishful thinking that almost before I knew it I had topped out on the sandrock ridge that overlooked the Kincaid ranch. Minutes later, I headed down the long slope through the bunch grass and junipers and rode Little Buck through Rolly's front gate.

Rolly Kincaid's place lay spread across rolling meadows and bottom land at the foot of the sagebrush hills. Made up mostly of irrigated pasture and hay meadows, the ranch was small but well kept, and it boasted good grass and tight fences. Shining like polished silver in the late afternoon light, a slim, brush-lined creek snaked its way across the valley and divided the ranch. Rolly's house stood trim and fresh-painted at the end of a long lane, and his yard held a garden and a good stand of apple trees.

Rolly had been a particular friend of Walt's, and he'd provided pasture for Quicksilver for as long as Walt had owned the animal. A dozen or so pairs, cows and calves, grazed in the upper meadow as I turned Buck through the gate and down the lane. I saw no sign of Quicksilver, but I figured he'd likely be in the lower pasture where Rolly kept his own horses.

As I rode up to the house Rolly's cow-dog Fred flew out from under the porch like a whirlwind and barked at me like he'd lost his mind, and Rolly came out through the screen door and barked at *him*. Even though I had traded howdies with Rolly at the cemetery just a few hours previous, he grinned like he hadn't saw me in a month of Sundays. "Afternoon, Merlin," he said, "light, and come inside. Can you stay to supper?"

Well, I do like to eat, and I have almost never declined an invite to chuck it in. That being true, you can imagine how it surprised even me when I heard myself turn Rolly down. Until then, I hadn't realized just how caught up I was in the prospect of collecting my equine bee-quest.

"Much obliged, Rolly, but I'm here to fetch Quicksilver. Danged if old Walt didn't leave him to me in his will."

"Hell you say. That Walt. He was the pure quill."

"He sure was, both ways from his belt buckle. Fine funeral, wasn't it?"

"Dandy. Gave him quite a sendoff, didn't we?"

"Well, you know. Folks liked Old Walt."

"Left you Quicksilver, you say? I'll be damned."

"Yeah. He still in the lower pasture?"

"Was, Tuesday week. Seen him down by the crick."

"Well, then, I guess I'll go fetch him. Much obliged, Rolly."

Rolly was still standing there in front of his house when I rode across the lane and stepped down to open the gate to the lower pasture. Waving then, he turned and went back inside. He was quite a Rolly.

19

It was Little Buck, of course, that seen Quicksilver first. I had scouted the coulees above the creek and had just commenced to turn the buckskin downhill to hunt the bottoms when Little Buck lifted his head and stared with his ears at something I couldn't see. The little horse froze in his tracks, tasting the wind, and I stretched tall in the stirrups, trying to see what he saw. Then, of a sudden, he whinnied, high-pitched and piercing, and from somewhere below came an answer.

Quicksilver stepped out of the willows along the creek bank like an actor in a stage play, and he was a sight to make even a horse-hater catch his breath. The big stud was tall and long of leg, graceful as a swan, and the muscles of his forelegs and the stifles in back showed plain he was built for speed. Quicksilver had the long topline and the small, well-formed head of the thoroughbred, and the way the late sun brought out his rich, blood-bay color almost made it seem like he had a light on inside him.

I had been struck by his beauty when first I saw him, and his spirit and heart had won me over altogether when I rode him, but never in my wildest dreams had I thought he might one day be mine. Now he was, left me by a man who had been both boss and friend. I don't mind telling you, I choked up some just knowing what that said about Walt's feelings for me.

I stepped down off Little Buck and walked up on Quicksilver, talking low and telling the big stud how handsome he was. I held my lead rope and halter behind me, reaching out to him with my other hand while I spoke his name. He studied me with some suspicion until directly he caught my scent. Then he lowered his proud head and answered me with a deep-throated nicker that was more like the rumble of distant thunder. I slipped the halter on, and then, while I stroked his silky neck, broke it to him gentle about Walt's passing and who his new owner was. I have to say he seemed to take it pretty well.

By the time I brought Quicksilver up from the horse pasture Rolly was out in his yard again. His dog Fred didn't bark at me that time, either because he forgot or because he'd finally figured out he wasn't supposed to. Anyway, Rolly and me passed a few pleasantries for the sake of politeness. He told me a joke and I told him one, which of course reminded him of another one, which he then told me. We discussed the weather and the condition of the range, we talked about what a fine feller Walt had been, and we shared what news and general gossip we could call to mind. Finally, I bade him good day and turned my horses out on the trail back to Dry Creek. That fool Fred dog barked at me all the way to the end of the lane.

The ride back was a pleasant one. Little Buck fell into his steady, clean-footed trot and Quicksilver came along easy at the end of my lead-rope, long legs flashing and his gait smoother than oil. The day was all but done. Sunlight born that morning had waxed strong and bold through the day, but had turned feeble and mellow by evening, painting the high plains a soft gold that would soon turn dusty rose.

Above the ridge, mud swallows darted and dipped as they hunted bugs, and somewhere out in the high grass a meadowlark yodeled his clear, cascading song. Farther on, I spied a fine doe antelope and her new-born, the fawn nearly invisible in the high, green grass. The doe straddled her baby, licking it clean and bidding it welcome to the world. She looked up once as I rode past, but seemed to figure I was no threat and turned her attention back to her young'un. He'd be up on shaky legs and having supper before I was out of sight.

Atop the low hills, jackpine and scrub cedar had gone black as ink, their trunks and branches sharp and detailed against the bright sky, and it almost seemed I could count every twig and needle. Long shadows stretched off to the east, where the rising bulk of the Brimstone range caught the last light on its snowy peaks and flung it back with a flourish. I was about as happy as ever I get, even though I still felt sad about Walt's passing and knew I would miss him plenty in the days ahead.

Sometimes it seemed that everyone I'd ever cared about had died and left me behind. I grew up on a hardscrabble farm north of Dry Creek, and I'd lost my mother to consumption when I wasn't but ten. For awhile there I thought I'd lose my Pa, too; he took to drinking, fighting, and riding bad horses like he didn't care whether he lived or died. Looking back on it now, I don't believe he did care. I reckon he was trying to find some way to go where mother was, although I don't suppose whiskey, bar fights, and mean broncs ever got anybody through the Pearly Gates.

Anyway, Pa finally remembered he still had me to raise, and he sobered up, healed up, and came to himself. We took to running mustangs together out in the Brimstone breaks and gentling them fuzz-tails for sale to the local ranchers.

"Gentling" might be too strong a word. What Pa and me done was take the rough off them broncs and work them 'til they would abide a saddle and rider for maybe five or ten minutes. If anybody ever really gentled them maniacs it was somebody else, not us. The way I seen it then, a man might as well try to tame a lightning bolt.

It was while Pa was "gentling" one of them mustangs that he'd got himself killed two years before. A wild-eyed black stud horse had bucked off a rimrock with Pa in the saddle, and they had both died in the fall. It occurred to me at the time that if Pa did follow Mother's trail to Heaven he made the trip on a high-spirited black stud, anyway.

After that was when Walt gave me the job at the Livery. Since that time him and me had come to be close as family. Now Old Walt was gone, too.

But I wasn't feeling sorry for myself, nor did I aim to. Dying is a thing we all must do, and I was grateful I'd had those special folks in my life as long as I did.

23

It was coming dark by the time I turned the horses onto Dry Creek's main, and only, street. The evening star blazed cold and bright above the rim of the world, and overhead the sky still held a hint of color, the dull gray-red of a hot stove, but it was fading fast. A cool breeze had come up with the setting of the sun, and I heard, though I could not see, the pattering leaves of the big cottonwood trees that slouched along the thoroughfare. Lamplight burned low in the window of Ignacio's Cafe and, farther up the street, spilled out across the boardwalk in front of the Oasis, but the hitchracks were mostly empty. It looked to be a slow night in Dry Creek.

I took the horses around to the corral behind the Livery Barn and slipped my saddle and bridle off Little Buck. Well, of course he took that occasion to get down and waller in the loose dirt just to show me how happy he was to get shut of my rigging. Fool horse made the whole thing look so pleasurable I came near to trying it myself.

A smoky lantern hung from a wire just inside the barn's open door, casting yellow light and deep shadows out across the stalls, and I knew Bummer, the night man, was on duty. Bummer had what some folks call a drinking problem, which is to say he had a problem getting enough cash to keep on drinking. Walt had gave him a job when nobody else would, and Bummer had never let him down. The only time I'd ever seen Bummer in the daylight had been that morning at Walt's funeral. He'd stood there cold sober

24

by the open grave with tears a-rolling down his craggy cheeks, and I knew he was yet another of Walt's many friends.

Bummer was a big man, big-boned and broad-shouldered, and well over six foot tall. He had a beat-up, weathered face and the red-rimmed, sad eyes of a bloodhound. His shoulders slumped as if he was apologizing for being alive, and his bony wrists hung three inches below the ragged sleeves of his shirt. It seemed hard for him to look a man in the eye.

He shuffled out of the office and stood watching while I led Quicksilver inside.

"Hullo, Merlin," he said, "What you doin' with Walt's horse?"

"Walt left him to me, Bummer. In his will. Dangedest thing."

"Left you Quicksilver? My, that's fine, Merlin."

"I'll need a stall for him tonight, and one for Buck."

"He'p yourself, Merlin. You want me to cool 'em out?"

"No, I'll do it. I see there's horses in the other stalls."

Bummer rubbed the three-day stubble of his chin with a work-hardened hand and nodded. "Circle F riders, in off the roundup. Your friend Orville Mooney is one of 'em. Said if I seen you I was to say come on down to the Oasis and help him spend his wages."

I grinned. "Reckon not. If I know my friend Orville he won't be happy 'til he's drunk more'n he can hold and started at least two good fights. I'll see him in the mornin' when he's sick, sober, and sorry."

Bummer sighed, and I smelled the sharp tang of cheap whiskey. His big shoulders sagged and he looked away from me, but not before I caught a glimpse of an old and private pain in his eyes. When he spoke again his voice had a lonesome sound. "Sick, sober, and sorry is where I *live,*" he said.

TWO
The Fanshaw and Mooney Racing Company

By the time I'd finished grooming the horses and had fed them each a flake of hay and a can of oats, I had almost got it through my head that Quicksilver really was mine. I stood there admiring the big thoroughbred by the lantern's smoky light, feeling puffed up and proud, and grinning like a possum eating a yeller-jacket. Bummer had wandered off somewheres, so he wasn't around to see me play the fool, and of course the horses never paid me any mind. I reckon horses have long since quit trying to understand humans, and anyway they have problems of their own.

I believe I may have mentioned my fondness for food. I was still kid enough then to be mostly appetite, and consuming vittles was high on my list of favorite pursuits. I do have to say, though, it never showed on me much. I stood five foot ten and a half, weighed one-thirty or so with my boots off, and was inclined to be narrow of hip and waist. Truth is, there wasn't much them days that could cause me to miss a meal, providing I had the means. That being so, I was more than a little surprised to find I had plumb forgot about eating until the sound of them horses a-crunching their grain brought it to mind. I recalled seeing the lights on earlier at Ignacio's cafe, and without further ado I set out in search of supper.

Ignacio Sanchez had gave up the sheepherding profession for the restaurant business, and far as I was concerned he'd made the right choice. I have no idea what kind of a mutton puncher he'd been, but his cooking was first-rate, and his cafe was the best in Dry Creek. I caught the smell of fried chicken and fresh-baked biscuits before I reached the front door of his place, and by the time I'd gone inside and set down at a table my belly was growling like a bulldog on a chain.

As it turned out, I had the place all to myself, owing to the lateness of the hour, I suppose. Old Ignacio shuffled out of his kitchen, wiping his hands on his apron, and gave me a broad grin. I never even bothered to look at the bill of fare; I had already smelled the chicken, so I just ordered by nose.

"I believe I'll have the chicken dinner," I told Ignacio, "I'd like it hot, quick, and plentiful."

Ignacio's chuckle came from deep inside him somewheres, and his smile showed big yeller teeth like kernels on a roasting ear. "That's how you *always* want it," he said with a shrug, "you celebrate your good luck, no?"

27

"So you heard about Walt leavin' me Quicksilver. News travels fast."

"¿*Si, como no?* Your friends are happy for you."

Ignacio's eyes went wide, and his smile growed even bigger. "Say, amigo," he said, "what you goin' to *do* with all that horse?"

"I don't know—race him, I reckon—if I don't starve to death first. You waitin' for that chicken to die of old age?"

Ignacio favored me with another of his deep-bellied chuckles and ambled back toward the kitchen. "Some good-lookin,' good-cookin' senorita goin' to catch you some day, amigo," he said, "she will use *comidas buenas*—good food—for bait, and catch you plenty."

Later, after I'd wolfed down most of a chicken, four or five biscuits, mashed taters and gravy, corn with chilies, a slab of apple pie, and three or four cups of coffee, I slumped back in my chair, stupefied by my gluttony but content. Ignacio set down across from me, rolled and lit a corn-shuck cigarette, and blowed blue smoke out his nose. "I don' think you like my cookin', Merlin," he said, pointing at my plate, "you din't eat the bones."

I favored him with a grin. "Reckon the grub wasn't quite up to your usual standards," I said, "but that's all right—I've decided to pay you anyway."

A wistful look came into Ignacio's eyes. "I'm goin' to miss Senor Walt," he said, "he was *un caballero grande*—a great gentleman."

28

Yes, he was that. For once, I could think of nothing to say, so I kept still and sipped my coffee.

"What's goin' to happen to the business now?" Ignacio asked, "Who's goin' to run the livery barn?"

"Rolly Kincaid told me Walt left the place to the widow Blair. Walt and her was longtime friends. I figure she'll hire someone to manage the place. Bummer will stay on as night man, I reckon."

"What about you? You goin' to stay on?"

"No, not me. I'm gonna work with Quicksilver some, then take him on the road and see if I can find him a horse race."

Ignacio's smile was a warm one. "When you do, I will bet on you," he said, "I can always use some more *dinero*."

I gave his smile back. "Maybe you'll lose," I told him.

Ignacio got to his feet and started to put out the lamps. "When a man bets on his amigo," he said, "he wins even if he loses."

It was late when I finally paid my bill and started back to the barn. A cold breeze sighed out of the west and swept along the dusty street, bringing the good smells of earth, new grass, and sagebrush. The only lights I'd seen when I came downtown were at the Oasis and the cafe; now, looking back over my shoulder, I could see Ignacio had closed up behind me, leaving only the saloon—and far up the street, the livery barn—still lit.

Dusty moths fluttered in and out of the light from the street lamps, looking like snowflakes in a storm.

29

Now and then a zig-zagging bat would catch light as it darted low and scooped up a moth, but other than that Dry Creek was about as quiet and peaceful as a town ever gets.

The night was clear, and there must have been at least a billion stars crowding the sky. Looking north, I could pick out both Dippers, Big and Little, and the cold, steady wink of the North Star that was even now guiding the big trail herds up from Texas to the Montana range.

I wondered if maybe Walt was up yonder beyond the stars somewheres, and I chose to believe that he was. If ever an old gent made it to Heaven, I figured Walt did, though I couldn't quite picture him a-playing harp and wearing a dress. I had seen pictures of flying horses and had read about winged Pegasus in a book about the old-time Greeks, and it occurred to me that maybe angels rode horseback on some of their longer trips. If that was so, I figured Walt might wind up running another livery barn up yonder, should the Boss okay the deal. One thing I knew about Walt—if them archangels, seraphim, and such ever went in for horse-racing, he'd have himself a seat in the very front row, right on the finish line.

Bummer was mending a buggy harness by lamplight when I got back to the barn. I looked in on Quicksilver and found the big thoroughbred deep in meditation, ruminating on whatever horses think about at such times. I didn't disturb him none, I just stood there and studied him awhile for the good feeling it gave me. Even in the darkness, he seemed to glow with a light all his own, like some rare jewel in a fairy tale.

Finally, I moved on, said goodnight to Little Buck, and went in search of my bed. I'd slept in the loft of Walt's Livery Barn as long as I'd worked for the old feller, and I climbed the ladder that night as usual and slipped between the soogans of my Pa's old bedroll. There was some open patches in the roof where the shingles had come loose, and here and there I could see stars through the openings, like bright, glittering pinpoints in the night sky. It was my intention to lay there awhile and think about Quicksilver and my plans for him, but I fell asleep before I could get started, so I dreamed about him instead.

I saw myself dressed like a nabob, wearing a silk hat, boiled shirt, and a clawhammer coat. I was crouched low over Quicksilver's withers; we swept past other horses and riders as if they was backing up. Crowds of people were cheering us on, the men throwing money while the womenfolk pelted us with flowers and fried chicken. Of course, we won the race easy, and once we'd crossed the finish line I stepped off Quicksilver and sort of floated to earth, where I went to gnawing on a drumstick and stuffing greenbacks and coin into my pockets. Folks had put a big wreath of flowers around Quicksilver's proud neck, and I got back up on him while the crowd bowed low and chanted our names: *Quick-silver! Quick-silver! Mer-lin! Mer-lin!*

Then we was off and away again, only this time we was *flying*. I seen without surprise that Quicksilver had sprouted great, white, beautiful wings and was using them to carry us high above the ground. He soared out toward the mountains in a long glide like a hunting hawk, and I felt ever so grand and free.

Looking down, I seen we was passing over the graveyard. Old Walt was standing there, leaning on his tombstone, and somehow my pa was there with him— they was both a-waving their hats and cheering us on. Walt grinned and slapped his skinny old thigh, and Pa winked the way he used to and gave me a thumbs up sign as I wheeled past overhead and headed into the sun.

Then everything turned a sort of greenish-gray and I found myself alone on a wide and windblown desert Quicksilver had disappeared. Grief swallered me whole; in the dream I fell to bawling like a baby. Tears streamed down my cheeks like spring runoff from the mountains, only they wasn't hot tears like you'd expect, but cold.

Of a sudden, I woke up to find a thunderstorm had blowed in and broke out over Dry Creek. The sky had been clear as a bell when I'd gone to bed, and I sure hadn't expected rain, but there it was anyway. It pelted down steady, drumming on the roof and dripping onto my face through a gap in the shingles, while lightning flashed and thunder growled. Wide awake, I took hold of the bed tarp and drug my roll over away from the wet.

For a minute, I just set there a-hugging my knees and shivering as I tried to shake the sad feeling the dream had brought me. Oh, I knew it had all been a fancy of the night, but losing Quicksilver had seemed so real. I felt gut-lonesome and hollow, the way I had when my mother passed on, or when Pa went to glory astride the crazy black stud, or when I first heard Old Walt had died. Finally, nothing would do but that I go and check on Quicksilver again.

He was there in his stall, of course. From the way he jumped when I came up on him I knew he'd been asleep on his feet and that the sound of my approach had startled him awake. My hand shook as I reached out to touch his proud head. His nostrils flared and his eyes glowed deep and warm in the darkness. I felt foolish because of my fears but relieved to find him still there. I stroked his neck and shoulders. I told him how handsome and fine he was and how glad I was that he was mine. After that, I felt better—if a little sheepish—and I climbed back up to the loft again.

I can't explain my behavior, even now, unless it was that I'd done so much losing in my brief twenty years that I had come to be fearful. I'd got to the place where I felt that whoever, or whatever, I cared for would somehow be took from me, and that I was born to be deprived. It would be some years before I understood that loss is but a part of life and that the Almighty hadn't singled me out for torment.

Back in the loft, I found a dry place in my bedding and slid back under the tarp and between the blankets.

It didn't take long for me to fall asleep again, just long enough to be grateful Quicksilver was still there and to marvel at what a late and fulsome supper can do to a man's dreams.

I was up the next morning before the sun was and naturally my first thought was of Quicksilver. I could hardly wait to see the big thoroughbred, and I vowed to spend the day a-working with him. The night's rainstorm had left the morning air new-washed and sweet, but there was a cold bite to it, too, so I wasted no time in getting dressed.

I had slept wet too many times in my life to enjoy it much, and I pulled my bedroll apart and spread the quilts and blankets around the loft so they could dry during the day. Then I climbed down the ladder and said my howdies to the dawn.

There was an old cannon stove in the office of the Livery Stable, and it had become Bummer's habit to build a fire in it and brew up a pot of coffee before he left for the day. It was a habit I approved of. I poured myself some and let the steaming cup warm my hands while I breathed in the rich aroma. As I often did, I burned my mouth with my first sip, but the coffee sure took the chill off and helped get my day a-going.

The saddlehorses of the Circle F riders were still where I'd left them the night before. There were three of them, including Orville's mouse-colored grulla. I watered all three, cleaned their stalls, and grained them before moving on to my own horses. Little Buck gave me a good morning whinny and nuzzled my face with his velvety nose, just to make sure it was me, I suppose. I turned him out into the pasture behind the barn and then I cleaned his stall. Walt told me once that a mature horse will produce five ton of manure in a year and a mature congressman maybe four times that much. Well, I didn't know any congressmen, but in the time I'd worked at the Livery I'd come to believe the figure for horses, at least, was maybe a bit low.

Once I'd cleaned all the stalls I gave Quicksilver a good currying, put him on a long lead, and walked him out to the big corral behind the barn. Passing out of the dark, the morning sunshine struck him broadside and his sleek hide gleamed like oiled and polished wood. I saw as for the first time the way the veins stood out on his strong, straight legs and chest, saw the ripple of muscle in his powerful neck and hindquarters, and I found myself dang near overcome by his beauty. Quicksilver was not only the finest horse I ever owned, he was the finest horse I'd ever seen, and he surely did cover all the ground he stood on.

Directly, I came out of my trance and began to exercise him there in the corral. I ran the big thoroughbred in circles at the end of his lead, reversed him and took him back around the other way, pleased by the clean, sure movement of his feet and the balanced way he held himself.

Quicksilver was unshod, of course; I had pulled his

shoes and put him out to pasture at Rolly's after he'd won his last race that spring. Now that I was fixing to ride him, I knew he would need shoes again, so I broke out my tools and put a set of training plates on him. I was about to fetch the racing saddle and take him out to the big flat east of town when I seen Orville Mooney come walking across the corral toward me.

Orville and me had both turned twenty that spring, and we'd been friends since our first day together at the Dry Creek school. At recess that day we'd locked horns—for no particular reason—in a combination fistfight and rassling match that nobody won—or maybe we both won, since the event marked the beginning of a close and lasting friendship.

Orville was taller than me by an inch or so, long of back and leg, and broad across his shoulders. He was dark-skinned, pale-eyed, and good-looking; women took to him like cats to catnip. He was normally quick and sure in his movements, although I have to say he wasn't moving very quick that particular morning.

Orville tended to be more particular about his dress and rigging than I was. Fact is, he liked to chide me for being casual about such matters. I guess that was just one of our many differences; I never cared all that much how a thing looked as long as it done the job.

For example, I carried my Pa's old wood-handled Colt's Dragoon in its well-worn, cut down Army holster. I kept the revolver's bore and action clean, but the blueing was pretty well gone and I guess a man could have found a rust spot or two had he looked.

Orville, on the other hand, packed a silver-mounted .44 Colt's Peacemaker with one-piece ivory grips in a custom-made holster, held up by a silver-buckled gun-belt that held a full box of fifty cartridges in its loops.

I can't tell you how much I admired that weapon. Orville had let me shoot it a time or two and I'd found it a well-balanced, sweet shooting revolver. Orville said he'd leave it to me in his will. "You never can tell," he said, "some jealous husband just might lift my hair some night. If I ever go belly up and shake hands with Saint Peter the Colt's and rig are yours."

Orville was particular about his clothes, too. My hat mostly kept the sun and rain off, but it wasn't much for pretty and it had lost considerable of its shape and stiffness. Orville's hat was a pearl-gray Stetson with a braided horsehair band, and it had set him back at least a full month's pay. My saddle was Pa's old Texas hull, not much for looks but long on service, and my good grass rope hung from its fork. Orville's saddle was a center-fire, full-stamped California rig with eagle-bill taps and a sixty-foot rawhide *reata*. In short, Orville was all the things I wasn't, and I guess I admired his sense of style.

Like me, Orville was an orphan. When he was twelve, his Pa had drowned trying to swim a herd across the Yellowstone, and his Ma took sick and died of pneumonia two years later. Orville was wild as a root-cellar rat and could be bad-tempered as a wolverine, while I tended to be more easygoing and good-natured. I believe that difference was one reason we'd come to be friends in the first place; our opposite natures tended to bring about a balance that was good for both of us. Orville kept me from being a total stick-in-the-mud, and I kept him—well, sometimes, anyway—from going altogether hog-wild and snake crazy.

Anyway, as he came sauntering toward me through the mud of the corral that morning, I could see by the way he held himself—neck straight and head canted at a careful angle—that his evening's debauch had bought him a fine morning's misery. His shirt was torn at the shoulder and there was what I took to be blood spots on its front.

Orville grinned at me in his old careless way and squatted down, his back against a corral pole. "You missed a helluva night, Merlin," he said.

"That was my intention," I told him, "and seein' you this mornin' tells me I made the right choice."

He yawned. "Wish I could remember more about what-all I done last night," he said, "from the taste in my mouth I must've had supper with a coyote, or maybe a buzzard."

"Well, you can read sign, I reckon. You've got a split lip, a bruise on your jaw, skinned knuckles, and your eyes look like two burned holes in a blanket. What conclusion would you draw from that?"

"I had a good time?"

"Must have." I couldn't help but grin.

I hunkered down on my bootheels beside him. Orville's eyes were closed, his head resting on a corral rail.

"You all done with the roundup?" I asked.

"Yep. Wagon's still out, but they're fixin' to bring it back in to the home ranch today. Some of the older hands are scourin' the breaks for slicks, but the rest of us have drawed our time and moved on."

He opened one eye a crack and looked at Quicksilver. "That is one fine-lookin' thoroughbred," he said, "you still ridin' races for Walt?"

"You ain't heard the news," I said, "Walt died this week. We buried him yesterday."

"Damn," Orville said, "sorry to hear that, Merlin. I know how you felt about the old feller."

"Yeah. Walt was like family, and I guess he liked me some, too. He left Quicksilver to me in his will."

Orville opened both eyes when he heard that. His head lifted clear of the corral rail and he stared at me. "The Hell you say. You ain't a-foolin' me, are you? That horse is yours now?"

Half the fun of good news is sharing it. I grinned at Orville and said, "Lock, stock, and barrel, legal and proper, one hundred per cent mine. You're lookin' at a man of property, pardner—a racehorse man."

"You lucky som'bitch. I swear, Merlin, you could step in a cow pie and scrape nuggets off your boot. You made any plans yet?"

"Mostly, I've been too busy gettin' used to the idea that I really do own Quicksilver. But yeah, I've got some plans. Thought I'd work the horse this week, then take him over to Shenanigan and try him in some races.

"I was gonna ask you to pardner up with me, but I

39

s'pose you spent all your money on whiskey and low women last evenin'. Besides, you prob'ly druther chase calves and ride bog for thirty a month than be a filthy rich race-horse man."

"Not so! I'm a true-blue friend, Merlin. Somebody has to go along and take care of you, make sure you come in out of the rain and all. So if you're fixin' to run in fast company I reckon I'm willin' to be your nurse-maid. As to money, I've got almost eighty dollars left, and I'm willin' to bet it all on that ugly nag, just out of loyalty."

Whereupon Orville gave me a sappy grin, we shook hands, and right there the Fanshaw and Mooney racing company was born.

An old-time cowpuncher told me once, "the good old days was when you was *young*." Well, if that's so, I reckon that day in Dry Creek was among the best of my good old days. Orville and me was young, sure enough, and full of plans. But plans are hopes that haven't come true yet, and I've found they don't always work out the way a feller expects.

Old Robbie Burns said it best in a poem he wrote:

"The best laid schemes o' mice and men
    Gang aft a-gley."

Damn straight, Rob. They sure as Hell oft-times do.

THREE
Off to the Races

During the week that followed, Orville and me spent long days working with Quicksilver in an effort to build up his stamina and speed. We gave him grain each morning and rode him out on day trips into the rough and broken hills above Dry Creek. We marked off a race course on the big flat east of town and ran him against time over distances of a quarter-mile to a mile and better, and the big thoroughbred seemed to grow faster and stronger each time he ran.

I was a better rider than Orville, and he knew it, although his pride wouldn't allow him to say so. I was also a good twenty pounds lighter than him, and as I said, I'd rode Quicksilver in a number of races earlier that spring. I knew the horse and what he could do, and I was learning how to make the most of him at whatever distance he ran.

Orville and me would generally take a break during the heat of the day and daydream about our future success in the world of horse-racing. We'd set in the shade of the livery barn and drink a beer or two while we'd speculate on life in high society. We'd talk about how we were going to build up our stable and improve our bloodline and we'd argue about the races we'd enter and all the places we'd go. I recall Orville tended to favor Kentucky, with its blue grass and southern charm, while I felt that taking the waters at Saratoga, New York, and hobnobbing with the rich and famous would be prime. Of course, neither of us had ever been anywheres but Montana—we'd hardly been out of Progress County.

As for Quicksilver himself, it didn't seem to make any never mind to him how far the course was; he was bred to race and he loved to run. With his deep chest providing the wind and his mighty hindquarters furnishing the power, he'd explode off the starting line and streak toward the finish like an arrow from a bow.

Walt had bought a good pad saddle and I'd learned to use it, riding a long seat well up over the horse's withers, my knees high and my thighs almost horizontal to the ground. It felt like a funny way to ride at first, and I wouldn't have wanted to go very far that way, but it was all part of giving Quicksilver every chance to run his best.

In the cool of late afternoon we'd take the big horse over the course again. Mostly, I'd act as jockey, but Orville took his turns in the saddle as well, and when he did I found almost as much excitement in watching the thoroughbred run as I did in riding him. With his strong neck stretched forward toward the finish, his mane whipping in the wind of his passage like a flag, and his flashing legs and hooves carrying him onward, Quicksilver was a sight to take a man's breath away.

As the sun went down and the sky caught fire, Orville and me would walk the horse around the big corral awhile to cool him out, then stable him for the night.

Generally, we'd eat supper at Ignacio's, then bed down up in the loft of the Livery Barn. You'd think that after being together all day Orville and me wouldn't have much left to say to each other, but we'd usually lay up there in the dark and chatter like magpies until one or the other of us finally drifted off to sleep.

Orville was pure cowboy, with all the good and bad qualities of the breed, and in normal times he'd have spent his nights drinking whiskey and playing stud poker at the Oasis till all his money was gone. But Orville and me had us a plan and a goal now, and we was investing our money in our dream.

Some nights I'd lay there awake in the dark, watching the stars through the gaps in the barn roof, and think about Old Walt. I'd remember his kindness and the way he'd always built me up. The old feller had worked me hard, but he'd been generous in his praise and with his time. He'd taught me what he knew about horses and how to care for them, but more important, he'd made me feel he believed in me. In his quiet way, Walt had taught me a good deal about character, and about how to be a man.

I'd never had a whole lot in the way of earthly goods, but I had mostly been content. I'd been raised on a hardscrabble farm by folks who loved me, and my mother taught me early that our family wasn't poor—we just didn't have any money.

It touched me that when it came time for Walt to make the big jump, he'd wanted to leave Quicksilver to me. He could not have gave me anything better. Not only did I value and appreciate the big thoroughbred, I saw the horse as a gift that could maybe change my circumstances and help me to be a better man at the same time.

As I laid there and pondered those far away, glittering stars, I hoped the preacher was right. I hoped Old Walt was up in Heaven, doing whatever it was that gave him joy. I hoped he was "Old Walt" no longer, but *young* Walt again, with all his teeth and hair, riding horses with beautiful wings and looking at high and shimmering mountains. Most of all, I hoped he knew the way I felt about him and how much I valued his gift.

The next morning dawned clear as spring water, and dew still sparkled amid the buffalo grass and wildflowers as Orville and me took the road west to Shenanigan for our first big horse-race. The town of Shenanigan lay maybe fifteen miles due west of Dry Creek as the crow flies, but there was no black feathers on Orville or me so we covered the twenty-odd miles by road.

Orville was mounted on the tough little grulla he called Mouse, and of course I rode Little Buck and led Quicksilver. We'd put together a camp outfit and had packed it and our bedroll on a white, glass-eyed gelding Orville was breaking. "Som'bitch is still too snaky to

44

ride," he said, "but that don't mean he gets a vacation. Damn churn-head has to earn his keep *some* way"

The day was the kind a man dreams about all winter. The sky was blue as paint, with only a few scattered clouds hanging over the distant mountains to ease the eye against its brightness. The tender green of new grass, the soft blue-gray of sagebrush, and the red dust of the roadway pleased my eye and made me glad to be alive. Meadowlarks stood their ground and sang their bright songs, or flew low and wobbly up a coulee to draw us away from their nests.

In the distance, below the red buttes that reared up above the valley floor, a scatter of pronghorn grazed—orange, black and white against the green prairie. I looked around for the scout and saw him standing head high and watchful on a low hilltop, sharp-eyed sentry for the herd.

Orville looped the reins around his saddle horn and rolled himself a smoke, setting loose and careless in the saddle. He grinned at me. "You're the book reader," he said, "what's that thing about June you always say?"

"You mean the poem? It was wrote by a feller name of James Russell Lowell. I don't know all of it, but it starts out:

'And what is so rare as a day in June?
Then, if ever, come perfect days;
Then Heaven tries earth if it be in tune,
And over it softly her warm ear lays.' "

Orville struck a match and lit his quirly, hands cupped against the breeze. Blue smoke drifted past his ears and disappeared. "That's the one," he said, "old Jim sure got that right, didn't he?"

I gave back his grin. "Yeah," I said, "but I figure he bet on a sure thing. *Everybody* likes June."

Shenanigan was the seat of Progress County and the center of the area's horse-racing as well. Once winter was well past and fair weather had come again, race-horse men, gamblers and their ladies, and horse fanciers of every stripe made their way to the town for the Saturday and Sunday races.

These races were held on a long flat north of Shenanigan and matched one horse against another in races of a quarter to a mile in distance. I'd been there a few times with Walt, and far as I was concerned there was nothing like a day at the races to get a man's blood up.

Orville and me had arrived after dark the night before and we'd camped up the draw a piece in a patch of cottonwoods. Come sunup I grained Quicksilver as usual and we brushed and curried him until he shone like a new penny. The big thoroughbred somehow seemed to know where we was taking him. He rolled his eyes and bowed his neck, snorting and prancing at the end of his lead-rope, and acting generally like a banty rooster in a new henhouse.

I noticed some of the same attitude in my pardner, as well. Orville had brushed his Stetson, slicked his hair back, and tied a bright silk bandanna around his neck. He'd already had a couple of drinks that morning—I caught the sharp smell of whiskey as we rode toward the race course, and I noticed he was wearing his old go-to-hell grin.

"Celebratin' a little early, ain't you?" I asked.

Orville's grin just got wider. He pulled a pint bottle out of his saddlebag and held it out to me. "Yes, mother," he said, "reckon I am, but this leopard sweat does wonders for a man's confidence. Have a drink."

"You've got confidence aplenty for the both of us," I grumped, "besides, you know I don't usually drink hard liquor."

"Suit youself," he said, taking another pull at the pint, "but drinkin' this stuff is the only way I've found to get it down."

Laid out along a grassy plain on the banks of Careless Creek, the Shenanigan race course was a regular beehive of busyness when we came in sight of it that morning. I saw saddlehorses, racehorses, teams, wagons, and buggies from every part of Progress County and beyond.

Townsmen, merchants and gambling men laughed, joked, and argued the merits of this horse or that, putting their money where their mouths was.

The womenfolk were mostly gathered in their own groups underneath the towering cottonwood trees, chatting and socializing among themselves. Some of the ladies had spread blankets in the shade and had set out picnic lunches, while others sat sewing and doing handwork or watching the young'uns to make sure they didn't get too close to the creek.

As for the young'uns, they was full of the dickens as children generally are. They played Run, Sheep, Run, leapfrog, and such in the mottled sun and shade along the creek bank. Some pretended to ride imaginary race-horses, galloping and laughing as they whipped their legs with willow branches and drove for the finish line.

Flirty-eyed young ladies in frocks and parasols strolled among the trees in pairs and groups of four, all smiles and giggles, and both Orville and me set a little taller in the saddle as we rode past. Them ladies paid special notice to Orville the way females always seemed to, but I believe there might have been one or two who took particular interest in me as well.

There was a six-passenger surrey parked down by the racetrack, full of calico queens from Bertha Mulloy's sporting house. The girls seemed to be having a high old time on their outing, all bright-colored silks, satins, and feathers, and they passed a silver flask around as they watched the races. Of course, they also took note of Orville. As we came abreast of their surrey, he flashed them his bright, reckless smile, tipped his hat, and made Mouse rear up on his hind legs like a circus pony.

A match race had just finished as we rode up, and the space around the finish line was crowded with horses, owners, riders, and trainers. Men were settling their bets, with much back-slapping, laughter, and beer-drinking from the kegs that stood pyramided alongside the track. Walt had warned me once about horse racing. "It's the awfullest disease there is," he'd said, "and once a man's caught it there ain't no cure, not even religion." The funny thing was it had been Old Walt who warned me about the racing fever, but he's the very one who gave it to me. Anyway, right about then I felt a relapse coming on.

Orville and me stepped down off our horses, loosened the cinches, and tied Mouse and Little Buck back among some alders next to the creek. By the time we'd led Quicksilver out into the sunlight and saddled the big horse I saw we'd begun to draw a crowd.

"Handsome beast, that. 'Strord'nary."

The feller who'd spoke turned out to be a chubby, pink-faced gent of about fifty. He wore a checkered coat and matching vest over a well-rounded paunch that told me he hadn't missed many meals of late. His expression was open and friendly, and he had the bluest eyes I'd ever seen. He was a big man with bushy white eyebrows and muttonchop whiskers, and instead of a hat, he wore what looked like some kind of helmet.

Orville's curiosity got the better of him. "No offense, mister," he said, "but what the Hell is that thing on your head?"

"*Topee,*" the feller said, "grew accustomed to wearing the beastly thing while I was in In'ja. Made of cork, you know."

The gent's smile was wide and warm. He looked at

49

Quicksilver again, and I could tell he was pleased by what he saw. His smile grew bigger, and it was as if a sunbeam had lit up his face. I can't tell you why, but I decided right then and there that I liked him.

"I'm Charles Bannerman, gentlemen. Do a bit of stock-raising north of the Musselshell. Splendid animal, that. Yours?"

I smiled, and we shook hands. His grip was firm, warm, and dry. "Merlin Fanshaw," I said, "from Dry Creek. That purty feller in the gray hat is my pardner, Orville Mooney—and yessir, this is my horse."

"Delighted," the man said, shaking hands with Orville, "jolly good to meet you! Please, gentlemen—call me Charlie."

From the frown on Orville's face, I decided he either had the beginnings of a bellyache or he was trying to remember something. He studied the gent's face for a second or two, then of a sudden he lost his frown and his eyes went wide. "Say," he said, "you wouldn't be 'Colonel Charlie' Bannerman from up near Judith Gap, would you?"

"Indeed," the Colonel said, "raise a few horses there, actually."

Well, when I heard that, I sure knew who he was, and so did Orville. I'd heard about Colonel Charlie Bannerman since I first started working at the Dry Creek Livery. Old Walt told me once that Bannerman had been a British cavalry officer and that he'd served in India for some years before he quit the army. Somehow, he'd found his way to Montana Territory and had turned his hand to the raising of blooded horses up beyond the Musselshell. The Colonel was considered a good rancher and was well-liked and respected by both his neighbors and the men who worked for him. According to Walt, Bannerman was also a crack shot with a rifle, and he'd put at least two horse thieves in the ground to prove it. But most of all, Walt had said, "Colonel Charlie" loved good horses and horse racing.

"Brought some rather good horses here myself," the Colonel said, looking thoughtful. "See here—what would you blokes say to a match between your animal and mine?"

Behind the Colonel two men were saddling a dapple-gray quarter horse. Smaller than Quicksilver and shorter in the legs, the animal was far from showy. He stood quietly as the men handled him; the horse was so peaceful, in fact, he seemed downright sleepy. I wasn't about to let appearances fool me, though—I'd heard the great Texas quarter horse Steel Dust hadn't been all that much to look at either. Steel Dust had looked drowsy, too—when he wasn't running like the wind. He'd been a far different horse in a race; Steel Dust had outrun just about everything that had legs and had gone on to sire a line of the finest quarter horses in the country.

"That your horse, Colonel Charlie?" I asked.

The Colonel laced his fingers together across his vest and smiled. "Indeed so," he said, "Name's Colonial Boy. Fast as bloody lightning over a quarter mile."

I didn't doubt it. For all I knew, the horse could well be out of Steel Dust's line himself. "Well, Colonel," I said, "I sure do believe you. Trouble is, my horse Quicksilver runs best at a full mile's distance."

Colonel Charlie looked thoughtful for a moment, then he smiled. "I say—suppose we split the difference? What about a half-mile?"

Back in Dry Creek, Quicksilver had run some of his best times at a half-mile. I looked over at Orville and raised an eyebrow. Orville had been studying Colonial Boy, and his face was serious. He caught my eye, and nodded.

"Agreed, Colonel," I said, "what's the bet?"

"Just a sporting wager. Best two out of three heats. For say, a hundred?"

I glanced at Orville again. A hundred dollars was just about the total resources of the Fanshaw and Mooney Racing Company. Orville shrugged. "We came to gamble," he said, and the race was on.

Men commenced to gather around us, placing their own bets on the outcome. I learned later that most of the betting favored Colonial Boy, but there were many who remembered Quicksilver from his Dry Creek races, and the big horse had his share of backers.

I gave Orville my spurs, hat, and gunbelt, took the short jockey's bat in my teeth, and swung up onto Quicksilver. Awiry, bowlegged little feller—one of the two men I'd seen with the Colonel's horse—mounted Colonial Boy. The other man took the horse by its bridle and led it to the starting line. Orville done the same with Quicksilver. I could feel the big thorough-bred quiver beneath me, feel the heat of him and the ripple of his muscles, and I knew that racing fever was a thing both men and horses could catch.

Tom Dollan ran the saddle shop in Shenanigan, but he told me once he only built saddles to support his horse-racing habit. On that particular day, Tom was starting the races.

I grinned and said, "Howdy, Tom" when we came up to the line, but I reckon he was too full of himself, being official starter and all, to let his hair down much.

He gave me a jerky little nod and said, "First of three heats at a half-mile distance. Jumpin' the gun or interferin' with the other rider or his horse will be grounds for disqualification."

He stepped back to the edge of the track, stopwatch in his left hand and pistol in his right. I could see people talking, but the sound seemed to fade away until all I could hear was the beating of my own heart. I set my feet in the stirrups, took a good hold on the reins, grabbed a handful of Quicksilver's mane, and leaned low over his withers. Orville grinned and gave me a thumbs up sign. Tom Dollan pointed his pistol at the sky. Tom, Orville, the crowd, the horses—every-thing seemed frozen in time like an artist's painting. Then, sharp and sudden, Tom's pistol barked, and the "painting" came to life with a whoop and a holler!

FOUR
Win, Place, or Showdown

Quicksilver exploded off the mark like a skyrocket. I felt his powerful muscles bunch and ripple under me, felt the heat of his sleek body as we swept out onto the track. The shouts of the crowd washed over us in a great wave of sound as I hunkered low in the saddle, urging the big stud onward, though he scarcely needed urging. Quicksilver was a racehorse born and bred, and it was clear he had come to run.

The air had been still at the starting line, but as the thoroughbred took the course the wind of his running roared past my ears like a gale through the piney woods. Looking to my right, I saw Colonel Charlie's dapple gray close alongside, dead even and pulling ahead. I hit Quicksilver once with the bat and felt him surge into a gait I didn't even know he had.

I thought the big horse had already been running his best, but his new pace made the old seem like a Sunday canter to church. From the corner of my eye I could see Colonial Boy still close beside. His jockey was bent low, eyes squinted against the wind, and whipping the little gray with a steady stroke. I knew I was in for a horse race and then some.

We thundered past the halfway mark, the horses' hooves throwing rock and dirt clods high into the air. For a moment Colonial Boy fell behind almost a length, but he quickly commenced a drive that brought him dead even with us again. I was surprised; I had believed the little horse would lose ground at the quarter mile point, that being his natural distance. Sure enough he'd done so, but then he'd won the lost ground back and was challenging Quicksilver for the lead.

The little quarter horse was drawing ahead, no doubt about it. I leaned forward along Quicksilver's powerful neck, asking still greater speed from him, and he gave it—but it was too late. Suddenly, we were pounding across the finish line Colonial Boy was the winner by a nose!

Standing in the stirrups, I began to rein the big thoroughbred back to a lope as he galloped down the track. Colonial Boy's jockey did the same, and soon we had turned and were back at the finish line. Orville caught hold of Quicksilver's headstall and gave me a wry grin as I slid from the saddle and dropped to the ground.

Colonel Charlie was all smiles and good humor, so tickled I couldn't help smiling myself. He was pleased his horse had won, of course, but I got the feeling the Colonel was a true sportsman and that he would have been happy no matter which horse won.

"Good show!" he hollered, "Jolly good riding, lads! Strord'nary!"

I'm afraid the Colonel had me beat six ways from the deuce when it came to being a sport—it made a *heap* of difference to *me* who won.

In the second heat Colonial Boy got off to a quick start and led by more than a length for the first quarter mile, but Quicksilver had his blood up by then; just as he'd done back in Dry Creek, the big horse only got faster each time he ran. At the halfway mark I gave him a smart whack with the bat, and he shot past Colonial Boy to finish more than a length ahead. The crowd cheered, Orville throwed his hat in the air, and Quicksilver swept on down the track like a runaway train. I slowed and finally turned him. Prancing and proud, he trotted back to the line with his head high and his nostrils flaring and red in the sunlight.

No sooner had my foot touched ground than Orville caught me around the neck in a bear hug that like to strangled me. His breath was anyway ninety proof, and I knew without seeing that his pint bottle had gave up its spirits, so to speak. Orville yelled above the clamor of the crowd, "That's more like it, pardner!"

Orville told me once he only drank to calm his nerves, but I think he was just trying out the idea when he said it and didn't really expect me to believe him. The truth is, he never seemed to need much reason to pull a cork. I'd seen Orville drink for celebration and consolation, when he was alone, and in the company of friends. He drank when he could afford it, he drank on credit when he couldn't, he went without when he had to, and no matter how much he drank, whiskey never seemed to make him mean.

Whiskey did seem to make him more friendly to

people he already liked and less friendly to people he didn't. It also tended to make him more reckless and wild than he normally was, which in my opinion was already aplenty.

One of the reasons I mostly stayed clear of booze myself was the way I'd seen it change people. I told Orville I had enough trouble being who I wanted to be without having to deal with too many drinks of sheepherder's delight. Orville said whiskey didn't so much change a man as it magnified him and made him more of who he was already.

Whatever the truth, I didn't trust whiskey, and I walked wide of it when I could. Now it may sound strange if you ain't familiar with the times I'm talking about, but there was occasions them days when a man couldn't avoid drinking, try as he might. Booze was a part of business deals, part of celebration and hospitality, and it was considered the worst kind of bad manners to turn down a drink when it was offered.

All of which is the long way around of saying I had me a couple of drinks before the third heat of our race. Colonel Charlie brought out a bottle of whiskey he said came all the way from Scotland, and he offered some to me and Orville. I took a drink or two (to be polite) and found it to be a warming whiskey, with a taste somewhere between woodsmoke and iodine. I'd never had liquor so fine, and it went down smooth as cream.

As we stood there drinking with the Colonel and the high-rollers at the finish line I found myself in two places at once. My body was laughing and joking, talking with the sporting gentry about horses, racing, and such as we sipped on the Colonel's scotch whiskey. But my mind was elsewhere; it had gone on ahead of me to the third and final heat of the race. I was remembering every bump, dip, and low place along the track and concentrating hard as I ran the final race in my imagination. No one had to tell me how important the upcoming heat was: the count stood even at one for Quicksilver and one for Colonial Boy. Whoever took the next heat would win it all.

In my mind's eye I got off to a fast start and quickly pulled ahead of the Colonel's gray. I saw myself reining Quicksilver over ahead of Colonial Boy as our lead grew to two lengths, then three, and I heard the crowd roar as we flew across the finish line in victory.

That's how it played in my mind, anyway. The way the race really turned out was different, to say the least, but then I don't reckon even my imagination was wild enough to think of every possibility.

When Tom Dollan's pistol barked to start the third heat, Quicksilver sprang off the starting line with a suddenness that surprised me—for a second there he almost lost me. I tightened my grip on the reins, leaned low over the big horse's withers, and urged him to even greater speed with quick, sharp strokes of the racing bat. He ran flat out as I knew he could, and his manner made it clear he figured to give the race his all.

My eyes watered and my vision blurred from the

wind of our passage. I turned my head to see that we had indeed left Colonial Boy and his rider a length and more behind. I swung my gaze forward, looking toward the finish line, feeling the thoroughbred's power through my legs and hands as if he was some great unstoppable machine. Then to my surprise Colonial Boy was alongside again. The Colonel's jockey was bent low and whipping the little gray with every stride as he turned his face toward me and smiled.

Colonial Boy moved up. He was ahead by a nose, and then by a neck, close in on Quicksilver's right shoulder. Then I saw the jockey rein the gray sharply toward me and felt a sudden, hard jolt as the two horses collided. For a moment Quicksilver was knocked off his stride, and in the time it took for him to get back into it again Colonial Boy pulled around us and ahead, pounding hard for the finish line.

Quicksilver ran on heart, racing after the little quarter horse, but it was plain we wouldn't be able to catch him. My heart sank as I seen the race was all but lost. Ahead, the jockey shifted in his saddle and looked back over his shoulder to see how close we were. When he did so, he must have pulled the gray's head to the side in mid-stride—that, and the shift in weight, unbalanced the gray; I saw the little horse stumble and fall, his front legs slowly folding under him like a horse in a dream.

Then horse and rider were down, directly in front of us. There seemed no way to avoid the tangle—I was all but certain we were going down, too. Then, at the last moment, Quicksilver gathered himself and cleared the fallen gray in one great leap. The big horse came down hard and running, swept across the finish line and beyond—we had won the heat, and the race!

Slowing the big thoroughbred was no easy matter. His blood was up and in his excitement he fought the rein with a will. Directly, though, he slowed, his smooth gait becoming a stiff-legged dance that rattled my backbone and bounced short, choppy grunts out of both him and me.

I got him turned at last and took him back to the finish line at a brisk trot. Colonial Boy was on his feet again and walking and so was his rider. I could see Colonel Charlie, Tom Dollan, and Orville all gathered around the two of them, but neither the little gray nor his jockey seemed to be hurt. When I reached them I drawed rein and slid down off Quicksilver. "You all right?" I asked.

"Right as rain," grunted the jockey, "Had me bleedin' bell rung and et a mouthful of dirt, but I'm all right." He stuck out his hand and favored me with a tough, gap-tooth grin. "Good race, mate."

Colonel Charlie knelt in the black dirt of the track, his fingers probing the knees and pasterns of the little gray. He looked tense, his face tight with concentration as his hands moved carefully over the animal's legs. Finally, the Colonel seemed satisfied. He got stiffly to his feet, and his face took on its old jolly appearance again.

"Good race indeed," he said, "Nice bit of riding, Fanshaw. Strord'nary."

"Much obliged, Colonel. Your horse had me beat till he fell. Bad luck."

The Colonel was already counting out the hundred dollars he'd bet. One by one, he placed five gold double eagles in my hand. "Fortunes of war, Fanshaw, fortunes of war. Deucedly fine thoroughbred, your Quicksilver. Should you ever consider selling him I hope you'll allow me the privilege of making an offer."

"I surely will, sir, but I ain't fixin' to sell. Reckon I'll be keepin' him."

The Colonel smiled as he shook my hand. "Can't say that I blame you. Splendid animal, that. Well, then. Best of luck, lads."

I appreciated the Colonel wishing me luck thataway, but I have to admit I was riding pretty high right then and didn't really figure I needed any more good luck. Seemed to me I had the world by the tail on a downhill pull, and nothing could possibly go wrong.

Of course I should have knowed better. Things can always go wrong. Things oft-times *do* go wrong. And when they do, there's no limit to *how* wrong they can go.

After the race, Orville and me walked Quicksilver around until he cooled out, then set him to graze on a picket rope. Winning over Colonial Boy made the big thoroughbred—and us—the center of attention for awhile, which didn't hurt our feelings a bit. Orville set his pearl-gray sombrero at a jaunty angle and strutted past the young ladies with his chest pooched out, and they in turn fluttered their eyelashes and simpered like ninnies. We watched two or three races, drank a few beers, and basked in our new-found glory like turtles sunning on a log. As far as we were concerned the Fanshaw and Mooney Racing Company was well begun and headed for the Moon.

That evening, back at our camp in the cottonwoods, Orville cooked up a bait of beef stew and biscuits while I gave Quicksilver an extra ration of oats. The sun was just setting, and I remember thinking that day had been among the best I'd had. I wanted to hold back the sun; I didn't want the day to end.

The light had turned a soft gold and had painted the grass and treetops with brightness. Purple shadows deepened and stretched long across the land. Birds sang their urgent goodnight songs and grew still, as a cool breeze stirred the big, heart-shaped leaves of the cottonwoods and set them to pattering in the stillness.

I staked Quicksilver out on the tall grass along the creek, hobbled the other horses, and glanced back at Orville. It was the strangest thing, but sometimes when I looked at Orville he seemed to sort of glow with his own bright fire, the way a burning pitch log blazes hot and bright, or the way Quicksilver some-times seemed to shine as if from some inner light.

Anyway, there was Orville, hunkered down at the cookfire, stirring the stew. He'd acquired another pint bottle of whiskey from somewhere, and when he seen me looking his way he flashed his old reckless go-to-hell smile and saluted me with the pint. Then he took a long pull, made a wry face, shuddered, and corked the bottle.

Dusk had fell upon the land by then, and the light of day was almost gone. As I walked back to where Orville squatted by the fire, I heard what sounded like the snap of a dry stick back among the trees. I swung my gaze in the direction of the sound, which is when I first saw the strangers.

It was like those times hunting deer when you're looking at a shady patch in the woods and all of a sudden, out of the gloom, a big muley buck takes shape. One minute there was no one there, and the next minute there was—three men, standing off a piece from the fire, watching us. Seeing them made me feel a mite edgy. I wondered how long they'd been there, and I took it on myself to do some sizing up of my own.

The men were hard-looking hombres, and no mistake. As I drawed closer I could see that one was solid-built and stocky, with big hands and a potbelly. His legs were bowed and seemed too short for his body. He had a cast eye and wore a sort of drowsy look, with a slack-jawed grin that made me think he was maybe six cards short of a deck. All told, he put me in mind of a big, sleepy old bear.

The feller standing next to him looked more like a coyote than a bear. He had a pinched, sly face, crazy yellow eyes, and a wolfish grin that made me dead sure

63

I didn't want him anywhere behind me. Each man wore a belted six-gun; Mister Coyote was packing *two*.

The third man looked like some kind of high-roller. He was maybe six foot tall, and he wore a black frock coat over a fancy checkered vest. Beneath his coattails a bone-handled Colt's revolver rode his right hip, butt forward in the cavalry style, and a rawhide quirt hung from his wrist. Beneath a wide-brimmed hat that must once have been white, his hair was uncommon long— down to his shoulders, dirty and lank.

His face was brown from the sun, but badly pock-marked. A black moustache and goatee framed a set of strong, white teeth. He bared them ivories wide when he seen me looking at him, and you couldn't have asked for a more friendly smile. Trouble was, it was only his mouth that smiled—his eyes were fixed on me, but they were guarded and cool. It was like meeting a snarling dog with a wagging tail—at such a time it's hard to know whether to believe the snarl or the wag.

"Can I help you gents?" I asked, but there was no friendliness in my question. Even to my own ears the tone of my voice made the question sound more like "What the Hell do *you* want?" I didn't like the way they'd slipped up on our camp without calling out.

Up to that point I don't believe Orville knew them fellers was there. I seen his head jerk up when I spoke, and I felt, rather than saw, him grow tense and watchful.

Mister high-roller kept his smile, but his eyes stayed careful. He kept glancing toward the meadow where

Quicksilver grazed at the end of his picket rope. "Saw you ride that horse today, boy," he said, "Would that be the stud they call Quicksilver? Used to race over Dry Creek way?"

"Yessir, it would," I said. The man's voice had a haughty edge to it, like he was accustomed to giving orders. I wasn't all that happy about the way he called me "boy"

"I'm told that horse belongs to an old-timer named Walt Finkelman. Know where I can find him, boy?"

"Yessir, I do. Ain't his horse, though."

High-roller squinted his eyes and traded his smile for a frown. "No? I understood it was."

"Didn't say it wasn't. Said it *ain't*."

For a moment he just looked at me. Then he said, "See here, boy—are you tryin' to mock me?"

"No, sir. Walt Finkelman's in the Dry Creek cemetery. He died more than a week ago. Quicksilver *was* his horse. Ain't *now*."

Mister high-roller was commencing to look annoyed. Behind his back, the other two men was grinning and rolling their eyes like the whole thing sure tickled them. High-roller caught them at it out of the corner of his eye, and it seemed to make him madder yet. He took a step toward me, and when he spoke his voice grated like fingernails on a slate.

"Damn you, boy," he said, "I'm gettin' tired of your smart mouth. I asked you who the new owner is. Are you simple, or just rude?"

Orville had stood up from his place beside the fire

65

and stood watching our visitors. The thumb of his right hand was hooked in his gunbelt, close to his holstered Colt's. He was wearing his wild, careless smile, and I knew he was hoping high-roller and his sidekicks would turn hostile. I also knew the situation was getting close to the edge and that I should back off some, but by then I was commencing to feel a mite warlike myself.

"Well," I said, "for openers, my name ain't 'boy.' It's Merlin Fanshaw, and I'm the new owner. The gent there at the fire is my pardner, Orville Mooney. Now who the Hell are you?"

High-roller stopped in his tracks like he'd run into a wall. His eyes went wide, his face turned red, and his teeth showed again, but not in a smile this time. His hand jerked, and for just a heartbeat there I thought he might pull his pistol. As it turned out, he didn't. The man took hold of himself, the high color faded from his face, and the moment passed—much to Orville's disappointment, I'm sure.

"No offense, Merlin Fanshaw," he said, putting on his smile again, "My name's Turk Fontayne, and I'm from over at Maiden, in the Judith Mountains. I deal in horses."

"No offense taken," I told him, "but like I said, Quicksilver ain't for sale."

"Now don't be hasty, Mister Fanshaw. You ain't heard my offer."

It was the second time since Old Walt died someone had called me mister. I reckon becoming a man of

66

property changes the way folks address a feller. I mistered him right back. "You haven't heard me, mister Fontayne. It don't much matter what your offer is— that particular horse ain't for sale. Fact is, he's about the *most* ain't for sale horse you ever saw."

"It's not that I don't believe you, son," he said, "but in my long experience I've learned that most everything is for sale if the price is right. What would you say to two thousand dollars cash?"

Now you have to realize that in the year 1884 two thousand dollars was a heap of money, even for a horse as fine as Quicksilver. For just a moment there, my resolve went slack as I pondered what-all two thousand dollars might buy. But Quicksilver had been left me by a man I'd loved like a grandpa, and besides, the horse was what I saw as the means to my fortune and my future.

"This here is your lucky day, Mister Fontayne," I told him, "because you're fixin' to learn somethin' new. There are some things that ain't for sale at any price. Quicksilver is one of them things."

"Now hold on, son. Like I said, I deal in horses. Your Quicksilver is a good horse, but I believe he can be a great one. As a sporting man, I'm prepared to invest money in his training and development so that can happen.

"Now obviously, you are also aware of his potential. However—and I'm just guessin' here, you understand—I don't believe a young man like yourself has the resources to help him reach that potential."

Orville broke in. His voice was calm and controlled, but there was an edge to it like broken glass. "Mister Fontayne," he said slowly, "my pardner just told you the horse ain't for sale. Is there somethin' wrong with your hearing, or are you just stupid?"

Fontayne's smile was rueful. He shrugged and showed me the palms of his hands. "All right, son, you win. I admire a man who knows his own mind, and I respect your decision. But before I go I'd like to be certain you really are Quicksilver's lawful owner. Would you mind showin' me your bill of sale?"

Again Orville's voice broke in, cold and flat. "We don't have to show you a damn thing, mister! My pardner's told you three times the horse ain't for sale, and there's nothin' more to say. I'm thinkin' it's time you boys made tracks."

The moment was tight as stretched wire. I held my breath and heard the beating of my own heart loud in my ears. Fontayne's gaze was intense as he studied Orville. At last he smiled his cold smile, and the tightness left his shoulders. "Appreciate your time, boys. I've got a feelin' we'll be seein' each other again."

He stepped slowly back a pace or two into the gathering shadows. The other two men followed him, their eyes on us. At the edge of the fire-light, the coyote-looking hombre turned and pointed the forefingers of both hands at us. His raised thumbs dropped suddenly, like the hammers of pistols, and his wolfish grin widened. The three men turned and disappeared into the darkness.

FIVE
Pride Goeth Before

The strangers had gone, but the bad feeling hadn't. Menace hung in the stillness like the woodsmoke from our cookfire, and remembrance of the men left a dark stain on the brightness of my day.

I tried to turn Orville's thoughts back to the horse race and the money we'd won. I imitated Colonel Charlie's English accent, I teased Orville about all the pretty girls who'd gave him the eye, and I tried to get him talking about where we should race next. I'd heard there was a dance over in town that evening, and I done my best to talk Orville into going. I even boasted that I was a better rider than he was (that had *never* failed to get a rise out of him), but he scarcely seemed to hear me. He just set there a-staring into the flames, his face hard and angry and his mind far away in some place of its own.

Finally, I gave up and fell to wolfing down beef stew and biscuits. Orville only picked at his food some and set his plate down by the fire. His eyes held a troubled look, and he took another long swig of whiskey from his pint.

"I seen them three birds at the track today," he said, "they couldn't take their eyes off Quicksilver. I don't trust them som'bitches. They're trail trash if ever I seen it."

"Lookin' don't do no harm. Quicksilver is mighty easy to look at."

"Didn't like the *way* they was lookin.' That tinhorn in the checkered vest just set there on his high-headed claybank and studied our horse like a duck lookin' at a water bug. I think them boys are horse-thieves, Merlin.

"All three of 'em was ridin' hot-blooded horses, born and bred to cover ground, and that Fontayne feller said he was from Maiden, up yonder in the Judiths. Well, you know as well as I do that whole country is crawlin' with rustlers, clean over to the Musselshell and north to the Missouri Breaks."

"If he's a horse thief, how come he offered to *buy* Quicksilver?"

"Hell, I don't know. Maybe to feel us out, see what we'd say. I'm tellin' you, Merlin, them boys are up to no good."

"Well, then, I guess we'd best be on our guard. You and me can set up tonight and watch Quicksilver in shifts."

To tell the truth, I really didn't think such drastic action was called for. Fontayne and his boys were a hard-looking lot, all right, but that didn't mean they was a danger to us or that they aimed to steal Quicksilver. I'd sort of planned on celebrating our success by going in to the dance and giving them town girls a whirl, but here my pardner had clouded up and rained all over that plan with his talk of horse thieves, rustlers, and what-not. I found his gloom to be contagious; Orville had got me to worrying, too.

"All right," he said, "I'll take first watch. You clean up camp and get some sleep. I'll wake you at midnight." Then he took up the rifle and a blanket and walked on over to the meadow.

I didn't fall asleep right away. I laid there between the soogans of my bedroll and watched the flickering light of the dying fire. I ran the events of the day through my mind like pictures in a magic lantern show I saw again in memory the Colonel's gray stumble and go down before me in the final heat. I remembered the way Quicksilver had gathered himself and cleared man and horse like a fox hunter jumping a wall. I remembered the cheers of the people, and Colonel Bannerman counting out the hundred dollars into my hand. I thought of Old Walt, too, of how pleased and proud he'd have been. I found myself wishing the old gent could nave been there with us that day, and then I thought well, maybe he had been. Maybe, somehow, he knew.

A cool breeze had rose up with the coming of evening, and I listened as it sighed through the cottonwoods, telling of the places it had been. Somewhere upwind an owl called, and far off in the rolling hills beyond the creek coyotes yodeled and yipped to the full and rising moon. Then at last sleep dropped over me like a blanket, and I drifted away to a warm dark place of peaceful slumber.

I awoke with a start, as from a nightmare, yet I could recall no dream. My breathing was shallow and ragged, my heartbeat loud in my ears. A feeling of dread had come upon me, yet I could neither name it nor tell its cause. The camp was dark; the fire had long since gone out and the moon lay hidden behind the clouds. To the north the sky was clear, the Pole Star glittering cold and bright among its neighbors.

I sat up in my blankets: something was wrong. Through the night the Big Dipper had rode its circle around the North Star and now sat nearly level just above the horizon—the time was almost four in the morning.

Where was Orville? He was to have woke me at midnight. Had something happened to him? My heart beating even faster than before, I found my boots and pulled them on. I took up my belted Colt's Dragoon and buckled it on as I headed through the trees for the meadow.

In my haste I tripped on a half-buried rock and sprawled headlong. As I got to my feet again the moon drifted out from behind the clouds and flooded the meadow with light. I figured Orville would have took his place somewhere in the darkness of the trees along the creek, but I didn't know where. The meadow was bright in the moonlight, and I made a swift count as I crossed it. There was Little Buck, Mouse, and the packhorse, hobbled and grazing. Where was Quicksilver? I looked again. I had not hobbled the thoroughbred but had staked him out on a picket rope instead. He had to be there in the meadow—he had to be, but he wasn't.

72

I hurried to the place I'd staked him, found his picket pin, drew the limp stake rope up out of the wet grass to its end. The rope showed not a break but a sharp, clean cut. The story was plain, there could be no doubt—Quicksilver had been stolen!

I found Orville slumped in the shadows of the trees, facing the meadow. His back rested against a fallen log, his blanket across his shoulders Indian-style, like a coat. The Winchester lay cradled in the crook of his left arm, his right hand resting on the stock.

The sense of dread I'd felt when I awoke came back full upon me. My throat felt tight and my hand shook as I reached out to touch him. "Orville," I said, "are you all right?"

Then I caught the strong smell of whiskey and saw the empty bottle in the grass beside him. I took hold of his arm and shook him. "Orville," I said, "wake up Quicksilver's gone." Concern for him gave way to anger as rage swept through me in a rush. At that moment I believe I could cheerfully have killed him.

He stared at me then, confusion in his eyes, trying to understand my words. "What? What time is it?" he muttered. His voice was thick, heavy with sleep.

"It's past four," I told him, "Quicksilver's been stolen!"

Orville lurched to his feet and shuffled, unsteady and halting, toward the moon-flooded meadow. He stopped and turned back to me. "Lordy, Merlin!" he said, "I—I just closed my eyes for a minute—"

"Yeah. Well, somebody slipped up and cut Quicksilver's picket rope. The other horses are still there."

Even by moonlight the remorse on Orville's face was plain to see. Fact is, he looked so miserable I commenced to feel sorry for him, and my anger melted like a snowflake on a stove. I thought of Bummer, back at the Dry Creek livery, and his words: "Sick, sober, and sorry is where I live." I had faults aplenty of my own, far too many to set myself above other men, but I felt grateful to the Almighty right then that a weakness for whiskey wasn't among them.

We saddled our horses in the gray light that comes before dawn and Orville scouted the flats and coulees for the better part of an hour while I rode the creek bottoms. I suppose we did so on the off chance Quicksilver had merely broke free and strayed, but neither of us really believed that was the case. Even as we were looking for him we both carried in our minds the picture of that clean-cut stake rope in the meadow. A cut rope meant a stolen horse, and no mistake.

Neither of us had much doubt but that Fontayne and his hardcases had took Quicksilver. What we didn't know was whether those boys were still in the area somewheres or if they'd lit out during the night. In the woods and clearings around the race course the early risers was already up and stirring as they made ready for another day of racing. Orville and me rode slow and watchful among them, looking for some sign of Fontayne and the boys or of Quicksilver, but saw none. Of course there was horse tracks everywhere— far too many to single out any particular hoofprints. At length we turned back to the meadow, packed our camp outfit on the glass-eyed packhorse, and set out on the road that led to the county seat of Shenanigan.

Orville was in a killing mood. There was blood in his eye and war in his heart, but I told him we needed to report the theft to the law before we took matters into our own hands. I guess I figured we'd made enough mistakes at that point and needed to do things by the book. Orville made it plain he didn't much like the idea, but he finally agreed.

Trouble was, I didn't have all that much confidence in the law right then myself. Oh, I believed in law and order, all right; but I didn't have much faith in the man who carried the law for Progress County.

The sheriff's name was Ernie Fillmore, and until two years previous he'd been town marshal in my home town of Dry Creek. When the former sheriff of Progress County got himself killed back in the fall of '82 Ernie had shook hands, bought drinks, kissed babies, and promised everything to everybody until he got himself elected.

In my opinion Ernie Fillmore was a poor excuse for a peace officer. When he was town marshal at Dry Creek he'd been a great one for bullying drunks and kids, but he'd managed to be away "on business" whenever a real hardcase hit town. I believe he would have soiled his breeches if he'd ever been called upon to arrest a bona fide outlaw.

Ernie was a short man, narrow of shoulder and mind and wide of hip and haunch. He nourished a potbelly the way some folks tend a rose garden. I never could understand why, but Ernie seemed to be mighty swole up with himself—no pun intended—and he wore his nickel-plated badge as if it was a medal from Congress.

If all this sounds to you like I didn't admire Ernie Fillmore I have to admit that you're right. Ernie didn't like me much, neither—I think he knew I'd seen his hole card and hadn't been impressed. Then, too, we'd had a few personal run-ins in the past. I recall on one particular occasion I'd called him a whey-bellied, gutless, chicken-stealing dog, and the term "horse's ass" may have come up in that same conversation, I don't recall.

Anyway, Ernie was a proud man so I believe he may somehow have took offense at my words. Since that time he had become high sheriff of Progress County. I was going to have to report Quicksilver's theft to him, but I had scant hopes that any good would come of it.

Far as I know, there are two different streams in Montana called Careless Creek. One of them rises in the Big Snowy foothills south of Lewistown and wanders on south and east with many a mosey and meander until it empties into the Musselshell River. The other one flows out of the Brimstone range past the towns of Dry Creek and Shenanigan, and that's the Careless Creek I know best. Orville and me had camped on its banks the previous evening, the night Quicksilver was stolen. Next morning at sunup we followed it two miles upstream until we came to the town of Shenanigan itself.

Sunlight was just painting the hilltops west of town as Orville and me crossed the bridge and turned our horses onto Front Street. Even at that early hour folks in town were up and doing. There were cowpunchers eating breakfast at the Red Rooster Cafe, their horses lined up at the hitchrack out front. Three doors down a storekeeper was sweeping the sidewalk in front of his place. From Tanner's Livery came the ring of hammer on anvil, and I figured some traveler was having his horse shod for a journey.

Over on Main Street the Progress County courthouse stood tall against the sky, the tip of its dome catching the early light, as I turned Little Buck in that direction. Beside me, Orville's face was grim, his jaw set and his eyes restless as he studied the tied horses and the occasional passing rider. I knew he was rawhiding himself over the loss of Quicksilver. I wished there was something I could do or say to help him, but I knew there was not. I figured whatever I said just then, no matter how well intentioned, was likely to make matters worse. My pardner was spoiling for a fight, and I knew him well enough to know that if he couldn't find one elsewhere he'd settle for one with me.

We'd just turned the corner onto Main when I saw the horses. There were two of them, saddled and loose-tied to the hitchrack in front of Tanner's. They stood hipshot and sleepy in the shade of the barn, and even though I'd never seen them before, somehow I knew them both on sight. Orville had described them well—they were "hot-blooded horses, born and bred to cover ground," and *one* of them was a claybank!

Orville was already out of the saddle. I heard the rowel of his spur ring as his foot struck the rutted street. "It's them, Merlin!" he said, "that high-headed yeller stud is Fontayne's horse! Them thievin' bastards are here somewheres!"

I knew it was no use, but I tried anyway. "Dammit, Orville, wait! We agreed—"

Turk Fontayne stepped forward into the open doorway, and the two-gun man with the crazy yellow eyes stood beside him. Fontayne looked cool as January. "Howdy, boys," he said.

Orville took a step forward. He spread his feet and planted them wide and solid in the loose dirt. Fontayne's eyes were wary, but his smile was friendly. When he spoke, his voice was a lazy drawl. "You boys change your mind about sellin' that race horse?"

"Hell no, we ain't," Orville said, "and you damn well know it!"

Fontayne didn't lose his smile. Carefully, slowly, he brought both hands up to grasp the lapels of his coat. "I do?" he asked, "and why is that?"

"Because you and your thievin' henchmen *stole* the horse last night, *that's* why!"

Fontayne looked past Orville to where I still sat astride Little Buck. "You'd best take charge of your pardner, kid," he said, "I b'lieve he's fixin' to draw cards in a game he can't win."

"Talk to *me,* you damn horse thief!" Orville said.

Words, I thought. Words had power. They could give hope, they could comfort and encourage, or they could challenge and accuse. And, like the firing of a bullet, once they were loosed they could never be taken back. There on that patch of dirt in front of Tanner's, Orville's words were taking him—taking us—to a dark and unknown place we hadn't meant to go. At least I hadn't.

A cold breeze was rising there on the street, but I felt a chill inside me that had nothing to do with the weather. Not only could I see where the words were taking us, I saw the why of them—Orville's reckless pride, his guilt because he'd fell asleep on guard, his wild, crazy temper. I choked, and found my voice again. "Orville!" I shouted, "Come away now, you hear?"

The two-gun man had been leaning against the door frame, watching. With a quick, shrug-like move he pushed himself away from the door and stepped out into the street. His face was a hard mask as he fixed his cold, yellow eyes on Orville.

"You'd best listen to your pardner," he said, "while you still can."

Orville's hand hung near his holstered Colt's, his body poised and tense as a cougar on a rock. "Who the hell are *you?*" he snapped.

"My name's Portugee Gossert," he said, "I do some

of Mister Fontayne's light work, and I'm gettin' real tired of your mouth, cowboy."

Fontayne spoke from his place inside the barn. He wasn't smiling any more. "You're walkin' on mighty thin ice, boy. You've called me a thief without cause or proof, you've cursed me, and you've insulted me and my friends. Even so, I've tried to be patient with you.

"Now I reckon anybody can make a mistake, so I'm givin' you one last chance. Either beg my pardon and back off, or pull that pistol and go to work. There ain't no other choices."

Right then I think even Orville saw he'd gone too far. He looked from Fontayne to Gossert and back again. His body was still tense as stretched wire, but his face had lost some of its reckless anger. For just a moment I thought the danger would pass.

"Come on, Orville," I said softly, "this ain't the way, pardner."

And then, suddenly, everything came undone. I saw Orville reach for his revolver, fast but still too slow, much too slow—Gossert smiling, his guns flashing, filling his hands, coming up. Then I was throwing myself from the saddle, trying to get between Orville and Gossert, hearing a word, a shout—somebody's voice—my voice—saying, shouting, screaming, "NO!"

Gossert's gun bucked in his hand. I saw orange flame stab from its muzzle—saw the slug take Orville high and hard in the chest. The sound of the shot was

80

loud in my ears—it racketed off the buildings of Main street and died in the chill morning air. Orville swayed, his knees buckling, his face strained, as he tried to bring his own gun to bear. Then his eyes, wide and stricken, the pistol firing once into the dirt at his feet and dropping from his fingers as he fell himself and sprawled face down.

A wild fury took me then—I must have gone plumb loco. Rage boiled up into my throat and like to strangled me. I was filled brimful with anger—anger at Gossert and Fontayne, anger at my hot-tempered pardner, anger at my damn self, and anger at God. That's when I grabbed for my own revolver. Through a red haze I saw Gossert's cold smile and looked into the muzzle of his gun.

Then the ground seemed to shake beneath my feet— I saw Gossert's gaze shift to a point beyond and behind me, and I felt pain explode through my head in a bright flash that went to black and dropped me off the edge of the world.

SIX
Taking the Trail

When I came to myself I was sure I had died and gone to Hell. I didn't smell sulfur nor see a lake of fire, but the torment I felt was intense and abundant, like the preachers always said it would be.

My head throbbed with a grievous ache that left me feeling deep-belly sick all over. Pain came in throbbing waves each time I moved or breathed, so I made every effort not to do them things.

My innards rolled and boiled in queasy surges that made me fear I was about to air my paunch. I sure wasn't looking forward to the experience—I knew how *that* would make my head feel. My mouth was dry; my tongue felt big as a cow's, and my ears rang with a steady, high-pitched drone. I decided I hurt too much to be dead, and for a time feared that I would die. Then, as the pain seemed to worsen, I became briefly afraid that I wouldn't.

I laid there with my eyes closed tight, moving nary a muscle. It was my belief at the time that staying perfectly still would help keep the hurt at bay, and maybe it did, I don't know. Something was tugging at the sleeve of my memory, demanding my attention. Whatever it was seemed important, but I paid it no heed. I was too busy with my pain.

I had quite a debate with myself about whether I

should open my eyes or not. After a time curiosity got the better of me, and the vote went from maybe to should. I cracked an eyelid and found I was not in Hell after all but merely the Progress county jail.

I was laying on my belly with my face pressed into a scratchy gray blanket that smelled of old, rank sweat and dried puke. I turned my head to the side and seen I was in a corner jail cell maybe twelve by twelve, with iron bars on two sides from floor to ceiling. The walls were made of granite blocks, with a narrow, barred window high up one side. In the far corner of the cell a chipped enamel slop-bucket stood awaiting my convenience.

My brain showed signs it was ready to go back to work again, and the first thing it done was ask what I was doing in the hoosegow. I had no answer, but right then the events at Tanner's barn came back to me, first slow, in scattered pieces, and then with a rush, like a man dumping taters in a bin.

I closed my eyes and saw again the cold, hard smile of the man called Portugee Gossert. I watched as Orville's hot temper prodded him over the edge. In memory I seen him make his play, too slow—forever too slow. Then Gossert's gun belching fire and smoke, the slug hitting Orville like a hammer. Inside my mind I heard again my own scream as I grabbed for my Colt's dragoon, felt the blow to my head from some-where behind me, and took my tumble into blackness and silence.

I swung my legs off the bunk and sat up, but the

results of that action made me wish sincerely that I had not done so. A wave of pain rocked through my head like a dynamite blast through a canyon and caused me to repent of my rashness. I sat there a-gripping the edge of the bunk, my eyes shut tight, and let the pain have its way with me. Then, when the hurt began to ease up a mite, I heard a door open and the sound of footsteps in the hallway.

"Howdy, Merlin," a voice said, "How you doin,' hoss?"

Opening my eyes again was the hardest thing I'd do all day. I squinted through the hurt and seen the speaker was Glenn Murdoch, chief deputy to Sheriff Ernie Fillmore. He stood just beyond the bars of my cell, holding a whiskey bottle and a tin cup. His smile was broad, and there was sympathy in his faded blue eyes.

I'd always liked Glenn. He'd cowboyed for some of the biggest outfits in the county until his horse fell with him during a cattle run and left him with a full-time limp. Until then, he'd been knowed by one and all as a top hand. Far as I was concerned he still was, lame leg or not. To my way of thinking, it was Glenn who should have been County Sheriff, not Ernie Fillmore.

Glenn unlocked the door and let himself into the cell. He poured the cup half full and handed it to me. "It was me hit you upside the head," he told me, "Sorry I had to, but it was a matter of life and death, as they say—your life. Your death.

84

"If you recall, you was pullin' your gun against a man who already had the drop on you. If I hadn't stopped your play you'd be dead as your pardner."

My heart fell. A great sadness swept through my vitals like a cold prairie wind. I took the offered cup and watched my hand shake. After a bit, when I figured I could keep my voice steady, I asked, "Orville's dead?"

"Afraid so. Sheriff and me was on our way back from breakfast when we happened onto you boys. You and Orville seemed to be havin' words with them strangers in front of Tanner's Barn. Then all at once we seen Orville draw against the two-gun man, saw him take a bullet and go down. I got to you just in time."

"Yeah. Did Orville say anything?"

"He said, 'Tell Merlin I'm sorry.' Said he had no kin—left everything he owned to you."

That's when I choked up. The thought came to me again that most everybody I'd ever cared about had took the big jump, one way or the other, leaving me behind and lonesome. My mother, my Pa, old Walt, and now my best friend Orville, had all gave up the ghost and went on up the trail ahead of me. At the time all I knew to do was feel sorry for myself. Right then it almost seemed them folks had all done it a-purpose, just to get shut of me. Grief took hold of me with its bony fingers and pulled me down a cold hole. Glenn nodded at the tin cup I held. "Drink up, hoss," he said, "it'll make you feel better."

He lied, or maybe not. Anyway, the whiskey sure primed my pump. It seared its way over my swollen tongue, descended my gullet, and touched off the explosion I'd feared. I dropped the cup and made a beeline for the slop-bucket, retching and heaving until I'd brought up everything that was in me. I knelt there a-gasping like a trout on a creek bank, all but convinced I had turned myself inside out. It wouldn't have surprised me none to find I'd thrown up some of my internal organs. Anyway, after I'd knelt there a-hugging the bucket awhile, I had to admit Glenn had been right; I did feel some better. Not much, but some.

While I was entertaining myself in the manner just described Glenn set down on the bunk, rolled himself a smoke, and patiently waited for my return. Directly, I done so—returned, I mean.

"Much obliged," I said, "I think maybe I'm goin' to live."

"Glad to hear it, Merlin. Keepin' you alive is the reason I thumped you in the first place."

"How'd you come to lock me up in this here cell?" I asked.

"Seemed like a good idea at the time. Orville drew on the stranger, and the stranger beat his hand and killed him. Strictly speakin', that made the shootin' self-defense. Had to let 'em go.

"I figured to head off more trouble by providin' you with room and board here in the county jail till them fellers had time to put some coolin' off distance between you."

86

"Them strangers stole my horse, Glenn, leastways I believe they did. I take it bad of you, protectin' 'em like that."

Glenn stood up and pushed the cell door open wide. "Why hell, Merlin," he said, "I wasn't protectin' them—I was protectin' *you*."

When Glenn led me into the sheriff's office, Ernie Fillmore was setting at his big roll-top desk doing paper work—concerning Orville, I supposed. Ernie was a short man, and his pantslegs were stuffed inside a knee-high pair of fancy boots with heels three inches high. He wore a high-crowned white Stetson hat that looked wider than his shoulders. Just looking at the pear-shaped lawman riled me; I had nearly forgot how much I disliked him.

He didn't look up when we came in, but went on writing like he was much too busy to take note of anything as no-account and piddling as me. After a bit, Glenn cleared his throat and said, "It's Merlin Fanshaw, sheriff. He's ready to go."

Ernie reared back in his swivel chair, looked down his nose, and curled his lip. "Oh," says he, "it's you."

I complimented him on his powers of observation. Him and me had come from the same little town, we'd knowed each other for anyway ten of my twenty years, he had only that morning caused me to be locked up in his dang jail, and just like that he recognized that I was *me*.

To give the man his due, there have been times in

87

my life when I made a better appearance. I had no mirror right then, but I had a pretty good idea of how I must have looked. There was a lump the size of a pigeon egg back of my right ear, tastefully accented by dried blood and matted hair. I smelled of whiskey and disgorged material from the depths of my innards. No doubt my eyes were red and my features haggard, and I'm dead certain my breath could have backed a vulture off a gut-pile.

Ernie leaned back in his swivel chair, put his feet on the desk, and laced his fingers across his belly. "Well?" says he, "you want to tell me what led up to the shootin' this mornin'?"

"Somebody stole my horse Quicksilver while Orville and me was camped over on Careless Crick. I have reason to believe the thieves was them strangers we seen at Tanner's."

"I see. What makes you think it was them?"

"Well—the big feller, the man called Fontayne, seemed to want my horse mighty bad. He tried to buy the animal, but I said no. Then later that same night somebody cut Quicksilver's picket rope and made off with him."

Ernie snorted. His feet came off the desk and hit the floor hard. He leaned forward and glared at me.

"Did you see them take the horse? Did you find the animal in their possession? Did Fontayne tell you they stole it? Maybe the horse ain't stole at all—maybe it just strayed!"

"And maybe it cut its own picket rope, too, but I doubt

88

it! No, I can't prove them fellers stole Quicksilver but I believe they did. Orville believed it, too—that's why he braced those birds, and that's why he's dead now."

Ernie stood up from his swivel chair and walked over to the stove. A coffee pot steamed atop the heater, and Ernie picked it up and poured himself a cup. He didn't offer me one, of course.

"In the first place," he said, "Orville's dead because he was a hot-head who picked a fight with the wrong man. In the second place, you have no evidence those men took your horse—you can't prove it was stolen at all. In the third place, I don't like you much, nor do I ever expect to. You have used your smart mouth on me one too many times, Merlin Fanshaw, and I believe you'd be better off takin' your troubles to someone who cares."

Ernie fished his dollar watch from a vest pocket and eyed its face. "And in the fourth place, I've got a *real* crime to investigate. Buford Suggs' stepdaughter, Pandora Pretty Hawk, broke an axe handle across his skull and ran off somewheres with all his money. It may not be the crime of the century, but it's a helluva lot more interesting than *your* complaint."

"And just about your *speed,* too," I told him, "you might almost be lawman enough to arrest a young girl without even callin' out a posse. Of course, if you have to *track* her any distance you'll be in trouble— it's common knowledge you couldn't track an elephant with a nosebleed through a *snowdrift*."

"Get the hell out of my office," he replied.

We held Orville's funeral the next morning at the Shenanigan cemetery. Orville had no kin that I knew of, nor any special attachment to the town of Dry Creek, so we buried him where he'd fell, like a soldier on a battlefield. There was no church service, and the event was nowhere near as well attended as old Walt's had been. Fact is, if you don't count "Bones" Jefferson, the grave digger, there was only Glenn Murdoch and me. Still, I reckon Orville got himself grieved for about as well as most dearly departeds.

For a minute or so I got plumb religious. I stood next to the open grave and asked the Lord to please cut Orville out a good circle horse, give him big country to ride in, and let him have a drink of whiskey now and again, if such was permitted.

I talked to Orville some, too. Oh, I know the part of him that was there inside that pine box didn't hear me, but that wasn't all there was to Orville, not by a damsite. I told him a couple of jokes I thought he'd like, recalled some of the good times we'd shared, and I made him a promise or two about getting Quicksilver back. I also discussed the two-gun man who'd killed him and made a promise about that feller, too. At which point I got religious again and wound up by saying, "God willing."

Afterward, I talked to Bob Tanner down at the Livery and asked him about Fontayne and Gossert. He said all he knew was they rode good horses and paid their bill. Gossert's horse had throwed a shoe and the black-smith next door had set a new one for him. They'd paid the smithy, too.

No, Tanner hadn't seen Quicksilver, not since the race, and he'd seen nothing of the third man—the one who looked like a bear—neither. He said Fontayne and Gossert had rode out right after the short arm of the law told them they could, but he hadn't noticed which way they went.

Tanner gave me a sheepish grin and said he was sorry he had so few answers to my questions. I told him that was all right, he couldn't know what he didn't know, and I thanked him for his time.

I asked if I could leave Orville's horse and saddle with him at the Livery for awhile, and he allowed that I could. He said he'd always liked Orville, so he didn't figure to charge me board. I said I appreciated his kindness and told him much obliged from both me and from Orville.

I felt mighty bad about Orville's murder—for murder is what it had been, to my way of thinking. Already, I missed his company. Even so, I couldn't help but notice (with some disgust) that my grief hadn't hurt my appetite none. I tied up at the Red Rooster and had me a big T-bone steak, four eggs, a mess of fried taters, half a pie, and a quart of black coffee before I high-heeled it out the door and put the streets of Shenanigan behind me.

It was late afternoon that same day that I took the road west for Dry Creek. The day was middling hot, and big thunderclouds stacked up white and billowy against a sky so blue it hurt my eyes. As always, I rode Little Buck, bringing the packhorse along at a go-to-work trot. The hollow echo of the horses' hooves on the planks as we clattered across the Careless Creek bridge caused me to recall the sound the dirt clods had made as they fell on Orville's coffin.

I found I was commencing to feel unsure about how I should proceed. Much as I hated to admit it, Ernie Fillmore had been right; there was no proof Fontayne and his boys had stole Quicksilver. Yes, they'd offered to buy the horse, but so had Colonel Charlie, and I didn't suspicion him. Surely a man could look at a horse, admire a horse, offer to buy a horse, without intending to steal it.

Even so, I remembered what Orville said about the way Fontayne looked at Quicksilver that day at the races. I'd made light of Orville's worry at the time, but the truth was I'd seen something that troubled me the night Fontayne and his boys came to our camp. Even while he was talking to us, Fontayne had kept a-glancing toward the meadow where Quicksilver grazed. His face that night had the look prospectors and gamblers sometimes wear—hard and hungry, with the wanting plain to see. Remembering that look, I knew a thing I couldn't prove—Fontayne *had* stolen Quicksilver, oh yes he had indeed.

Well, I didn't have any idea which way them boys had gone. All I knew to do was start out on the road and hope maybe some passing traveler might have seen them. As it turned out, I hadn't gone but a mile or so when I happened onto a barefoot kid, riding an old work mare and herding twenty head of milk cows toward Shenanigan. There was Jerseys and Guernseys and even some range cows in the bunch, but all of them was milkers and all of them was moving slow and easy as they plodded up the road. I pulled off to the side and waited till the boy drew nigh.

"Afternoon," says I with a grin, "you must be quite a hand to move a big trail herd like that all by your lonesome."

The kid reined the old mare to a stop. He wore no hat, and his fine yellow hair flamed bright in the late afternoon sun. The boy gave me a sort of sideways look and said, "You're funnin' me, I reckon, but herdin' these cows is my job, mister."

"That a fact?"

"Yessir. I take 'em out to graze every mornin' after the folks that own 'em finish their milkin.' I let 'em graze durin' the day and fetch 'em back to town again come evenin'."

"Sounds like a big job. Folks pay you by the head?"

"Yessir. I get two cents a day for each cow. My ma takes in washin' and the money helps out."

"You sound like a real go-getter," I said, "and a man who keeps his eyes open. Might be you could help me. You see, I'm tryin' to catch up with some fellers, and I thought maybe you might have seen them."

"Maybe," the kid said, "I don't miss much."

"There'd be two men, ridin' hot-blooded horses and

maybe herdin' some others. See anyone like that today?"

"Hard to say. What might it be worth if I did?"

I stood in my stirrups and dug two silver dollars out of my britches. The coins glittered in the sunlight as I held them up. "Five days wages, cowboy," I told him.

The boy put on a poker face, but his eyes never left the money. "Two men this mornin'," he said, "one tall, ridin' a yeller claybank. Other man smaller, on a blue roan. Two-gun man. They was headed south, toward the mountains."

My heart went into a gallop. Now it was my turn to wear a poker face. "Just them two?" I asked, "how about a third man—big feller, built like a bear? Maybe herdin' some loose stock?"

"No, sir," the kid said, "just them two."

"Much obliged, pardner," I said, handing him the coins, "you don't miss much at that."

I had already started to ride away when the kid's voice stopped me. "Mister," he said, "that other man you asked about? Like I said, he wasn't with them two. I seen him earlier, before sunup, ridin' fast and leadin' a blood bay thoroughbred stud. He was goin' toward the mountains, too."

It's curious, the way things work out. Only minutes before I had no proof other than my feelings that Quicksilver had been stolen at all. I didn't know which way Fontayne and Gossert had gone and I knew even less about where the third feller was. Then in one

94

short pow-wow with a tow-headed cow wrangler I'd learned the answers to all them questions. Fontayne and his boys were headed south, the kid had said, and my horse was with them.

I thought I knew where the horse-thieves was bound. Fontayne had said he was from the town of Maiden, up in the Judith range. If that was so, there was only one way to get there from Shenanigan and that was by way of Brimstone Gap. The gap was the only pass through the mountains for fifty miles or more; it led to Silver City and from there east across the Yellowstone and north to the Judiths.

Whatever doubts I'd had before were gone. I don't recall even considering going back to Sheriff Ernie Fillmore with what the kid had told me for I was convinced it would do no good. Instead, I intended to follow them thieves myself wherever they went, and one way or another I would take my property back. I'd made promises to Orville and to myself, and I meant to keep them. Without so much as a backward glance I turned my horses off the road and into the broken country leading south.

For the first three or four miles I held Little Buck to a steady trot, and the packhorse kept pace with little effort. The glass-eyed gelding led well; the only time his lead-rope tightened at all was when Buck jumped a wash-out or dodged a badger hole and the packhorse had to look to his own footing. Twice I stopped to check the pack, but it hadn't loosened. The second time I gave the horses a breather, then moved on.

The air turned cold as the sun dropped behind the mountains, and long shadows stretched out over the hills to the east like thin, blue paint spilled from a bucket. A meadowlark exploded out of a sage thicket, gliding and fluttering in mock distress as she tried to lead me away from her low-lying nest. I admired her spunk; somehow seeing her buck the odds on behalf of her young ones helped keep my own spirits up.

Above the mountain peaks, clouds took on a gilt-edged glory as the sky below went red as warpaint, faded, and went gray. By the time I'd reached the road again at Brimstone Gap the light was nearly gone. I turned my horses upward through jet-black trees, fallen rock, and quaking aspen, looking for a likely place to camp. Directly I heard, more than saw, a thin stream chuckling and dancing over rock, and I followed the water uphill.

The source of the stream turned out to be a good spring in a patch of quakers, and them trees was living up to their name. A cold breeze had rose up with the setting of the sun, and it caused the dollar-sized leaves to tremble and patter with a sound not unlike the water itself.

The grove stood on a grassy bench below a granite outcrop maybe a hundred yards above the road, and I knew I'd have a fine view of the country with the coming of daylight. I pulled the pack off the gelding, unsaddled Buck, and staked the horses out to graze.

By the time I'd rolled out my bed and got a fire going it was full dark with the first stars of evening seeming close enough to touch yet at the same time more distant than a man could begin to understand.

My appetite was a constant marvel to me. In spite of my big breakfast at the Red Rooster I was hungry again. In less time than it takes to tell it I'd greased a skillet and cooked up a mess of bacon and beans that would have fed a logging camp. I done my best but there was more vittles than even I could do away with so I put the lid back on the skillet and figured I'd finish the job come morning.

As I set there staring at the embers of my dying fire I thought ahead to the finding of Fontayne and his pardners and of getting Quicksilver back. I knew not when, but I was dead certain I'd find them boys and recover my stolen horse. When the showdown came, I aimed to set things right, no matter what that should require.

I was no gunman, but neither was I a stranger to the use of weapons. I had hunted since I was just a button and was considered a good shot with both rifle and shotgun. My Pa never allowed me to handle a revolver much. He said carrying a short gun would only get me in trouble and that packing a six-shooter had put more young men in the graveyard than the cholera.

After Pa died, I'd strapped on his old Colt's dragoon and shortly discovered he was right. I wound up riding for a season with Original George Starkweather's outlaw band, and during the time I was with them boys I had occasion to kill a feller in a shooting affray.

The man was a bounty hunter, and he was trying to kill me at the time, while I was doing my best to prevent that outcome. Truth is, the feller pretty much stumbled into my bullet, but he died sure enough and it was my shot that took his life. I wish to God it hadn't happened. I'll not forget the man though I live to be a hundred.

I believe a man must stand for the right and that he is bound to defend himself against them that would steal from him or abuse him, even to the use of deadly force. I hoped it would not come to that this time, but I was prepared to do what I had to.

I don't have any idea how long I set there staring at the embers and pondering my pursuit of the horse-thieves. I recall feeling drowsy and telling myself I should go check on the horses and turn in for the night. My belly was full, I was warm from the fire, and a soft breeze played among the aspens and brought the soft patter of leaves to my ear. It was a sound like hundreds of tiny hands a-clapping from a long ways off.

My eyelids felt heavy. Twice, my eyes closed and I jerked awake as my head nodded slow towards my chest. Somewhere far back in the pines a night bird cried. I could hear the horses grazing easy out on the bench. I crossed my arms, leaned back against Pa's old Texas saddle, and drifted off to sleep.

I have heard it said that the slightest sound from a sleeping baby can bring its mother wide awake if that sound is anything different than what she knows to be normal. Well, I'm no mother, nor am I likely ever to be one, but it was a sound—a different sound—that woke me, woke me sudden, my heart pounding. The fire had long since gone out, and the night was darker than I'd have believed it could be. Even the moon had gone into hiding behind the clouds and shed no helpful light.

I caught my breath and held it, the better to listen. What had I heard? What was it that had brought me full awake and staring into the darkness? Then, I heard it again—Little Buck's familiar, deep-throated nicker, that nervous rumble that told me something was wrong. I saw nothing, yet I knew Buck would be standing, his head high, his ears pointing and alert, and his nostrils wide as he sniffed the cold night air.

Then, of a sudden, I sensed something, or someone, close by in the darkness. I don't remember reaching for it, but my Colt's dragoon was in my hand; my thumb eared the hammer back to full cock, the double-click sounding clear as a sidewinder's rattle. My voice was harsh and tight; I didn't recognize it myself.

"Who's there?" I rasped.

The answer came, soft and breathy, a woman's voice, and young.

"Don't shoot me, Merlin," it said, "you'll feel bad if you do. And I won't feel so good myself."

SEVEN
Pandora's Story

The hair on the back of my neck stood straight up. I was drowsy no more, but suddenly wide awake. The woman's voice had sounded very near, and I stared hard into the darkness, trying to locate its source.

"Who are you?" I asked again, and this time at least I sounded a little more like myself.

The voice had a smile in it, "You don't remember me? You're breaking my heart, Merlin."

My own heart had jumped from a slow walk to a high lope when first I sensed her presence; now it began to settle back to a more normal pace. I eased the hammer down on my six-gun. My ears felt hot, and I knew I was blushing. I was glad right then it was dark.

"I ain't in the mood for games," I huffed, "Who am I talkin' to?"

For a long moment there was no reply. Faintly, I heard a soft rustle, as of clothing, and I caught just the faintest trace of a sweet, musky fragrance.

"I'll strike a match," says she.

I heard a scratching sound, then bright flame popped to life and punched a hole in the darkness. Directly across from where I set, the woman's cupped hands held the blazing match before her face, and the face smiled.

"It's me, Merlin," she said, "it's Pandora."

100

Pandora Pretty Hawk! And pretty she surely was. The match flame made tiny bright spots in the blackness of her eyes and cast deep shadows behind her high, wide cheekbones. Beneath a battered felt hat, her straight black hair hung loose, shining and sleek in the yellow light. Then the match burned out, and the darkness was darker than before.

I had set aside a dead pine branch to start my morning fire. Groping, my hand found it and laid it atop the ashes of the fire pit. Seconds later, my own match burst into flame and I held it to the dry needles until they caught. Soon, I had a good blaze going, and I took a closer look at Pandora.

It had been nearly four years since last I'd seen her, but she hadn't changed all that much. Pandora had always been a beauty, and if anything she had grown even more so. She was two years younger than me, but I had known her since we was in school together at Dry Creek.

Pandora was half Crow Indian on her mother's side, and even when she was little she had moved with an easy grace that put me in mind of a mountain lion prowling a rimrock. Pandora had took the name "Pretty Hawk" as a last name, after her Crow grandpa, and that name alone gave her a certain flair at school. I'd always liked Pandora, even back there in grade school when I hated females on principle.

It seemed to me then that girls was mostly nuisances and more dang trouble than they was worth. You was always supposed to treat them gentle, and if you ever did accidentally get a little rough with one she'd go a-crying and sniveling to the teacher. Then a feller would likely wind up getting a whipping by the schoolmaster and another one by his Pa when he got home. Anyway, I didn't admire girls much in them days.

Except for Pandora; even then the girl was different. She could out-run, out-climb, and out-fight most of us boys, and the one time I did get rough with her she bloodied my nose. Later, when we got to be around thirteen or fourteen, she used to flirt with me some—trying out her weapons, my Pa said.

She'd crowd me into a corner somewheres and stand up real close, to where we was almost touching each other and talk all quiet and whispery until I fell to blushing and stammering. Or she'd walk off a ways, look back at me over her shoulder kind of sleepy-eyed, and smile like she knew some special female mystery, which maybe she did.

Anyway, at them times I'd go clumsy and foolish as ever a boy can. I'd either get plumb tongue-tied or babble like a idiot. I would feel such sweet confusion and at the same time such a terrible fright I'm sur-prised I didn't perish altogether right on the spot.

There was talk, of course. Seems like there always is with a girl like Pandora. A few of the boys hinted she was wild and tried to make out they had personal knowledge of the fact. Some of the girls were of a similar opinion or said they were, but I figured they was talking out of jealousy. Many of the girls her age was every bit as flirty, but it was Pandora that turned the boys' heads. All them girls was fishing the same waters, but Pandora was a born fisher of men, if you take my meaning, and her bait was better.

She was a natural beauty and she had a way about her that surely was special, but Pandora never put on airs. She didn't even seem to know how fine she was, though us boys all did. Pandora was just her natural self and she done things her own way. I will confess, though, there was times I wished she *was* wild, and that she'd be wild with *me*.

But that was then. I had become a man since those days, and I aimed to let her know that. I took it on myself to lecture her some just to get my dignity back.

"It's good to see you, Pandora," I said, "but you took quite a chance, sneakin' into a strange camp after dark. I might have shot you for a thief."

Her smile was a bright flash in the firelight. "I *am* a thief," she said, calm as you please, "I've had no food in two days, and I was looking to steal some from you. As for shooting me, I believe you'd need to be *awake* to do that."

"I still say you took quite a chance. I could have been anybody."

"You are anybody. You're somebody with a pack-horse and food. I've been watching since before sun-down. Even from a distance I thought it was you."

"Why didn't you call out then?"

"I thought it was you, but I wasn't sure. I needed to be sure."

I moved the beans back onto the fire and took a clean plate out of the pannier.

"Yeah, I heard. Fearless Fillmore's on your trail. He told me you laid your stepdaddy out with an axe-handle and stole all his money."

"There's some truth in the worst of lies," Pandora said, her eyes fixed on the skillet. Her hand shook as she reached out and took the beans off the fire. "I'll tell you about it later, but right now I need to eat something. And it don't need to be warmed up, either."

Well, Pandora lit into them beans with considerable zest and I just set back and admired her style. Some of my interest was professional in nature; like I said before, the consumption of vittles is among my main pursuits, and I feel I've achieved a degree of skill at it. The other part, to be plumb honest, was just that I found Pandora mighty good to look upon.

She ate with real gusto, yet with a certain delicacy I found impressive in one so hungry. When she finally set the skillet down, there was scant need to clean it.

"A-ho," she said, using the Crow word for "much obliged."

Pandora leaned back against one of the panniers from my pack outfit and closed her eyes. I started to ask her more about the trouble she was in, but by the time I got around to it she had already fell asleep where she sat.

I took a wool blanket from my bedroll and the old star quilt my mother had made and covered her. Then, while the fire burned low, I watched her by its flickering light. I speculated, as I have many times before and since that night, on the way trails sometimes cross and how chance meetings can change a man's life. Finally, I shucked my boots, slipped into my roll, and laid back to ponder the situation. I studied the night sky for a minute or two, started in to corral my thoughts and go to reflecting on them, and promptly drifted off to sleep like a milk-fed pup by a warm stove.

I came awake to cold morning air and the rich smell of fresh coffee. My mind tried to keep hold of a busy dream I'd been having, but lost its grip and let the reverie fade. Then I recalled some of what had took place over the last few days and the previous evening, and I remembered Pandora Pretty Hawk.

The canvas tarp that covered my bedroll was wet and stiff with the morning dew, but I was warm inside my blankets. I rolled over and opened my eyes. Pandora was busy at the cookfire, her movements practiced and sure, and I laid there and took pleasure in the watching of her.

She wore a faded blue flannel shirt, open at the throat, and a choker collar of white and turquoise beads. I seen with some surprise that she wore men's britches made of canvas ducking and held up by galluses. Women didn't wear pants much in them days, at least not decent women, nor did they ride astride, neither. But Pandora never did pay much heed to custom. She mostly did just about whatever she had a mind to. I admired that about her, and I suppose envied her some, too.

She wore the star quilt I'd covered her with the night

before across her shoulders like a shawl, and high-top Crow moccasins of white deer-skin covered her tiny feet. In the warm morning sunlight her skin was tawny and red-gold, and her long, straight hair was the blue-black color of a raven's wing. Pandora Pretty Hawk was altogether a sight to behold, and I laid there and beheld her for some time.

She turned to put another stick on the fire and caught me looking at her. I set up in bed, put my hat on, and yawned as if I'd just woke up. "I see you're still here," I said, "I suppose that means I'll have to feed you again." I don't reckon I fooled her much; my eyes had already told her I was glad to see her.

"I'm feeding myself, as it happens," she said, "but there's enough for you, too, if you're through sleeping your life away."

My boots were cold and stiff, and it took some effort to pull them on. I stood and stomped around some until my feet set themselves for the day. Pandora poured a cup of coffee and handed it to me.

"You're pretty sassy, for a charity case," I told her, "but I'm feelin' generous this mornin.' I guess I'll let you stay to breakfast."

She smiled. "You always *were* a sweet-talker," she said.

Pandora surely had learned to cook, I'll give her that. She'd made fry bread and another batch of bacon and beans, and I found the meal as good as any I ever had. Even her coffee was better than mine, or just as good anyway, though I wasn't disposed to tell her that. I hunkered down by the fire, poured a second cup from the battered pot, and thought about Pandora.

I never knew what happened to Pandora's real Pa, but Buford Suggs took her and her mother in when she wasn't but ten years old. Buford had a little farm west of Dry Creek where he raised hogs, did a little farming, and, some said, used a long loop and a running iron on his neighbors' cows.

Buford was known as a hard man, and local gossip held that he worked Pandora and her Ma like field hands. I recall Pandora used to fall asleep in school sometimes from pure tiredness, and there was often blisters on her small hands.

There was other things, too. I remember times she came to school sporting a black eye, and other times when she had bruises on her arms or legs. Pandora never complained, though, and when the teacher asked about her hurts she'd say she fell down, run into a door, or something. Like I said before, Pandora had a graceful, steady way about her that was almost unnatural in a child. I never believed she could be hurting herself because of clumsiness.

I always believed it was Buford who put them marks on Pandora. Because she wouldn't say so there wasn't much anyone could do about it, even if they was so inclined, and nobody was. To most folks around Dry Creek, Pandora Pretty Hawk was just a half-breed child Buford Suggs had took in. If anyone except me worried about her, I never saw much sign of it.

Her mother died the year Pandora turned thirteen, and Buford took her out of school and set her to working full-time at home. I saw her only once after that. It was on a gray, snowy afternoon in February, and the wind that howled down out of the Brimstones gave real teeth to the cold. Buford and Pandora had come to town in his wagon, and I seen her late in the day, huddled on the wagon seat outside the Oasis saloon. She was waiting for Buford to come out, and it looked like she'd been there awhile.

I said howdy, and she seemed happy to see me. She asked how I was and I said I was fine as frog-hair and asked how she was making out. She said, oh, pretty good, that she was working hard keeping house and helping with the work. Said old Buford had promised her wages of ten dollars a month and that she planned to save up her money so she'd have a grub-stake of her own some day.

About that time, Buford came a-staggering out of the saloon, drunk as a lord, and hollered at me to get away from Pandora, so I did. What I wanted to do was kick his sorry ass, or at least talk back, but I didn't. I wasn't but fifteen myself and no match for the mean old devil. Besides, she *was* his step-daughter, and I reckon he had the right to say who she could talk to.

Even so, I sometimes used to daydream about giving Buford Suggs a licking in front of the whole town and making him promise to treat Pandora right. I never did any such thing, of course; I suppose I was just a dang coward. Daydreaming is easy, but trying to really be a hero can get a feller killed.

Pandora had filled the dutch oven with water from the spring and had set it on the coals to heat. She knelt there beside the fire, her back straight and her small hands resting on her thighs. A frown creased her brow and shadowed her face the way a storm cloud blocks the sun. For a time, she gazed far out toward the valley and the distant blue line of mountains beyond. Then, with an impatient toss of her hair, she turned her attention back to me.

"I said last night I'd tell you more about my trouble later," she said, "Well, this is later—and as good a time as any."

I stood up and cast the dregs from my coffee cup into the fire. "There's no need, Pandora," I told her, "I'm glad I could help, but I've got business of my own on up the road, and it can't wait."

"I need to tell somebody, Merlin. I need to tell *you,*" she said, her eyes big and serious, "It won't take long."

Well, damn. What could I do? Fontayne and his pardners already had almost a day's lead on me, and I had lost their trail. I knew I was burning daylight. I wanted to be saddled and gone, but Pandora said she needed me to listen, and I didn't know how to say no. I squatted back down onto my boot heels and nodded.

She dropped her eyes to the fire, and her voice was so soft I could hardly hear her.

"Even before he made me quit school," she said,

"Buford took to comin' at me, like a slobberin' dog. Not all the time, but every now and then, when he was drunk. He'd try to catch me, put his hands on me, you know. I felt disgusted and scared when it happened, and sick to my stomach.

"Mostly, I could get away—I'd go off in the woods someplace and hide until he sobered up. But—sometimes I couldn't get away, and those times were bad. I would fight him like a cat, teeth and claw, but he was strong. He'd hold me and hit me until my strength was gone, and then he would have his way with me. This happened three times before I turned thirteen.

"Each time he came to me later and told me how sorry he was. He said it was the whiskey that made him crazy, and he swore on the Bible it would never happen again. He said I dare not tell my mother because she would blame me and hate me. I didn't know what to do. I didn't want my mother to hate me. I didn't want to hurt her. So I said nothing.

"At first, I even felt sorry for Buford. One time he got down on his knees, hung onto my skirt, and bawled like a baby. He begged me to forgive him, and he cried great, ragged sobs like something had broke inside him. I was just a kid; I'd never seen a grown man cry like that. It scared me, and I didn't know what to say. So I told him I forgave him.

"But then time would pass, Buford would get drunk again, and he'd come at me again. I told him I'd put the law on him, but he said, 'who you gonna tell— Ernie Fillmore? He's a damn joke, everybody knows that. Anyway, you think he'd believe you? More likely, he'd try to bed you his own self,' and he laughed like a crazy man.

"I said I'd run away, someplace where he couldn't find me. 'You do that, girl,' he said, 'and I'll have the law on *you.* The law *will* believe *me,* and the law will bring you back.' Well, I figured he was right about that, so I stayed."

Pandora was quiet for awhile then, and there was naked hurt in her dark eyes as again she stared out across the wide valley. I was quiet myself as I watched her. I wanted to say something to help, something to let her know I understood, something to soften her pain, but I didn't know what to say and I didn't understand. A hot anger toward Buford Suggs had took hold of me, there was a bitterness like gall at the back of my throat, and I don't believe I could have said anything right then if I'd wanted to.

Pandora looked down at her hands and spoke again, and this time her voice sounded older, and tired. "Then my mother got sick with a fever and took to her bed. I sent for the medicine man and the missionary priest, and they both came. The medicine man sang over her and burned sweet grass. He drummed for her and he shook his rattle, but the sickness didn't leave. The priest read from a little book and prayed for my mother. He talked to me about God's will and God's grace, but still the sickness didn't go away.

"I rode to Dry Creek and asked Doc Taggart to come see her, and he did. Buford told Doc he hadn't sent for any damn sawbones, and he wasn't going to pay for one. Doc said he didn't care about Buford's money, he cared about my mother. He said he was going to doctor her whether Buford liked it or not. Doc told me she had typhoid fever, and he done the best he could, but it was too late. I'll never forget how hard she fought to stay alive, or the way the room smelled. Did you know typhoid fever smells like fresh baked bread? Anyway, Mother died that night. I felt like part of me died, too.

"Buford took her dying hard. He cried that night like a child, and he wouldn't eat or take care of himself. Her funeral was the worst of all. Buford took hold of her casket, pulled a gun, and said nobody was going to put his dear, sweet, wife in the cold ground. He wailed and hollered and moaned something awful, but after awhile I was able to calm him down and get him home.

"I was going to leave right then, and I should have, but Buford seemed so hurt and lost I just couldn't. That's when he said he'd pay me ten dollars a month if I'd stay, and I finally said I would. I told him if he ever came at me again the way he had before I would leave for good, and that I'd go so far away he'd never find me. He said I didn't have to worry, that was all in the past. He said them times before had been the whiskey's fault and that he had quit drinking. He swore on the Bible again, and I believed him again.

"For awhile he was as good as his word. He still got drunk now and then, and he worked me hard, it's true, but he paid me like he said he would and he didn't abuse me or come at me again.

"Remember that old lard bucket I used to bring my lunch in when we were in school? The one with the lid? Well, I put the money I saved in that bucket, and kept it underneath my bed. I told Buford I would stay on the place and work for him until I'd saved $500. Then, I said, I would go find work somewhere else and start my own life. He told me I'd have his blessing when that day came and said he was grateful I'd stayed on."

Pandora had been cleaning up the pots and pans while she talked. Now she got to her feet and began to pack the grub, skillet, dutch oven, and such back in the rawhide panniers. She stood then and looked into my eyes, and her voice sounded flat and hard.

"On the first of the month, he paid me again. I counted my money and saw I had almost four hundred dollars—in just ten months I'd have the stake I'd worked so hard for.

"I was happy that day—happier than I had been since my mother died. It was a pretty spring day. The country was all fresh and green in the sunshine, and the birds were singing everywhere. I saddled my horse and rode out across the prairie and down along the crick for nearly two hours. As I was coming back to the farm, a big cloud shut out the sun and darkness fell over everything. All at once I felt afraid, like something bad was going to happen. I put my horse in the corral and went up to the house.

"And there he was—Buford. He was in the kitchen, drunk and dirty. He looked like he'd threw up on himself, and there was mud and grass on his clothes, like he'd been sleeping with the hogs. He was at the kitchen table with the tin bucket from under my bed, and he had my money in his filthy hands.

"I screamed at him—I asked him what he thought he was doing—and he called me a name and stuffed my money in the pockets of his coat. He said he was going to buy some whiskey, that the money was really his anyway. When I tried to stop him he hit me with his fist and knocked me to the floor. He tried to go outside, and I held onto him and kept screaming that he had my money and he had to give it back. Then he said by God he'd had enough of my bellering—he called me a redskin bitch, and he hit me again.

"Seemed like he went crazy then. He threw me to the floor and came at me like he had those times before, tearing at my clothes and calling me bad names. I guess that's when I went a little crazy myself.

"Buford had been working for the last couple of weeks on a new hickory handle for his axe, and it was leaning against the wall, beside the stove. As he forced me to the floor, I caught hold of it and rolled out from under him. That's when I hit him the first time."

"The *first* time?" I said, "Didn't that stop him?"

"It stopped him a little. But I was mad—crazy mad.

I hit him some more, hard as I could. Even when he quit moving and lay still, I hit him. I broke the axe handle. I thought I'd killed him."

"Too bad you didn't, if you ask me. Seems like he was still alive enough to tell Ernie Fillmore you tried to, anyway. What did you do then?"

"I took my money, got on my horse, and left there."

"Left there in a hurry. You didn't think to bring any food, or blankets, or anything. You didn't even bring a gun."

"I just wanted to get away—as far and as fast as I could. I spent that night, and the next two days, in the mountains near here. Then, last night at sundown, I saw you."

Again, she stared out beyond me at the valley and the road leading back to Dry Creek.

"I'm sorry if I've caused you trouble," she said, "I appreciate you letting me talk."

I wanted to put my arms around her and hold her, I wanted to more than anything. I didn't know how she'd take it, so I hesitated, and the moment passed.

"There's no need to thank me," I told her, "I'm glad I was here, and you haven't caused me no trouble."

"Maybe not *yet,*" she said, her eyes looking beyond me at the valley, "but if I'm not mistaken, that's sheriff Ernie Fillmore and a three-man posse, coming this way."

EIGHT
Hide and Seek

Pandora was right. Four riders were coming fast up the road, and there was no mistaking Sheriff Ernie Fillmore's big white hat or his pear-shape build. I got my Pa's field glasses out of my saddlebags and took a closer look.

What I seen was just about what I expected. There was Kip Mefford and Coley Peters—both loafers and sometime county deputies—and Stub Hathaway, a storekeeper's kid. More than anything, Hathaway hankered to be a lawman, and Ernie Fillmore was his hero, if you can believe that. Anyway, there they were, armed to the teeth and coming straight toward us.

I wasn't all that worried; there was no way they could see us from the road. We were a good hundred yards above them, screened by aspen groves and pine, and our morning fire had long since gone out—there would be no smoke to give us away. I figured they was a-hunting Pandora, all right, and I had to grin; Ernie really *had* called out a posse to catch one lone girl.

I figured they would ride on past us through the gap and we could pack up, slip out behind them, and go easy on our way. It was not to be. Ernie reared back in the saddle, his hand in the air and his belly a-jiggling, and pulled his horse to a sliding stop. His intrepid

116

deputies done the same, more or less. Hathaway had a little trouble controlling his steed and rode on past the others a ways before he could get it stopped and turned around.

Ernie held a war council then, all puffed up for his posse and pointing in all directions with many a bold and sweeping gesture. Hathaway mopped his brow and blowed his nose on a big bandanna, while Mefford rolled himself a smoke and Peters got down, walked off a piece, and relieved himself. Pa's old field glasses were good ones; I was enjoying the way I could watch the possemen without them knowing it.

"What's going on?" Pandora whispered. She had crawled over beside me, and I smelled the same sweet, musky scent I'd noticed the night before.

"Looks like Ernie is makin' a speech to his troops," I told her, "but they don't seem all that impressed. I have a feelin' they've heard it all before."

"You think they're looking for me?"

"I don't know, but I can't think of any other reason they'd be out this way. Your stepdaddy must have offered a reward or somethin'. Ernie don't usually set foot outside the city limits."

I handed the glasses to Pandora. She brought them to her eyes, watching the parley below us. "Where's your horse?" I asked her.

She lowered the glasses and handed them back to me. Her eyes looked up, beyond the rocky bench above us. "Up there," she said, "in a clear place beyond that spruce grove. I staked him out there last night."

"You might want to slip up there and get him," I said, "It would be a good idea for us to be saddled and ready to ride, should it be needful."

Pandora moved off, silent as smoke, and disappeared among the shadows of the trees. I laid on my belly in the grass among the aspens, braced my elbows, and studied the posse again. The boys had all got down off their horses by then, and Ernie still seemed to be caught up in his own oratory. Hathaway pulled out a pint whiskey bottle, and the boys passed it around, setting cross-legged in the grass near the road.

I thought I knew how the talk was going. Ernie was getting nervous. He was just a mile or two from the county line; the Gap marked the boundary between Progress and Brimstone counties. That meant Ernie was pritnear out of his jurisdiction. I figured he'd do what he done best, which was palaver and speechify, and then him and his intrepid posse would turn back from the border and go somewheres else.

I left the boys to their picnic and made my way to the meadow where I'd staked out the packhorse and Little Buck. Pandora had already repacked the panniers, so it didn't take long to throw my bed together and pack up the gelding. By the time I had Buck saddled I'd commenced to wonder what was keeping Pandora. I thought maybe her horse had got loose and wandered off during the night. Then I heard a hoof strike rock somewhere in the timber above me, and I knew she was on her way.

Over east, the sun had begun its slow climb up into the morning sky, and the warmth it gave felt mighty good after the cold of the night. I put the glasses on Ernie and the boys again. They were still hunkered in the grass, enjoying the sunshine and the whiskey. Kip Mefford lay stretched out with his hat over his eyes. Coley Peters was setting next to Ernie, and he took a drink from the bottle and passed it on to Stub Hathaway. The horses stood nearby, ground-tied and grazing. Only Stub and Ernie had aholt of their bridle reins. It occurred to me that if they really was a posse they was a pretty sloppy one.

Pandora broke out of the trees, crouched low and leading her horse. I had just time enough to see that her mount was a deep-chested Indian paint, a little over 14 hands high, with good legs and a deep chest. Then, all of a sudden, the apple cart upset.

Like trouble sometimes does, it came as a total surprise and from the last place I expected—from my own saddle horse, Little Buck. When he caught sight of Pandora's pony, he threw up his head, stared, and let out a high-pitched, piercing whinny that could have shattered glass. Through the field glasses, I seen sixteen eyes—eight human and eight horse—stare directly up at where we was.

I knew the fat was in the fire. Ernie's posse would be amongst us in minutes, and both Pandora and me would be arrested and took back to the Shenanigan jail. I just couldn't let that happen because I had men to find and a horse to find, and I didn't figure Pandora deserved to be drug home and turned over to her damn stepdaddy neither. In my mind's eye I could already see Ernie Fillmore's smug and prideful look as he brought us in. I determined then and there that such an outcome must not and would not occur.

I pulled the Winchester from its scabbard, jacked a shell into the chamber, and took aim. "Hold the horses, Pandora!" I hollered, and squeezed the trigger. The sound of the rifle was loud there next to the ledge. It echoed back and forth among the rocks and trees like the clatter of a rockslide in a canyon. As I meant for it to, the .44-40 slug gouged up a gob of dirt a foot from Ernie's horse. The animal shied and reared back as Ernie jumped to his feet, and I saw the bridle reins jerked through his hand.

My next shot set Ernie's and two other horses to running, but Stub Hathaway still held onto his mount. He swung into the saddle, but his horse was scared and goosey. When I fired again, it went to running and bucking. Stub was all over that horse from croup to withers. I thought he made a pretty good ride, seeing as he never did get all the way mounted. About the fourth jump, his horse swallered his head, popped his backbone, and left young Stub up yonder where the dickie birds roam.

Dirt flew up in a cloud when Stub came back to earth. He landed forked-end up, and I could hear the sound all the way to where we was. By then, the horses was flying, too, and Ernie and his posse had been set afoot.

Pandora's face beamed like the morning sun itself. She handed me the packhorse's lead-rope as I swung up onto Buck. We rode on down through the trees to the road and swung out toward Silver City at a high lope.

I could hear Ernie cussing us, even above the breeze of our passing and the sound of our running horses. Either him or one of the boys must have pulled a pistol and fired after us; I heard at least two shots as we rode out. I didn't give it much thought, in any case. I knew none of them boys could hit a moving target with a short gun, and Pandora and me sure was a-moving.

We crossed the county line twenty minutes later and slowed the horses to a walk. There was no sign of pursuit, nor did I expect any. I'm sure Ernie Fillmore was mad enough right then to follow us across the line, but I knew he had other things to do. I figured him and his deputies would be occupied the better part of the day just rounding up their horses.

Pandora stepped down off her pinto and walked on up the crick a piece while I turned my back to give her some privacy. When she came back she was smiling at me like I'd hung the moon.

"You've got style, Merlin," she said, "but I don't believe you made a friend of Ernie Fillmore today."

I grinned back at her. "Ernie's gettin' too fat," I said, "I noticed he could use some exercise, so I just gave him the chance to do a little walkin'."

Pandora's face turned serious. Her dark eyes studied me with some interest, and I had the feeling she was trying to read my thoughts. "What now?" she asked, "where do we go from here?"

Caught in the frankness of her gaze, I felt my ears grow warm and knew a blush was coming on. I turned away and pretended to check the cinch on my saddle. "Why, I don't reckon *we* go *anywhere*," I told her, "You're free to go any place you've a mind to, and I've got business of my own."

"You carry a rifle, a revolver, and plenty of cartridges," she observed, "looks to me like your 'business' is huntin' men."

"Three men," I said, "they killed my friend Orville Mooney and stole my horse. I aim to find them and get my horse back."

Her eyes never left my face. She smiled, reached out her hand and touched my arm. "Tell me about it," she said, and of course I did.

I told her about Walt and the way I'd felt about him, I told her about Quicksilver, his speed and his beauty. I told her about Fontayne and his men and about the way Portugee Gossert had gunned Orville down. Through it all, Pandora just listened, that soft half-smile on her lips and her eyes gone warm and deep.

"Let me come with you," she said, "I'll help you get your horse back."

Well, I have to admit I wanted to say yes. I knew the trail ahead was likely to hold many a twist and turn, with danger at each of them turns. It would be a lonesome trail as well, and I expected it would take me to new country—places I'd never been before. I surely could use a pardner on such a trip, but Pandora was a woman, and I could not ask her to take such a risk. I tried to let her down easy.

"Much obliged for the offer," I told her, "but I reckon not. The road up yonder is liable to get long and hairy before it ends. I'd be worried about you when I should be thinkin' about Fontayne."

Then I said something really dumb, even for me. "Besides that, I expect it will take more than a hard lick with an axe handle to stop *them* boys."

I don't know to this day why I said that. I was trying to make a joke, I guess, but it fell flatter than a cow pie on a frozen pond. The fuse I lit was a short one. Pandora looked at me like I'd struck her. Her eyes went kind of glassy, then they flashed fire and she blew up like a black powder bomb. I hadn't seen her so mad since she punched me in the nose back in school.

"What you mean is I'm just a woman, and couldn't be much help," she said, "I thought better of you, Merlin. I can do many things, some of them—*many* of them—better than *you!*"

She caught me by the arm again, and her fingers were like steel. "Come over here," she said, "I want to show you something!" She led me to a grassy patch maybe fifty feet distant, near the crick. "What do you see here?" she said, pointing at the ground.

"What am I *supposed* to see?" I asked, "I see a patch of grass by a crick!"

"There's more," Pandora said, "use your eyes! Two men, an older one ridin' a sorrel and a younger one on a strawberry roan, stopped here less than an hour ago. They watered their horses and took a rest. The older man chews tobacco—he's a big man, 220 pounds or better. The younger one rolls his own and smokes Bull Durham cigarettes. He has a hurt leg—his left one. They stayed here maybe twenty minutes, then crossed the crick and rode on toward Silver City."

I stared again at the grassy patch but could see nothing. "Now how the devil could you know all that?" I asked.

"Footprints," Pandora said, "hoof prints. Flattened grass where they walked, where they stood. Horse hairs there—where the sorrel rubbed his head against his foreleg. Other hair there by the water, where the young one's spur rowel dragged the ground. Older man's step shorter, toed in, foot dragging—his prints deeper in the dirt. His horse's prints deeper, too. Younger man's prints uneven, more weight on his left foot than the right. Tobacco, where the older man spit. And," Pandora bent down and straightened again. In her fingers were a burnt match and the flattened stub of a cigarette. "younger man's smoke, where he stepped on it. His boot print."

Pandora tossed her head, and her long black hair swept about her shoulders like cascading water. "You look for the men who robbed you. Do you think they'll make it easy for you? There are things I know, Merlin Fanshaw, and things I can do—*tracking* is one of them."

I stared again at where she'd pointed. Had she really seen all them things in that small patch of ground? Even as my mind asked the question I knew she really had. Pandora stood there, head high, eyes flashing, her cheeks flushed with color. She looked proud and untamed as a mustang filly, and I thought right then I had never beheld such beauty.

I was blushing again, but this time I made no effort to hide it. I even took my hat off to her. "I sure stuck my foot in a dog-hole that time," I said, "I'm plumb sorry, Pandora. I never meant no offense."

Her face softened a bit; she even gave me one of them quick, flashing smiles of hers. "I know," she said, "you were just tryin' to protect me. You've been a friend at a time when I needed one. You fed me last night, you covered me with your blankets when I fell asleep, and you listened when I needed to talk. You were there for me this morning when the lawmen came. Let me ride with you, Merlin—I want to help."

I put my hat back on and stuck out my hand. "All right, pardner," I told her, "but you do the cookin' and the trackin.' I don't want this outfit poorly fed, nor lost."

Her smile was bright as summer lightning.

My Pa used to say that a man had to make his start from wherever he was. Where I was right then was beside a creek with a good-looking pardner and no idea where to look for my racehorse and the men who took him. Silver City wasn't but four miles away, and

I knew a few people in that town. I figured Fontayne and his boys had likely passed through there and that maybe someone had seen them. It wasn't much, but Pa was right—a man had to start from where he was.

I left Pandora camped among the cottonwoods and willows and told her I'd go scout the town and find out what I could. She was to stay in camp and lay low in case Ernie had telegraphed her description ahead from Shenanigan, or had notices on her printed up. She gave me some money and asked me to buy her a saddle slicker and a few other necessaries, and I told her I would.

Little Buck took the road with the eager spirit he always showed when he was in new country. His ears up and taking in every sound, he carried me toward Silver City at a steady, clean-footed trot. The fancy came to me that I was setting out on my horse-and-man hunt in the company of two pardners, one of them a fine-looking woman and the other a good horse.

Little Buck and me had been through many a hap and mishap since we'd met, and I pretty much knew what he'd do in most every situation. Anyway, I thought I did. Oh, he'd cross me up every now and then, like he had that morning, but mostly he was tough, willing, and reliable at all times.

Pandora, on the other hand, was five cards dealt face down. She could turn out to be a royal flush or a busted straight; there was just no way to predict which. I had known one or two ladies in my brief twenty years—and a few who *wasn't* ladies—but Pandora was different from any female I could recall. I remembered her as a schoolmate, yes, but she'd growed into a woman since then. From what she'd said, she'd been through some mighty bad times with that stepdaddy of hers, and I had no idea what that might do to a person.

Like most men, I let on that I knew more about women than I really did, but I couldn't lie to myself. The truth was I knew next to nothing about a good many subjects, womankind among them. Like I mentioned, my mother had passed away when I wasn't but ten, and except for school I had lived with my pa in the world of men. Him and me had mostly spent our time hunting and breaking wild horses. Only once in a great while would I even meet a lady, and when I did all I knew to do was be polite, tip my hat, and hobble my lip so I wouldn't offend by cussing or calling manure by its right name.

Most of what little I did know about womenfolk came from books, for I was a great reader. During the brief time I'd rode with the Starkweather gang the year before, I had took to reading books again, not because I had to like when I was in school, but because I wanted to. Even on this trip, I had brought a volume or two along. I liked all kinds of stories—pirate tales, stories of knights who rescued damsels (seems like damsels always needed a heap of rescuing), and tales of the old-time Greeks and Romans.

I remembered the legend of Pandora, who was made out of dirt like old Adam, and who got all kinds of gifts from the gods. Way the story goes, Zeus gave Pandora a jug full of trouble and she went and pulled the cork on it, letting every kind of misfortune loose on the world. She was sort of like Eve, in the Bible, who let a snake talk her into going against the Almighty and got the human race off to such a bad start. Anyway, I hoped Pandora my pardner wouldn't be anything like her namesake. I had all the trouble right then I could use.

Maybe, I thought, Pandora would turn out to be more like the sore-footed lion in the story of the Roman slave Androcles. It's true I hadn't pulled no thorn out of her paw like Androcles did for the lion, but I had done her a kindness. That's the way some good friendships start, I told myself, and I hoped for the best.

The day had dawned sunny and bright, but by late afternoon when I reached the outskirts of Silver City, dark, soggy-looking clouds had filled the sky and a cold breeze had put a chill on the day. I thought of Pandora, back by the creek, and hoped she'd make out all right if a hard rain should come. Then, almost as soon as the thought crossed my mind, I knew she would. The way she'd read them tracks back at the grassy patch told me she was sure no hothouse flower and knowing that helped put my mind at ease.

Silver City was a good-size settlement, and growing. It had been a rip-roaring mining camp back in the sixties, but by the mid-seventies the ore had commenced to play out. For the town's boosters it was root, hog, or die. Many another mining town had played out when the minerals did, and there were ghost towns in many a gulch to prove it.

Silver City made the switch. The city dads had turned their eyes to new ventures and had made the town into a supply and shipping center for the cowmen and nesters of the region. Their spirit and enterprise had got the settlement named the Brimstone county seat, and they hit the jackpot when the railroad built a station there.

The streets were busy as I rode in. A high-sided freight wagon was unloading in front of the Silver City Mercantile, jump-seat delivery wagons scuttled to and fro, busy as ants, and a beer wagon clattered along Plata street, iron wheels stuttering over the cobblestones. Farm wagons and buckboards passed each other as ranchmen and sodbusters went about their business, and there was surreys, buggies, and hackneys aplenty, as well as cowhands and townsfolk on horseback.

Little Buck was wild-eyed and goosey as we made our way up the busy street. I could see his ears a-working on all the new sounds, and his nostrils flared as he tried to sort out the strange smells. I had to laugh because if I'd hollered "boo" or made a sudden move right then I believe Buck might have jumped clean over the hotel.

There was three livery barns in Silver City, but the main one—and the one I knew best—was the Blue

Dog, on Galena Street. I passed the time of day with a young hostler who worked there, but he didn't recall seeing anybody like Fontayne or his pardners, nor a handsome, blood bay thoroughbred like Quicksilver neither.

I then made inquiry at the other two stables, with the same result. The storekeeper at the mercantile sold me a slicker and a change of clothes for Pandora, but other than that he wasn't much help. He thought he might have saw a feller like Fontayne, but he wasn't sure. Said he thought maybe he'd run into him once over at Bozeman, or maybe Helena, but then again maybe not.

It was pouring down rain when I left the store, and lightning snapped and crackled overhead like dry sticks a-breaking. Wind gusts swept paper and trash along the street, and thunderclaps grumbled up yonder among the big-bellied clouds. Little Buck stood all a-quiver at the hitchrack, cold water streaming down his flanks. If he could have talked, I believe he would have said, "Let's leave this madhouse, boss—I've had me a bellyfull of city life."

I put my bundles in my saddlebags, slipped into my slicker, and spread Pandora's new oilskin out over the saddle to keep it dry. I left Little Buck humped up and sulky, high-heeled it up the boardwalk until I came to Kelly's Saloon, and went inside.

I was no drinking man, then or since, but I knew saloons were where high-rollers like Fontayne were likely to be found. I stopped just inside the door and shook the water off my hat. It was only early evening, but the room was already dark from the storm outside, and the swamper had begun to light the lamps.

Men stood elbow to elbow along the polished wood of the long bar. Others set at tables along the wall and in the middle of the room, playing cards and talking. A piano player in shirtsleeves and galluses ran his fingers over the keys, but it was hard to hear the music above the talk and the clatter of poker chips and glasses.

Nobody had took note of me when I came in, and I made my way through the cigar smoke, trying to find an open spot at the bar. I was slightly acquainted with the barkeep at Kelly's, and I hoped he might have news of the horse-thieves. I found me a half space between a couple of drinkers, and elbowed my way into it. Just then, the feller on my left stepped back and we bumped into one another.

"Sorry, pardner," I said as he turned to see who had jostled him. His eyes went wide, both the good one and the cast eye, and my heart like to quit beating altogether. I was nose to nose with the big, potbellied feller who'd last been seen riding south with my horse Quicksilver!

NINE
When it Rains, it Pours

The big feller stared, and his jaw went slack. I could see he recognized me, as I did him, and I reckon we was both plenty surprised to find ourselves facing one another at Kelly's long bar. He wore his sixgun on his left hip, butt forward, and I saw him make a grab for it, trying at the same time to back up and get some shooting room between us. All of this happened fast—faster than I can tell—but the strange thing was it didn't seem fast, but gradual.

Like the slow movements in a dream, I could see the surprise on the man's face, his staring, bloodshot eye, stubble of whiskers, and his stained and broken teeth. His right hand reached across his belly toward the handle of his pistol, and I fumbled for my own but could not grasp it beneath the folds of my slicker.

My Pa once gave me his advice on the manly art of fist fighting, and I had followed it on several occasions with some success. "When you see there's no way out and you are headed into a fight," Pa said, "be sure you get in the first lick and hit the other feller smack on the nose. Hit him just as hard as ever you can. That will do two things—hurt him like Billy Hell and cause his eyes to water to where he can't see. Then you need to keep on a-hittin' him until there's no fight left in him and the encounter is concluded in your favor."

I throwed my right hand from the shoulder with everything I had and caught the big feller dead center. He had put me in mind of a big old bear the first time I saw him, and he looked even more like one now. He stumbled back into the other men at the bar, still trying to pull his gun, and I stayed on him, hitting and hammering with both hands like a man possessed.

Mr. Bear's gun came clear of the leather, but I caught the hand that held it with my right and hung on, still hitting him with my left as we slid along the bar scattering beer steins, glassware, and customers. I felt my boots slip in the loose sawdust on the floor but kept on swinging and punching as the two of us continued our fistic fandango. Then his foot caught in the brass footrail and he buckled and fell backward with me on top of him, holding his gun hand with all my strength.

I saw boots, brogans, and the legs of men shuffling around us as we struggled there amid the sawdust and spittoons. Twice, three times, using both my hands now, I slammed his gun arm hard against the floor. He lost his hold, dropped the weapon, and one of those shuffling feet I'd saw kicked it away and out of reach. Mr. Bear hit me a hard, glancing blow to the side of my head, and I pulled in my neck like a turtle, grabbed him by the throat, and hung on. He was reaching, claw-like, for my eyes, when I let go of his throat with my right hand and hit him in the nose again. That seemed to take some of the starch out of Mr. Bear. He was still a-punching at me, twisting and moving underneath me, but I truly believe I had him whipped at that point, or pritnear, anyway.

Then something struck the base of my skull, and the pain was so fierce I couldn't believe it. Behind my eyes, it seemed I saw the sun explode and scatter flaming chunks of itself out in every direction. White light flashed and vanished, and when the sun went out, so did I—out into a darkness so dark it held no light at all.

When I came to, it was like swimming up from the bottom of a deep lake. I seemed to rise out of the depths toward the light, but when I broke through and breathed deep once again, the pain hit me like a sledge hammer.

It still wasn't all that light, wherever I was. I was laying on a narrow bunk in some kind of small room, but everything was dark and gloomy and I could not make out any detail as to my whereabouts. Off to my left I could see a faint strip of light near the floor, and I swung my legs off the bunk and tried to set up. That proved to be a mistake, far as my throbbing head was concerned, but I just shut my eyes and let the pain run its course.

After a bit my eyes growed accustomed to the gloom and I began to see things clearer. The sour, rank smell didn't give it away nor did the cold stone walls, but when I seen the iron bars that made up one side of the room I sure knew where I was. I'd woke up in a hoosegow only two days previous, and there was no doubt I had done so again.

I tried to think, to remember what I'd done to get myself throwed in the pokey, but at first I could not. Then, slowly, the ache in my head began to let up some, and I recalled my scuffle with Mr. Bear. I was still wearing my slicker, and my hat was laying nearby on the floor. My cartridge belt, holster, and six-shooter were gone, of course, so I could tell right off that particular jail was a first-class operation.

Gingerly, I touched my fingers to the back of my head and found a new lump there to match the one Glenn Murdoch had so recently gave me. That would surely account for the hurt I was enjoying, as well as the way my rassling match had ended. My guess was the barkeep at Kelly's had chose to restore order by thumping my melon with a bung starter. Thinking back on it, I couldn't blame him none. I had gone to war with that big feller as soon as I laid eyes on him and without so much as a by your leave. The bartender must have thought I'd been eating loco weed.

I saw that the narrow strip of light came from under a door across the way, and I thought I heard someone moving around in the room beyond. Feeling in need of some conversation I stumbled over to the bars and took hold of them. "Hey!" I hollered, "Is anyone out there?"

I heard what sounded like the squeak of a chair, then heavy footsteps. Light flooded the cell as the door swung open, and a big-shouldered jasper with a star on his vest bulked up the doorway.

135

"Well, looky who's awake," he said, "the great John L. Sullivan, bare-knuckle champeen of the world. What d' you want?"

"I want out," I told him, "what do you think I want?"

"People in Hell want lemonade, I'm told. That don't mean they get it."

"I take your point. Who might you be, sir?"

The badge toter leaned up against the doorframe and thoughtfully scratched his crotch. "I'm Joe Farraday," he said, "overworked, underpaid city marshal. It was me fetched you here from Kelly's last night and provided you with this handsome lodging."

"Mighty neighborly. Refresh my memory—what exactly did I do?"

"Attacked a peaceful citizen while he was mindin' his own business, namely drinkin' beer. Lucky for you, he left town without preferrin' charges. Bartender didn't prefer charges neither. Said some glassware got busted, but no other damage."

"Then what am I charged with?"

The marshal looked thoughtful again. "Well, now, I ain't sure. How about disturbin' the peace? Or maybe creatin' a public nuisance? I've got to charge y'all with *somethin'*."

"Why's that, Marshal?"

"The town of Silver City has more law than you can shake a stick at. There's a U.S. Marshal above the post office, there's the Brimstone County Sheriff over to the courthouse, and there's me here at the city jail. Uncle Sam pays the U.S. Marshal, the county taxpayers pay the sheriff, and *nobody* much pays me. This office winds up drinkin' at the last titty on the sow, so to speak. I am kept out of the poor house only by the fines levied against no-account, trouble-makin' drifters like y'all."

"And who levies them fines?"

"The city judge does, at ten o'clock weekday mornin's. If he's sober, that is. If he ain't, it could be a week from now, and I'll have to feed you 'til then."

"With all due respect, Marshal, couldn't we come to some kind of accommodation?"

"I'm listenin', son."

"Well, it occurred to me I might repent of my wicked ways, promise never to dark up your doorway again, plead guilty, and pay you ten dollars gold to satisfy the requirements of the law."

He still leaned against the door jamb, but his eyes took on a gleam of interest. "How do I know you *have* ten dollars?"

"You've got my gunbelt in yonder," I told him, "The cartridge belt is a money belt, and there's two eagles and two double eagles inside."

His smile was a wide one. "My missiz will be pleased," he said, "I just might buy her a *turkey* for dinner this evenin'."

Three minutes and ten dollars later, I was a free man once again.

According to Pa's old silver watch, it was 8:32 in the morning when I left the marshal's office and stepped

137

out onto the street. Rain was still falling in a steady, soaking drizzle, and the sky was the color of lead. Plata and Galena streets were paved with cobblestones, but the rest of Silver City's byways were gumbo mud, ruts, deep holes, and puddles. I ain't sure what street I was on right then, but it could well have been Quagmire Avenue. A duck would have felt right at home.

My first thought was of my horse, Little Buck. I'd left him tied in front of the Silver City Mercantile, and I set out to find him. The wet boardwalk was slick as ice, and once or twice my boots nearly went out from under me as I hoofed it on up the street. My head still ached aplenty, though not as bad as when I first woke up, and I took extra care so as not to slip and fall.

Buck must have heard the jangle of my spurs as I rounded the corner, for he lifted his head, whinnied, and gave me a look as if to say, "Where have you been?" He was alone at the hitchrail, and he was wet and a little stiff, but I seen he was all right. I rubbed his neck and gave him a handful of oats from my saddlebags, and he seemed to forgive me.

I felt guilty about leaving him for so long, but I reckon that's because I was thinking like a human, which of course is what I am. I sure wouldn't want to be tied up to a hitchrail overnight, but I ain't sure that's the way horses think. I know they can't tell time—ten minutes or ten hours may be pretty much the same to a horse.

Pandora's new slicker had kept the saddle dry. I

rolled it and tied it behind the cantle. Then I tightened the cinch, stepped up onto Buck, and turned him up the street toward Kelly's Saloon.

There was a poker game already in progress, or maybe it was still going on from the night before. An old-timer stood at the far end of the bar, lost in his thoughts, drinking memories with his beer. A drunk slept in his chair, his feet propped up on the rail of the Sunshine stove, maybe dreaming of whiskey or better days. Other than that, Kelly's had quieted down considerable from the night before, and the crowd had all went home or somewheres else.

Big Paddy O'Rourke, the barkeep, was polishing glasses and smoking a black cigar when I ambled in. He wore his usual expression, which was somewheres between "I've seen it all" and "I ain't impressed," and he didn't bother to change it on my account. He did take the stogie from his mouth and gave me the slightest of nods as I walked up to the bar.

O'Rourke looked wary. Carefully, he placed one of his big hands palm-down on top of the bar. His other hand was out of my sight, beneath the bar, and that's the one I worried about.

"Merlin Fanshaw," he said, drawing the name out like he didn't know what to say about it, "sure, and haven't you already caused me enough trouble?"

"I ain't here to cause no trouble, Paddy," I said, "that was not my intent last evenin', neither."

"Nevertheless, you do seem to have a certain talent

139

for mayhem. What was last evenin's donnybrook about, if I may ask?"

"Three men stole a fine race horse from me this week over at Shenanigan and one of 'em killed my pardner. I came to Silver City to look for 'em. When I walked in here I bumped smack into that big feller and seen he was one of the three. He recognized me, too, and went for his iron. That's when I hit him."

O'Rourke was silent for a second or two. Then the tension seemed to leave his shoulders and he brought his other hand up from behind the bar and placed it on top. I was relieved to see it come up empty.

When he spoke, there was a smile in his voice. "Sure, and when I saw you strike the gentleman, with nary a word spoken between you, I thought you'd gone stark, starin' daft."

O'Rourke drawed a beer and set the stein before me. "This is by way of makin' amends, lad," he said, "It was me knocked you out and sent for the marshal. No hard feelin's, I hope."

"Much obliged," I said, picking up the beer, "no hard feelin's. You got to preserve decorum in a nice place like this." Over at the poker table, one of the players hollered a cuss word so foul I wasn't sure at first I'd really heard it.

O'Rourke took a drag on his stogie and blowed blue smoke out into the room. He looked thoughtful. "Three men, you say. One of 'em a sportin' man with long hair, wearin' a frock coat and a checkered vest? Another one a pinch-faced, yellow eyed, two-gun runt? And the third your dancin' partner of the afternoon?"

"Sounds like you saw 'em, all right."

"They were in here yesterday mornin', drinkin' to their good fortune and celebratin' the way they got the better of some Dry Creek bumpkins. One of those bumpkins, I trust, would be you?"

"It would."

"I've seen 'em in here before, once or twice. It was a quiet mornin', they were my only customers at the time. They did a good deal of talkin' and, as I had little else to do I confess I did a bit of listenin'. The sport goes by the name of Turk Fontayne, and the runt is a would-be gunfighter who calls himself 'Portugee' Gossert. The great bear of a man you tangled with is 'Cock-eyed Clarence' Williams.

"Fontayne and Gossert left town about noon yesterday. There was some argument on the part of Williams, who said there was still whiskey and women in Silver City and he wanted to stay on for awhile. Fontayne said all right, stay then. He could catch up with him and Gossert later, over at Stillwater on the Yellowstone.

"As for Williams, he left in a hurry right after you'd gone off to dreamland. I suppose he's bound for Stillwater, too."

I drank the beer down and set the stein back on the bar. "Many thanks, Paddy," I said, "if there's ever anythin' I can do for you, all you have to do is name it."

"There is one thing. Don't start any more fights in Kelly's."

141

By the time I took the road back to where I'd left Pandora, the rain had growed from a drizzle to a downpour. Water swept along the roadside like a live stream and cascaded down coulees that was normally dry. As I rode, the downpour growed into a gully-washing frog-strangler that put me in mind of Sunday school stories and caused me to consider taking up ark-building.

I thought about Pandora then, caught out in the storm and waiting for me, and my guilt came back. Maybe a horse couldn't tell time, but Pandora could. She'd be worrying and fretting by now, maybe plumb frantic, wondering where I'd got to and what had happened to me. She'd be miserable from the wet and the cold, not even able to keep a fire going. Maybe she'd be hostile again, the way she'd been at the crick when I made the dumb remark about the axe handle.

Well, I'd done the best I could—it hadn't been *my* fault I'd got hit in the head and throwed in the city jail, had it? I'd come back as soon as I could—I didn't even take time to have me any breakfast.

The rain wasn't my fault, neither. How was I supposed to know the Almighty would pick that particular day to start Him a new flood? I had done what I set out to do—I'd met one of the three horse thieves up close and personal, I'd learned their names, and I'd found out they were headed for Stillwater. Pandora just better *not* be mad at me, that's all.

I reined Buck off the road toward the place our camp

was. The little crick was muddy and swollen to nearly twice its size, and the bank that led down to it was steep and slick as calf slobbers. Little Buck took it slow, his nose almost to the ground and placing each foot with care. I leaned far back in the saddle, shifting my feet forward in order to help his descent, and he half walked, half slid, down to the cottonwoods and willows along the stream.

Minutes later, I rounded a bend and pulled up near a fallen tree where our camp had been. There was no sign anyone had ever been there. Oh, yes, I'm sure the great Pandora Pretty Hawk could have wrote a *book* based on the sign *she* could see, but all I saw was wet grass, dead wood, and mud. Where was she?

Then I noticed Little Buck. His head was up, sniffing the wet air, his ears pointed uphill and toward the rising foothills of the Brimstones. I gave him free rein and he struggled back up the slippery incline and moved out toward a low-lying fog bank that was drifting down the slope. Then I heard it—somewhere up ahead a horse whinnied, high-pitched and shrill. Buck whinnied back and quickened his pace.

Ahead lay a stretch of limestone cliffs, dropping sheer from the cloud-shrouded upper slopes. Buck surged ahead at a fast walk through a patch of scrub cedar, and then, of a sudden, we broke out of the fog and mist. A large and spacious cave, maybe sixty yards long by a hundred feet deep, stretched along the base of the cliff, and there inside it set Pandora.

She had a fire going, and she knelt before it with my

star quilt over her shoulders in the Indian fashion. She was dry as a bone and pretty as a picture, and when she smiled her whole face lit up.

"You made good time," she said, "have you had breakfast?"

As I stepped down off Little Buck and moved into the shelter of the cave I felt a strange mixture of happiness and confusion I didn't understand at the time. I savvy the feeling better now; I have felt it many times since that day. In my case, at least, it seems to be caused by associating with womenfolk, who seldom if ever do what a man thinks they will. I have known one or two men over the years who claimed they understood women, but I found they lied about other things, too.

I slipped my saddle off Little Buck, rubbed him down, and set him out in his hobbles to graze. I could feel the damp and the chill clean to my core. Pandora poured me a cup of coffee and I hunkered down by the fire and warmed my hands on the steaming cup. The cave was warm and dry; it was good to be in out of the rain.

"After you left, I saw the clouds move in," Pandora said, "I knew we were in for a hard rain. I rode out and looked the country over until I found this cave. Then I went back, packed up, and came here. Just in time, too—it couldn't have been ten minutes later the rain started."

Whatever she had a-cookin' smelled mighty good. It was all I could do to keep from drooling like a hound.

"You've been a busy one," I said, "What's for breakfast?"

"Rabbit," she said, "I snared two cottontails this morning. There's biscuits, too, and rabbit gravy."

Pandora always did know how to get my full attention.

By the time I'd had four or five biscuits, most of a rabbit, and cleaned up the gravy, I was feeling like myself again—even the hurt in my head had mostly gone away. The fire had burned down to embers, and Pandora knelt across from me, the glow of firelight playing upon her face. I gave her the saddle slicker and the clothes I'd bought her, and she smiled like a kid at Christmas time. You'd have thought I'd done her some sort of special kindness.

I told her of my adventures in Silver City—of my encounter with Williams, my passing the night in the city jail, and my later discussion with Paddy O'Rourke. Because I was telling the story, I left out most of the dumb things I'd said and done. I told it in such a way that I'd look more smart and resourceful than lucky.

I'm not sure I fooled her. Maybe it was because of the way she could read tracks and such, but I had the uneasy feeling that Pandora was more than able to separate truth from fiction. When I'd told her all, she closed her eyes and was silent for a long time. Then she looked up into my face, and asked, "This town—this place called Stillwater—is it far?"

"Two days ride, maybe. It's one of them new railroad towns on the Yellowstone. The Northern Pacific built a station there last year."

I walked to the mouth of the cave and looked out at the falling rain. "I'm thinkin' we need to get travelin', Pandora. Fontayne hasn't been in much of a hurry so far, but once Williams catches up with him he'll know I'm trailin' him. When he does I expect he'll take my horse and go to ground somewhere or set up an ambush and lay in wait for us."

I wasn't looking forward to going back out in the rain, and I said so. "I sure druther not be startin' out wet, but we don't have much choice. The way this storm is settin' in it's liable to last all day"

Pandora lifted her sloe-black eyes to the lead-colored skies. She looked like she'd asked an unspoken question, and was waiting for an answer.

"Sit down, Merlin, and rest," she said, "The rain will end in an hour. Maybe less."

I mostly tend to be good-natured, but right then I very nearly held the woman up to ridicule for trying to predict the weather that way. As it turned out, I'm glad I didn't.

Forty-seven minutes later the rain stopped and sunshine lit up the land.

TEN
Beyond the Yellowstone

After the rain the country seemed brand new. Out across the valley raindrops clung to grass and trees, sparkling like diamonds in the sunlight. Meadowlarks warbled their cheerful songs, mule deer grazed among the rolling hills, and the air smelled sweet, cool, and fresh-washed.

A hawk spiraled upward on a rising current, seeming not to fly at all but simply to drift like a youngster's kite. He was a red-tailed hawk, and as he circled high overhead his tail feathers caught sunlight and glowed soft rose against the sun.

Pandora and me rode down off the benchland and into the valley, moving through jackpine and scrub cedar past outcroppings and ridges of sandrock. Everywhere I looked there was green grass and wild-flowers, and I just rode along leading the packhorse, breathing the air, and letting the beauty of the countryside take hold of my heart.

Pandora Pretty Hawk had commenced to take hold of my heart some herself. I had thought she would be trouble to have around, but I'd been wrong. Pandora had turned out to be steady, hard-working, good natured, and pretty to look at as well. She was a born rider, she savvied nature's ways better than I did, and she talked just the right amount for a trail pardner, neither too much nor too little.

She rode up alongside me on her tough little paint and smiled her bright flash of a smile. "This is fine country, Merlin," she said, "the land of my mother's people. Isn't it beautiful?"

Pandora's happy smile and her soft voice made my chest feel tight. I gave no answer to her question for a long moment. She was right, of course, the country *was* beautiful, but for some reason I couldn't bring myself to say so. No, I had to be contrary and act like a man of the world, as if I'd seen it all and the glories of that June day were nothing special.

"Oh, I don't know," I said, "I guess I've seen better."

Pandora raised an eyebrow, looked at me for a second, and gave a slight shake of her head as if I was plumb obtuse. Her smile didn't fade, but it changed from friendly to amused. She didn't pursue the point; instead, she changed the subject.

"How did you get the name Merlin?" she asked, "Did your folks name you after that old wizard in the story books?"

"Not hardly," I said, "truth is, my mother named me after a pigeon hawk. When she and Pa came west in '63 Mother took a real interest in the birds out here. She liked redwing blackbirds, meadowlarks, prairie chickens, robins—she even liked crows and magpies. One of her favorite birds was the little falcon they call a merlin. Merlins are fast and bold, you know—they're good hunters."

"Like you?" Pandora said, her black eyes merry. I

felt she was mocking me, and I believe I might have took offense except I sort of figured I had it coming.

"Well, yes," I said, "I reckon you could say that."

"What do these merlins eat?" she asked, smiling, "everything, like you?"

Now I knew she was trying to get my goat. The heat in my cheeks and ears told me I was blushing. "No," I said, "they mostly eat young grouse, doves, and such."

"Well," she said, finally letting up on me, "I guess I wouldn't say no to a grouse for supper myself."

Which is what gave me the notion to show off a mite. We'd seen grouse several times that afternoon, and I figured Pandora would be plumb impressed if I brought down a couple with a six-shooter.

I had taken to wearing Orville's Peacemaker since his death at Shenanigan and the gun was as different from my old Colt's Dragoon as a saber is different from an axe. The weapon was chambered for .44-40, which was also the cartridge the Winchester took. I could use the same ammunition in both six-gun and carbine.

Now in the first place I'm a fair to middling shot with a short gun, but I sure ain't good enough to hunt grouse with one. About the only grouse I'd be likely to hit with a revolver would be a fool hen, but fool hens live up in the mountains, not down where we was. In the second place, I hadn't so much as fired the weapon since Orville left it to me. I didn't know whether it would shoot true or not, but I had an ace up my sleeve Pandora didn't know about.

149

That day in Silver City when I bought her saddle slicker I picked up a few shot-shells that would fit Orville's gun in case I should happen into snake country. As I rode I shucked the bullets from the gun, stowed them in a vest pocket, and replaced them with the shot-shells.

Sure enough, a mile further on two grouse exploded out of the tall grass to my right and flew up and away into the low sun, stubby wings whirring frantically. Holding Little Buck steady with my left hand, I drawed and fired the .44 twice with my right. Both them birds stopped in mid-flight as if they'd run into a wall, then dropped like stones out into the tall grass.

White smoke drifted out into the still air. I returned the Colt's to its holster with a flourish, then twisted in the saddle and looked at Pandora. "What'd you think of that?" I said.

Her nose wrinkled and her lip took on a slight curl as she looked out toward where the grouse had fell. "I'll cook them," she said, "but *you're* gonna have to pick out the buckshot."

Another thing about Pandora, she surely was observant.

We made camp early that evening in a grove of cottonwood trees above a clear, fast-moving stream. While Pandora set up camp I put the horses out to graze. The little stream gabbled and splashed over its rocky bed, and I set there and let it talk to me. After a bit, I came to believe the stream might have some trout in it, so I cut me a pole, tied a hook and line from my war bag on it, and went to fishing.

Truth is, I wasn't all that serious about catching fish, but fishing is a good way to loaf without causing comment. If I'd told Pandora I was fixing to set by a stream and just think, she might well have demanded I fetch her some more water, or wood, or build her a dang house, for all I know. Pa always said women can't abide seeing a man set and relax too long; it makes them nervous. Anyway, Pandora just nodded when I said I was going to fish awhile before supper, and I walked over and put a line in the water. I didn't bait my hook, though; I didn't want no fish a-bothering me while I was fishing.

It was mighty pleasant, setting there on the bank of that stream in the early evening. The light turned soft gold and shadows stretched long across the land as the sun sank lower and got ready for bed. Upstream, a mulie doe came walking, stepping cautious then stopping, her big ears flicking nervous-like, alert for the sound of danger. I set still as any statue, watching her. The doe drank, raising her head from time to time to listen. Then she high-stepped into the stream, crossed over, and with a flip of her tail disappeared into the willows on the other side.

The sound of the water was soothing. As I set there and listened my thoughts drifted back over the events of the past week while I tried to sort out what had happened and speculate on what was liable to. I knew I'd have to make a plan and ride it through with care if ever I hoped to get Quicksilver back.

Of a sudden, remembrance of Orville and the shooting at Shenanigan came upon me again, catching me off guard and wrenching my heart. Memories of that day were never far away, laying at the edges of my mind like coyotes watching a sheepfold. Mostly, I was able to keep such thoughts at bay by staying busy and by crowding them out with other, better thoughts. It was during the quiet times, when my guard was down, that they snuck up and busted through my defenses—times like first thing of a morning, or just before sleep, or while setting by a stream, pretending to fish.

Running into Cock-eyed Clarence back in Silver City had been the worst kind of luck. I hadn't been ready, and as a result I had lost whatever advantage surprise would have gave me. If Fontayne was in Still-water, and if Clarence got there before I did, them thieves would be warned of my coming. I figured Fontayne and his boys would then either try to bush-whack me or light out and put distance between us.

I was moving into country I didn't know. Livingston, Stillwater, the new town of Billings, were all settlements on the Yellowstone river and on the Northern Pacific's main line. Settlers were still few in that region and for good reason. Like Pandora had said, this was Crow country. We was near the heart of the Crow people's reservation, and fine country it was, too. Because it was Crow country, their longtime enemies the Sioux and Cheyenne sent a steady string of war-parties in a-hunting Crow ponies, captives, and such. The trouble was, them war parties wasn't all that particular. They'd just as soon raid a cowman or a sod-buster, and a blonde or auburn scalp made as good a trim for their leggins as a black one. So, like I said, settlers tended to be scarce thereabouts.

And what about Pandora? I still wasn't sure Ernie Fillmore and his posse was a-hunting her, but I believed they was. I'd took a hand in helping her get shut of them, and I didn't figure they would keep on a-coming. Ernie was sheriff of Progress county, and his jurisdiction ended at the county line. In any case, I had fired on Ernie and the boys and had set them afoot. I knew I'd be about as welcome back in Shenanigan as a mad dog at a birthday party.

Then there was Buford Suggs, Pandora's stepdaddy. If he had put out a reward for her return, there could be others on her trail, too. Suggs might even come after her himself; the old skinflint was sure mean enough.

I had no wish to put Pandora at risk by taking her with me, but I could find no way around it. She had nowhere else to go, and I had agreed to let her ride with me. All I knew to do now was keep a-going and do the best I knew how. I hoped it would be good enough.

The next day dawned bright, warm, and sunny—you could almost hear the grass grow. Pandora and me rode easy through low hills and green valleys through the day and camped that night along a swift-flowing creek under cold, bright stars that seemed close enough to reach out and take hold of. We saw no other riders, but saw game aplenty—whitetail in the bottoms, mule deer on the ridges and in the breaks, and antelope on the flats by the hundreds. We even saw a few little bunches of buffalo, though no big herds.

On the afternoon of the third day we spied smoke on the skyline and knew we had reached our destination. We rode up a slope, topped a ridge, and there it was— a cluster of log and frame buildings scattered out beyond the river on a broad tree-lined flat—the town of Stillwater.

Stillwater, Montana Territory, had quite a history. First, there'd been a stage station—the old Countryman station—called Stillwater. Later, a small settlement called Eagle's Nest sprang up a mile or so to the west. Then there was a trading post called Sheep Dip, and finally in 1882, when the Northern Pacific came through and set up a station there, the town took the name Stillwater and settled down to being more or less permanent.

One thing was sure—Stillwater sure had been set in a pretty spot. A broad valley, bordered by low, pine-studded hills and buttes, stretched away green and shining in the late afternoon light. Nearby, the Yellowstone river poured over its rocky bed as it rolled east and north to meet the Missouri. Off to the south the mighty Beartooth range reared up against the sky like mountains in a dream of glory, and farther east the Pryors lay in the mist of distance like sleeping buffalo.

Tall cottonwood trees lined the banks of the Yellowstone, seed pods drifting on the breeze like summer snow. As Pandora and me rode down to the river, a bald eagle swept low, skimming the high, muddy water. We watched as the eagle suddenly struck out with its talons and snatched a trout from the current. It slowly rose above the river, wings battering the air with the sound of a flag whipping in the wind.

Across the river, people went about their business with an industry common to new settlements. Men on foot and horseback moved along the dusty streets, and wagons rumbled under their heavy loads. The sound of a blacksmith working an anvil rang clear as a church bell across the river, and from somewhere in the settlement came the sharp racket of a carpenter's hammer.

Beyond the town, out on the flat, a jerk-line team approached, twelve horses pulling three high-sided freight wagons loaded with grub, whiskey, and all the paraphernalia folks deemed necessary to conduct their lives and work. It came to me that the days of the horse-drawn freighter were fast drawing to a close now that the railroad had come to Stillwater, but I was glad to see they weren't through yet. Closer in, the rails of the NP tracks caught sunlight as they knifed through Stillwater and beyond. From where we were I could make out the station, but there was no train in evidence.

Pandora set her pony with an easy grace, studying the town. I twisted in my saddle and turned to face her.

"I'm askin' you to stay behind again, Pandora," I said, "If them thieves are in Stillwater, there's liable to be shootin' before the day is out. If you ain't in the vicinity, you can't catch a bullet."

Her voice was soft when she replied, but firm. She shook her head. "No," she said, "this time I go with you. I said I'd help get your horse back, and that's what I'm going to do."

I started to protest, but I could see by the set of her jaw there would be no changing her mind. "Well, all right," I told her, "but you're about half stubborn, you know that?"

She shrugged. "I'm your partner," she said, "I'm entitled to my half of this outfit's stubbornness."

Before we set out, I stepped down off Little Buck and checked the action and loads of both my revolver and the Winchester. Then I dug Pa's old Colt's dragoon out and gave it to Pandora.

"I don't reckon you'll have cause to use this," I told her, "but it's better to have it and not need it than to need it and not have it."

Pandora took the heavy weapon from me and carefully placed it in the waistband of her britches. Her black eyes shone and her face was serious, as if I'd just gave her a treasured family heirloom. Which, as I thought about it, I guess I had.

"My Pa carried that piece during the war," I told her, "and it shoots where you point it. But, like I said, it ain't likely you'll need it."

Then she smiled her soft, sweet smile and reached out to gently touch my face. "You're concerned for me," she said, "That's sweet, Merlin, but I'll be fine. Don't worry."

"Hell, I ain't worried," I said, turning away to get back up on Little Buck, "I'm just tellin' you what I think."

It has always been a mystery to me the way some women can read a man's thoughts. It occurred to me that if a feller ever had a wife like Pandora Pretty Hawk he'd have no choice but to spend his whole life telling her the absolute truth.

The Yellowstone ran high, muddy, and rolling, but we found a ferry a mile or so upstream of the town and paid the old-timer who ran it to take us and our outfit across. Had it not been for Pandora, and for the heavy laden packhorse, I believe I might have swum Little Buck over. The buckskin was a strong swimmer and had ever proved steady and sensible in the water.

As it turned out I was glad we took the ferry. Once we reached the other side I seen that swimming it would have been chancy even for Buck, and I was glad I had chose the safer way. The Yellowstone wouldn't reach its high water mark for another week or so when the last of the snow melt came down, but it was already higher than I first thought and too high to take a chance on.

The town of Stillwater was busy as a beehive as Pandora and me crossed the tracks and turned our horses up the main street. Most of the buildings had a rough and unfinished look, and a number of them sported canvas tops and sides. We passed a meat market which featured deer, elk, and buffalo, as well as a clatter of mangy dogs and a generous population of bluebottle flies. There was a couple of hash-houses, three or four saloons, a dry goods store, and a mercantile. Farther up the street a sweating blacksmith was fitting a tire to a wagon wheel with many a lusty hammer blow while he muttered cuss words hotter than his forge. A two-story structure marked 'Hotel' stood just beyond, and still further on was a fair-sized livery stable and corrals.

I rode slow and watchful among the tethered horses, looking for three I'd last saw in Shenanigan—a sorrel, a blue roan, and a high-headed claybank stud. I was hunting the men who rode them, too, but most of all, I was looking for a blood bay thoroughbred that shone like he had a light on inside him, my horse, Quicksilver.

I didn't only rely on my own eyes, neither. I had described the horses to Pandora, and while my pride wouldn't let me say so, I knew it was likely she'd spot them before I would.

The sun had set by the time we got to the end of the street. It was plain by then that the horses we were hunting weren't in town. Pandora and me even rode the alleys. We talked to the hostler at the livery barn, but he'd saw neither the horses nor the men we described. At that point, my spirits sunk low as a bullsnake's belly—it seemed clear that Fontayne and his henchmen had moved on to parts unknown—if they'd ever been there at all.

"Well, there's no point in spendin' money we don't have to," I told Pandora, "we'll just go on down along the river somewheres and camp tonight."

Downriver, a quarter-mile from town, we found the horses. A pole corral, set back among the big cottonwoods at the riverside, sported a homemade sign that read "Clifton's Livery Stable and Feed," although there wasn't no stable but only the corral. Inside was maybe a dozen horses, among which was the sorrel, the blue roan, and Fontayne's claybank. Most important of all, at least to me, there at last was my horse Quicksilver.

The big thoroughbred stood in the corral among the others, but in a corner and in a class by himself. Everything about him was the way I remembered it— his shining coat, his small, perfect head, his deep chest, his long and graceful legs. I stepped off Little Buck and put my hand on the gate.

"Can I help you folks?"

I turned to see a young feller standing nearby, a half-filled grain sack in his left hand. Beneath a shapeless cavalry hat his hair was straw-colored. His smile was equal parts friendly and cautious. A wall tent and a lean-to full of saddles, blankets, bridles, and such stood behind him near the corral.

"We was just admirin' the horses," I said, "they yours?"

His chuckle was a dry rumble. "No, sir, they ain't," he said, "I'm Clifton Miller, and what I do is board

159

them animals, just like the stable in town does, only I board 'em for less.

"Fact is, I aim to have the second livery stable in Stillwater, soon's I can raise the money to get 'er built. Second stable, and the best."

Pandora still set astride her paint, her long, straight hair blowing slightly in the breeze off the river. The future stable owner looked at her in just about the same way a cat looks at cream, which ruffled my feathers some. Still, I couldn't blame him none. Pandora was, as I've said, a real beauty.

I saw confusion in his eyes, too. His hand rose toward his floppy hat brim but stopped halfway there. On the one hand, he surely could see she was a handsome woman. On the other hand, Pandora was wearing britches and riding astride, which a lady didn't do, and she looked like she might be an Indian woman, to boot. The feller was rimrocked by his prejudices. He didn't know whether to feel superior or inferior. I could've told him, had he asked. Around Pandora Pretty Hawk, a man mostly was inclined to feel inferior.

Pandora favored him with her brightest smile. Her voice was low and warm, almost a whisper. "I was admiring that blood-bay stallion," she purred, "Could you tell me where we might find the animal's owner?"

Clifton's eyes took on a sort of glazed look and his mouth fell open. He not only tipped his hat to Pandora, he took it off and crumpled it before him with both his hands.

160

"He—he never told me his name, ma'am," he said, "but I believe he's some kind of sportin' gent. Him and the two fellers he rides with mostly spend their nights playin' poker in the back room of the Great Northern."

Pandora's eyes widened slightly and her mouth took on a pretty pout. "Thank you, Clifton," she said, her voice now even lower, "you've been most helpful."

I don't know why exactly, but I was feeling grumpy as a wet owl as we rode away from the corral. "Maybe I can't read sign like you," I told Pandora, "but I'll bet I know what that feller's gonna be *dreamin'* about tonight."

ELEVEN
Stillwater runs Deep

I was hotter than a coal-oil fire in a tin stove. I'd found Quicksilver, and I'd learned where the dang horse-thieves was. I told Pandora I had half a mind to charge right into the Great Northern like General George Custer and take Fontayne's greasy scalp. She said I sure did have half a mind and she reminded me what had happened to General George Custer. She also advised me to take hold of myself.

"The last thing we need right now is for you to go off half-cocked like you did in Silver City," she said, "this time you need to face those thieves with the law at your side."

161

I was some offended by her words. Running into Williams the way I had was pure chance and no fault of mine. At the same time, I knew she was right about calling in the law, but that knowledge only made me crankier. I was sure getting tired of Pandora being right all the time.

"I've *got* the law with me, little girl," I said, "it's here in this holster on my right hip."

"I like you better when you're not talking like a dime novel," she sniffed, "and I haven't been a little girl for some time now."

We moved on down the riverbank another quarter mile, unpacked the packhorse, and staked him out on a grassy patch. I stacked the pack-saddle, panniers, and bedroll under a big cottonwood tree, and set my eyes toward town.

"Let's get it done," I said.

Full dark had come by the time we got back into Stillwater, and the night side of town was commencing to come alive. It was a warm evening, and the saloons had their lamps lit and their front doors wide open as Pandora and me rode by. Music was playing at most of the whiskey joints. I heard a fiddler tuning up at one, a banjo picker plunking out "Oh dem Golden Slippers" at another, and somebody playing a lively dance tune on a piano at yet another.

Pandora and me loose-tied our horses in front of the Great Northern, and I was halfway through the door before I noticed she wasn't with me. I turned back and seen she was still standing at the hitchrack between Little Buck and her paint pony.

"What's wrong?" I asked her, "Ain't you comin'?"

"I can't go in there, Merlin," she said, "You know they don't allow Indians inside a saloon. If I go in there they'll tell me to leave, then you'll stand up for me, get lippy with the barkeep, and get us both thrown out.

"Why don't you go in, find out who carries the law in this town, and come back for me? I'll wait here."

My blood was up. "You can dang well go in there if you want to," I said, "Maybe they will throw us out, but if they do it'll be after the *fight*. Anyway, you're only half Indian."

"See? You're gettin' feisty already. Go on, Merlin."

It didn't set well with me, but I had to admit Pandora was right. Full blood or half, she did look Indian. That's all the barkeep would see.

I gave her a grin, and then I gave her a hug. "Well, all right, darlin'," I said, "you just wait here, scrape a hide, do some beadwork, or somethin.' I'll be back faster'n a turpentined cat."

Far as I could tell, the Great Northern wasn't much different from any other saloon, except maybe it had more trimmings. Three or four fellers stood drinking at a long bar which looked to be made of cherry wood or some such, and a couple of cold-eyed calico queens worked hard at prospecting the customers.

There was fancy wallpaper and pictures in gold leaf frames on the walls, and the spittoons, lamps and

163

footrail were all of polished brass. A couple of poker games were running there in the main room, and at another table a mixed bunch of muleskinners, railroad men, and drifters were bucking the tiger against a sleepy-looking faro dealer.

I sauntered up to the bar and set my elbows upon it. The young bartender had been combing his hair by the backbar mirror, and he looked at me like I had interrupted a great artist at his easel. His hair was red, parted down the middle, and plastered back both ways with enough grease to fry a buffalo. His moustache was waxed and well-clipped, and I noticed he couldn't seem to keep his eyes off the chippies who were working the bar. Maybe, I thought, he wouldn't have throwed Pandora out after all.

"What'll you have, buster?" asked the bartender.

"Why, a beer, if it ain't too much trouble," I told him, "and maybe the answer to a question."

He drawed a beer and set it before me. "That'll be ten cents for the beer, buster. I ain't in the answer business."

I hadn't come that far to be put off by a sassy bartender. I drawed Orville's .44 and cocked it. "I was goin' to ask where I could find a peace officer in this town, but since you ain't in the answer business and are surly to boot I believe I'll just start shootin' up this whiskey joint and see if a lawman shows up."

The barkeep's eyes went wide, then narrowed to a squint. I had his full attention now, and he wasn't looking at the ladies of the evening no more, but at my gun. "N-Now, you just hold on a minute, buster," he said, "You don't want to do that."

"No, I don't want to," I said, "but I need me a lawman, and if you won't tell me where one is—"

"Horace Wisdom is constable here in Stillwater," the barkeep said, nodding at a closed door beyond the faro table, "He's playin' poker yonder in the back room."

I paid him for the beer and holstered the .44. "See what you just done?" I said with a grin, "You answered a question and prevented a fracas. You ever think about goin' into the answer business?"

Before he could answer I was already headed for the back room.

When I got to the door, a big-shouldered plug-ugly with short hair and a fighter's nose blocked my progress. "Sorry, bub," he said, "that's a private game in there."

I was beginning to grow tired of rudeness. In my first few minutes inside the Great Northern I'd been called 'buster' and 'bub' and now I was being denied entry into the one place I needed to be.

"I have to see Horace Wisdom, pronto," I said, "A whole mess of white folk have been killed by Indians."

Doubt drifted over the man's face like cloud shadow over a meadow. It was clear he'd been told to keep strangers out of the back room, but I had presented him with a bigger problem than he knew how to deal with, and what's more I had mentioned the constable's name. He frowned, trying to catch hold of the situa-

165

tion. "Indians, huh?" he said, "Wait here."

Seconds later, he came back with a heavy-set man in a high-crowned hat following close behind. Inside the big man's frock coat a nickel-plated badge caught lamplight and told me I had found the constable.

Horace Wisdom looked annoyed, like he'd left the poker game in the middle of a winning streak. He was a slope-shouldered man with a double chin and a belly like bread dough in a sack. His eyes were close-set and suspicious. "All right," he said, "who the Hell are you and what's all this bull about white folk bein' killed by Indians?"

"My name is Merlin Fanshaw," I said, "and I have reason to believe you're playin' high stakes poker in that room with the sons o' bitches who stole my horse."

Wisdom's mouth opened and closed once or twice, but nothing came out.

"As for the Indian trouble, I just said that to get your attention. It did *happen,* though, over on the Little Big Horn back in '76. You remember, it was in all the papers."

"You are a smart-mouth troublemaker, ain't you, boy? What did you say your name was again?"

"Merlin Fanshaw, from Dry Creek."

"I see. You wouldn't happen to know a female person of the opposite persuasion who calls herself Pandora Pretty Hawk, would you?"

The question came as such a surprise that I nearly told the truth before I could think to do otherwise.

166

"Why—uh, no," I stammered, "Why do you ask?"

Wisdom's face didn't change, but a short-barreled revolver appeared in his hand and stared at my belly with its cold, black eye. "I believe I'll just take your weapon, Merlin Fanshaw," he said, "and we'll go outside and see if there's anybody waitin' on you."

Pandora was waiting out front, sure enough. She stood at the hitchrack, holding the bridle reins of both her pony and Little Buck. Wisdom prodded me out ahead of him, and when Pandora saw us a smile lit her face, then quickly faded as she sensed trouble.

Constable Wisdom was polite but professional. "Miss Pretty Hawk?" says he, "I'm afraid you're under arrest, miss. Please turn loose of them bridle reins and raise your hands."

Pandora hesitated, and I knew she was considering flight or fight. I feared for her safety. If I'd read Constable Wisdom right, either one of them actions could lead to the worst possible result.

"Do what the man says, Pandora," I told her, "He's the law, and he's holdin' the high cards."

"Young Fanshaw is givin' you good advice, miss," Wisdom said, "should you try to run or draw a weapon, it will be my sad duty to shoot you down. I don't believe any of us wants that to happen, do we?"

Well, I sure didn't, and to my relief it seemed Pandora didn't either. She hesitated for just a moment, then slowly raised her hands above her head. Wisdom reached over and took my old Colt's Dragoon from the waistband of Pandora's britches. "Excuse me, miss," said he.

Behind us, a plump lady of the evening had jiggled out onto the veranda of the Great Northern and was watching us with some curiosity.

"Frankie Jo," said Wisdom to the lady, "I will require your assistance over at the jail. Come along with us, if you please."

The four of us made quite a procession as we moved on up the street. Pandora and me was in the lead, our hands shoulder high as we made our way along the muddy thoroughfare. Wisdom came next, leading Pandora's paint and Little Buck with his left hand while holding his short-barreled revolver on us with his right. Bringing up the rear, came the dancehall woman Wisdom had called Frankie Jo, delicately holding her skirts up to keep the ruffles and ribbons out of the puddled ruts and horse apples.

The Stillwater jail stood off by itself north of the town's main street, and we arrived there without incident. One or two town dogs—maybe the same ones we'd seen at the meat market—barked sort of half-hearted at us, but I had the feeling they only done so to be polite. Dogs tend to bark at what they don't understand, and I'm sure they didn't understand us. I can't say I understood much right then myself.

I tried to tell Wisdom about Fontayne and his boys and the way they'd gunned Orville and stole my horse back at Shenanigan. I tried to find out how come he'd

168

arrested us, but without success. Each time I tried to speak the constable replied with the general recommendation that I shut up, and when I persisted he knocked me down for emphasis. At no time did he seem even mildly annoyed; he just appeared to know what he wanted of us and required that we do it.

For a mostly law-abiding young man, I was fast becoming an expert on the hoosegows of Montana. During my single-minded pursuit of justice over the past few weeks I'd been imprisoned at Shenanigan, incarcerated at Silver City, and was now fixing to be jailed at Stillwater. Looking on the bright side, I told myself I was at least *conscious* for a change.

A quick once-over convinced me that the Stillwater jail was a tad more primitive than the aforementioned two had been. It was a low-ceilinged affair, maybe 30 foot square, built of cottonwood logs over a stone foundation and floor. Two cells ran half the building's length with a log wall between them. Instead of a bed, each cell was furnished with a threadbare blanket and a straw-filled pallet on the floor. Of course, that made things more convenient for the local vermin; they could get to the jailbird without having to climb up the leg of a bed.

The only light came from outside through the dirty window of a small office or from the hanging oil lamp that Wisdom then proceeded to light. By the dim glow I could see both cell doors were open, and that their iron bars offered both visibility and security from the office area.

169

Once inside, the constable made me lean against the wall while he searched me. He took my pocket knife, gunbelt, and spurs, and locked me in. Then he turned his attentions to Frankie Jo and Pandora.

"Frankie Jo," said he, "I require that you search the young lady, and that you do so in a thorough and expeditious manner. I wish to make sure she has no concealed weapons, money, or contraband on her person. If she resists, or gives you any trouble, it shall become my unpleasant duty to do the job myself."

Turning then to Pandora, he says, "Do I make myself clear, miss?"

The color was high in Pandora's cheeks and her eyes flashed fire and ice. "You do, constable," she said quietly, "Just exactly what are you looking for?"

Wisdom picked up a folded piece of paper from a cluttered desk near the door. "Why, stolen money, for one thing," he said, "about four hundred dollars as I understand it."

Wisdom produced a pair of gold-rimmed spectacles from a vest pocket, put them on, and unfolded the paper. "I received this telegram yesterday from Sheriff Fillmore over at Shenanigan. According to his message, you and young Fanshaw are wanted in Progress County on a variety of charges. These include aggravated assault, attempted murder, robbery, resistin' arrest, unlawful flight to evade prosecution, and interferin' with a peace officer in the performance of his duty.

"In summary, the sheriff says you tried to brain your stepdaddy with an axe handle and stole a horse and four hundred dollars of his money. Then you joined up with your accomplice, young Fanshaw yonder, who helped you escape by openin' fire on the sheriff and his lawful posse with a rifle."

Turning his attention back to me, Wisdom said, "Now I ain't interested in hearin' your side of things, nor any bull about some fellers killin' your pardner and stealin' your racehorse. All I'm concerned with is keepin' you two on ice till Sheriff Fillmore can come pick you up. That, and gettin' back to my poker game."

I couldn't see from where I was inside my cell, but I reckon Frankie Jo finished searching Pandora because I heard her say, "The girl don't have a blessed thing on her, Horace, except a body I would kill for. Can I go on back to the Great Northern now?"

"Yes, you may, Frankie Jo," the constable said, "I shall accompany you."

Then he closed and locked the door to Pandora's cell, turned the lamp down low, and him and Frankie Jo went off into the night. There have been times in my life when I felt if it wasn't for bad luck I'd have had no luck at all. That evening was one of those times.

The silence that fell upon the jail after Frankie Jo and the constable left was tomb-like and total. For a while I just set there in the gloom and listened to the sound of my own breathing. I could hear nothing of Pandora in the cell next door, and after a minute or two I came to worry about her.

"Pandora?" I said, "You all right, pardner?"

Her voice was tight and strained when she answered. "Yes," she said, "I'm all right. I didn't much enjoy bein' searched, probed, and pawed by that painted cat from the saloon, but I'm all right. How about you?"

"Feelin' sorry I got you in this mess."

"You never, Merlin. It's just that sometimes the wrong people have the power. Life isn't always fair."

"No, it sure ain't. But somehow, deep down, we keep expectin' it to be. I wonder why that is."

"I don't know. When my mother died, the priest told me all people everywhere, from little children to the oldest of the old, have that feeling. He said it's sort of a deep knowing that life should be fair, and one of the proofs that God exists."

Pandora was quiet then for what seemed a long time. When she spoke again, her voice sounded quiet and small. "I—I don't do well in dark, closed-in places," she said, "I feel trapped and helpless.

"Could you go to the front of your cell and reach toward mine through the bars? I think I'd feel better if I could hold your hand."

I done as she asked. I found her slim, strong hand in the darkness and, laying close to those cold iron bars, took it in mine. I reckon it did help her to feel better, and somehow it helped me.

"Try to get some sleep, darlin'," I told her, "Things will look better in the mornin'."

She didn't answer me, but she gave my hand a squeeze. I was still holding her hand when I drifted off to sleep.

Well, I was wrong. Things didn't look better in the morning. If anything they looked worse. A surly, gray half-light flooded my cold and clammy cell, showing the dirt and shabbiness that had been hid by darkness the evening before. I was chilled and stiff from laying on the floor, and my sunny disposition had gone into total eclipse. What with the skeeters and bedbugs staking claims to my person all night, I had slept poorly. At one point I'd heard the nervous scratch and skitter of what could only have been a rat. A dusty spider web filled one corner of the cell, complete with a couple of mummified flies, and the bleak walls held the names and thoughts of former inmates as well as rude drawings I could only hope Pandora's cell didn't have.

I was worried some about Pandora. I remembered the lost, hopeless way her voice had sounded the night before, and I determined I would do what I could to lift her spirits. I waited until I heard movement in the cell next door, then, cheerful as a chipmunk, bade her good day.

"Good mornin', pardner," says I, "how're you feelin' today?"

For a long moment there was silence. When Pandora finally answered, her voice sounded lorn and far away. "I—I don't feel much like talkin' right now, Merlin," she said, "all right?"

"Why sure, darlin'," I told her, "I just wanted you to know I'm here if you do feel like it. I've cancelled all my appointments."

I'd hoped Pandora would reward my poor jest with her merry laughter, but she did not. Well, I didn't blame her none; I wasn't feeling all that pert right then myself.

It's peculiar, but I've noticed that time don't always pass at the same rate of speed. There have been occasions in my life when a minute seemed to last all day, and other times when a day seemed to race past in a few hours. I can neither account for that mystery nor can I explain it; all I can do is take note of it. There's one thing I do know jail time passes slowest of all.

Over that day and the next Pandora and me saw little of the constable. Instead, a coon-footed old-timer with two beady eyes and an equal number of teeth brought us our meals. Breakfast was cornmeal mush and sorghum, while supper was some kind of catchall stew and hardtack. There wasn't no midday meal.

There also wasn't no conversation. I tried to pass the time of day with the old gent, but he just squinched up his eyes and shook his head like he didn't savvy my lingo. He never stayed around long, neither just enough to give us the vittles and shuffle on back out the door.

In some quarters, anyway, news of our arrest must have got to be general knowledge. During that first afternoon Clifton Miller, the young feller who aspired to build Stillwater's second livery barn, came by the jail. He still wore that same sappy smile Pandora had put on his face the day we arrived, so I knew he hadn't come to see me. He just stood there outside the cell doors with his hat in his hands and gazed upon Pandora like she was the Queen of Sheba or something. I admit his manner irritated me considerable. There he stood, making calf's eyes at Pandora and ignoring me altogether, while I couldn't even see her from where I was.

"I don't know what you done," he said to Pandora, "but I think it's a dang shame, you being locked up and all. I just wondered if there's anything I can do for you."

Pandora made no reply, so I took it on myself to answer him. "That's mighty neighborly of you, bub," I said, loud enough to get his attention, "You don't have any dynamite on you, do you?"

At least that caused him to look at me. "Dynamite?" he said, "Gosh, no! I don't—Oh, you're joshin' me, ain't you? Dynamite. That's a good one. Haw, haw."

His gaze went back to Pandora like scrap iron to a magnet.

"Say, pardner," I said, "would you do me a favor?"

"Uh—yeah, I guess so. What is it?"

"Our packhorse is staked out about a quarter mile below your corral, along with my bedroll and the rest of our plunder. I'd appreciate it if you'd look after the animal and our outfit till I can come back for it."

Clifton looked doubtful. "How do I know you'll be back?"

"You know because I *say* I will. When I do come back I'll pay you for the horse's keep and somethin' extra for your trouble."

175

It was clear Clifton would rather look at Pandora than talk to me, but my mention of future payment had stirred up his commercial nature. He squinted at me sort of suspicious-like and said, "Yeah, but what if you don't come back?"

By that time I had commenced to feel just a touch hostile toward young Clifton, but there was iron bars between us so I couldn't lay hands on him. I took a dally on my temper and answered him as pleasant as I knew how. "If I don't come back, you've got yourself a horse and a good pack outfit. If I do—that is, *when* I do—you get well-paid in cash money and I get my property back. All right?"

He pondered that for a second or two. Nobody could accuse Clifton of being the impulsive type. Finally, he nodded his head. "All right," said he, "it's a deal."

Reaching through the bars, I shook his hand. "Good," I said, "Now there's one more thing. That blood bay thoroughbred stud you had in your corral yesterday. Is he still there?"

"No, he ain't. That sportin' gent and his pardners took all their horses, includin' the thoroughbred and rode out at first light."

"Didn't say where they were goin', did they?"

"Can't say as they did. Why do you ask? They friends of yours?"

The thought of Fontayne and his trail trash riding off again with my horse Quicksilver was almost more than I could bear. I slid down the wall of my cell and just set there in a funk. Now it was *me* who wasn't looking at *Clifton*. "No," I said, "I don't reckon 'friend' is exactly the word."

Sometimes, when I was working for old Walt back in Dry Creek, I'd get to feeling downhearted over one thing or another. At such times Walt used to grin, slap me on the shoulder, and say, "Cheer up, kid—things could be worse." After Clifton left I tried to follow Walt's advice. I worked hard on my thoughts, and by afternoon of the next day I had cheered up considerable. Sure enough, things got worse.

After two days Constable Horace Wisdom finally came back to his jail. With him were Sheriff Ernie Fillmore and Pandora's stepdaddy, Buford Suggs.

TWELVE
Act of God

Nobody was smiling when the constable brought us out into the sunlight, least of all Pandora and me. Our horses were saddled and waiting at the hitchrack, and Little Buck raised his head when he seen me and nickered as if to ask "Now what kind of mess have you got yourself into?"

Ernie Fillmore had been in the saddle and away from his swivel chair for two days, and the man looked trail-weary and put-upon. As he stepped down off his horse he passed me a look that seemed to say I had caused all his problems. Well, I hadn't, of course, not all of them, but that's how Ernie looked at me, and at the time I almost wished I had. I know I hadn't ought to have felt that way, but there was something about Ernie Fillmore that just made a person—all right, that made *me*—want to cause him trouble.

All knees and elbows, Buford Suggs slouched in the saddle atop his pudding-footed mare. Raggedy overalls hung loose upon his lanky frame, and his big feet were shod in lace-up work shoes that barely fit his stirrups. A twelve-gauge shotgun lay across his thighs, and he glared hot-eyed and furious at Pandora. If looks could kill Buford's surely would have, and it wouldn't have surprised me to see him go to foaming at the mouth like a mad dog. Beneath his battered hat, he had a bandage wrapped around his skull that put me in mind of a turban on a Hindoo. His beard was matted and tobacco-stained, and he worked a quid in his cheek like a hog eating turnips. Staring at Pandora, his face went beet-red and frog-eyed. He spat a brown stream out onto the street and pointed a bony finger at her.

"I got you now, you redskin bitch," he said, "I'll learn you to lay wood to a man and steal his money!"

"Speakin' of money," said Constable Wisdom, "I found three hundred dollars in the girl's saddlebags."

"Good work, constable," said Sheriff Ernie Fillmore.

I knew it would cost me to speak, but I couldn't help myself. "Oh, my yes, good work, constable," I said, "but I reckon what you really found was four hundred. Are you keepin' a hundred as a finder's fee?"

The constable hit me, of course, a hard blow to the

belly that took my wind and dropped me to my knees in the dirt before him. I wasn't able to breathe, but I did manage to grin and give him a wink before he hit me a second time.

"Say, now, that's right," Buford said, "*Four* hunnert is what she stole. How is it you only found three hunnert?"

Wisdom rested his hand on the butt of his holstered Colt's and gave Buford a look that could have froze hot coffee. "Three is what I said and three is what I found, Mr. Suggs. Or do you mean to call me a liar?"

Buford's face turned snake belly white. "Why—no sech a thing, constable," he whined, "damn squaw must've *spent* a hunnert, that's all."

Wisdom kept his icy stare on Buford another ten seconds, then turned his attention back to Ernie.

"I've done my duty, sheriff," said the constable, nodding toward the doorway of the jail, "the money and the prisoners' personal effects are inside, in my safe. I'll need you to sign for 'em."

"Certainly, Constable," said Ernie. As he started to follow Wisdom inside, he turned and nodded at Suggs. "If young Fanshaw there tries to escape, you have my permission to stop him, Buford," he said, "whether it requires one, or *both,* barrels of that scattergun."

Buford smiled at last, but it wasn't what anybody would call a *pretty* smile.

The four of us—Buford, Ernie, Pandora, and me—left Stillwater about four-thirty in the afternoon, crossing the Yellowstone on the same ferry Pandora and me had come over on. The day was passing hot and still. Off to the east thunderclouds towered blue-black as a bruise, topped off by a spreading anvil shape. I figured rain would surely come upon us inside the hour.

As we headed south into the low hills beyond the river, the thought crossed my mind that Quicksilver and the men who stole him were no doubt riding *north* at the same time. After all I'd gone through to find the horse, every passing minute was now taking us farther apart. I felt despair fall over me like a wet blanket, but I done my best to fight it. No man is ever licked until he allows he is, and I wasn't ready to give up just yet.

Ernie led our little procession, of course, setting puffed up and proud on his buttermilk gelding, with me behind him on Little Buck. Pandora rode next to me, and Buford brought up the rear. My belly still hurt where the constable had hit me, but I took my mind off the pain by watching Ernie's back. His fat ass filled his saddle to overflowing but he set tall and pompous as a field marshal. His narrow shoulders were throwed back and his chest was pooched out almost as far as his belly. I had to admit sheriff Ernie Fillmore had a rare gift—somehow, he had learned to strut setting down.

Riding close beside me on her paint pony, Pandora's face was sad and her eyes downcast. She looked older, somehow, and weary. I knew the despair I'd felt had come upon her, too. During the brief time we'd rode together I had growed accustomed to her laughter and bright smile, and I found that I missed them. I'd took considerable pleasure in feeling I had rescued her from her troubles and had become her protector. Now Dame Fortune had quit smiling upon us and had gone to frowning. I felt I had let Pandora down. I longed to brighten her spirits and rekindle her hope.

"Don't give up on me now, darlin'," I told her, "You know what they say about silver linin's, dark clouds, and all."

She looked not at me, but at the threatening sky. "Yes," she said, "outside every silver lining there's a dark, dark cloud."

For the next hour or so Ernie led us down out of the hills and into the wide valley that stretched south toward the mountains. Away from the river, the air was hotter still. Sweat crawled out from underneath my hatbrim and trickled down my face. Ernie had gave up his fearless lawman pose and slumped in his saddle like a sack of wheat on a stump. Far out across the valley, willows and low trees marked the stream Pandora and me had camped on only days before. I found myself wishing Ernie would let us stop along its banks awhile so we could shade up and partake of its coolness, but of course he did not.

Pandora and me had been neither tied nor shackled, but Ernie had made it clear he would not hesitate to shoot us if we tried to run. Behind us, Buford Suggs muttered threats and curses, fingering his shotgun as if he hoped we *would* break for the tall and uncut.

181

For a brief time I considered it. Little Buck was quick as a cat, and I figured if I could get beyond the range of Buford's twelve-gauge I stood a fair chance of getting away altogether. Even as the thought took shape I knew I could not run without Pandora. I recalled the pain in her voice the morning she told me about her life with Suggs. I glanced back and saw again the rage and hate behind his crazy eyes, and I knew I would never leave her in his hands if I could help it.

Right about then Ernie drew rein and pulled his horse around to face us. "There's an old trapper's cabin in a draw about eight miles from here," he said, "we'll put up there this evenin' and go on into Shenanigan tomorrow."

Across the valley, the storm swept toward us, ragged shirttails of cloud splayed out in its wake. Distant lightning stabbed the earth in bright, jagged streaks and I smelled the wetness on the wind as the storm came on.

"I don't much care for the looks of them clouds," Ernie said, "I reckon we're in for a storm, and a big 'un." Turning in his saddle, he untied the strings that held his slicker and slipped the garment on. "I'm puttin' my 'fish' on, and I'd advise you to do the same," he said, "but if you're thinkin' this would be a good time to make a run for it you better think again. If Buford don't get you with his shotgun, I surely will with the rifle."

In a trice, Suggs, Pandora, and me had pulled on and

buttoned up our slickers. The heat of the day had gone, replaced by a gusty, cold wind blowing out of the east, ahead of the rain. We rode on at a trot, the horses goosey and nervous, and I watched the storm sweep down across the hills and out into the valley. It was then I heard the sound.

Loud and growing louder as the first big raindrops struck us, the noise was a rattling, thunderous roar like a fast-moving train. I had heard that sound once before, while riding the plains north of Dry Creek with my pa. Of a sudden I knew we faced not just rain but something worse—*hail*.

I could see the white stones hammering the valley floor, bouncing high in the grass as the storm quick-marched our way. Then I saw the hail was no ordinary hail, but huge rock-hard balls of ice as big as hens' eggs.

I turned in my saddle and saw Suggs' eyes go wide and his jaw drop as he watched the storm sweep toward us. Ahead, Ernie's gelding rolled its eyes in fright and broke into a nervous dance as the sheriff tried to calm the animal. The rain and hail rattled toward us, slashing the earth and mashing the sage-brush with an avalanche of sound—then, suddenly, it was on us.

"Pandora!" I shouted, "Slip your saddle and step down quick! That's a killin' hail a-comin'!"

She stared at me, confusion in her eyes. I didn't know if she understood, but I hoped she'd watch me and do what I did even if she didn't savvy what I said.

Even as I called out to her I was taking my own advice. I swung down off Little Buck, jerking my latigos free as I did so, and slid Pa's old Texas rig off with me.

Suggs was blind to the danger. As he saw me step off Little Buck he swung the twelve-gauge around and fired into the space I'd only just vacated. The storm was so loud I couldn't hear the shot, but I saw the muzzle belch orange fire just as I hit the gumbo with my saddle in hand. Crouching into the slashing hail I hoisted the rig atop my shoulders and over my head. Ice balls hammered above and about me. One struck the fingers of my left hand and at first I was sure it had broke them.

My concern was for Pandora. I quickly scanned the area from beneath my makeshift shelter, fearing the worst. Then, sixty feet away, amid the hammering, rattling fall of the hail, I saw her. Like mine, her saddle was held atop and above her as a shield. I remembered to breathe again.

Ernie spurred his terrified gelding toward the distant tree line as hailstones struck him like frozen fists. His horse was being struck as well, and the animal lost all reason and fell to running and bucking. Pounded from above and below, Ernie hung and rattled for a jump or two, then lost his seat and fell heavily into a washout a hundred yards away.

The other horses were running, too, but I could see little save the slashing rain and hail. The roar of the storm seemed to grow even louder. I could feel the shock of the striking hailstones all the way through the saddle's bullhide cover and hardwood tree. It felt like crazy men was out there with sledgehammers, and I wished they would let up.

My pa told me about being caught once in a barrage of cannon fire during the war. He spoke of his fear and the feeling of helplessness that gripped him as he hugged the earth and prayed hot metal would not find his vitals.

"Lordamighty, Pa," I'd said, "what did you do?"

"Nothin' I could do," said he, "I knew I would either die or not, so I just hunkered down and waited to learn which it would be."

Well, once again there was nothing to do but hunker down and wait, so that's what I did.

I don't know how long I crouched there, but the noise was a constant roar and the buffeting of the storm seemed to grow stronger with each passing moment. Muddy water and ice swirled around my boots and my fingers throbbed from being struck by the hailstones. My hat was pushed up into the saddle's sheepskin lining, and my Navajo blanket had fell down across my shoulders, smelling strong and sour of horse sweat. The smell brought Little Buck to mind; I had set him free to find what shelter he could. With all my heart I hoped he'd be all right.

Then, as sudden as it had come, the storm passed. Water streamed off my rigging and ran inside the sleeves of my slicker. Hailstones, torn grass, and twigs floated in the muddy runoff around my feet. My shoulders ached from holding the heavy saddle above my head, but the pounding had stopped, and the noise faded as the tempest swept on across the flat and into the hills beyond. Slowly, I eased my saddle to the ground and took note of my surroundings.

The valley lay wet and battered as far as the tree line and beyond. Above, torn clouds let shafts of sunlight through and the plain was lit with brightness. Hailstones lay piled up in drifts and mounds around the battered sagebrush. Steam rose off the ice into the new-washed air, and in the sky a bright rainbow made mock of the storm's harshness.

I saw no movement anywhere in the valley, nor any sign of the horses. I hoped they had made it to shelter somewhere, maybe in the trees or beyond in the hills. Pandora's saddle lay atop her motionless form, the yellow oilskin of her slicker bright in the sunlight. I hurried to her, lifted the rigging off, and set it aside. She lay face down and unmoving, but as I bent down and touched her hair she turned and looked at me with wide, serious eyes.

"It's all right, pardner," I said, "the storm has passed." She tried to stand, but quickly sank back down and sat beside her saddle. "It—it's my ankle," she said, "I can't put my weight on it."

I loosened the strings that tied her high-topped moccasin and slipped it off. Gently, I rotated her foot, wincing as I felt her stiffen with the pain of it. "It ain't broke," I told her, "likely you sprained it when you stepped off your pony. Just set easy awhile—I'm gonna find out what happened to Ernie and Suggs, then see if I can locate a horse."

I found Ernie in six inches of muddy water with his head partway under a big patch of sagebrush. He was breathing but bloodied, and it was plain the storm had gave him quite a beating. I drug him up out of the washout and laid him in the sunshine, then I borrowed his six-shooter and gunbelt and went a-hunting for Suggs.

By the time I'd walked the half-mile to the trees, I'd almost come to believe Pandora's stepdaddy had vanished into thin air. There had been no sign of him as I crossed the flat, nor had I seen anything of the horses. Green leaves and broken branches littered the creek banks and gave evidence aplenty—as if I needed any—of the power of the storm. The brush was thick in places and I went careful and slow as I worked my way downstream. Back among the trees, hailstones lay unmelted in the deep shade and the stream gabbled softly over the boulders in its bed. From somewhere close by a songbird chirped a bright melody, but other than that the woods were silent. Every now and then I'd stop and listen, but I heard nothing.

I was about to turn back and take my search upstream when I heard movement nearby in the brush.

"Buford?" I called, "Is that you?" No answer came, though I waited a spell and called out a second time.

Then, once again I heard something moving ahead

in the brush and a deep grunting sound. I bent low, pushing my way through the tangled branches, and broke out into a small clearing. It was there, among the thick trees and deadfall, that I finally found Buford Suggs—and his pudding footed mare.

The horse stood, muddy and bleeding from a score of cuts and scratches, in a tangle of fallen timber. The mare gave a pitiful whinny when she seen me, and I could see, by the unnatural angle at which she held it that her right foreleg was broken. On her nigh side, his foot still caught in the stirrup and the rest of him stretched out flat and limp as any doll, lay Buford Suggs. Somehow he'd run his foot through the stirrup when the storm broke and been dragged to his death by the terrified mare.

I don't mind telling you the whole scene gave me a queer feeling. Buford had been a hard man to like, and after Pandora told me of the way he'd done her I reckon I'd come about as close to hating a man as ever I could. He'd been Pandora's stepdaddy, but he'd not only failed to care for her and protect her like a daddy ought to, he'd been the very one who hurt and abused her. I tried to feel glad he was dead, but somehow, seeing the poor devil sprawled limp and lifeless there in the mud, I felt my anger drain away like water from a leaky bucket. His staring eyes had already filmed over, and his gaping mouth seemed to ask the questions I suppose all men ask when the end comes. Maybe, I thought, he knew the answers now. Anyway, I can't say I felt much one way or the other, except to wish he could have took the hurt he'd caused Pandora with him when he left.

There was nothing I could do for Buford, but I could still help the mare. I loosened the girth on the saddle and let the rigging slip to the ground. Then I pulled Ernie's nickel-plated six-shooter, drew a bead midpoint between her eyes, and put an end to her pain forever.

When I got back to where I'd left Ernie, Pandora was tending his wounds. Somehow she'd limped or crawled over to where he lay and was washing the cuts and bruises the hailstones had put on his face. The sheriff of Progress County lay there in the grass with his head on Pandora's lap, whimpering like a whipped dog, and I marveled at the picture they made.

"He still hasn't come around," she said, "I think maybe he's in shock."

Her long black hair hung lank and wet across her face. She smoothed a strand of it back, shading her eyes against the sun as she looked up at me. I reckon the look on my face must have answered her question.

"Buford's—dead, isn't he?"

"Yes, he is. Got his foot hung up and died of it. I carried his body out of the trees."

"I heard a shot."

"His mare. Broken leg."

I tried to read Pandora's face, but could not. There was no relief, no satisfaction, no gladness at the news of her tormentor's passage that I could see. Instead, a sad, wistful look came upon her features, and I saw tears well up in her warm, dark eyes.

When she spoke, her voice was almost a whisper. "Poor Buford." she said.

THIRTEEN
A Bath and a Burial

Pandora had pretty much got Ernie's bleeding stopped, but the lawman had took quite a pounding, both from the hailstorm and from getting bucked off into the washout. He had knots on his head, cuts and bruises on his face, and his right eye was puffed up and going to black. I laid my hand upon his brow and discovered his skin was moist and clammy as a carp. Putting my ear to his chest, I found his heartbeat weak and faint but racing like a scared rabbit's. Pandora was right; the sheriff of Progress County had gone into a state of shock.

I knew shock oft-times followed a serious hurt and could be worse for a person than the injury that caused it. Doc Taggart had told me once that a big danger to shock victims was losing their body heat and that it was important to get, and keep, them warm. Keeping Ernie warm, as I saw it, presented a few problems.

In the first place, he was pretty well soaked to the skin from laying in the cold water of the washout. In the second place, because the sun was about to set, I could already feel the temperature dropping. We were going to need a fire, and soon. It had long been my habit to carry matches in my vest pockets, but the constable at Stillwater had took mine when he throwed me into his two-bit jail. Looking through my saddlebags, however, I found nearly a full box. The problem would be finding dry wood. All there was in our immediate vicinity was damp sagebrush, and I knew that wouldn't serve. Even when it was dry, burning sagebrush tended to make more smoke than fire.

"We'll have to get him out of those wet clothes and find a way to warm him up," I told Pandora, "which means I'm gonna have to move him. I figure I can find dry wood down along the crick, get a fire goin', and make us some kind of camp. By mornin', he'll either be better or Progress County will need a new sheriff."

Ernie outweighed me by at least forty pounds. Hefting his bulk onto my shoulders and packing him down to the tree line was no easy matter. He was dead weight and heavy as a November bear. I had to let him down and catch my breath four times before ever I reached the trees. Pandora said that watching me carry Ernie in his bright yellow slicker was like watching a bow-legged ant carrying a lemon.

Once there, I found a fairly level spot under a good-sized tree about fifty feet from the creek. There was a rock shelf nearby that I figured would reflect the heat, and I rustled up enough wood to get a blaze going. I stripped Ernie buck naked, then wrapped him in my flannel shirt and both his slicker and mine. Hanging his clothes near the fire to dry, I propped his feet up on a log and made my way back to fetch Pandora.

The sun had gone down when I got back to where she was. As I came near, I saw she had taken the saddlebags and my lariat from our saddles and was hopping toward me on one foot through the twilight. I had to grin. She looked for all the world like a little girl playing hopscotch.

When Pandora and me reached our camp on the creek, the fire had pretty well burned down, and Ernie had slipped farther away in his spirit. I knew Pandora's ankle was hurting her plenty, though she never showed it. She just knelt down by Ernie's side and gave his chest and arms a brisk rubdown while I rustled more wood and built up the fire again. The sheriff was deathly pale and still. The side of him that had laid next to the fire was warm enough, but his other side had that cold, clammy feel he'd had when we first found him.

I was worried about him. I knew we had to keep him warm, but I didn't know how to do it. We couldn't keep a-turning him from side to side like a hotcake on a griddle, and building a fire on each side of him didn't seem like a practical answer either. It was Pandora who came up with the solution.

"My mother's people use the *awu'sua*—the sweat lodge—for religious reasons, but also for keeping clean and for healing. We could make one for Ernie— it would sure warm him, all right."

192

Well, I had of course heard about the sweat lodge. I knew it was a kind of Indian steam bath, but I have to admit that's about all I did know; however, with Pandora's supervision and a jackknife I found in Ernie's britches, I commenced to build one. First, Pandora had me to fetch about a dozen good-sized rocks and put them in the fire to heat. Then I cut twelve willow shoots from the creek bank and set them into the earth in a circle maybe six foot across. I couldn't see what difference it made, but Pandora insisted the doorway to the bath had to face east and no other direction, so that's the way we done it. While I scooped out a firepit just inside the door, Pandora wove the ends of the willows together in a dome shape and tied them in place with strips of willow bark.

Next, she showed me how to use a pair of heavy forked sticks to move the rocks from the fire to the pit inside the lodge. While I was doing that she covered the willow framework with our saddleblankets and slickers until no light from outside could be seen at all. Only the glow of the nearly white-hot rocks inside the pit showed, ghost-like and spooky to behold.

I stripped Ernie to his drawers and done the same myself. Once again, I hefted the sheriff of Progress County onto my shoulders, and, on my knees, carried him into the sweat lodge. As soon as him and me was inside and more or less settled, Pandora adjusted the covering again from outside where she tended the fire. I set there, holding Ernie at my side, and felt the heat of the rocks fill the lodge with a dry, baked smell.

Then Pandora handed me the battered tin cup I carried in my saddlebags, filled my hat with water from the creek, and passed that inside as well.

"Wet your hair down, and your face," she said, "Ernie's, too." I did so, feeling helpless, and a little edgy. Then she said, "Now use the cup to splash water on the stones," and I done that, too.

Water hit the rocks with a sound like a pistol shot and steam filled every square inch of the lodge, which, by the way, was dark as the inside of a moose. The steam sizzled and popped in the blackness, and I was plumb certain I was going to suffocate, be boiled alive, or both. I would have hollered as much to Pandora, who had got me into all this, except that I could not breathe. I set there, a-hugging Ernie while my eyes felt they was about to explode and the top of my head seemed to have caught fire.

Pandora called from outside and assured me that everything was normal and the way it was supposed to be. I confess I had my doubts; all I wanted to do right then was somehow live through the event. I had me a quick but desperate talk with the Almighty during which I made a whole mess of promises on the condition He would somehow allow me to survive.

Through the entire ordeal, Ernie never moved a muscle. Water dripped off the both of us like hot rain, and then, to my surprise, I discovered I was able to breathe again. I figured the Lord had wrought a miracle on my behalf, and I was so grateful that for a time I actually meant to keep my vows. During the next few minutes I found I was actually growing accustomed to the heat, if you can believe it, and time and time again I used the cup to dash water from my sombrero onto the stones. Each time I done so the heat seemed greater than before; then, after awhile, the rocks began to cool.

"Now," Pandora called from outside, "throw the cover off the door and jump into the stream!"

Well, I remembered from the time I'd spent fishing that stream just how cold it was. Every part of my body seemed to pucker in horror as my mind considered her words.

"What?" I choked, "I'll shatter like glass!"

For the first time in days I heard Pandora's bright laughter, and I was pleased to have caused it. "No, you won't," she said, "Do it, Merlin—you'll feel wonderful."

I flung the slickers back away from the entrance and made a wild dash for the creek. I know I yelled something at the top of my voice, not a word exactly, but a high, shrill sound—a sort of cross between a beller and a shriek. When I reached the bank I jumped high and came down into the water like a hot cannon ball.

Now I half thought my heart would quit beating the instant my body hit that ice-cold water, but no such a thing. I hardly felt anything at all, except a cool, relaxed pleasure and a kind of pure joy. It seemed like I weighed nothing at all, as if I could just float up beyond the treetops and into the soft evening sky like smoke. I didn't know right then if the sweat lodge had helped Ernie, but it surely had helped me. I even considered throwing him into the stream, too, but thought better of it. Our purpose was to get the man warm, not kill him.

By then Ernie's clothes had dried, so I dressed him, bundled him up in his slicker, and bedded him down by the fire again. He still hadn't come to, but he'd lost his clammy feel and it seemed to me his heartbeat was a bit stronger.

As night fell over the grove, Pandora and me set and studied the flames as the dry wood crackled and snapped in the stillness. Neither of us was in a mood to talk much, so we didn't. The birds of the day had gone silent, but from somewhere close by I heard an owl hoot, short and breathy as the low notes on a flute. The creek made a pleasant sound as it chuckled over the rocks, and the feeling came upon me that in spite of all our troubles everything was, and would be, well. I hollowed out a hip and shoulder hole in the soft dirt, stretched out, and closed my eyes. There was much to think about, and more to do, but there would be time for all that come morning. The last thing I recall was Pandora laying down beside me. Somehow her closeness seemed the most natural thing in the world, and I fell asleep a-holding her in my arms.

It was just past dawn when I awoke. Sunlight was slanting through the trees, turning the smoke from our campfire a soft pink. Near the fire, Ernie Fillmore was awake. He sat with his back propped up against a cottonwood log, while Pandora gave him what smelled like some kind of tea from my old tin cup.

"Good mornin,' Ernie," says I, "Looks like you're gonna live after all."

He was weak, but uppity as ever. "I'll bet you're *real* glad about that," he said. I hadn't gave it much thought up to then, but when I did I was surprised to find I really *was* glad. Maybe it was caring for him like we had, or the way he'd looked so frail and helpless, but whatever the reason I found I felt different about him, somehow, than I had before.

"I *am* glad, believe it or not," I said, "I still don't like you much, but I do believe I'm gettin' used to you."

Ernie nodded his gratitude at Pandora and gently pushed the cup away.

"I believe that's aplenty, thank you," he said.

He looked and sounded tired, but he'd passed the crisis and was in his right mind, anyway. "That hailstorm," he said, remembering, "where's Buford?"

"Dead. Hung up in the stirrup and dragged to death when his horse bolted. Found him in the trees about a mile downstream. His mare had broke her foreleg. Had to put her down."

Ernie closed his eyes and leaned his head back against the stump. "The other horses?" he asked.

"Haven't seen 'em since the storm. Figured I'd go look for 'em this mornin'."

Ernie opened his eyes and studied me for a time before he spoke again. Then he said, "Looks like the tables have turned. I'm *your* prisoner now instead of

197

you bein' mine, and I see you're wearin' my gun."

"You don't see enough," I told him, "You had one foot in the Great Beyond when we picked you up. Pandora and me worked hard to pull you back over to this side again."

I got to my feet and put my hat on. "Now it does seem to me you could return the favor and cut us a little slack. I'm gonna go hunt horses now, but while I'm gone I'd like Pandora to tell you the truth about her life with Buford Suggs, and what really happened the night she left home. When I get back, we'll talk about your gun."

West of the treeline, long shadows stretched like fingers out across the plain. A fresh breeze stirred the tall grass, bending it in long ripples like water and rolling it on to the distant hills. The lawmen had left Pa's field glasses in my saddlebags, no doubt figuring I couldn't *look* myself into an escape, and I'd brought them along to hunt the horses. I stood there at the edge of the brush and studied the country, taking my time and seeing what there was to see.

Above the hills a hawk circled slow on the rising air, hunting the slow and unwary in the grass below. Across the valley floor, I caught movement partway up the hillside and for a moment thought I'd found Pandora's painted pony. But then I saw it was just a lone antelope, far away and grazing easy along the sunlit slope.

Seeing the pronghorn woke up my appetite, which wasted no time in reminding me I hadn't had any food in awhile, and for a time thoughts of breakfast filled my mind. I knew if I walked slow and easy along the shady side of the creek there was a better than even chance I'd run onto a deer. I knew, too, that even if I did I had only Ernie's nickel-plated six-shooter to do my hunting with. Boasting to Pandora aside, I knew I wasn't that good with a revolver.

Walking slow and holding to the shade, I moved on down the treeline to where I'd left Buford's body. I'd wrapped him in his slicker and piled brush on him the evening before and had brought his saddle and bridle out as well.

I heard the magpies before I saw them, and of course I knew what they was up to. Their raucous cries told me they were gathering for a feed and that old Buford was the main course. As I came around a bend in the brush I seen that I'd sure called the turn. A half-dozen of them long-tailed carrion eaters flew up in a clatter of black and white feathers and settled down again a short distance away.

There was no getting around it. I would have to find a way to bury Buford. Now I have never been over-fond of working with long-handled tools such as shovels, rakes, or hay forks. Oh, I've used such blister-makers when I had to and expect I will again, but given the choice I druther perform my labors from the back of a good horse. Anyway, at the time I'm speaking of I sure could have used a shovel, but that need was, as they say, academic. I had neither shovel nor horse, and I still had me a man to bury.

A quick search of Buford's saddlebags produced a half-pint of whiskey, a good supply of jerked beef, and a dozen shotgun shells. There was shells in his pockets, too, as well as a tobacco plug, a whetstone, and nine dollars and thirty-two cents in coin. Best of all, in a scabbard beneath his shirt I found a well-honed bowie knife with a twelve-inch blade.

In the time since Buford had gone on to a better world or wherever, his carcass had took on a distinctive aroma. This smell may have appealed to the chattering magpies, but I have to say I didn't care for it much. I wet down my bandanna at the creek and pulled it up over my nose road-agent style. Then I took up the Bowie knife and fell to gouging out a resting place in the earth for Pandora's dear departed stepdaddy.

An hour later I finished my labors, rolled Buford in a shallow hole, and covered him over with dirt and rocks. It was the first grave I'd ever dug, and it was no prizewinner, but I hoped it would keep the varmints at bay until old Buford could be moved to a deeper hole.

Finding the shotgun shells reminded me of the first moments of the hailstorm when I'd quit Little Buck and Buford had cut loose at me with the twelve-gauge. Someplace between that point and the creek he would have dropped the scattergun, and I set out to find it.

It didn't take a Pandora Pretty Hawk to track the path of the run-away mare. Buford had fallen just after the storm struck, and the marks of his dragging were plain. I found the shotgun in the grass by a big sagebrush, not far from where the hail first hit us. It was muddy and dull, and rust had already begun to appear on the metal. I wiped the gun as clean as I was able and made certain both barrels were loaded. Then I moved back into the trees and waded the creek.

Low hills and shallow coulees marked the east side of the treeline, with a few flat-topped buttes in the middle distance. I climbed up through loose rock and scrub cedar to a point where I could pretty well scout the whole country. Once there, I hunkered down cross-legged and made a slow, careful scan of the land. Dry washes and sagebrush flats stretched far away as tomorrow, and off to the east the mountains lay in a misty blue haze, but I saw no trace of the horses.

Back at the creek, I broke the fast with a hunk of Buford's beef jerky and a long drink of cold water before I made my way upstream to our camp. More than anything, I needed to find our saddlehorses, but I knew they could have run miles ahead of the storm—they could even have quit the country altogether.

I missed Little Buck, of course, but Ernie's horse held my special interest, and for good reason. Wherever that animal had got to, it had carried off most of Pandora's and my earthly goods. The Winchester carbine and scabbard, Orville's six-gun and belt, my old Colt's dragoon—even my spurs and jackknife—had all been on the gelding when he'd dumped the sheriff and took off for parts unknown. Our money had been in Ernie's saddlebags, too, three hundred dollars of

Pandora's and just over two hundred of mine. In my opinion, the buttermilk steed from Progress County had chose a mighty poor time to go off sightseeing.

I thought about Pandora. Since the night she took refuge in my camp I'd come to admire her more each day. She'd been a good pardner for the trail, doing more than her share. She had a pleasant disposition and was cheerful, mostly, in all circumstances. Also, as I may have mentioned before, she was mighty good to look at. Not only had Pandora broke into my camp the week before, I reckon she had also broke into my heart.

Maybe it had all started long ago, as far back as our school days in Dry Creek when she'd first stirred up them strange, wild feelings in me. I knew Pandora and me would go on with our lives from where we was, but I wasn't sure we'd be going on together. Whatever happened, there was no reason for her to ride my trail any longer. Her stepdaddy, Buford Suggs, was dead—dead of a hailstorm, a spooked horse, and lace-up work shoes that trapped his foot in the stirrup. Suggs was no longer a threat to her or anyone. No matter what Sheriff Ernie Fillmore chose to do, Pandora would soon be free to find and build a new life. Knowing I might not be a part of that life left me feeling hollow, somehow, and lonesome.

I suppose it was thinking such thoughts about Pandora that set me on an old track, the counting of my losses. Once again, I brought to mind those people I'd cared for who had gone out of my life. I recalled the way my mother had bought her ticket to Heaven, leaving me behind at the unripe age of ten. I remembered my Pa and how he'd gone to glory astride that crazy black stud, and Old Walt, who'd just wore out from living too long. He'd left me a gift horse and a legacy, but I'd lost his gift to thieves. I remembered my friend Orville, and the way he'd died of pride and a slow hand on the streets of Shenanigan.

Now I'd lost Little Buck and maybe Pandora, too. I told myself I'd had a bellyfull of losing, that it was time to cut my losses and go on back to Dry Creek. Why should I risk my life following Fontayne and his hardcases in a fool quest to reclaim my property?

Even as I asked the question, I knew the answer. The reason I had to keep going was *because* of the folks I'd lost—because of mother who had dreamed of the man I might become, because of Pa who'd loved me better than he loved himself and had taught me how to be a man, because of Walt who'd left me a racehorse and a dream, and because of Orville, my friend, who'd lost his life trying to get that dream back for me.

Most of all, I would go on for my own sake, no matter what it cost and no matter where the trail led. I would go on because I couldn't live with myself if I didn't and because going on was the right thing to do. I asked myself, "is a principle worth risking my life for?," and my answer was, "You bet."

There's a curious thing that happens when a man decides what's right and determines to do it. He may not know the how, and he may not have the means, but the moment he makes the decision all those things are somehow taken care of.

That's the way it happened that day. I made my way through a tangled thicket into a clear space among the trees, and it was there that I found our missing horses.

FOURTEEN
Going our Separate Ways

When I said I found the missing horses, that ain't quite the whole truth. What I found was two of the three missing horses. Little Buck and Ernie's gelding stood inside the clearing, all but hidden by thick brush and the low-hanging branches of a great box elder tree, but Pandora's pinto was nowhere to be seen.

Little Buck spooked as I stumbled through the tangled growth and into his view. He'd heard me crashing through the underbrush, of course, and I reckon he was waiting to see what kind of critter was coming upon him. When it turned out to be me instead of a bear or a horse-eating catamount, I think he was glad, but I'm not sure. He acted kind of stand-offish at first, like he was mad at me or something. Maybe he thought the hailstorm had been my fault and that I'd started it just to cause him grief, I don't know. Anyway, he laid his ears back and gave me a sort of walleyed look while he was making up his mind. I tried to put my hand on him, but he shied and snorted nervous-like when he seen me reach out, so I quit trying, hunkered down on my heels, and gave him some more time.

Little Buck *had* looked better. One eye was bruised and nearly closed, from a hailstone, likely. His black mane and tail were matted and tangled, and his tawny hide showed scratches, bruises, and open cuts. He still wore his bridle, but he'd stepped on the dragging reins and had broke off all but a foot or so of the nearside one. Flies were a-working on both horses, and the animals stood together in the clearing, head to tail, switching the pests away from each other as horses will.

Ernie's buttermilk gelding looked no better. Like Buck, he wore cuts and bruises from the storm, and his proud head hung low and sullen as he watched me. He still carried Ernie's saddle, but only barely. The rigging had turned, and it hung nearly upside down back near the horse's flanks. It looked like the gelding had made an effort to rid himself of it altogether because the saddle was muddy and bore hoof-marks where he'd tried to kick it free. The Winchester had fell from its scabbard somewhere, but I was glad to see the saddlebags were still in place.

There was good grass there in the clearing, and even though both horses still wore their bridles they'd been able to graze and go to water. I stood up sudden, spooking them on purpose, and watched as they quick-stepped away from me. I was pleased. Both animals were stiff and sore, but sound of limb; they would heal.

Again, I held my hand out to Buck. He sniffed it,

wallered the smell around in his memory some, then nickered low with a deep, rumbling sound and came to me. I was mighty glad to see the little horse alive and well. There in that clearing, I hugged his strong neck and told him so.

Ernie was setting in the shade when I got back to camp. Pandora was nowhere to be seen, but I didn't figure she'd gone far. Even though she tried not to show it, I knew her ankle still hurt her plenty. She'd made herself a crutch from a stout tree branch, and even though it helped her to get around, I don't guess it had done much to ease the pain.

"Well?" says Ernie, with his usual charm, "did you find the horses?"

"As it happens, I did. Yours and mine, anyway. Where's Pandora?"

"Slipped out of camp nearly an hour ago. Didn't say where she was goin', and I didn't ask."

I had reclaimed our property from Ernie's saddlebags back in the clearing and had tucked away Pandora's and my money inside my shirt. I was wearing Orville's gun once again, and I made sure Ernie saw it. Carefully, I placed his revolver and gun belt on a nearby log.

Producing Buford's pint whiskey bottle, I pulled the cork and said, "Magpies was prospectin' Buford when I got there, so I buried him, in a temporary kind of way. Found this flask of prairie dew among his personal effects and figured maybe we should use it to tell him good-bye. Here's how."

I tipped the flask up and took a healthy swig, although the word "healthy" don't sound quite right, somehow. The whiskey was homemade, harsh, and vicious; it seared my mouth and closed my gullet, and I couldn't have spoke right then for a hundred-dollar bill. My eyes watered as I passed the bottle to Ernie, who took it, said "how," and drank.

For a minute or so it was pretty quiet around our camp. I suppose that was partly because we were remembering the dearly departed, but I believe the stillness had more to do with trying to catch our breath than grieving the absence of Buford's. Ernie was the first to speak.

He throwed out his chest, cleared his throat, and said, "Now see here, Fanshaw—Miss Pretty Hawk gave me a full account of the circumstances surrounding her life with the late Buford Suggs. She particularly described the events of her last night under his roof, and the factors that led her to hit him upside the head with an axe handle.

"I am inclined to believe her story; therefore, as far as the law is concerned, I'd say the young woman is free to go wherever she wishes. When she's able, of course."

Ernie got to his feet, picked up his gun belt and buckled it about his chubby hips. He frowned, then fixed his gaze on me. "Your case, however, is a different colored horse entirely. You opened fire on me and my posse from ambush that day at Brimstone Gap. That act constitutes assault with a deadly weapon

207

and quite possibly attempted murder besides."

I grinned. "That dog won't hunt, sheriff, and you know it. I fired only to spook your horses and set you afoot so Pandora could cross the county line. Had I been trying to kill you I can assure you this here conversation would not be takin' place."

Ernie wouldn't meet my gaze, but dropped his eyes and made his face hard. He acted as if he'd bit off a piece of tough steak and could neither spit it out nor swaller it. Finally, he cleared his throat and gathered up his dignity.

"Well," he said, "be that as it may—I'm inclined to let bygones be bygones this time. Miss Pretty Hawk also told me all you done to help me after the storm, and I ain't an ungrateful man.

"You asked me this mornin' to cut you some slack and so I shall. I still find you to be a cocky young whelp and a smart-mouth troublemaker, but I'm prepared to dismiss all pending charges against you."

I grinned again. "Why, Ernie," I said, "are you tryin' to thank me for savin' your life?"

Ernie's face turned the color of ripe watermelon. "No, damn you, I ain't," he snapped, "As sheriff, I'm merely extendin' you clemency on a onetime basis."

I took his hand, ignoring his outburst. I put a quaver in my voice and a wide-eyed, sappy look on my face. "You're more than welcome, Ernie," I said, "don't mention it."

His face went from red to thundercloud purple, and he stomped off toward the creek.

I had to smile again as Ernie fussed and fumed like some kind of damp firework. The poor man had no sense of humor at all, and it was both his mistake and misfortune that he oft-times took me too serious. Even worse, he took *himself* too serious.

I fetched my curry comb and brush from my saddlebag and groomed Little Buck as best I could. I had to go slow and careful on account of the cuts and tender places the hail had put upon him. His legs and feet were sound, and there were no serious sores on his back, but I was worried some about his eye. The eyelid was swollen, puffy, and nearly closed, so I could see little of the orb itself. Some matter had formed around the lid, and I rinsed it away, gently bathing the area with cool water from the creek. Ernie tended his horse, too, but there was little either of us could do for the animals beyond brushing them some and staking them out on good grass.

When I let myself think about it I found I was hungry as a winter wolf. I figured Ernie was, too, so I offered him some of Buford's jerky, but he just shook his head and moved off a piece. I reckon he was still mad.

About that time Pandora came back, supported by her crutch and moving smooth and easy over the uneven ground. She wore her bright smile and carried two rabbits by a thong tied to their legs. The hand that gripped the crutch also held her bandanna, which looked to contain a quantity of fresh-dug roots. I returned her smile, surprised by the gladness I felt at sight of her.

"I see you've been down to the market, Pandora," I said, "how'd you come by them rabbits?"

"I set some snares last night after you and Ernie were asleep. If someone will get a fire going, we'll have them for dinner."

Using Buford's pocket whetstone, I put a good edge on my jackknife, skinned out the rabbits, and quartered them. The campfire had died out, but I built it up again, laid on some dry chokecherry wood, and soon had a good bed of coals ready. Using forked willow sticks, we cooked the rabbits over the embers and wolfed them down. By the time we finished there was nothing much left but the bones. I don't believe there was enough meat left to interest a fly.

The roots Pandora had brought back turned out to be what some folks call prairie turnips. She washed them in the creek, wrapped them in wet leaves, and cooked them in the coals. I'd never ate them before, but I decided they was plumb tasty. I don't know if I'd have thought so if I hadn't been half starved, but anyway I did. Hunger makes a fine garnish.

After dinner we broke camp and prepared to part company. I showed Ernie where I'd buried the late Buford Suggs, and we hung his saddle in a nearby tree. I borrowed a rein from his bridle to replace the one Buck had busted, and we both saddled up.

Pandora's horse had lit out for parts unknown, and she sure couldn't do much walking on her sprained ankle, so I knew she'd have to go with either Ernie or me. I knew what I wanted her to do, but the choice was hers. I tried not to let my feelings show.

"Well, Pandora," says I, "I reckon you can go any-where you've a mind to, now that you ain't a desperate fugitive no more. What's your pleasure?"

She put her hands on her hips and gave her long black hair a saucy toss. "As I recall, you and me are pardners," she said, "and we still have a racehorse to find." Her dark eyes fixed on mine, and her smile seemed bright as the sun. "As for what my *pleasure* is, Merlin Fanshaw, a gentleman wouldn't ask, and a lady wouldn't tell."

My smile might not have been as bright as hers, but I reckon it was just as wide.

Ernie Fillmore had little to say as we parted company and set out on our separate ways. Just in case we ran into that Stillwater constable again, I asked Ernie to give me a note saying all charges against Pandora and me had been dropped, and he wrote one out for us. Ernie said his plan was to spend the night at the trapper's cabin he'd spoke of earlier and try to make Shenanigan by sundown the following day. I figured he'd likely send a man back for Buford's body later in the week.

As for Pandora and me, we turned our faces back toward Stillwater in the hope of somehow picking up Fontayne's trail. Pandora rode Little Buck, while I walked ahead and led him. By the time I'd tramped a mile or two across that short grass plain I was sore-footed as a sheepdog in cactus. Pride of appearance soon took a back seat to comfort, and I would have traded my fancy-stitched riding boots for Buford's high-top work shoes in a heartbeat.

For a time we rode double on Little Buck. Pandora sat the saddle skirts behind me, her hands at my waist or clasped close about me. For all our misfortune, she seemed happy as a child again as we traveled over the plain toward the Yellowstone, and the town of Stillwater. Her voice was cheerful and relaxed, and she spoke of simple things—the beauty of land and sky, memories of her mother, a favorite doll she once owned.

I mostly just listened, thankful Pandora had found herself again. A following breeze traveled with us, keeping the sharp, clean smell of sagebrush in our nostrils as Buck's hooves crushed the silver-gray leaves. The breeze also brought the sweet, musky scent that was Pandora Pretty Hawk, and the combination was like some mysterious perfume. Now and again she would hug me close about the body and press her face against my back, and I found myself wishing our ride would never end.

It had to end, of course. Little Buck was willing, as always, and double tough, but he'd been ill-used by the storm and I knew I must take care lest I wear him out. So, from time to time, I would step down again and walk, sore-footed and leg weary, but feeling better in my mind.

The shadows of late afternoon stretched long upon the land, and the light turned pink as a maiden's blush.

There are no clouds like the clouds of late June in Montana, towering billows of brightness and shadow, rolling and building high above the plain. As the sun dropped toward the edge of the world the clouds caught fire, ablaze in brief glory against a great spread of sky that made a man and his troubles seem small.

The trip back to Stillwater seemed longer than the ride from there with Buford and Ernie had been, I suppose because we made a late start and had to travel slower. Pandora and me stopped for the night alongside a spring-fed creek at the head of a grassy draw where a small grove of cottonwoods offered firewood and shelter. Riding down toward the grove I had spied the mottled gray-brown of sage hens in the grass as we came upon the place. Ernie had kept Buford's scattergun, but I still had some of the shot-shells I'd bought for my six-shooter. In a matter of minutes Pandora and me had the makings of our evening meal.

Afterward, we sat close together, watching the embers of our fire glow dull red and fade to gray like an old man falling asleep in his chair. From time to time a cool breeze swept through, rattling the big heart-shaped leaves of the cottonwoods and stirring the fire to life again. The day had been a warm one, and the night wind brought the smell of earth and growing things. Somehow, all that gave me hope.

In the stillness we could hear Little Buck grazing on the tall, rich grass of the coulee, shuffling easy on his picket rope. As the first stars came out and took their places in the summer sky, Pandora and me heard the distant clamor of a coyote choir. Pandora shivered at the wild sound and snuggled closer to me, and for the first time in my life I found myself feeling grateful to them yodeling song-dogs.

We didn't talk much, nor did we feel the need. It was enough and more just setting close and sharing the sounds and smells of the evening. Pandora turned and looked into my face, a question in her dark eyes I neither knew how to read nor answer. Soft as rose petals, her fingertips touched my face and gently traced my lips. Then to my surprise, she kissed me, tender at first, then harder and more ardent. I felt myself catch fire.

I'd kept the lid on my lustful feelings for Pandora up until that night, but I can't deny I had them. If the truth be known I reckon I'd had them as far back as our school days. She turned in my arms, and I felt her body press hard and bold against mine as she kissed me again and yet again, more urgent and wholehearted each time. I tried to think, to understand the why of her sudden ardor, but I couldn't—my mind had took the night off and left my body in charge. I felt her arms draw me down atop her into the high grass, heard the passion in her breathing, and I flung whatever resistance I had left to the winds.

Now I ain't the kind of man to go telling tales of conquest, believe it or not. If things had kept a-going the way they was headed I'd pull down the curtain on my account right here and say no more. But the fact is things didn't keep a-going the way they was bound. They stopped, sudden and short. I felt Pandora stiffen within my embrace and pull away. I reckon her brakes were better than mine; I'd been slower getting started but was finding it a good deal harder to stop, and at first I did not. Pandora's hands pushed hard against my shoulders, shoving me away; her eyes in the dim light were wide and frightened. She seemed to panic, and her small fists struck against my chest and face as she squirmed frantically to break free.

Then she was out of my arms, rolling away and stopping, her knees drawn up and her back turned toward me. The only sound was the fast rise and fall of our breathing. Pandora's actions confused and confounded me, to be sure, but I have to admit I wasn't all that concerned about her right then. There was a stampede in my blood and I was trying to turn the leaders and get the herd to milling. In brief, I was trying to catch hold of my feelings and get settled and quiet in my mind again.

Then from someplace deep inside her came a small, sad, moaning sound—a sort of hopeless whimper that hurt me just to hear it. Her voice was choked and *angry* when she spoke.

"May God—forgive—Buford Suggs," she said, "for I don't think I can." She turned toward me then, and even in the gloom I could see the glistening tears on her face. "He's dead at last, and gone—but he left the hurt behind."

She came back into my arms, gently now, and I held her the way a man might hold a lost and hurting child. From somewhere far away, the coyote choir joined in her crying.

In time, Pandora slept. I laid her gentle on my saddle blanket and covered her with a slicker, then rolled over onto my back and stared up into them star-filled heavens. Somehow in my entire life I never found a better way to ponder the riddles of life than looking up into the great, glorious mystery of the night sky.

Original George Starkweather started me reading a play called *Julius Caesar* during that summer I rode with his gang. The play was written by a English feller name of Bill Shakespeare, and old Bill was supposed to be about the best play writer there ever was. I liked what I read, though I didn't understand all of it, and it seemed like a lot of what Bill wrote was sad as a trail song. Anyway, I never finished reading the play, but I recall one part that surely had the ring of truth to it.

Some fellers had ganged up on old Julius in the Roman Senate and had killed him dead as a bearskin rug. Later on, Caesar's pardner, Mark Antony, gave a speech at the funeral in which he said:

"The evil that men do lives after them,
The good is oft interred with their bones."

Well, I had buried Buford Suggs, and I don't know how much good got planted with his bones. But it surely did seem that the evil he'd done to Pandora was still alive and well.

I laid there in the grass and thought about good and

216

evil, life and death, love and lust, and all them over-size topics until my head commenced to hurt from the very bigness of it all. Then I just watched the sky and thought about nothing in particular.

Now and then a shooting star would streak across the heavens like God striking a sulfur match. I must have counted at least ten of them as I lay there, and I reckon there was plenty more that came later. I never saw them later ones, though, for by then I had fell asleep.

FIFTEEN
Backtracking

A little past noon the next day Pandora and me rode Little Buck down off the low hills south of the Yellowstone and drew rein once again at the river's edge. The day was hot, as befits late June, and if there was a breath of air moving anywhere I sure didn't feel it.

Across the river the cottonwood trees stood tall and stolid, their leaves motionless as painted leaves in a picture. Beyond on the sagebrush flat, the town of Still-water dozed amongst the heat waves and waited for the cool of evening. All the usual sounds—the rumble of freight wagons, the busy racket of hammer and saw, the ring of the smithy's anvil—were missing on that early afternoon. Even the dogs had fell silent. In the flat light of mid-day the whole town had a raw, temporary look about it, but to Pandora and me right then it was the most welcome sight this side of Paradise.

For most of the morning, I had walked and led Little Buck while Pandora rode. Her ankle was much improved but still swollen nearly twice its normal size. Before we broke camp that morning she had made herself a poultice of bear-root and moss and had tightly bound her ankle with cloth strips.

We had not spoke of the previous evening and its events, nor would we. With the coming of sunrise, Pandora had took on a bright and cheerful air, acting as if nothing out of the ordinary had happened the night before. I was more than glad to do likewise or try to, anyway.

I've never been one to let a bad thing stand if there was something I could do about it. In the case of Pandora's trouble, there wasn't a blessed thing I could do except be her friend, and I was that. I would cheerfully have killed old Buford for what he'd done to her, but the old devil had proved contrary to the bitter end. He'd gone and got *himself* killed, which pretty much interfered with my rubbing him out for vengeance sake.

The Yellowstone was still running high, so with Pandora in the saddle I led Little Buck upstream, figuring to cross over on the ferry as before. When we reached the crossing the boat was tied up on the far side and the ferryman was nowhere to be seen. I figured he'd gone off somewheres for a snooze and a cold beer, and that he had closed up shop for who knew how long.

Pandora and me were left with a simple choice—shade up somewheres and let the skeeters feed on us

218

till the ferryman came back, or swim that cold, fast-flowing river on our own.

Looking across at the sleeping town, I said, "Well, Pandora, I don't know about you, but I ain't inclined to set here and wait. I've been promisin' myself a set-down dinner at a hash-house for the last thirty mile or so, and I've about run out of patience. Which, when it comes to food, I never did have all that much of, anyway. Patience, I mean."

I led Little Buck through the willows and down to the water's edge, his hooves clacking upon the river rock. Pandora slid off his back and into my arms, favoring her sprained ankle as she did so. I loosened the saddle's cinches to give the little horse breathing room, pulled off my gunbelt and boots and hung them on the saddle's fork. Pandora likewise took off her high-top moccasins, and I pushed them well down inside my boots, hoping they would stay dry.

"Take hold of his tail," I told Pandora, "and don't let go 'til we're across and on dry ground."

Limping a bit, Pandora took a firm, two-handed grip on Little Buck's tail as I led him to the water's edge. Legs braced, the horse bent his neck, sniffed the water, and blowed his nose. Then with my right hand gripping his mane and my left guiding him with the nigh rein, I urged him onward. Buck took one step, then two, and walked out into the rushing stream.

For twenty feet or so Little Buck walked the river's bed with the swirling, surging cascade up to his belly. Then he dropped off into a deep hole, plunged beneath the surface, and came up swimming. Suddenly, I was wet to my shoulders. The coldness of the river took my breath away. Glancing back, I saw Pandora stretched out behind, holding Buck's tail with a death grip, only her head above water. Carried downstream by the current, the little gelding swam steady and strong toward the bank, slowly drawing closer. Then we were across, water streaming from man, woman, and horse as Pandora turned loose of her tail hold and Buck lunged up the rocky bank and into the shaded grass beneath the trees.

We found young Clifton Miller asleep in the shade at his open-air livery stable. He lay stretched out inside his tent by the corral, his shoulders propped against the bedroll I'd left behind and his hat pulled low over his eyes. I coughed. I spoke his name, quiet at first, then louder.

"Clifton," I said, "Hey there, Clifton."

He didn't move a muscle. I kicked the turned-up sole of his boot. "CLIFTON!" I said, "Wake UP!" His breathing was deep and regular. If anything, it grew deeper. Still dripping wet from our crossing, I took off my sopping bandanna and wrung the river water out of it onto Clifton's belly. "Look OUT, Clifton!" I said, "get out from under that horse!"

He came awake, sudden and all at once. "Say, now," he said, scrambling to his feet and away from the falling water, "what the Hell—?"

My smile was pleasant as I could make it, considering I was soaking wet, dog tired, and hungry enough to eat my saddle. "Afternoon, Clifton," says I, "Remember us?"

His face lost its color, and his eyes went wide and staring. He remembered us all right. "Mister Fanshaw!" he said, "but I thought you—"

He was staring, calf-eyed again, at Pandora. Clifton had a habit of looking at her while talking to me, and it had commenced to irritate me some.

"—was going to jail over at Shenanigan," said I, finishing his thought, "well, we didn't. I told you I'd be back."

There were horses in the corral, but our packhorse was not among them. "I've come to pick up what we left behind," I said, "beginnin' with some dry clothes from that bedroll you've been leanin' on. Miss Pretty Hawk and me aim to get us some dinner over in town, buy a few things, and come back here.

"At that time you can help me pack the glass-eyed gelding we left in your care, and maybe we'll even buy a saddlehorse from you if the price is right."

Somehow, Clifton managed to look surprised, confused, and guilty all at the same time. "But—I—that is, I didn't think you were comin' back! I—I *sold* that white horse yesterday!"

I'm not sure why, but somehow I wasn't surprised. I think I half expected some such action on his part. "Now see, Clifton, that's where you're wrong," I said, taking my gunbelt and boots from the forks of my saddle, "you didn't sell that horse because you don't *own* it, and you can't sell what you don't own. Now we'll be over in town for an hour or two, after which time we will return. I'll expect my packhorse to be here, ready for the trail."

I buckled the gunbelt about my waist, checked the loads in my revolver, closed the loading gate with a snap, and holstered the weapon. "If that horse ain't here for some reason," I said, "I'm gonna be *awful* disappointed."

Clifton made no reply; he was already saddling a horse. I unrolled my bed and shared the dry clothes I had with Pandora. By the time we'd changed, Clifton was long gone.

When I led Little Buck across the railroad tracks and turned him up Stillwater's main street, I had already sweated through my last semi-clean shirt. It must have been anyway a hundred in the shade that day, and like the feller says there wasn't any shade.

The Great Northern Saloon had its doors open, front and back, in hopes of catching a cooling breeze, but the breeze was like the shade I mentioned—there wasn't any. Two rangy saddlehorses slept at the hitchrack with only their restless, fly-switching tails awake. From somewhere inside came the low murmur of voices and the sour smell of spilled beer. It was a relief to find the town wasn't dead after all, but merely hunkered down in the heat of day like a bull in the willows.

Two saloons and a sleeping dog past the Great Northern, we came upon a restaurant called the

Rosebud. That Bill Shakespeare feller I mentioned once wrote that a rose by any other name would smell as sweet, and I sure knew what he meant. It wouldn't have made any never-mind to me if the place had been called the Carrion Cafe or the Buzzard's lunch—it was an eatery, and I was a quarter past hungry and five minutes to grouchy as Hell.

I loose-tied Little Buck out front, helped Pandora get down, and we stepped up onto the gallery and went in. It was dark inside after the brightness of the street, and at first I couldn't make out a blessed thing. Then my eyes commenced to adjust.

I seen I was in a spacious room that held maybe eight tables, all topped with white tablecloths. There was a plump, rosy-cheeked family of four eating roast beef and mashed taters at one table, and it took all the self-control I had not to jump their claim and wolf down their vittles, I was that hungry. Just the smell of that grub nearly locoed me.

At the far end of the room, a heavy-set gent with bushy white eyebrows and muttonchop whiskers had finished his meal and sat reading a newspaper. There was something familiar about him, somehow. I knew I'd seen the man somewhere before, but at first I couldn't rightly say where.

Then he looked up, laid the paper down, and said, "Merlin? Merlin Fanshaw? Is that you?" He stood then and came toward us, a broad smile on his face and his blue eyes a-twinkle. "It is, by Jove! Delighted to see you again! Strord'nary!"

It was then the cogwheels of my memory slipped into place, and I recognized Colonel Charlie Bannerman. It seemed a hundred years since the races at Shenanigan and even longer since Pandora and me had seen a truly friendly face. The Colonel wore the same odd helmet he'd worn back then, and he took it off and held it before him as he beamed at Pandora.

"This here is Colonel Charles Bannerman, Pandora," I said, "Colonel, I'd like you to meet my friend Pandora Pretty Hawk."

She offered her hand, and the colonel took it and bowed over it as if it was some rare and precious treasure. "Charmed," he said, "Delighted to meet you, miss Pretty Hawk."

"See here," he said, herding us toward his table, "you two simply must join me. The food here is plain but nourishing, and I'd very much like you to be my guests."

I grinned. The colonel sure was a likeable cuss, and a hard man to say no to. "You don't know what you're askin,' Colonel," I told him, "it's been three days since we had a square meal. I can't speak for Pandora, but *my* plan is to fork it in until I founder."

The Colonel laughed. "In that case," he said, "there isn't a moment to lose."

Colonel Charlie set us down across from him, pulling out Pandora's chair for her like a real gent. He bellered for a waiter, and not one but two of them worthies

224

popped out of the kitchen like they was escaping from a fire.

"Bring these young people an abundance of whatever you have prepared," Charlie ordered, "and be quick about it."

The waiters nodded their heads, ran back to where they'd come from, and returned directly with steaming plates of stew, roast beef, mashed taters, fresh-baked biscuits, butter and jam. By the time I'd run through three or four such plates full, drunk nearly a pot of coffee, and consumed the better part of a pie and a half, I wasn't plumb full yet but I had begun to take the edge off. Pandora was more ladylike, which is as it should be, and she made do with two helpings of stew, three biscuits, and a single wedge of pie, though it was a big one.

Through it all, the colonel just set there and marveled, as though he had a seat at the opera and was watching true artists at work. Which in a way I suppose he was. I don't mean to boast, but when it comes to the finer points of gluttony there ain't many who can hold a candle to me. I truly believe consuming great quantities of food is one of my true callings.

The curious thing is I never seemed to gain any weight, no matter how much I ate. At the time I'm speaking of I weighed between one twenty-five and one thirty soaking wet and was inclined to be snake-hipped and withy. Pandora teased me about it some, said it was because I was still a growing boy. Maybe so, but for all I ate I never seemed to do much growing. Of course, I'd like to think all that nourishment went to my brain, but I never seen much evidence of that neither and I'm not making the claim.

Anyway, I pushed away from the table and slumped back in my chair in a stupor. I had a bulge in my middle like a bullsnake who'd swallered a rabbit. The waiters were standing by with their mouths open, and I halfway expected to see them break into applause. Then the Colonel snapped his fingers and them boys came out of their trance and cleared away the crockery.

"Strord'nary!," the Colonel said, "Bloody marvelous! You're a born trencherman, Fanshaw—I could fairly see the sparks fly! Devilishly fine form!"

"Much obliged, colonel," I said, a mite embarrassed. I tried to change the subject. "I sure didn't expect to run into you here in Stillwater."

"Just a brief stop on my way back to Judith Gap," he said, "I recently returned from Billings. Did a bit of racing there this past week."

"Running Colonial Boy?"

"Yes. Did rather well, actually. I do have a bone to pick with you, though."

"Why, what's that, Colonel?"

"If you recall, I offered to buy your horse Quicksilver after our race in Shenanigan. You declined, understandably. I then said that should you change your mind in future I hoped you'd permit me to make an offer. You said, I believe, that you would."

"Yes, sir, I did. But—"

Colonel Charlie frowned. His bushy eyebrows came together like a collision of caterpillars. "Well," he said, "dash it all! You can imagine my surprise to find you sold that splendid animal to someone *else*. There the beast was, at the Billings races, running like winged Pegasus and winning money for that jackleg gambler Turk Fontayne!"

I didn't jump the table, but I sure came out of my chair. "'Scuse me, Colonel—did you say you saw my horse Quicksilver at Billings? Racing for *Turk Fontayne?*"

"I did indeed. Blighter must have won nearly a thousand dollars during the two days I was there."

My first impulse was to light out at a high lope for Billings and lift Fontayne's greasy scalp, but Pandora gently took hold of my shirtsleeve and I calmed down some. I looked Colonel Charlie in the eye and told him the cold and unvarnished truth. "I never sold that horse, Colonel—Fontayne and his trail trash *stole* Quicksilver from our camp the night after the Shenanigan races. I've been tryin' to pick up their trail ever since."

I don't quite know how to explain what happened next, or why. Maybe it was like I said before Colonel Charlie's had been the first friendly face we'd seen in quite a spell—or maybe there was just something about the man that made me trust him. Anyway, I opened my mouth and the words poured out like water through a sluice box. I looked into the Colonel's honest blue eyes and told him just about everything that had happened to me, from the day Old Walt had left me Quicksilver to that morning Orville had perished of pride and the slows in Shenanigan. I told him of the peace officers and jails I'd seen since I took the trail, I spoke of Pandora and of how we'd come to be pardners, and I gave account of the hailstorm we'd survived and our tough trip back to Stillwater.

Finally, when I'd told it all, my talk slowed to a trickle and stopped. Thinking back on it, I don't believe I was looking for either sympathy or advice. I guess I just needed was to tell somebody and to hear myself do it. The Colonel said nothing; he just set back in his chair and took on a thoughtful look. The chubby pink family had paid their bill and gone, the waiters had cleared the tables and swept up the debris, and we three had the Rosebud Cafe all to ourselves. The only sounds I heard were the hollow ticking of the clock on the wall behind me and the lazy buzzing of a wandering fly.

The colonel leaned forward and fixed his gaze upon me. His honest blue eyes took on a troubled look, and his voice was soft when he spoke. "Sorry, old chap," he said, "should have known you'd not sell the thoroughbred. My apologies, young Fanshaw.

"May I assume you intend to continue your quest," he went on, "and that you plan to pursue the blighters until you recover Quicksilver?"

"Way I see it, Colonel, it's a thing I have to do."

"Yes, of course. Still—rather a risky undertaking, what?"

228

He fell silent again. Carefully, he brushed a crumb from his vest. "See here, Fanshaw—Miss Pretty Hawk—what I'm about to tell you must be held in strictest confidence. Livestock losses to thieves in eastern Montana have in recent months gone beyond the serious to the extreme. Because they have, certain plans are now being implemented which I believe will remedy the problem.

"What I'm saying is you might wish to let those plans unfold a bit before risking your lives further in a personal quest."

"I appreciate your concern, Colonel," I said, "but gettin' Quicksilver back is mine to do. I wasn't brought up to let others carry my load."

"I understand. I wish you Godspeed, young Fanshaw. If I can be of any assistance, please call on me. My ranch is just south of the Snowies, on Careless Creek.

"In view of your decision, there is one more thing which may interest you. I can't imagine why, but for some reason the anniversary of America's independence from Mother England seems a major cause for local celebration. Further, it appears that one such celebration is to include a full day's horse-racing at Lewistown.

"The interesting part is this just before leaving Billings, I overheard Fontayne challenge the sporting crowd to *meet* him there on July Fourth."

Behind me, the ticking of the clock seemed to speed up, and so did my heart.

The bill of fare for the Rosebud Cafe was printed on a single sheet of paper. Colonel Charlie took one from our table, turned it over, and with quick, sure strokes of a pencil from his vest pocket drawed us a rough map of the region.

"It's a good three days' ride to Lewistown," he said, "and much of the country is dry and open. If I were you, I should go north and west until I struck Sweet Grass Creek below the Cayuse Hills, then proceed north to the Musselshell and on to Lewistown."

The Colonel paid the bill, gave me the map, and we walked outside together. Once again, he took Pandora's hand. His blue eyes twinkled and his smile was warm as August.

"Pleasure to meet you, Miss Pretty Hawk. Delighted, by Jove. Strord'nary!"

I thanked him for the vittles and for his friendship. His grip was firm as he shook my hand. "Not a bit of it. Pleasure is mine," he said, "Good luck to you both." Then he smiled, turned on his heel, and marched up the street like the soldier he once had been.

I'm not plumb sure, but as he walked away I think I heard him say, "Good hunting, young Fanshaw."

The first thing Pandora and me seen when we got back to Clifton Miller's outdoor livery was our glass-eyed packhorse, standing in the shade of the big cottonwood trees and eating oats from a feed bag. Clifton had not only fetched the gelding back from wherever it had been, he'd combed and brushed the animal and had tended to its shoes.

I'd bought a Winchester rifle and a good used saddle and bridle for Pandora at a second hand store on our way back through town. We'd also picked up some groceries and possibles at the Stillwater Mercantile and Pandora had upgraded her wardrobe by a shirt, two pair of britches, and some lady fixin's that were none of my business.

The day hadn't growed any cooler, and by the time we got back to Clifton's I'd sweated through my shirt again and had little salty tributaries a-crawling out from under my hatband and rolling down my face. Clifton stood just outside his wall tent, looking bright-eyed and eager to please. As usual, he stared at Pandora while he talked to me.

"I got your horse back, mister Fanshaw," he said.

"Why, yes, Clifton, I see that you did. That'd be the big white thing standin' over yonder, wouldn't it?"

I picked up our pad and packsaddle from the jumbled pile of tack inside the tent. "Now, if you'd be so kind as to help me pack the animal I believe I can promise not to become unduly hostile. That is, if you can take your eyes off Miss Pretty Hawk for a minute."

It took a few seconds for my speech to soak in, but it finally did. "Huh?" he observed, "Oh—sure. You bet."

Once I'd got Clifton's attention, it didn't take long for us to pack the glass-eyed gelding and throw a diamond hitch on the outfit. He did keep his eyes off Pandora—for the first few minutes, anyway—so I decided to cut him some slack. It was too hot to box his ears anyway.

All there was left to do was buy a horse for Pandora, settle up with Clifton, and ride out. I'd had a grand plenty of the boy for awhile so I squatted on my spurs in the shade and told Pandora, "I'll let you dicker for the saddlehorse—you're the one who'll be ridin' it. Besides, I figure you can get a better price, seein' as you're the object of young Romeo's worship."

As usual, just seeing Pandora's bright smile lifted my spirits and brightened the day, "It's a deal, O jealous one," she said.

Ten giggles, eight smiles, and a bunch of eyelash flutters later, Pandora Pretty Hawk had bought a handsome six-year-old Palouse gelding for half Clifton's asking price and had even got him to saddle it for her. I reckon if she had gave him two more smiles and a slow wink he'd have cancelled our stable bill altogether, but I wasn't mean-hearted enough to allow that so paid him in full.

As we took the trail north into the rolling hills above Stillwater, Clifton Miller stood and watched us till he growed small and lonesome in the distance.

SIXTEEN
The Nature of Evil

Pandora and me took Colonel Charlie's advice, moving away from Stillwater into the big open country below the Cayuse Hills. We made late camp that night maybe twelve miles from town and was up and riding the next morning before sunup.

We struck Sweet Grass Creek that day and followed it west, rolling out our soogans on its banks come evening. I laid awake for a time while the fire burned low, just pondering the night sky and thinking them big thoughts I mentioned before. I had quit trying to count the stars the way I used to, but near as I could tell they hadn't growed any fewer.

The next day found us heading north and making good time. To the west lay the Crazy Woman mountains, their brief span rising craggy and tall in the sunshine, proud and set apart from their distant neighbors. Behind us the grassy hills and high plains fell off through sandrock coulees, scrub cedar, and jackpine to the valley floor and the Yellowstone. Ahead lay the windswept open country that led to the Musselshell River and beyond, all the way to Lewistown.

Pandora was as fine a pardner for the trail as a man could ask for, always ready to do her share and more, but she seemed thoughtful since Buford's death and a little distant. I suppose she was considering what she might do with her life now that she was truly free to go anywhere and do anything.

By the end of the second day her ankle was pretty well healed. When I remarked on the power of her bear root salve she gave me some to use on Little Buck to heal his hurts from the hailstorm. I believe it helped him, too, and I was relieved to find he'd suffered no harm to his eye but only to the lid where the hailstone had struck it.

Pandora seemed pleased with her new horse. Truth to tell, the gelding did appear to be a strong and reliable mount. I had long since come to expect the worst when buying or trading horses, and I reckon it was my Pa who had helped make me that way. Pa had been a fair to middling horse trader and I'd seen enough tricks of the trade when I was growing up to make me feel uneasy about any new horse until I'd rode him at least a month.

It was just past noon when we came onto a sheep ranch. Pandora and me had seen big bands of woolies off in the distance twice that morning, but they was too far away for us to see or talk with the herders.

That country is mostly rolling hills and prairie all the way to the far mountains, and settlers thereabouts was scarce as hens' teeth. That being so you can imagine my surprise when we topped a low hill and looked down on a spring-fed pond and a scatter of buildings that bespoke a tidy, well-kept ranch.

Across the yard from the main house stood a sod-roofed horse barn that opened onto a sizeable corral, but the gate stood open and there was no horses inside. It was different at the main house. A work team stood hitched to a wagon out front and a saddlehorse was tied to the tailgate. A gusty wind had come up and was blowing directly into us as we came over the rise. As Pandora and me started down the hill it was the horses that seen us first. They looked our way and the saddlehorse shrilled a loud whinny which Little Buck, sociable as always, felt bound to answer.

A couple of sheepdogs lay in the shade of the house and when they heard the horses greet one another they commenced barking like they was afraid they'd lose their jobs if they didn't. I reckon they was embarrassed they'd been caught napping and had allowed the horses to see us first.

The dogs was still a-barking as we rode down to the house and drawed rein. Right then the front door flew open and a tall, rawboned feller stepped out. In his hands was the biggest-bore shotgun I'd ever seen, and it was pointed straight at Pandora and me.

"Get your damn hands up and do it fast," he said, "this house has seen trouble aplenty for one day."

The man's voice was bitter and hard-edged as a file on metal. He held the shotgun as though he hoped we'd make a warlike move, but that was the last thing I intended. I took a wrap around the horn with the reins and lifted my hands like a sun-worshipper. Pandora did the same.

"We ain't in the habit of troublin' folks," I told the

man, "we're just passin' through."

"Them other sons o' bitches was just passin' through, too, before they gunned down Bob Mac-Donald and stole six of his horses."

"Mister," I said, "I'm plumb sorry for whatever misfortune has come upon this place, but we ain't the ones who brought it. I'd appreciate it if you'd put the gun down."

"Damn if I will! This range is crawlin' with horse-thieves and killers, and I've got no way of knowin' you ain't two more of the breed!"

"You said Bob MacDonald. This his place?"

"Was, till them three hardcases showed up and blowed out his lamp. Shot him down in front of his wife and rode off laughin' while she tried to hold his head out of the dirt."

I was scared. I could hear the outrage in the man's voice, and I knew there was no way I could reason with him. Pa used to say "Life is a gamble, and I came to play." Well, that's kind of how I felt right then. I lowered my hands and stepped off Little Buck with my back to the scattergun.

"I ain't a killer nor a thief, Mister," I told him, "but if you figure I am I reckon you're just gonna have to shoot me in the back."

Usually Pandora's voice was soft and gentle, but not that time. "And if you do," she told the man, "you won't have time to get off a second shot."

I glanced at Pandora. She'd lowered her hands and her right one held my old Colt's Dragoon, its hammer thumbed back and its muzzle centered on the man with the shotgun. Somehow, the feller managed to look crazy mad, confused, and fearful all at the same time. His eyes darted from Pandora to me and back again. I reached out and carefully pushed the shotgun's barrels aside.

"You don't want to shoot anybody, Mister," I said, "why don't you put that goose gun down and tell me what happened here?"

He dropped his eyes and lowered the weapon. "Sorry," he mumbled, "reckon I ain't myself right now." He looked like he was about to cry. I grinned, hoping to lighten the moment some. "I ain't always *my* self neither," I told him, "but today I am. Name's Merlin Fanshaw, and I'm from down Dry Creek way. The lady yonder with the big Colt's revolver is Miss Pandora Pretty Hawk."

Pandora put the pistol back in the waistband of her britches and favored the man with her bright smile. He looked bashful, uncertain. His big hands fumbled with the shotgun as though he didn't quite know what to do with it. Finally, he propped the weapon against the house and nodded at Pandora.

"I'm Kip Nelson," he said, "I work for Bob Mac-Donald. This is his place. It was about eleven-thirty this mornin' when I came in from tendin' his camps. Found Bob layin' in his own blood over yonder by the corral. Missus MacDonald was a-holdin' him and cryin' like her heart was broke. She seen the whole thing."

237

His voice broke then, and he fell silent. Only his eyes spoke, and the naked pain and grief I saw in them caused me to look away. Between the wind gusts, I could hear sobbing from someplace back inside the house.

"Where's the man's body?" I asked. Nelson nodded toward the open doorway. "Kitchen table. I covered him with a blanket."

Inside, the kitchen was long, narrow, and low of ceiling. A big cookstove crouched against one wall, and shelves and cupboards lined the other. The room was clean and tidy, except for the dark blood that spattered the floor and dripped from the blanket-covered form atop the table. At the room's far end a sheet of muslin closed off the doorway. Pandora slipped through the curtain and disappeared from view. I knew she'd gone to offer such comfort as she could to Bob's widow, and I was glad.

Nelson's hands had commenced to shake, and he set down on a bench beside the table, staring at the dusty boots that stuck out from under the blanket. I opened a cupboard door beside the table and hit paydirt first thing. There on the top shelf was a nearly full quart bottle of bourbon. I lifted it down, pulled the cork, and handed the whiskey to Nelson.

"Don't know if you're a drinkin' man," I said, "but if you are, have one on Bob. This here's a time for clear minds and steady nerves." Nelson took the bottle, his eyes wide and questioning.

"If you're wonderin' how I knew where to find it," I

said, "I just got lucky. My pa used to keep his jug on the top kitchen shelf. Figured maybe old Bob did, too."

Nelson took a long drink. When he came up for air I motioned to him to have another. Then I raised the bottle in salute to the dead man, and drank to him. "Now, then," I said, "tell me again."

"Like I said, I wasn't here when it happened. Bob sent me out yesterday to tend his sheep camps, and that's what I done. Took a saddlehorse along behind the wagon so I could ride the rough country should I need to. Bob told me to come back about noon today and have dinner with him and the missus—he wanted to hear how the sheep were doin'.

"When I came in sight of the house I seen the missus down in the dirt a-holdin' Bob. She was wailin' like a lost soul, nearly out of her mind. It was some time before she'd let me bring her back up to the house. I don't know how long Bob had been dead but he was white as chalk. It looked like he'd pretty well bled out where he lay.

"She told me Bob had gone out about ten o'clock to see to his horses. He'd just bought six head from a feller up north. They was good horses, and Bob was proud of 'em.

"The missus said next thing she heard was Bob talkin' loud and angry to somebody. She went to the door and seen three strangers settin' their horses down by the corral and Bob lookin' up at 'em. She said one man had long hair and wore a black frock coat over a

239

checkered vest. Said the man was mounted on a yeller claybank and that it looked like Bob was arguin' with him.

"One of the riders—a big feller, she said—rode over and opened the corral gate. He left it open, rode inside, and commenced drivin' out Bob's horses.

"That's when the third man stepped down. Missus MacDonald said he was a smaller man and that he wore two guns. Bob wasn't armed. He turned and started for the house. That's when the two-gun man shot him in the back. Bob went down, but he was tryin' to get up when the feller kicked him over on his back and shot him a second time. Missus MacDonald said she screamed and ran out of the house toward where Bob lay dyin'. The two-gun man laughed when he seen her comin' but he didn't stay to face her. He swung back into the saddle and the three of 'em rode off with Bob's horses."

Nelson reached a shaky hand for the bottle and took another drink. When he spoke again his voice sounded sad and old. "For a long while I couldn't get the missus to leave his side. Finally I persuaded her to go to the house and lay down—said I'd stay with Bob. I had just got him inside and was settin' here wonderin' what to do when I heard you ride up."

"Well," I said, "I reckon the first thing we need to do is get old Bob out into the wagon and clean up this kitchen. How far is the nearest law?"

"Merino's the nearest town, up on the Musselshell, but there's no peace officer there. Ain't much of anything there except a post office and a store or two. I guess the nearest lawman would be over at Fort Benton."

"Then that's where you'd best take him. Stay with Bob's wife till she's up to the trip, then take her along, too."

We wrapped Bob's corpse in an old canvas tarp, carried it out to the wagon, and loaded it in the back. Then we filled a couple of buckets at the well and scrubbed the table and floor clean. Nelson helped himself to the bourbon twice while we worked, and I could see his nerves had got about as steady as they needed to be. I took the bottle and closed the bar.

"You're gonna need to be sober to make that drive to Benton," I told him, "and Missus MacDonald is gonna need somebody she can depend on."

Sad-eyed as a bloodhound, Nelson watched as I put the whiskey back on the shelf. I knew he might get into it again after Pandora and me rode on, but I hoped I'd reminded him he still had a man's work to do.

We'd finished our chores just in time. Beyond the curtain I heard women's voices and the sound of footsteps coming. Then Pandora lifted the curtain aside, and I got my first look at the widow.

She was short and stout, with ruddy cheeks and pale blue eyes, and her hair was a sort of strawberry roan. She wore a dark woolen shawl about her shoulders, and the sleeves and bodice of her simple dress were dirty and bloodstained. Pandora was at the woman's elbow guiding her, and she led her to a rocking chair

241

near the stove and helped her to set down. The woman glanced at me, then looked quickly away. Her gaze seemed to jerk around the room as though she was watching a butterfly on the move, and she kept fussing with the bloody bodice of her dress.

"Oh, my," she said, "I must look a fright. I really do apologize—I wasn't expecting company"

I took my hat off and held it before me. Pandora said, "Ruth—this gentleman is my friend, Merlin Fanshaw. Merlin, this is Ruth MacDonald."

"Howdy, ma'am," I said, "I'm real sorry about your husband—"

"Oh," she said, "Bob isn't here right now. He'll be powerful sorry he missed you. Bob and me don't get much company here, you know."

Outside, the wind had picked up. A sudden gust rattled the window, wailing as if it too was grieving for Bob, then swept off up the valley with a lonesome, moaning sound. Ruth MacDonald stood up from her chair and picked up the coffee pot from the stove.

"Oh, dear," she said, "coffee's cold, I'm afraid. I can hot it up in a jiffy."

Pandora caught my eye and sadly shook her head. There were tears in her dark eyes and anger, too. I knew how she felt; I was clouding up pretty good myself and there was a lump in my throat the size of Colorado.

"Uh—no thank you, ma'am," I told her, "I wouldn't care for no coffee. Please don't trouble yourself."

"Oh, my, it's no trouble," she said, "It's so nice to

have visitors. Like I said, Bob and me don't get much company out here—" She paused. Her expression was a mixture of confusion, fear, and doubt. It was as though a cloud shadow passed over her face. At length she smiled a sad, rueful smile and said quietly, "But I guess I said that before, didn't I?"

She snugged her shawl close about her shoulders and closed her eyes. The only sound was the moaning of the wind outside and the slow creak of her rocking chair. Then she opened her eyes, turned to Pandora, and asked in a small, lost voice, "My Bob's dead, ain't he?"

Pandora didn't answer; I don't reckon she could. She looked at Ruth, her eyes brimming, and nodded.

"Yes," Ruth said, "yes, I remember now. Please excuse me, but I got to go lay down again. It was mighty nice to meet you, Merlin Fanshaw."

Pandora helped the woman to her feet and guided her back through the muslin curtain. I put my hat on and turned to Kip Nelson. "See to it she makes it to Benton," I said, "and see that Bob gets a proper burial and all. You just got done tendin' his camps—his herders will be all right for a week or so."

"I'll do it," he said, "You and the lady goin' on?"

"Yes, we are. I believe the men who killed Bob and stole his horses are the same three I'm lookin' for. They stole a horse from me, too, and they killed my pardner."

Nelson nodded, his eyes downcast. Of a sudden, he lifted his head and looked directly into my face. His face was tight with rage, and his voice was harsh as a whiplash.

"When you find that laughin' two-gun bastard," he said, "gut-shoot the sonofabitch."

Outside, the wind rattled sand against the window pane and shrieked like a banshee.

I neither speak nor savvy any Indian tongue but I've been told the Indian people oft-times have ways of saying how they feel that beats us white folk six ways from the deuce. As Pandora and me watered our horses down at the pond, I recalled one such saying— I believe it was from the Cheyenne—that pretty much summed up my feelings for poor Ruth MacDonald: My heart is on the ground because of your trouble.

Pandora and me had left the house in silence, each of us lost in our own thoughts, and we said nothing as we made ready to take the trail again. What was there to say? Calamity had fell upon the MacDonalds sudden and without warning. Three strangers and two bullets had ended her husband's life and had brought such pain to Ruth that her mind could scarcely take it in. That first night at the Stillwater jail, Pandora and me had talked about how life ain't fair. We'd agreed it was curious the way people kept expecting that it would be, and yet there I was once again trying to find meaning in the meaningless and a pattern within the random.

Thinking about the MacDonalds and the nature of evil soon set me on a downhill slide to melancholy. I felt my anger growing, too—anger at Fontayne,

Gossert, and Williams, of course, but anger at God as well. Oh, I didn't figure the Almighty had personally sent them killers to the ranch, nor that He had took Bob's life neither, but the way I looked at it, He surely had *let* it happen. I spent the next few minutes taking God to task, and I suppose I'd have been doing so yet if I hadn't begun to feel foolish.

When I finally came up out of the slough of despond I seen that Pandora had mounted her horse and rode him over by the barn. There was a dark stain on the ground where Bob had bled his life away, and I watched Pandora ride a slow circle around it and step down. Bent low at the waist as she studied the ground, Pandora slowly worked her way around the corral and out again. I knew she was reading tracks, gathering sign from the dirt like a prospector washing nuggets from sand. She swung back into the saddle and turned the gelding into the gale, waiting for me. Leading the packhorse, I rode over and reined up beside her.

The wind whistled across the barnyard as before, pausing, then gusting in sudden blasts that tugged at a man's clothes and blowed grit into his eyes. I took hold of my hatbrim and squinted at Pandora.

"Three men, all right," she said, nearly shouting against the wind, "riding north, loose and careless. They're not expecting anybody to come after them."

"In that case," I said, "I'd have to say they're mistaken."

Pandora nodded, her mouth a tight, hard line. She said nothing, but pointed north to the rolling grassland that seemed to stretch on forever. I gave spur to Little Buck, and Pandora and me turned our faces into the wind.

I looked back just once. There, near the corral, the dogs were lapping at the blood-soaked earth.

SEVENTEEN
Across the Musselshell

The sky was a dirty, sullen gray as Pandora and me pointed our horses north, and somehow my feelings were the same. Even at the best of times there is the hint of an old and lonesome sadness about that high plains country, as if the land itself was grieving some long-remembered loss. I felt myself growing more gloomy with every mile.

The wind had eased a bit but it hadn't quit. It swept in sudden gusts across the low, rolling hills like an ill-tempered bully, forcing the sagebrush and buffalo grass to bow down before it. Black as my mood, Little Buck's black mane whipped in the breeze before me like a tattered flag. I hunched my shoulders and turned my face into the squall.

Up ahead, Pandora rode her spotted horse through the sage at a fast walk, her eyes fixed upon the ground. I knew she was tracking the killers, reading signs in the dirt as though they was words on a page. Not for the first time, I envied her skill.

We hadn't spoke since leaving the ranch, nor did we

need to. As far as Pandora knew she was tracking Bob MacDonald's killers. She hadn't heard Nelson describe the three men so I wasn't sure if she knew the men who'd gunned MacDonald were the same three we'd been hunting. There was no doubt in my mind. Nelson couldn't have described Fontayne, Gossert, and Williams any better if he'd been an artist and had drawed their pictures.

Twice in the first hour I reined up and scanned the country with the field glasses, but in all that big open land nothing moved except the wind. Now and then we'd come to a deep coulee or dry wash and Pandora would step down off her horse, kneel, and study the ground at close range. I'd set my saddle and wait, knowing she would read the tracks and the sign, then lead us on in the right direction. Every time, she did.

I was puzzled by my gloomy outlook. Mostly, I tend to be cheerful even in the worst of circumstances, but something was troubling my mind. I told myself I should be glad. I hadn't expected to catch up to Fontayne and his boys until we hit Lewistown, but we'd got lucky and had cut their trail by pure chance. Even though they didn't seem to have Quicksilver with them at present I knew Fontayne planned to race him at Lewistown over the Fourth of July. He'd have to pick up the thoroughbred sometime before then, maybe dropping off the stolen MacDonald horses at the same time. That meant Fontayne and the boys likely had a hideout somewhere nearby. I figured that's where I'd find my horse.

247

Ahead, in a washout between two low hills, Pandora stopped again. She leaned out, looking down, and I could feel her concentration as she scanned the loose earth at the bottom of the draw. For a long moment she sat, still as a cat by a mouse hole, her eyes downcast and her small feet set firm and solid in the stirrups. Only her shining black hair moved, flowing and rippling in the wind. After a time she straightened in her saddle, looked back at me, and smiled. Then, touching the Palouse with her heels, she turned him downhill and rode on.

Always before, Pandora's bright smile had lifted my spirits and brought me joy, but on that particular occasion it brought a feeling of sadness. I felt a great melancholy deep inside, and something else, something very like *fear.*

Well, I told myself, it was only natural I should be afraid, at least a little. We were going up against men who had already killed at least twice, and I knew they wouldn't hesitate to gun us down too, should they find it in their interest.

Then, all at once, my scattered feelings came together clear and sharp, the way the country does when a fog lifts—*I was afraid for Pandora.*

Pandora had drawed cards in my game; she had backed my play, and now her life was at risk because of me. I recalled Orville's lifeless body laid out at the funeral parlor in Shenanigan, I remembered cold, dead Bob MacDonald, wrapped in a tarp in the back of his wagon, and I knew what I had to do.

I was determined not to let the Reaper take Pandora Pretty Hawk because of me, for I knew if that happened it would surely break my heart. Pandora had been the best of companions. She had lightened my load through her sharing and she had brought happiness to a cold and lonely trail. It had been her skills as a tracker that had helped bring us that far. I could no longer let her put her life at risk. I would send her away from danger. I would make her go somehow, no matter what I had to do.

We struck the Musselshell River in late afternoon and crossed at a point maybe six miles east of Merino. Fontayne and his men had stopped for a time in the shade of the cottonwoods, and the tracks of men and horses along the muddy riverbank were clear and sharp as a new brand.

"They took themselves a rest when they hit the river," Pandora said, "They were here maybe half an hour."

"That puts us thirty minutes closer. I guess you know them boys are the same ones we've been huntin'."

Pandora must have heard something in the tone of my voice. She looked up sharply and studied me the way she studied tracks.

"I *didn't* know, but I thought they might be. Ruth MacDonald told me something of how the men looked. Sounded a lot like your description of Fontayne and his crew."

She frowned, and her dark eyes were troubled.

"Something's on your mind, Merlin. What is it?"

I couldn't meet her gaze. I turned my back to her and fooled with the latigo on my saddle. For a time I said nothing. Then, when I figured I could trust my voice again, I said, "This is as far as you go, Pandora. You've been a good pardner, and I'm obliged for your help, but from here on I play a lone hand."

"But—you can't take on those killers by yourself—there's *three* of them!"

"I guess I'll do what I have to," I said stiffly, "that ain't for you to worry about. I'll need to travel light, so I'm ridin' Little Buck and leavin' the packhorse with you. The town of Merino is just west of here. I reckon you can find a place there to put up for awhile, or you might want to head on back to Dry Creek."

The hurt in her voice was like a knife in my vitals. "I—I don't understand, Merlin," she said, *"why?"*

I turned on her. "Because I said so, dammit! I've got a dirty job to do and I don't want no damn female in my way. The *last* thing I need is having to take care of *you* when I go up against Fontayne and his boys."

She held her head high, pride in every line of her, but her lip quivered and she looked as though I'd slapped her. "I—I didn't know I was a burden," she said, "I thought I'd been doing my share."

Now it was Pandora who turned away. For a time she stood looking out across the river. When at last she spoke again her voice sounded small and lost. "I don't know why you're saying these things, Merlin. I can't believe you really mean them."

"What part of 'no' don't you understand?" I said, "I let you ride with me awhile and now it's time to split the blankets, that's all."

She turned around and looked into my face, seeking truths it was my intention to hide. Her black eyes were wide and staring, and I saw she was trying hard to hold back her tears.

"I thought we shared more than just two people riding the same trail," she said, "I thought there was something *special* between us—"

My belly felt like I'd swallered a cold boulder. I wanted Pandora with me so much it hurt, but I couldn't weaken now. I had to make her leave for her own sake. I knew she wouldn't go if she knew the truth, so I lied. I played my trump card and said the one thing I knew would make her leave. "Yeah, I thought so, too—until that night after we left Ernie the last time."

Pandora seemed to buckle. She swayed, turned, and looked up at the sky as if she hoped to find understanding and comfort there. Her hand shook as she took my Colt's Dragoon from her waistband and gave it to me.

"I won't need this," she said, "I have the other rifle."

She tightened the cinch on her saddle, picked up the packhorse's lead rope, and swung up on her Palouse gelding.

"Good luck and Godspeed, Merlin," she said. Then she was gone, riding off up the river toward the little sheepman's town of Merino.

I felt so miserable right then I nearly gave up trying to be noble altogether. I had lied to the person I cared most in the world about. I had hurt her on purpose. I had drove her away from me when I wanted and needed her to stay, and I'd done it all for the purpose of keeping her safe. Now you might think all that nobility would make me feel like one Hell of a feller, but it didn't. It made me feel like something I'd scrape off a boot down at the stockyards.

All of which proves, I guess, that feelings are a poor guide when it comes to doing right. Oh, I know folks say "Let your conscience be your guide," but I don't generally seem to get much guidance from *my* conscience until it goes to telling me I shouldn't have done whatever I just *did*. It could be, I guess, that I just don't know how to listen.

Anyway, I knew I couldn't spend the rest of the day a-pondering morality there on the banks of the Musselshell. Thanks to Pandora's tracking skills and Fontayne's thirty minute rest, I was a good deal closer to the horse thieves than I had been. I figured it was time to close the gap. I checked the loads in my revolvers and rifle, pointed Little Buck north, and touched him with my spurs. Head high and clean-footed, he took up the chase at a high lope.

Now I'd like to tell you I followed them boys to their lair through my outstanding ability as a tracker and plainsman. I'd like to say I caught up to them fellers through my superior knowledge of outlaw nature, or by my skill and savvy in the fine art of man-hunting. I'd like to tell you them things, but they just ain't so.

What really happened was I kept Little Buck covering ground, riding the coulees and creek bottoms and staying off the hilltops so I wouldn't be seen. Now and then I'd crawl up a hill and peek over a ridge Indian-style, but all I got for my trouble was a dirty shirt and sore elbows. I seen grasshoppers, sagebrush, and one time a jackrabbit, but no sign of Fontayne and his men nor the MacDonald horses neither. I finally came to believe them fellers had a bigger lead on me than I'd thought, and I gave Buck his head and went back to riding the bottoms again.

The sun had gone down like a burning ship, and daylight had turned to dusk in the low places. Overhead, the sky still held some color, but darkness was coming on fast. I rode Little Buck through the twists and turns of a dry riverbed. A steep cutbank, topped by a scatter of cottonwood and box elder trees, marked one side of the wash, while thick brush clumb partway up a low hill on the other side. Underfoot, the soft, loose dirt, as fine as talcum, muffled the sound of our passage and rose up beneath Buck's hooves in a cloud.

Then, sudden as summer lightning, I came around a bend and nearly ran into the hideout. I drew rein, set Little Buck back on his haunches, and we slid to a stop in the powdery dust. Stepping down, I led him back sixty yards or so and tied him to a chokecherry bush. Then I shucked my spurs, pulled the rifle from its scabbard, and made a slow, careful stalk back to where I'd been.

Across a small, bowl-shaped clearing, inside a pole corral half-hidden by brush and trees, were six sweated horses I judged to be the MacDonald stock. Two saddlehorses grazed in their hobbles outside the corral, and my heart went from a lope to a gallop when I saw one of them was Turk Fontayne's yellow claybank. Both horses had took note of us, heads high and alert, but they'd made no sound. For a mercy, neither had Little Buck.

On the near side of the clearing a low, sod-roofed cabin showed a dim light behind its dirty window. A thin thread of smoke wisped upward from the cabin's stovepipe and disappeared into the darkening sky. From the corral came a sharp squeal and the quick scuffle of hooves as the horses worked out their pecking order, and somewhere nearby an owl asked who I was.

The layout sported one other feature. A ramshackle outhouse, tilted ten degrees off the level, leaned in the shadows at the edge of the wash. It was toward this slantwise hooter that I made my approach, walking slow and stopping every few steps to watch and listen. I saw no sign of Quicksilver among the other horses or in the clearing, and I had no idea which or how many of the outlaws might be inside the cabin.

My mouth was dry and my hands were wet, which struck me as being bass-ackward of the way things are supposed to be. My heart was pounding so loud I feared it could be heard inside the cabin. I had no real plan of attack. Surrounding a place ain't easy when you're by yourself, so that never really was an option. All I knew to do was make a sneak upon the cabin, kick the door in, and hope to get the drop on whoever was inside. If I managed to accomplish that, I would take it from there. If I didn't, I wouldn't require no further plan.

It surely wasn't my conscience, but someplace inside my mind a voice kept trying to tell me all the things that could go wrong with my plan. I tried not to pay the voice any heed. Instead I gave it a chance to come up with a better idea. When it didn't, I dried my hands on my britches, jacked a shell into the Winchester, took a deep breath, and made my move on the cabin.

The trouble with the unexpected is that it always comes when you don't expect it. Just as I was easing around the corner of the outhouse its door swung open, and I found myself dang near nose to nose with my old sparring pardner from Silver City, "Cock-eyed Clarence" Williams!

I don't know who was more surprised, him or me, but I believe it must have been pretty close to a tie. Clarence stumbled out of the outhouse, still adjusting his britches, his holstered revolver draped over one huge shoulder. When he seen me his eyes bugged out like a stomped frog. He took a clumsy step backward and pulled his weapon.

I was too close to bring the rifle to bear so I done the next best thing and swung it like a club. The barrel caught Clarence just above the ear with a sound like a thumped pumpkin, but it didn't put him down. I hit him again and seen his eyes go glassy as the six-shooter dropped from his hand.

I thought I had him whipped at that point, but Clarence was nothing if not game. His big hand darted down to his boot and came up with a Bowie knife that looked big as a plowshare. He swung it in an arc that surely would have made me a man of parts had it found its mark, but I dodged back just in time. That's when I swung up the rifle butt and knocked Clarence on *his*.

Standing astraddle of the big outlaw, I poked the Winchester's muzzle into his paunch and asked him politely to hold still. He done as I asked.

"If you move, or call out, your innards will be out yonder in the grass behind you," I said, "You get my drift, Clarence?"

His nod told me he did, but the look in his eyes could have burned a hole in boiler plate.

"Now who's in the cabin yonder—Fontayne? Gossert? Both of 'em?"

Clarence turned his head to one side and spat. There was blood on his mouth from where I'd hit him. "Nobody," he grunted, "Ain't nobody in the damn cabin. I'm here alone."

"Now why don't I believe you? Maybe it's because Fontayne's yeller claybank is eatin' grass yonder in the meadow. I'm gonna ask you just one more time—who's in the cabin?"

"I told you—*nobody!* Fontayne and Gossert went to Lewistown. Left me here to watch the horses."

I stepped back and turned so I could keep an eye on the cabin. "Get up," I told him, "we're gonna go see if you're tellin' the truth."

Clarence had told the truth; there was nobody inside the cabin, at least nobody human. I had in my time seen some lousy living quarters, but I do believe that boar's nest in the clearing topped them all. The rusty cookstove was black with grease and littered with moldy pots and pans. Here and there, nameless chunks of charred food stuck to the stove's surface. Woodsmoke had painted the ridge pole and rafters a sooty black, and even the cobwebs had took on a charcoal hue.

I said there was nobody human inside the hideout and there wasn't, but there was other critters, large and small. When first we came inside, a packrat big as a bobcat scuttled off to a dark corner and disappeared under a pile of trash. Bluebottle flies held a family reunion atop a rough-sawn table, and a big-bellied spider hung out his welcome mat in a corner nearby.

Cans, bottles, and old clothes littered the dirt floor together with dried mud, horse manure, and cigar butts. At the back of the room, what I took to be Clarence's bedroll was spread against the wall, its stained canvas tarp partly hiding tattered blankets that were glazed with dirt. I reckon them outlaws had somehow growed accustomed to living in such conditions, which just proves a man can get used to most anything.

I kept Clarence covered with the Winchester, and you can believe I kept a careful eye on his every move. Even though I had took away his weapons, the man outweighed me by a good seventy pounds. I well knew he could snap me like a twig if I gave him half a chance.

Inside, I allowed he could turn about and face me, although I still required him to keep his hands up. Clarence glanced briefly at the rifle, then looked into my face with a kind of bemused curiosity, as if I was some strange kind of bug he hadn't seen before. Then he grinned a gap-toothed grin and shook his head. "Damn, kid," says he, "You're about half crazy, you know that? If you keep comin' after us somebody's gonna snuff your candle."

"Could be," I said, "but I wasn't brought up to let my horse get stole and just set home suckin' my thumb."

I shifted my hold on the Winchester and gave Clarence my nastiest grin. "Speakin' of my horse," I said, "where is that fine thoroughbred?"

Clarence cleared his throat and spat on the floor. "Go to Hell. You ain't scarin' me with that rifle-gun, kid. Takes more sand than you've got to gun down a unarmed man."

"Oh, I ain't fixin' to shoot you, Clarence," I said,

258

"but I think maybe I bent the barrel a mite when I laid it upside your head. I might have to straighten it by tappin' you once or twice on the *other* side."

The big outlaw gave me a scornful sneer, but I saw doubt in his eyes. He studied me for a time, then shrugged. "Fontayne and Gossert took the horse to Lewistown. Figure on runnin' him in the races there."

I stood up. "You know, I believe you, Clarence. Not because I think you wouldn't lie, but because I already guessed that was Fontayne's plan.

"Tell you what. I haven't had much luck with lawmen so far, but I'm gonna take you over to Lewistown and locate a good one, if they have such a thing. Then I'm gonna tell him how you boys stole my horse and how you murdered that sheepman back yonder and stole *his* horses. Then, after they lock you birds in the crowbar hotel, I'm gonna take my fine thoroughbred back home to Progress County."

And that was my intent. But less than a minute later my best-laid plans once again went to Hell in a handbasket.

The gunshot was a sharp, loud boom, the kind a buffalo gun might make. In the split-second it reached my ears the cabin's only window exploded in a shower of shattered glass and a heavy-caliber slug slammed into the opposite wall.

I blew out the lamp, stumbled through the clutter to the cabin's broken window, and took me a careful look outside. The moon was up, and it hung swollen and bright just above the far hills. The clearing and the high ground beyond were bathed in ghostly light. There, at the edge of the clearing, sat a dozen riders on their horses, moonlight glinting on the barrels of their rifles. Other men had dismounted and stood facing the cabin from the brush. Two of them held burning torches.

A little apart from the others, a big man on a pale horse raised himself in his stirrups. When he spoke, his voice was clear as a hell-fire preacher's at a camp meeting.

"You, in the cabin!" he shouted, "Come out o' there *now,* or we'll *burn* you out!"

I can't say as I cared much for either choice.

EIGHTEEN
The Big Jump

The man on the pale horse had gave me a choice that was no choice at all. Now it was up to me to call his bet or fold. Clarence's voice was a tight, hoarse whisper. "There's a rifle in my bedroll, kid," he said, "Let me fetch it and we'll stand them boys off together."

I was hunkered down in the shadows, looking back at Clarence. Caught in the shaft of moonlight that slanted through the window, the big outlaw stuck out his jaw and hunched over like an old boar grizzly. His eyes had took on a wild and desperate look, and he kept clenching and opening his hands.

"I ain't real crazy about the odds," I told him, "I counted more than a dozen men out yonder, and those are only the ones I could see."

I turned the Winchester on Clarence and cocked it. The hammer went back with a solid click that sounded loud in the darkened room.

"Tell you what, Clarence," I said, "you get your hands up and go on out that door ahead of me. You can thank me later for savin' your life."

Clarence did what I told him to, but he wasn't happy about it. "If them boys is who I think they is, you ain't savin' my life, kid, you're just puttin' my *death* off a little while."

Hands high, he shuffled over to the door and stepped outside. I held the Winchester high above my head with both hands, swallered hard, and stepped out behind him.

Seconds later, the men rode into the clearing and gathered close around us. By their manner and their outfits I judged them to be cow-punchers, and by the light of their torches I seen what I took to be a D bar S brand on several horses. One of the riders took my weapons while another searched Clarence. The big man stepped down from his horse and grinned.

"Evenin', Clarence," said he, "who's the pup?"

Clarence shrugged again, and spat. "Nobody much. He ain't no pardner of mine."

"I sure as Hell ain't," I said, "Clarence and them desperados he rides with stole my horse. I tracked them here."

261

"Is that a fact? This stole horse you're talkin' about—is he one o' them yonder in the corral?"

"No, sir. My horse is a thoroughbred stud, a race-horse. Clarence told me them other birds—Fontayne and Gossert—took the animal to Lewistown just before I got here."

"That is quite a story," said the big feller, "and part of it may even be true. It does seem to be a fact Fontayne and Gossert ain't here, and that's a disappointment. But old Clarence is here and so are you, so our visit ain't a *total* loss."

I took a closer look at the man. He was big-bodied and raw-boned, but his bulk went to muscle, not fat. A high-crowned Stetson set square and level above faded blue eyes, and his sun-browned face wore a look that said he'd seen most of what life had to offer and he hadn't been all that impressed. The way the others stood back and let him do the talking made it clear he was the he-bull of the outfit. All at once I felt like a January breeze had blowed cold along my backbone.

"I'm not sure I get your drift, Mister," I said, "I'm Merlin Fanshaw, from Dry Creek, Montana, and I just captured old Clarence yonder. Now who might *you* be?"

"Why, bless you, son, I ride for the D H S and I work for Mr. Granville Stuart. Me and the boys here are part of a rustler roundup for the Montana Stock Growers, and you and Clarence have just joined our little herd." The man smiled then, but his smile held neither mirth nor warmth. "More to the point, kid," he said, "*I'm* the

262

man who's gonna *hang* your sorry ass."

He turned then and walked over to the cabin. I was still trying to talk to him when some of the men took hold of me and tied my hands behind my back. Nearby, I heard a scuffle and cussing. When I looked that direction, I seen the boys had trussed Clarence up, too.

Riders had gone inside the cabin and had lit the lamp again. I heard somebody say, "If livin' in filth was a crime them boys would be hung already" A young cowhand with buck teeth and freckles went inside and came out carrying a short-barreled carbine. So much for the rifle in Clarence's bedroll, I thought.

By the time the big man came back the boys had built a bonfire in the clearing and had set me and Clarence down next to it. The evening was warm, but I felt a bone-deep chill that had more to do with the big feller's words than the weather. He walked slowly over to where we sat by the fire and looked down at me.

"It don't seem to matter to you much, but I'm no rustler, mister," I said.

"What *matters* is puttin' a stop to the stealin' of honest ranchers' livestock, son. I *know* Clarence there is a thief. I ain't had the pleasure of your acquaintance, but you're holed up here with Clarence at this rustlers' roost so I figure you're a thief, too. Innocent men don't hobnob with horse-thieves and killers much.

"Besides which, somebody killed Bob MacDonald south of here this mornin' and stole six head of his horses. The horses in question turn out to be them yonder in the corral."

263

"I know that, mister! I follered the killers here from MacDonalds'. You've got to listen to me—I'm not a rustler!"

The big man took out his makings and commenced to roll himself a smoke. He raised his eyes, looked at me, and grinned his humorless smile. "That's another thing about rustlers, kid," he said, "they *lie*."

Clarence had been staring glumly into the bonfire's flames, He raised his eyes to the big man and said, "Oh, Hell. Let the kid go, Sam. He ain't no thief."

The man Clarence called Sam twisted the paper on his smoke, stuck it in his mouth, and lit it. He let smoke drift out through his nostrils and spun the match away into the fire. "See what I mean, kid? Rustlers *lie*."

"Let me get this straight," I said, "If a man admits he's a rustler you take that as proof he's guilty. If he says he ain't a rustler then he's a liar and likewise *that* proves he's guilty. What happens if you hang a feller and find out later he was innocent?"

The man called Sam grinned again. "Why, son, we don't hang innocent men. If we hang a man, that proves he was guilty. Now you'd best settle your affairs, make your peace, or whatever—you and old Clarence are both gonna swing come sunup."

Well, there it was. It was not only hard to argue against such logic, I found it to be impossible. No matter what argument I came up with the big feller had an answer for me, and always the same one at that. I'd been found in the company of a known rustler so I must be one, too. Case closed, as they say. The man seemed so dang positive I even commenced to wonder myself if I might be guilty. I didn't wonder long, understand. It came to me I was either innocent or crazy, so of course I chose to believe the former.

The freckle-faced puncher moseyed over to where Clarence and me set by the fire, I suppose to get himself a better look at us desperate outlaws. There was neither anger nor sympathy in his expression, but a kind of thoughtful curiosity. He stood there and studied us both like he wanted to memorize what we looked like. I thought if he watched us stretch hemp in the morning he'd remember what we looked like all right. I'd never seen a hanging myself, but I'd talked with men who had. From what they'd told me remembering wasn't the problem, *forgetting* was.

"Say, pardner," I says, "how about doin' me a favor?"

Freckles looked startled when first I spoke to him, but he got over it fast. "Anything but turnin' you loose," he said.

"There's a good buckskin horse tied to a chokecherry bush maybe sixty, seventy yards up that dry crick bed yonder. I'd surely appreciate it if you'd unsaddle him and take him to water."

The puncher grinned. "You bet," says he, "ain't a horse's fault his rider's a thief."

"Glad you feel that way. I was afraid you fine-haired sons o' bitches might hang him, too."

Freckles never cracked a smile, but just sauntered off to fetch Little Buck. Sarcasm is lost on some folks.

The moon painted the clearing with soft, cold light. Before me the flames flickered and guttered, casting a red glow onto the faces of the men who sat or stood nearby. The riders mostly bunched together in groups of two or three, either near the fire or back in the shadows. Some talked low of cows and horses and girls of the night, but most were quiet and there were several who kept to themselves, eyes downcast, and lost in their own thoughts.

There was swearing, and laughter now and then, some of it louder and longer than seemed needful, like men trying to keep unwanted thoughts at bay. From over near the cabin I could hear somebody playing "Aura Lee" on the mouth organ, and I found myself nearly moved to tears.

It wasn't because I was scared, neither. I can't explain it, but for some reason I wasn't as worried right then as I had cause to be. It hadn't yet crossed my mind that I really was going to die. Still, there was something about that song.

I closed my eyes, trying to run the string back, and then all at once I remembered. The sweet, sad melody brought memories of my family back at our Dry Creek place when I was just a kid. Pa used to play the fiddle after supper sometimes, and mother would sing along in her sweet, clear voice. I had nearly forgot what my mother looked like until that night, but there in that

266

moonlit clearing her face and form had come back clear and sharp on the lonesome quaver of a harmonica.

It has always been a wonder to me the way a song, or a smell, or the way the light strikes a meadow or mountaintop, can stir up memories from somewhere so far back inside a man he plumb forgot they were there. That's the way it was for me that night.

I glanced over at Clarence and was surprised to see he'd slumped back against a log and had fell fast asleep where he set. I recall being both surprised and impressed he could snooze at all, knowing what waited for us at sunup. Clarence was built of sterner stuff than me, I thought. I couldn't have dozed off for a thousand dollar bill.

Once again my body made a liar of my mind. The next thing I knew I woke from a deep sleep with a start. The fire had gone out, and I felt chilled and stiff. Overhead a few scattered stars still clung to their places, and in the east the sky was already growing light.

Around the clearing, men were moving about in the predawn darkness, talking low as they groomed and saddled their horses. Smoke drifted up from the cabin's stovepipe and lamplight glowed orange in the window. The man called Sam stepped out through the cabin door and spoke to a rider who nodded, turned his horse, and moved off toward the corral. Minutes later, the rider rode back at a trot, hazing the Mac-

Donald horses ahead of him on their way back home.

Clarence was awake, too. He leaned against his log as before, with only his eyes alive and moving. I figured his thoughts, like my own, were fixed on daybreak and the fate that waited for us beneath the spreading branches of a cottonwood tree.

While I'd slept, fear had seeped into my bones along with the chill night air. I fought panic the way a man fights pain, keeping a tight rein on my imagination and trying to fix my mind on pleasant things. I recalled wildflowers in mountain dells and the way a bull elk moves proud and graceful across a clearing. I thought about my horses—about Quicksilver, who ran like the very wind and gleamed in the sunlight like some rare, polished wood, and about Little Buck, tough, wiry, and willing as ever a horse could be.

I thought of Pandora and of the way her long, glossy hair caught light and rippled in the wind. I closed my eyes, breathing deep, and remembered her warmth and her sweet, musky scent them times I'd held her close. I recalled her tears, and I remembered her laughter, bright and cheerful as birdsong.

I wondered: was Clarence remembering, too? Was he thinking of elk on a high country morning, or of some special woman somewhere? There was no way of knowing. I reckon it was none of my business anyway.

It came to me then that I really was going to die, and the full force of that knowledge was almost more than I could bear. I fixed my eyes on the distant mountains far to the east and on the one brightest patch of sky behind them. I tried with all my strength of will to hold the coming sun back, to keep it from rising that morning, knowing all the time it would come up as it always had.

It seems like I mostly go to praying as a last resort, when I've got myself rimrocked and can't find my way out. The thought has oft occurred to me that if I took to praying sooner and more frequent I might not get into some of them messes in the first place. But each time, as soon as the trouble is past, I seem to forget. I don't mean to—I reckon it's like not fixing a leaky roof when the weather's fair and remembering it needs doing only when the rains come.

I tried to recall the store-bought prayers of my childhood, but all I could think of was "Now I lay me down to sleep." Somehow, that didn't seem to fit my present circumstances but I prayed it anyway—I surely was fixing to lay me down to the *big* sleep.

I took to bargaining. I asked the Almighty to save me from the rope and to spare my young life. I told him every reason I could think of why he ought to. I promised I would give up cussing and forsake gluttony. I vowed I would no longer harbor lust in my wicked heart. I pledged I would go to church at least once a month and put two bits—or better, if I had it—in the collection plate. I dang near wore myself to a frazzle giving God my sales pitch, and finally I just sort of ran down like a windup monkey and quit.

I can't explain it, but when I finally quit struggling

a peaceful feeling settled over me and spread inside my chest like warm molasses. My breathing slowed, my heart done likewise, and somehow I wasn't afraid any more. I went to praying again, but it was different than before. I gave thanks for the calm, easy feeling, and I asked the Almighty, *por favor,* to stay close and not let me show yellow when my time came.

Old Clarence wasn't doing as well, poor devil. His eyes was wide and staring, his teeth was bared in a frozen grin, and he was quivering like a wet dog. When he seen me looking his way he stopped shaking and tried to spit, but without much success.

"I wish them som'bitches would get on with it," he grunted, "I'd like to be in Hell before they quit servin' breakfast."

The sun exploded above the far mountains and flooded the plains with brightness. Sunlight lit up the trees on the far bank, and long shadows jumped across the clearing. Somewhere nearby a meadowlark yodeled its bright song, and I marveled. Never, I thought, had anything sounded so clear or so sweet.

Then from someplace nearby I heard Little Buck's piercing, high-pitched whinny. I sat up and looked across the clearing. There, wearing my saddle and bridle and led by the freckle-faced puncher, the buckskin stepped toward me through the wet grass. He whinnied again when he caught my scent, and he looked at me almost as if he knew something was wrong. Beside him, also saddled, was the horse I'd seen grazing with Fontayne's claybank. The man called Sam rode his pale horse out around this procession and drew rein in front of Clarence and me. He folded his hands atop his saddlehorn, raised himself in the stirrups, and said, "It's time, boys."

Our hands were still tied behind us, but a couple of the D H S riders helped us to our feet and into our saddles. It felt good—natural, somehow—to be a-setting my old Texas rig again and to be astride of Little Buck. I knew well my last ride would be a short one, but the familiar feel of the tough little gelding helped calm me somehow. It caused me to marvel—even at the moment of my dying I took my comfort where I could.

A weathered cottonwood stood apart from its smaller kin at the edge of the clearing, and it was to that gnarled old tree the riders led me and Clarence. From a sturdy branch overhead two hard-twist ropes dangled, nooses already built for the morning's grim business. The riders stopped our horses beneath the limb, and the man called Sam rode alongside us and tightened the ropes about our necks. Then he rode over a ways, turned his horse to face us and commenced to speak.

Since earlier that morning when the peaceful feeling had come upon me so strong it seemed my senses were keener than ever they had been. I could smell woodsmoke from the cabin, wild flowers in the grass, a patch of mint somewhere nearby. I felt the cool, rising breeze upon my skin. I saw the dark green of

271

cottonwood and box elder leaves, the tawny yellow of meadow grass, the rich browns of wood and earth, and the deep blue of the sky, colors bright and details clear and sharp.

I heard sounds in a way I never had before—sounds of shod hooves striking rock, the ring of a spur rowel, the music of birds, the rise and fall of my breathing, and the steady thud of my heartbeat. I could even hear the rustle of my clothes against my skin as I moved. It was as if everything I saw or felt or heard had growed sharper somehow, the way a candle will sometimes flare its brightest just before it goes out.

Then the strangest thing happened. I looked at Sam as he spoke to us, I watched the movement of his mouth but I could hear *nothing!*

It was as though the senses that had so lately gone razor-sharp now were shutting down. I felt a kind of crazy fury; I felt cheated—I wasn't supposed to die until my *body* did. Somehow the sudden loss of my hearing seemed more unfair even than being lynched for something I hadn't done.

Blind rage took charge of me; for a moment I could neither hear nor see. Then my vision cleared, and I saw surprise cross Sam's face. I sensed movement beside me, and I turned my head to see Clarence dig his heels sharply into his horse's sides—the animal jumped forward, the outlaw's head snapped as the noose drew tight, and his heavy body jerked and struggled at rope's end. Slowly twisting to and fro between heaven and earth, Clarence swung in the cool morning air.

I did not see his face, nor did I want to. Like other men before him, Cockeyed Clarence Williams had took a hand in his own dying and had gone out game as a man can.

Then, from the corner of my eye I saw someone raise a rawhide quirt above Little Buck's hindquarters and swing it sharply down. The buckskin bolted out from under me, I felt the sharp burn of the rope as the loop closed about my throat, and all the world turned to darkness.

NINETEEN
Independence Day

It don't seem possible a man could be in two places at the same time, but somehow I was. The pain of the noose as the rope took my full weight was both grievous and intense. I tried to breathe, but I could not. Panic took charge of my mind as my body struggled in midair. I thought my chest would surely explode. Pressure built behind my eyes like steam in a boiler, and a fearful roaring sound echoed inside my head. Then came the blackness that eased my torment. It was as though I'd drifted into some quiet eddy in a rushing river. I quit fighting and let the current take me where it would.

Then I was somehow outside and *beyond* myself, looking down at the scene from above. My body hung limp and silent at the end of the rope, twisting slightly in the morning breeze. Looking more like a bear than ever, the body of Cockeyed Clarence Williams dangled next to mine. The man called Sam sat his pale horse, his face hard as he pondered his handiwork. Most of the other men looked on as well, although several turned away. Over behind a low bush, the freckle-faced cowboy had turned a pale shade of green and was retching into the weeds.

Little Buck had not run far; one of the DHS men had caught his reins and held him up. The little horse stood nervous and all a-quiver, tossing his head and rolling his eyes. I wanted to put my hand on him, to calm him the way I'd done so many times before, but even as the thought came I knew I could not.

The two riders came from the south, busting a hole in the breeze as they swept toward the men and horses beneath the cottonwood. I recognized Pandora first, her loose black hair shiny in the early light as she whipped her spotted horse to an even faster pace. Beside her, astride a lathered bay hunter, was a man who could only be Colonel Charlie Bannerman, spurring the horse onward and shouting as he raced toward the tree.

The man called Sam swung his horse about to face them, reaching for his revolver as he did so. Then he seemed to recognize the colonel, raising his hand in greeting as the fast-approaching riders came on. As for me, I was still in that curious condition I'd enjoyed since just before the hanging; I could see Colonel

Charlie shouting, but I still could hear nothing.

Sam seemed to hear him, though. His head jerked back to the hanging bodies. He spurred his horse forward, the knife already in his hand, as he reached up and cut the rope above my head. Pandora pulled her sweated gelding to a sliding stop, throwing herself out of the saddle and running through the billowing dust toward my other, former self.

Being apart and detached somehow from the scene below, yet at the same time observing it, was pleasant. A feeling of peace and well-being unlike anything I'd ever known came over me. Then, like a cloud blotting out the sun, the feeling changed. I felt the force of that other world take hold and begin to pull me. Somehow I knew I was being drawn back to that still, crumpled figure in the dirt, the one Pandora now held in her arms, but I truly didn't want to return. I saw Pandora's tears; I wished I could tell her not to cry for me, that everything was well, everything was beautiful. Then the pull grew stronger, like the pull of a magnet to steel, and I knew I could resist no longer. Suddenly, I was back—there was no longer two of me, but only one.

Pain was waiting for me when I moved back into my body, and so was Pandora. She fell to hugging and kissing on me, crying and calling out my name like a girl who'd just found her lost puppy. Her attentions embarrassed me somewhat, coming as they did in front of all them men, though I have to admit I found them pleasant enough elsewise. Pandora was carrying on in front of the colonel and the DHS riders as if she didn't care *who* seen her.

I found I could hear again, but it didn't help much because I'd forgot how to talk at that point and had somehow lost the knack of opening my eyes. I heard the man called Sam say, "Excuse me, miss," and then somebody—I suppose it was him—took hold of my belt and went to lifting and lowering my midsection in an effort to bring me around. I must say I found it curious that the man who'd just tried to kill me was now trying to save my life, but I'd long since learned that life is oft-times crazy as a drunkard's dream.

I knew I was back among the living, anyway. Dead folk don't feel the kind of pain I was enduring, for if they did there wouldn't be much point to dying in the first place. My head throbbed with a stabbing hurt that all but robbed me of thought, and my throat burned as though I'd swallowed hot coals. My neck felt like it was two foot longer than it used to be, and the rope burn that California collar had gave me seemed to go clean to the bone.

I don't know how long them efforts to revive me continued, but the fact is they finally took. I opened my eyes and found myself looking directly into Pandora's. Her smile alone was worth coming back for.

Once she seen I was going to be all right, Pandora dried her eyes, blowed her pretty nose, and went to playing nurse. She fussed and bustled, soothed my troubled brow, gave me water from her canteen, and generally took charge.

"Nice try, Fanshaw," she said, "that playacting you did back at the river had me fooled—for a little while. I was almost to Merino before I figured out what you'd done, and why."

She had me at a disadvantage. My throat tended to close up and go into a spasm if I even thought about talking.

"I remembered Bannerman's ranch was near Judith Gap on Careless Creek, so I decided to pay the colonel a visit. When he heard you'd gone after Fontayne and his boys alone, it didn't take him long to get horseback and come with me." Pandora poured water on a bandanna, lifted my head off the ground, and went to washing my face. "I was hurt when you told me I was a burden," she said, "but I got downright *hostile* when I realized you'd gone *noble* on me."

Pandora's smile was sweet as clover honey as she let my head fall to earth again. Shooting pains stabbed through my skull and caused me to fear I might not survive her tender care.

"If you recall," she said, "I signed on to be your partner, not your poor, helpless maiden in distress." Still kneeling beside me, Pandora gave her hair a toss and favored me with her brightest smile. "But I guess you meant well. I forgive you, Merlin," she said, "and I accept your apology."

I'll say one thing for Pandora; she had style. It's a rare person who can accept an apology that ain't been made yet.

Directly, I came to feel some better. I still wasn't up to a frolic or a footrace, but at least I could set up and look around some. I could even talk a little. As for Pandora, she was all smiles and chatty as a magpie. My Pa told me once there's few things that make a woman feel better than forgiving a man who's done wrong and has seen the error of his ways. I figured Pa should know if anyone did; he'd sometimes gave my mother the chance to enjoy that feeling two or three times a week.

Colonel Charlie Bannerman stood off a piece, deep in conversation with the big feller called Sam. They spoke earnestly for a time, then ended their palaver with a nod and a handshake and walked over to where I sat.

"Delighted to see you again, Fanshaw," said the Colonel, "Close bloody *call,* that. Beastly business, hanging."

I couldn't argue with that. My voice was a sort of raspy whisper and it still hurt considerable when I tried to talk. I gave him a grin instead.

"Sorry, kid," said the man called Sam, "but when I find a bushy-tailed critter in a coyote den I tend to figure it's a coyote. Colonel Charlie tells me you're more a coyote *hunter,* like us. Anyway, I'm glad you're alive, kid."

"Likewise," I whispered.

Sam's leathery face broke into a riot of wrinkles. He flashed a quick smile, then his expression turned sober again. Beyond the clearing's edge, the riders sat their horses, waiting.

The big man nodded in their direction. "Well, Hell, kid," he said, "we got to be goin'. Good huntin', son."

"Same to you," I rasped, and shook his hand.

With the departure of the hanging party the clearing almost, if not quite, took on a peaceful feeling. The morning sunshine felt warm upon my face and a soft breeze set the cottonwood leaves to pattering. Birds sang in the tree tops, and a bumblebee droned his busy way among the blossoms of the clearing. Sam and his men had taken Clarence's gelding and Fontayne's claybank stud with them, and our own horses grazed quiet and easy on the meadow grasses. Only the shadowed form of Cockeyed Clarence Williams, hanging heavy and silent from the tree limb, marred the morning's peace. A cold chill ran up my spine when I recalled how close I'd come to sharing his fate.

By the time I'd got to my feet and walked around some I felt pretty near my old self. Colonel Charlie gave me brandy from a silver flask and Pandora fed me some jerky from the saddlebags. For the most part she kept her eyes fixed on my every move, and I have to admit I felt plumb flattered by her devotion. Then I realized there was another reason for her attention. Pandora kept her gaze upon me so as not to look at Clarence. I sure didn't blame her none. The lately departed Clarence had been a hard-looking customer in life, and death by hanging had done little to improve his appearance.

"As you may recall," said Colonel Charlie, "I told you back in Stillwater that certain plans had been set in motion to deal with the cattle rustlers and horse thieves of the region."

"Yes, sir," I said, "it occurs to me I just had me a close *call* with some of them plans."

"Quite. This past April, at a meeting in Miles City, the Montana Stock Growers Association was formed. At that meeting plans were set in motion to rid the range of rustlers and horse thieves. Several cattlemen urged all-out warfare against the blackguards, but their proposals were rejected. Such direct action, some of us argued, would warn the rustlers and allow them either to organize a strong defense or escape the area.

"Instead, we decided in executive session to establish a vigilante organization to deal silently and swiftly with the scoundrels in a series of raids. These raids are now underway, led by our members in different parts of the territory—the Fort Maginnis section, the Little Missouri section, and the Tongue River section, among others.

"Now I know you've been pursuing Fontayne, Gossert, and Williams for good and sufficient reason. Our Association has also been on their trail. The group you encountered this morning began its work by removing the late Clarence Williams from the playing board. Other men, including Turk Fontayne and Portugee Gossert, are also on our list."

Colonel Charlie had hunkered down in front of me. He seemed to study his big hands for a time, lost in thought. Then he looked up sharply, and his bright blue eyes flashed.

"Now see here, Fanshaw," he said, "None of my bloody business, I know, and of course you may jolly well do as you please, but it strikes me your continued pursuit of the blighters may no longer be necessary. In all likelihood, Fontayne and Gossert shall meet the same end as the late and unlamented Clarence Williams. I'm also confident one of our several committees will recover your horse.

"Dash it all—what I'm trying to say is I rather *care* about you young people. It seems to me you no longer need risk your lives in this dangerous quest."

The Colonel fell silent then. He looked out across the prairie toward the distant mountains, his face flushed and his eyes restless. He was embarrassed by his strong feelings, I reckon, and I knew speaking up hadn't been easy for him. I glanced beyond him at Pandora to find her looking back at me in that honest, open manner of hers. As clear as words, her forthright expression said the decision was mine, but either way she planned to be at my side.

I liked the Colonel, and I respected him. I knew he'd spoke his mind out of concern, and I had no doubt he truly believed what he said. Because I respected him, I gave serious thought to his words, but even as I did so I knew what my answer would be, what it *must* be.

"Colonel," says I, "I appreciate all you've done for

281

us, and I reckon you may well be right. Just the same, I'm goin' after those two because the job is mine to do, and, well, because I have to.

"You say one of your hemp committees will likely catch Fontayne and Gossert and get my horse back. I reckon that sure could happen. On the other hand, them boys could slip away, maybe cross the border into Canada or go to ground somewheres.

"If I'm not mistaken, today is the Fourth of July, the day you said Fontayne planned to run Quicksilver in the races at Lewistown. For the first time them hard-cases and my horse are within reach, and I can't let the chance pass me by. Lewistown ain't all that far from here—I figure I can be there sometime this after-noon."

"*We* can," corrected Pandora.

Colonel Charlie was silent only for a moment. "Yes," he said, "we jolly well *can*."

While Pandora led the horses to water, Colonel Charlie and me took the late Clarence Williams down from his elevated position and buried him in a shallow grave at the edge of the clearing. When Pandora came back, we stepped astraddle of our horses and lit out at a high lope for Lewistown.

My life has always been eventful, but as I recalled everything that had happened since sunup that day I couldn't help but marvel. I'd been hanged to a cotton-wood tree at first light alongside a horse thief I'd been hunting, and I had *died*—in a temporary sort of way—as a result. Then I'd been rescued by a pretty woman and an Englishman, and been manhandled back to life by the feller who'd strung me up in the first place. Now I was traveling with my friends on a fast ride to a horse race and a showdown. At the time I told myself a day don't *get* much more eventful than that.

I was wrong.

Lewistown is situated in such a way as to surprise a person who comes upon it from the southwest as we did. All you see at first are rolling plains and a view of the Judith Mountains off to the northeast; then all at once you drop into a pleasant valley and there's the town.

I heard the gunfire before we came in sight of its source. At first I figured it was only the sound of fireworks as folks commenced their Independence Day celebration, but I soon had cause to know I was wrong.

We rode down off the bench and onto the wide street that marked the business district just in time to see what resembled the second battle of Bull Run, or maybe Custer's Last Stand. Two hard-looking gents, each armed with a pair of Colt's revolvers and a Winchester rifle, stood their ground on the wide, dusty street, firing away at the townsfolk. My first thought was that they might be Fontayne and Gossert, but they wasn't. One of the gents—a dark-faced, long-haired jasper—seemed to be wounded; he crouched unsteadily on one knee as he fired.

Citizens were blazing away at the men from the

shelter of the nearby buildings, which obviously gave them something of an edge. Out in the street where the two hombres were making their stand there wasn't anything bigger than a horse apple to hide behind, and I judged from the volume of the gunfire that the townsfolk had them boys outnumbered about a hundred to two.

The sound of the shooting was almost a continual racket. Gunsmoke blossomed and drifted above the street, and bullets whipped and whined as they gouged up geysers of dirt about the two men and now and then struck one of the gents themselves.

Pandora, Charlie, and me reined up our horses when we first came in sight of the battleground; we stepped down and led the animals around behind Crowley's Saloon and out of range. Going inside through the back door, I saw the place was nearly full. Men crouched beneath the front windows, cautiously rising now and then to catch a quick glimpse of the action out on the street. The slick-haired barkeep showed little interest in the gun battle, but kept the glasses and steins of the drinkers filled, conducting business as usual. At the front door, two men took turns firing outside, each one shooting and dodging back behind the door frame while the other did the same.

It was a one-sided contest that couldn't last long, and it didn't. Through the doorway I saw the long-haired gent fall facedown and lay unmoving in the street. The other hombre stood over him, swaying on his feet, and fired once again before two slugs from a building across the way struck him and put him down next to his pardner. The fight, such as it had been, was over, and the townspeople began to gingerly come out from hiding, like chickens after a rainstorm.

Folks were talking a mile a minute as they drew near the dead men. People who hadn't even been there during the shooting were bragging about their marksmanship. Even the barkeep left his post to walk out and study the carnage.

The bodies of the two men lay sprawled near the tent of a traveling photographer who had come to make pictures of the townsfolk as they celebrated the Fourth. I don't reckon he had expected the celebration to become quite so festive, but it was plain he knew how to take advantage of a bonanza when it fell on him. Before a man could wind his watch them corpses were tied to boards, propped up like scarecrows before the camera, and the picture maker was taking orders for photographs.

Colonel Charlie seemed to know some of the fellers who'd shot the men. I watched him speak to two of them at some length before he came back to where Pandora and me stood waiting on the boardwalk.

"The dead men were notorious rustlers," Colonel Charlie said, "partners in crime known as 'Long Haired' Owens and 'Rattlesnake Jake' Fallon. They were high on the Stockgrowers' list of wanted men. Blighters only recently returned to Montana from Wyoming. Bad timing, what?"

"It wasn't the Stranglers who got them," I pointed

out, "How'd them boys come to their one-sided battle with Lewistown?"

"Seems they came here to attend the races," the Colonel said, "They invested a portion of their ill-gotten gains in whiskey and lost the rest betting on the horses.

"They evidently lost their sunny dispositions as well. They pistol-whipped a local citizen named Bob Jackson for no other apparent reason than that the man was dressed in an 'Uncle Sam' costume. After abusing and humiliating the unfortunate Mr. Jackson, they turned their attentions to the town's business district. They undertook to shoot up the town, killed one young man and wounded another. The townspeople returned fire, and the hapless desperados ended up as you see them now."

Across the way, folks were still gawking at the perforated badmen. The photographer was still taking orders for his picture of the dead men, and a hard-eyed sport in a boiled shirt and derby hat was selling handkerchiefs that had been dipped in the outlaws' blood.

Colonel Charlie seen a feller he knew—I think it may have been one of the Stranglers—and went over to talk to him, but I was set on getting down to the racetrack as soon as possible. I stepped back out behind Crowley's and swung back into the saddle. Then I touched Little Buck with my spurs and he stepped out smartly and broke into a run with Pandora riding close behind.

• • •

The racetrack lay along a broad, grassy flat not more than a mile or so from the business district. I wasted no time in getting there; now that the Stranglers had commenced their work I figured Fontayne and Gossert would be wary as coyotes. If they were still in the area they had no doubt heard the gunfire from Owens and Fallon's last stand, and that would have gave them another reason not to linger long in Lewis-town.

The races had long since ended but there were still men and horses around the stables and in the paddock area. I eased Little Buck back to a walk, riding slow and careful as Pandora and me made our way among the tethered horses and wagons. I was some edgy myself because I knew Fontayne and Gossert had planned to bring Quicksilver to the races that day and I had pushed hard to get there, but had arrived late. Once again it seemed I was a day late and a dollar short. I was half past discouraged and on the verge of feeling sorry for myself. I was tired. I hadn't had a square meal in two days. My neck was stiff and sore, and sweat crawled down from under my hat and stung the raw rope burn at my throat.

At the far edge of the flat, a line of green trees rambled along beneath the hills and marked the meandering passage of a small creek. Out on the Fort Maginnis road, freight wagons clattered north, trailing a rising dust cloud behind them. Somewhere nearby a raven scolded, his cry brassy and raucous in the still afternoon. I shifted in my saddle and looked back at Pandora. Her raised eyebrows and the shrug of her slim shoulders told me she'd seen no trace of our quarry either.

A rickety wooden grandstand stood on the west side of the race course, casting its shadow out onto the grass beyond it. As Pandora and me rode out of the brightness, it took my eyes a second or two to adjust to the gloom. I eased into the coolness of the shade and let my mind go easy.

Looking back on that day, I can see I should have been more watchful. I hadn't found the men I was seeking nor my horse neither, and I let down my guard, pure and simple. It was like those times hunting in the high country when I had told myself the elk weren't nowheres nearby. It never failed. No sooner did I ease up a minute than some fine big bull would bound out of the timber like a runaway train. I'd fall all over myself, fumble for my rifle, and lose the chance I'd spent days trying to get.

It was Little Buck that brought me out of my trance. I felt the buckskin break the rhythm of his stride and heard his deep-throated nicker. I came alert then; Buck's eyes were wide and staring, his ears pointed toward something I could neither see nor hear. Then it was my turn to stare.

Sixty yards away, a man in a dirty white hat and black frock coat rode into view from the other side of the grandstand. He was leading a handsome, blood-bay thoroughbred and a second, smaller man rode behind him. The riders saw us as we saw them; our eyes met across the space between us and time itself seemed to stop. I'd have known those two men and that horse in Hell with their hides off—*I was looking at Turk Fontayne, my horse Quicksilver, and Portugee Gossert!*

TWENTY
Misfortune Favors the Brave

Gossert was fast, and no mistake. The cold-eyed killer turned his horse broadside to Pandora and me, his revolver already out of the leather and coming up. Beyond him, Turk Fontayne had his hands full, reining his saddlehorse with his left hand and holding Quicksilver's lead rope with his right. His eyes were wide with surprise and his teeth were bared like a wolf's as he recognized me; he bent low in the saddle and spurred his mount hard toward the distant tree line.

White smoke blossomed at the end of Gossert's hand and flame flicked out like a snake's quick tongue. The bullet whirred past my head, so close I could feel the wind of its passing, and the sound of the gunshot was loud and sharp in my ears.

Orville's silver-mounted .44 was cocked and in my hand, which surprised me some, for I do not recall pulling it. I swung Little Buck's head hard to the right, firing at Gossert across my left arm as I did so, but my shot went high and wild. Gossert fired again, then bent low in the saddle and sunk spur as he streaked out after Fontayne in a race for the tree line.

It was seldom that Little Buck ever gave me cause to fault him, so it surprised me some when he let out a squeal and swallered his head. I figured the gunfire had spooked him, or that maybe he'd just got confused, but the little gelding fell to pitching like some wild-eyed bronco. I had to postpone my gun battle in order to deal with his tantrum.

Pandora swept past me, the Winchester in her hand as she kicked her pony into a lope. Little Buck was still a-quivering like a wet dog, but he had quit his rebellion. I turned the little horse after Pandora and reminded him with my spurs that I was the rider and he was the horse, whether that arrangement was to his liking or not.

Fontayne had already reached the creek. Still leading Quicksilver, he hit the crossing at full gallop. I watched as his horse carried him across and lunged up the steep bank beyond with Quicksilver scrambling behind. At his pardner's heels, Portugee Gossert twisted in his saddle, shooting back at Pandora. She neither turned aside nor slacked her pace, but swept on, returning the killer's fire as she rode.

Then Gossert was across and spurring his horse up the hill. Following him closely, Pandora's spotted pony plunged into the stream and splashed across after him. She was just urging the animal out of the water and up the hillside when Gossert reached the top, turned in his saddle, and fired back at her again. I saw

Pandora lean away from the shot, her shifting weight and the taut rein pulling the palouse off balance. Then, fighting for a foothold, the pony fell hard on his side, pinning Pandora beneath him.

Everything seemed to happen at once. Atop the hill, Portugee Gossert jerked his horse about and disappeared from view. Below, at the muddy creek bank, the pony thrashed, legs flailing, trying to get back on its feet. Trapped beneath the animal, her eyes wide and her face pale, Pandora struggled to free herself.

All this I took in at a glance as Little Buck carried me toward the creek. The last thing I wanted was to let Fontayne and Gossert get away again, but Pandora was in trouble and my options were down to one.

Little Buck was laboring. Even as I felt the familiar bunch and ripple of his muscles I could feel his gait growing unsteady. The buckskin slowed just this side of the stream, his breath coming in ragged gasps. He stumbled, nearly fell, caught himself, and stopped at the water's edge.

Even as I stepped down off him I knew the little horse was hurt, but it wasn't until I saw the bright red blood behind his shoulder and the pink froth at his nostrils and mouth that I knew Little Buck had been lung-shot.

Across the creek, the Palouse pony had found his feet, although Pandora had not. She lay in the shallow water at the edge of the stream, her face tight with pain and her hands grasping her right thigh. Beyond her, the Palouse started up the steep bank, stepped on his trailing bridle reins, and turned back. He stopped at the bottom of the slope and stood shaking, his eyes confused and fearful.

I was at Pandora's side in a moment, but my hero act was tarnished some when I asked her the dumbest question I could have, under the circumstances.

"Pandora!" says I, "are you hurt?" Which was something like pulling a drowning man out of a lake and asking was he wet.

Pandora's face had gone white as chalk. She squinched her eyes tight closed, and when she spoke her voice was strained. "My—leg, Merlin," she said, "I—I think—it's broken."

Behind me, I heard Little Buck's breath coming in long, strangled gasps. I glanced back just as the buckskin slowly eased onto his hindquarters and lay down. I knew what I had to do. I bent over Pandora and brushed a long, wet strand of hair from her eyes.

"Be with you in a second, darlin,' " I told her, "Little Buck needs me first."

The buckskin lifted his head as I walked toward him. The awful rattle of his breathing was almost more than I could bear. He struggled, trying to get to his feet again, but could not. I loosened the latigo and pulled off my saddle. My hand shook as I aimed my revolver at a spot midway between his great brown eyes, made my mind a blank, and squeezed the trigger.

Tears streaked my face when I got back to Pandora, but I didn't care if she seen them. I could tell she was hurting plenty, but she managed a tight smile in spite of the pain. Her dark eyes had a fevered look, and there was something like sympathy in her gaze. "You—gonna shoot—me, too?" she asked. I gave her a tight smile of my own. "I haven't decided," I said.

I lay no claim to any great knowledge of medicine, but the years with my Pa had taught me one or two things about treating broken bones. In his profession of breaking wild horses Pa had also broke various parts of his personal anatomy. As a result, he acquired a certain savvy in the field of basic human repair. Some of this know-how he passed on to me for my general education, but also because he figured he might sometime need my doctoring.

He was right. Twice in three years I had been called upon to splint and bind up broken bones that had attended his horsebreakings, and while I may not have been as skilled as I might have been Pa had never complained.

With my jackknife, I slit the leg of Pandora's britches and found the damage to be serious, but not as bad as I'd feared. The bone was broken, all right, just above the knee, but it seemed a clean break. I could feel the grating of the broken pieces, but they had not pierced her flesh. Pandora had dropped the Winchester when her horse fell. I used the weapon as a splint, binding it to her limb from ankle to hip with strips of cloth and my bridle reins.

Dark thoughts tried to ambush my mind. Once again, Fontayne and Gossert had slipped my loop and had taken to the tall and uncut with my thoroughbred. Little Buck, more friend than saddlehorse, lay dead of an outlaw's bullet, and my own. Pandora Pretty Hawk lay hurting and broken on a creek bank, bravely fighting the pain her loyalty to me had brought her.

Blame and failure made a heavy load, but I was equal to it. I hefted it high and took its weight full upon my shoulders. Doing so, I found it more than I could tote right then. I told myself I would deal with it later, put it aside, and gave my full attention to caring for Pandora.

Behind me, I heard the sound of horses coming fast. I turned around just in time to see Colonel Charlie Bannerman bring his bay hunter to a sliding stop, dismounting on the fly. In his dust came other riders—from the racetrack crowd, I supposed—and a fat townsman driving a two-seated buggy.

Colonel Charlie splashed across the creek like some great long-legged bird, coattails flying and eyes wide and worried. His face was beet-red and his mutton-chop whiskers all a-quiver as he came panting up to where I stood over Pandora.

"Bloody Hell!" he gasped, "Appears you've had the devil's own time of it, Fanshaw!"

"You could say that," I allowed, "but the good news is there ain't much left that can go wrong."

Colonel Charlie's face was hard as flint, and his usually warm blue eyes had turned to ice. When he spoke I could hear the anger behind his words. "Fontayne and Gossert?"

I nodded. "They were just ridin' out when Pandora and me ran into 'em. They had my Quicksilver horse, like I figured. Gossert went to shootin', and we had us a runnin' fight all the way here to the crick. Then Pandora's horse fell with her and I stopped to help. Last I seen, Fontayne and Gossert were burnin' up the Fort Maginnis road."

It was late in the day. Already, the sun had set and dusk had fell over the valley like a curtain. I felt played out and bone weary, but Colonel Charlie had a way of taking charge. He throwed out his chest and commenced giving orders like a man accustomed to command, which I reckon he was. Some of the boys rigged a stretcher out of poles and a horse blanket from the stables and we put Pandora on it. Then, gentle as we knew how, we carried her over to the buggy and laid her across its back seat.

I stowed my saddle and bridle inside the rig, tied Pandora's spotted pony on behind, and took a seat up front next to the driver. Then, as I held Pandora's hand in both my own, our little procession made its way slow and careful back toward the lights of Lewistown.

According to Colonel Charlie, there were two doctors in Lewistown: one mostly drunk and the other either off somewheres tending to the hurts of country folk or trying to catch himself a fish. I cast my vote for the sober one if he could be found, and everybody in our little procession pretty much agreed. All the way back to town the fellers from the racetrack rode alongside and ahead of us, clucking over Pandora, calling her a poor little thing and what not.

One of the boys offered her a snort of whiskey from a pint bottle he carried, but Pandora shook her head no. The feller appeared to have consumed considerable of the flask's contents himself. He kept offering Pandora the bottle and wouldn't let up until I put my hand on my gun butt and firmly declined on Pandora's behalf.

It was coming dark when the townsman stopped his buggy at a small frame house near the edge of town. A lamp burned low in one of the front windows. A picket fence set the yard off from the dusty street, and a shingle on the gatepost read "H. Sorenson, M.D."

As it turned out, we were in luck. Doc Sorenson had just come back from what he called "a combination breech delivery and fishing trip" somewhere down the valley. In a voice that held more than a trace of Swedish accent he told Colonel Charlie he'd brought a baby into the world that day and took a good mess of trout out of it. The doctor was a tall, slim man, with thinning blond hair going to silver. He had a friendly, open expression and frank blue eyes that seemed to look straight through a feller. I liked him on sight.

Colonel Charlie introduced us, and I found the doctor's handshake dry and firm. He asked us to bring Pandora around to his office at the back of the house. When we'd done so he turned the lamp up higher and took a careful look at her injured limb. I could see her knee had swole up nearly twice its normal size, and the flesh near the break had turned an ugly, angry red. Pandora looked helpless and plumb pitiful, and I knew she was hurting plenty. Doc Sorenson's manner was gentle and practiced. As I watched, Pandora seemed to relax some and give him her trust. I began to breathe a little easier.

"Horse fell on her, Doc," I said, "It was me put on the splint."

"One of the better uses of a firearm I've seen," he said, "you did a good job, cowboy"

The doctor poured water into a china basin and began to scrub his hands with lye soap and a brush. "You gentlemen can wait in the parlor if you want to," he said, "Please tell my daughter Lena I will need her help."

Lena Sorenson turned out to be a female version of her Pa. Tall, slender as a reed, and rosy-cheeked, she wore her fine blond hair in a tidy, complicated braid. She looked to be about seventeen or thereabouts, with a warm and open smile. Like her daddy's, her eyes were a bright corn-flower blue. Before she left us to go help tend Pandora, she showed Colonel Charlie and me to the parlor and poured us each a cup of fresh coffee. Most women are inclined to be too generous with the water when they make coffee, but Lena's brew was strong, hot, and fine. After the events of the day, her coffee surely hit the spot.

The furniture in Doc Sorenson's parlor was Turkish Victorian in style, which means you didn't so much set *on* it as *in* it. I eased myself down onto a red plush overstuffed chair, and it swallered me up like a quick-sand bog. I sunk into it, helpless as a turtle on its back, and I don't believe I could have got up if I'd tried. All of a sudden I felt weak as a newborn pup; even the coffee cup felt too heavy to hold. Colonel Charlie was saying something to me, but I couldn't quite catch hold of his words or their meaning.

There was a ringing in my ears like a swarm of locusts. I couldn't seem to keep my hands from shaking. I felt light-headed, queasy in the belly, and in some danger of passing out. One part of my mind told me to get hold of myself and straighten up, while a second part told the first part to go to Hell.

"The kid's got every right to let down," the second part seemed to say, "He ain't hardly ate anything or slept in two days. He was hung to a cottonwood tree this mornin,' and he even died for a spell. Then the poor devil rode all the way to Lewistown, took part in a runnin' gun battle, and lost his racehorse again. He had to put his buckskin gelding down, and he seen his pretty pardner bust her sweet leg—excuse me, *limb*—in a horse fall. Now if all that don't qualify a man to ease up some, what does? Cut the kid some slack."

The second part must have won the argument. I don't remember another thing about that evening till I woke up next morning.

When next I seen the light of day I had no idea where I was. My unwashed young body was stretched out on a feather bed beneath linen sheets and a hand-quilted

298

comforter. A goose down pillow, trimmed in lace, supported my shaggy head. Overhead, I could make out a ruffled canopy covering the whole shebang, and I wondered if maybe it was there because the ceiling leaked.

Looking around, I seen I was in a small, tidy room full of female fooforaw and fancies. There was roses on the wallpaper, lace on the curtains, and carpet on the floor. A wash stand with pitcher and basin stood next to a closed door, and a mirrored dressing table and dainty chair stood across the room beside a handsome, carved wardrobe.

To the right of the closed door I found the only familiar items in the room. My hat, shirt, vest, shaps and britches were neatly folded atop a Windsor chair, and my revolver and cartridge belt was looped over its back. My boots, with spurs attached, slouched upon the carpet. I had never saw a room so clean, nor had I slept under a roof at all since the jail at Stillwater. I felt hemmed in, nervous as a hog on ice, and out of place as a skunk at a camp meeting.

I was still trying to solve the riddle of my whereabouts when I heard footsteps outside the door and seen the knob turn. I had no idea who might be coming through that portal so I pulled the covers up to my eyes in the interest of modesty. I figured the sight of my raggedy underwear could put a civilized person in shock. Then the door swung open, and there stood Colonel Charlie, looking bright-eyed and chipper as a songbird. My first thought was that I wished I felt as good as he looked.

"Wakey-wakey, young Fanshaw," said he, "It's daylight in the canyon, as you chaps say"

"Mornin', Colonel," I said, "You mind tellin' me whose bed this is?"

"Belongs to Miss Lena, actually. You met her last evening."

"Oh, yeah. Doc Sorenson's daughter. But how—?"

"I was offering my analysis of the day's events as we sat together in the doctor's sitting room. You dropped off to sleep during my lecture—bored, no doubt."

I scrambled out of bed and pulled on my britches. "I took that young girl's bed? Lordamighty, Colonel— where did she sleep?"

"She didn't, actually. Spent the night nursing our Pandora. Girl's doing well, by the way. Pandora, I mean."

It didn't take me long to get dressed. I felt plumb embarrassed. "Glad to hear Pandora's all right, but I still druther you hadn't put me in here."

"Not my idea, Fanshaw. Lena offered her bed and Doc Sorenson concurred. Good people, the Sorensons. Strord'nary."

Well, I couldn't argue with that. I washed my face and slicked my hair back as best I could. A sideways glance into the looking glass as I was leaving the room didn't show much improvement: I still looked like a cross between a border ruffian and the Wild Man of Borneo. They'd have to fumigate that room.

As Colonel Charlie led me through the Sorenson house the edgy feeling growed stronger. Wending my way cat-footed and careful among the bric-a-brac made me feel like a range bull in a glass factory. I went wall-eyed and goosey, scared I'd bust something and feeling just a whisker this side of a stampede. I'd been living in the outdoors too long, I suppose.

Doc Sorenson was in his office, and so was his daughter. The girl wore a starched pinafore and an apron, and she looked none the worse for having gave up her bed to a stranger. I snatched my hat off and took a grip on it with both hands. My ears felt hot so I knew I was blushing.

"I—I'm much obliged to you folks," I stammered, "but I sure don't feel right about putting you out of your bed, Miss Lena."

She smiled. "I was up with Miss Pandora for much of the night, anyway," she said, "but I did get some sleep. There's an extra bed in the sick room."

"Well," I said, studying the floor, "well."

Doc Sorenson nodded toward a half open door across the room. "I think the young lady is awake now, if you want to go in and see her," he said.

"Uh—thanks, doc," I said, "I'd sure like to."

Pandora lay upon a white-painted iron bed, her glossy hair loose and spread across her pillow in a fan. On a table beside her was a bunch of yellow flowers in a blue vase, a water pitcher, and a glass. Pandora wore a soft flannel nightgown instead of the trail clothes I was used to seeing, and somehow she looked smaller and more frail than I remembered. Her whole face lit up when she seen me.

"Mornin', pardner," she said, "it's about time you got up. Give a lazy man a soft bed, and he'll stay in it all day."

"Look who's talkin'," I said, "you ain't out of your blankets yet." My grin told her how glad I was to see her. If I'd had me a tail right then I would surely have wagged it.

Her injured leg was tightly bound by bandage and plaster strips in a splint that went from her hip to beyond the sole of her foot. The limb was raised above the foot of the bed and held there by a rope through a pulley in the ceiling. I set down next to her and took hold of her hand.

"You must not be as desperate a character as me," I told her, "I see they only hung part of you."

Her quick smile faded and her eyes looked troubled. "I—I'm sorry, Merlin," she said, "if it hadn't been for my horse wreck you might have Quicksilver back by now."

"Yes," I said, "or I might be dead from Gossert's bullet, like my saddle horse. Little Buck was breathin' his last by the time you went down anyway. I don't reckon he could have took me another step."

Still holding her hand, I leaned over and kissed her. "Anyway," I said, "you need to heal up now and get some rest. I reckon I might make a serious rim at you once you're back on your feet."

Pandora closed her eyes and kissed me back. "I'll hold you *to* that, cowboy" she said.

TWENTY-ONE
A New Horse and a New Town

Behind me, Colonel Charlie stepped through the door and cleared his throat. His voice was gentle when he spoke. "Not to worry, young Fanshaw," he said, "Pandora is doing well, you know."

I smiled. The colonel had seen the look on my face and figured I was worrying about Pandora. I was, but my thoughts had also moved on to the pursuit of the horse thieves. "I know she will," I told him, "I was thinkin' about somethin' else."

Colonel Charlie's eyes narrowed. He looked away, out across the sunlit valley toward where Fort Maginnis and the town of Maiden lay. "Yes," he said, "about Fontayne and Gossert. You're still determined to go after them."

It was a statement, not a question, but I answered him anyway. "Yes, sir, just as soon as I can. I was about to go hunt me up a hash house and feed my wolf. I haven't ate for so long I ain't sure I remember how. You care to come along? I'm buyin'."

"Another time, perhaps. I have to attend a meeting this morning."

His handshake was hearty. "Take care, Merlin," he said, "my best advice to you is well-meant but physically impossible, I'm afraid."

"What's that, Colonel?"

303

Colonel Charlie's expression turned serious. His grip on my hand tightened. "Watch your *back,* young Fanshaw."

I made my way downtown to a cafe called the Blue Oyster, but I can't tell you whether the food was any good or not. Truth is, I cared more about quantity at the time than I did quality, and I ordered—and consumed—most of what was listed in the bill of fare. By the time I'd wolfed down an appetizer of a dozen sourdough cakes, six eggs, and a plateful of fried spuds I was ready for the main course.

The beefsteak that came next was a good two inches thick and hung off the platter a full inch all around. When I got through with that morsel there was nothing left on my plate but the glaze, and I finished breaking my fast with a double order of biscuits and gravy, a wedge of cherry pie, and half a pot of coffee. I could have took on more, but I didn't want folks to think I was a glutton.

Midway through my repast the waiter called the cook out from the kitchen and they watched the show together. "Where are you *puttin'* all that?" asks the cook, "Last time I seen things disappear thataway was at a magic show in Kansas City"

"Sorry, boys," said I, "I never reveal how I do my tricks."

My shirt buttons strained the fabric some and I had to let my belt out a notch or so, but my *hat* still fit. I paid my bill and waddled out the door.

My next stop was a big, ramshackle barn maybe two blocks east of the Blue Oyster. The sign out front read "Snowy Mountain Horse Hotel—Horses for Sale or Rent," so I circled around back to size up the merchandise. As it turned out, the corral behind the barn held twenty-three horses of various sizes, shapes, and colors, but there was only about three in the bunch that I figured was really worth a damn.

I climbed to the top rail of the corral and continued my studies until I'd narrowed my attentions to a tough little Roman-nosed gray and a big-chested gelding of the Morgan persuasion. I figured either horse could meet my needs, but there was something about the gray that troubled me. He stood quiet among the others, but he never took his eye off me for a second. His little pin ears was laid back, and I had the feeling it would give him great pleasure to do me harm.

Now I was still young enough—and fool enough—in them days to think of such a horse as a challenge. At twenty, I figured I could ride most anything that had hair, and up to then I hadn't met my Waterloo. Even so, I knew that tracking down Fontayne and Gossert was a dead serious pursuit. I needed a strong, steady mount that would toe the mark and tend to business—in short, one that would be more pardner than assassin. I throwed a half-hitch on my pride and turned my gaze away from the gray and onto the Morgan.

He was big for his breed; I judged he'd weigh

maybe thirteen hundred pounds and stand a good sixteen hands high. As to color, he was a dark bay from head to hoof with only a white blaze down the center of his face to break the pattern. Like the gray, he'd gave me his full attention when I first appeared but he'd since returned to his meditations. I liked him; he seemed steady and calm, and his deep chest and good legs told me he could go the distance.

I'd been expecting the owner to show up at any time, and I wasn't disappointed. Just then I heard footsteps behind me and a voice that sounded casual, as I knew it would. "Somethin' I can do for you, young feller?" I had to smile. The game had begun.

I stepped down off my perch and turned around. The feller who'd spoke was somewheres in his mid-forties, with white hair and a four day beard. His gap-toothed smile *oozed* sincerity.

"I'm Delbert Hames, and I own this outfit," he said, "You lookin' for a saddlehorse?" His watery blue eyes seemed to have trouble meeting mine. I shook my head and went to go around him, but he blocked my way without seeming to.

"Yes, sir," I told him, "I need a good usin' horse, but I don't see such in your string. You got any others?"

As I meant for it to, my remark caught him off balance, but he made a good recovery. "Why, no," he said, "what you see is what I've got. There are some fine horses in that bunch, though. Could be you missed 'em."

I let him turn my attention back to the corral. "Now

you take that sorrel yonder—he'd make a man a good saddlehorse."

"Kid's horse," I said, "he won't weigh eight hundred pounds."

"Yes, he will. Well, how about that line-back dun by the fence? He'll go a thousand pounds easy."

"Cow-hocked and calf-legged," I said.

I leaned my arms on the rail and looked at the horses again. "Only one I see that *might* fill the bill is that snake-eyed gray. A man would have to work the kinks out of him, though. How much?"

"You've got a good eye, son. That's a fine horse."

"How much?"

"I'd let you have him for a song. Hundred and a quarter."

"That's quite a song. I'd give you fifty"

"Fifty? You don't know much about what horses bring hereabouts."

"Maybe not," I said, "Don't really want him anyway. Thanks for your time." I made a move to walk past him again, but Delbert took hold of my shirt and stopped me.

"Be reasonable, son," he said, "there must be *somethin'* in that string you like."

I looked back at the bunch. "Well. What about that Morgan? He some kind of carriage horse?"

"No, he's a saddlehorse. I'd sell him for a hundred and ten."

We dickered awhile, then Delbert broke out some whiskey and we set in the shade and socialized. Then we haggled for a spell. After awhile we walked among the horses and Delbert talked about their good points. I pointed out their bad ones. He put halters on a couple and led them around the corral while I watched. I mouthed a few (including the Morgan, of course) to check their ages and the condition of their teeth. I was pleased to find the Morgan had a full mouth; I figured him for five years old, going on six.

To make a long story short, we haggled and dickered and drank, then we drank and dickered and haggled. Delbert asked a hundred for the Morgan, I offered sixty. He acted like I was stealing bread from his children, but came down to eighty-five. I raised my offer to sixty-five and finally bought the horse for seventy. Delbert was happy with the deal (but not so happy that it worried me), and so was I. The whole process had took an hour and twenty minutes, but good things can't be rushed. Time flies when you're having fun.

Back at Sorenson's I looked in on Pandora, but found she was sound asleep so didn't disturb her slumber. I cinched my saddle onto the Morgan and rode him down past the racetrack to where Little Buck lay. The buckskin hadn't swole up much yet, but the magpies and crows had found him, of course. Except for the birds the little horse might almost have been sleeping in the sun the way he used to back in his pasture at Dry Creek. I gave a holler and them flying gut-eaters took to the air. They didn't go far, but lit a short ways off where they belly-ached and cussed me for interrupting their meal. I might have had more sympathy for them if their dinner hadn't been Little Buck.

The Morgan made his feelings clear. Muscles taut as fiddle strings and his big eyes fixed on Little Buck's mortal remains, he stood quivering and snorting in his fright. I didn't push nor prod him, but held him in place as I stroked his neck and spoke low in his ear. I told him there was naught to fear, that he was a good, brave horse and I was proud of him. After a bit, he settled down some and took hold of himself.

Taking my grass rope from the forks of the saddle, I stepped down and put a loop around Little Buck's neck. Then I mounted the Morgan again, took my dallies, and touched his sides with my spurs. The big horse moved ahead with a steady pull, straining against the weight, and we slid the little buckskin upstream beside the creek on his final trip. Directly, we came to a dry wash that had one time been part of the old creek bed. There I took my rope off the buckskin, caved a dirt bank down on him, and laid Little Buck to rest.

For awhile I just set there in the dappled sun and shade of the young cottonwoods and thought about the little horse and all the trails we'd rode together. It was as good a way to say good-bye as any. Then, after a time, I got to my feet, swung up onto the Morgan, and headed back into Lewistown.

Pandora was still asleep when I got back to Doc and Lena Sorenson's. Doc Sorenson himself was out either visiting patients or pursuing the wily trout, but I did talk to his daughter Lena. She said Pandora was doing well, "just catching up on her rest." I left ten dollars on account and told Lena I was going out of town on business for a week or so. Said to tell her daddy much obliged and that I'd settle up with him when I got back.

I had hoped to tell Pandora good-bye before leaving town, but figured I had pretty much done so earlier that day. I also felt the need to pick up the outlaws' trail as soon as possible. They already had nearly a full day's lead on me. I knew Pandora had chose to help track down the outlaws of her own free will, but somehow I still felt responsible for her getting hurt. I was glad she was in good hands and out of harm's way.

Downtown at the Lewistown Mercantile, I bought coffee, beef jerky, beans, and bacon, and a half sack of oats for the Morgan. I still had a full box of .44s for the rifle and Orville's six-shooter, but I figured it was better to have cartridges and not need them than to need them and not have them, so I bought another box. I had last seen Fontayne and Gossert on the road that led to the mining camp of Maiden, and I recalled that Fontayne had once claimed that place as his home range. I packed my saddlebags, tied my slicker and a blanket roll behind the cantle, and took the road north to Maiden.

The road ran due north out of Lewistown for maybe ten miles before turning east along Warm Spring Creek and into the mountains of the Judith range. The afternoon was hot and muggy, and I sweated through my shirt before I'd hardly rode two miles. Beyond the mountain peaks, big-bellied clouds reared up like fighting stallions, promising thunder, lightning, and maybe even rain come evening. I wasn't took in by their bluff; July clouds in Montana don't always keep their promises.

With every mile, I was more pleased with the Morgan. He seemed willing and easy-gaited, with a steady nature and no trace of the shadow-jumper or switch-tail about him. He carried his head high, watching as he went, and he paid heed both to his surroundings and my wishes. I still missed Little Buck, of course, but it felt mighty fine to be riding out on a good horse once again.

The storekeeper back in Lewistown had told me Maiden was a fair-size town, if a new one, with upwards of a thousand folks and more than a hundred and fifty buildings. It was a mining camp, he said, "wild and lawless, like all them boom towns." I reckon it was civic pride that caused him to add that Maiden wasn't civilized like Lewistown was. I never said anything, but I couldn't help grinning as I thought of how them "civilized" Lewistown folk had shot them two horse-thieves to ribbons the day before.

As to that, I had to ask how "civilized" I was myself. There I was, setting out to find Fontayne and Gossert and get my horse back—through deadly force, if need be. Some folks wouldn't think that course of action was civilized, nor prudent neither. I knew I stood a fair

311

chance of getting myself killed, and I sure had no wish to be dead. I also knew living wouldn't be worth much if I lost my self respect. I could quit the trail and turn back, all right, and maybe live longer, but I figured there's whole lot more to being alive than just not being dead.

There was traffic aplenty on the road. I passed a bull train, the yoked oxen stolid and plodding as they pulled the canvas-topped freight wagons. A bull-whacker trudged in the dust alongside, guiding the team with the crack of a twenty-foot whip and bellering like a man possessed. I howdied him as I rode past, but he paid me no mind; I reckon he was too busy a-telling them oxen his opinion about who and what their parents had been.

Two miles farther on a miner with a wagon load of lumber rattled past, followed by two fancy-dressed high rollers in a sidesprung buggy. No sooner had their dust settled than four troopers galloped past me on big blocky cavalry mounts. From the way them boys bounced and slid around on their horses' backs I judged they'd bought themselves a drunk back in Lewistown and were delivering it to Maiden, or maybe beyond, to Fort Maginnis. For their sake I hoped it was the former; if they returned to the fort in their condition they'd be shoveling horseshit and sleeping in the guardhouse for a week. Anyway, right about then is when I decided I'd ate enough dust for awhile, so I reined the Morgan off the road and into an

312

aspen grove across the meadow.

After my orgy that morning at the Blue Oyster I figured I wouldn't want no food for a week, but already my belly thought it was hungry. I fed it some beef jerky, drank a little spring water, and took me a *siesta* in the shade.

It was the wind that woke me. It swept down the gulch, rippling the tall grass and setting the nervous aspen leaves to chattering. I sat up and looked around. Out in the meadow, the Morgan grazed in his hobbles, his mane and tail blowing in the wind. The sky had turned gray as lead, with fast-moving thunderclouds rolling and boiling above the mountains. I could smell the coming rain on the wind, and I cussed myself for a fool. If I hadn't took time out for a snooze, I'd have been warm and dry in some Maiden saloon instead of traveling under a downpour.

I was a mite goosey still about storms; the memory of the hail that had struck us beyond the Yellowstone was still fresh in my mind, and I wanted no more such adventures. I caught up the Morgan, slipped into my slicker, and took his hobbles off. Then I tightened the cinch, swung into the saddle, and spurred him out across Warm Spring Creek and onto the road again. I was still three miles from Maiden when the storm broke.

Big raindrops spattered onto the roadway and lightning stabbed the peaks as I pointed the big horse into the storm. Ahead, the rain seemed a nearly solid sheet, marching down the road toward me with a drumming patter that grew into a roar as it came. Then it swallered us up, churning the dusty road into black, soupy mud and drenching the Morgan and me as if I'd rode him under a waterfall. I couldn't see; the world had turned to water. It wouldn't have surprised me none to see a family of trout swim past my nose. I pulled my neck down inside the collar of my slicker and gave the gelding his head. I hoped he could find the way; I knew I sure couldn't.

The cloudburst seemed to last a long time, but looking back on it now I don't suppose it could have been much more than ten minutes before the heavy downpour slackened and the storm tapered off to a drizzle. I was wet as a frog. There was water inside my boots and inside my slicker, and I was cold and chilled as a froze dog, but at least I could see again. Steam rose off the Morgans neck and withers. He took the greasy road at a steady pace as we came at last to the one long street that was Maiden's main drag.

The town lay sprawled across a broad, sloping meadow and was hemmed in on three sides by mountains. Pine, fir, and spruce grew upon the hillsides and here and there in the valley itself, but much of the nearby timber had been cleared to build the town. Most of the buildings were made of log, though many had made the jump to board siding. Some of the newer places were still unfinished. These ranged all the way from tents and lean-tos to log-walled structures with canvas tops.

The street itself was wide and rutted, filled with wagons, horses, and mules. The bull team I'd passed on the road was parked off to one side, oxen still in their yokes, some standing while others lay in the mud and chewed their cuds. To get the lay of the land, I rode all the way through town, taking note of the businesses as I passed. I counted six saloons and at least that many gambling dens and dancehalls. There was an assay office, three dry goods stores, a couple of eating places, a hotel, a hardware, and two livery barns. Up at the far end of the street a funeral parlor stood right next door to a gunsmith's shop, which struck me as sort of fitting somehow.

You know how sometimes you can be someplace and a sound or a smell—or maybe the weather or the way the light falls—takes you back to some other time and place? Well, right then, just as I was riding past the bigger of the two livery stables, one of them recollections came over me like a spell. It seemed like I was back at the livery barn in Dry Creek with old Walt, and for a minute there the feeling was so strong I felt like I'd stepped through a hole in time.

I drew rein and just set there in the drizzle a-staring at the stable. Its big front doors stood open, and a lantern hanging just inside cast a soft yeller light out onto the street. The office was to the left of the big doors, with a small door all its own, and there was a light on in there as well. I caught the smell of woodsmoke from the office stove even before I seen it drifting from the stovepipe. The familiar odors of hay and horse wafted out onto the street, and I have to say they smelled mighty good to me. I can't tell you why, but it almost seemed like I'd come home.

Just then a feller appeared in the doorway. He was backlit by the lantern so I couldn't see his face, but he seemed to be studying me. For a minute we just held our places and looked at one other.

Then he says, kind of impatient-like, "Well? Are you gonna set there in the rain all night or are you gonna bring that animal inside?"

His words snapped me out of my trance and reminded me where I was. I rode the Morgan to the open doors and stepped down into the muck.

"I'm bringin' him in," I said.

Inside the barn, I doffed my hat and slapped the water off. The feller who'd spoke was shorter than me, around five foot five, and looked to be somewhere in his fifties. He wore a long rubber coat, open down the front, and high-topped gum boots. His short white beard reminded me of pictures I'd saw of Robert E. Lee, and his bowed legs told me he'd seen a horse or two sometime before. I grinned.

"My mama always said I didn't have enough sense to come in out of the rain," I told him, "Looks like Ma was right again."

The feller didn't smile, but he looked like he was trying not to, which was just as good. "We'd all been better off if we'd listened to our mamas," he said, "You want to put your horse up?"

"How much?"

"Two bits a day. Forty cents if you want him grained."

"How much if I stay, too?"

"Make it fifty cents. You can bunk in the loft."

I fished out a four-bit piece and handed it to him. His eyes never left my face as he took the coin and put it in his vest pocket.

"You look like a drowned mush-rat," he said, "When we've took care of that chesty Morgan, why don't you come on in the office and dry out by the stove. I might even find you a cup of coffee."

The liveryman showed me to a stall and I rubbed the gelding down with a grain sack, pitched a couple forks of hay into the manger, and poured him a can of oats. Then I walked back to the office.

The room was warm and dry. I set down next to the potbellied stove and shivered as I waited for the heat to do its work. Good as his word, the liveryman poured coffee into a tin cup and handed it to me.

"Much obliged, mister," I said, "I figure the man who first brewed a pot of coffee went straight to Heaven, no matter what else he might have done in his life."

"Might not have been a man. Could have been a woman. We already agreed mamas do most things right."

We both fell silent for a time. The stove glowed dirty red around its middle. It popped and groaned in the silence as the hot metal expanded. The liveryman took a short-stemmed pipe from his shirt pocket and filled it from a beaded pouch. When he'd got it tamped and lit, he spoke again.

"I know that gelding of yours," he said, "used to belong to Delbert Hames over at Lewistown."

"That's right," I said, "I bought him from Delbert this morning."

"I hope the old skinflint gave you a bill of sale. He don't always."

"He did. I just *told* you I bought him."

"Yes. No offense meant, son." The liveryman didn't meet my gaze, but studied his pipe with some care. "I know it's hard to believe, but some men around here been known to ride horses that don't *belong* to 'em. There are others who take *exception* to the practice."

"As they should. I've come a long way lookin' for the men who stole *my* horse."

The liveryman stood. "None of my business, son," he said, "sometimes I talk too much." He smiled then. "I'll be headin' out now," he said, "My night man will be along directly. But you make yourself at home. Maybe I'll see you tomorrow, unless you're leavin' early."

"Expect I'll be around a day or so," I said, "thanks again."

As I watched the man walk out into the dark, I somehow knew I *would* see him again. What I didn't know was the way our trails would meet and weave together in the days to come. And what I *surely* didn't know was that our meeting that rainy night in Maiden would change both our lives in a mighty big way, and forever.

TWENTY-TWO
Sunday Dinner

After the liveryman left I set there by the stove for a spell, soaking up heat like a lizard on a rock. It had been my intention to go out to supper before I bedded down, but I found myself nodding off in my chair and so changed my mind. I climbed the ladder to the loft, rolled out my damp blankets, and fell asleep before my head hit the hay.

When next I awoke I had no idea where I was. It seemed I'd been in the midst of a pleasant dream of some kind, but try as I might I could neither recall its nature nor return to it. I laid there in the gloom and considered my situation. The sweet, musty smell of timothy and bluestem told me I was in a haymow somewheres, and the first thing that came to mind was the livery barn at Dry Creek where I'd slept so many nights. After a time my brain shook off its cobwebs and commenced to function once again. I recalled the events of the previous day—my ride, the storm, and the liveryman who'd bade me welcome—and I set up in my blankets, donned my hat, and pulled on boots and britches. My first full day in Maiden, Montana, had begun.

The sun had only just topped the ridge when I stepped out onto the street. Its warm rays lit the wet grasses of

319

the meadow and painted the storefronts a soft rose. On the opposite side of the street cold shadows stretched long across the muddy thoroughfare, and puddled rainwater reflected red clouds against a blue-gold sky.

The town was awake and going about its business. Teamsters and bullwhackers hitched up their teams and off-loaded freight at rear door loading docks, merchants in aprons swept their boardwalks, and miners walked and rode out of town on the way to their claims. At Gie's Saloon a sullen swamper swept a litter of old playing cards, dried mud, and cigar butts out onto the street. Gray woodsmoke from chimney and stovepipe turned bright pink as it caught sunlight, and from a cabin somewhere back in the trees came the clear, sharp chock of an axe splitting wood.

I follered the crowd to an eatery called the New Chicago and took on a breakfast of batter cakes and sausage, with enough black coffee to bring a man full awake and well begun upon his day. Afterward, I moseyed up and down the street, talking with whoever would, and asking—in the most casual manner I could assume—about a blood-bay thoroughbred horse and *hombres* who might fit the descriptions of Turk Fontayne and Portugee Gossert.

The results of my inquiries were disappointing. When first I'd met him Fontayne told me he was from Maiden, but the folks I talked to that morning either didn't know the man or weren't inclined to say they did. As for my horse Quicksilver, no one claimed to have laid eyes on him either. One feller said he might have saw such a horse at the races down at Billings, but he couldn't say for sure. By noon I'd decided Fontayne and Gossert either really hadn't been around Maiden lately, or I hadn't spoke to the right people.

When I got back to the stable, the liveryman was there again. He was shoveling wet straw and horse manure into a wheelbarrow with a fork, and he looked mad as a wet eagle. I throwed him a cheery good morning but he chose not to catch it. His faded blue eyes flashed fire, and he just grunted in reply. It was plain he was carrying more of a mad than he could rightly contain, and I figured he needed some help turning it loose. I primed his pump when I asked, "Somethin' wrong?"

He flung the manure fork to the stable floor and glared at me. "Somethin' wrong? Why, yes, you might say so," he said, "I ran into my night man just after I left here last evenin'—som'bitch gave me two seconds notice and quit me on the spot. Got *gold* fever, if you can believe that. Quit me to go be a *millionaire,* by god. Fool kid can't find his butt with both hands, but he's fixin' to go find *gold.*"

He was just getting warmed up. "Worst damn stable boy I ever saw," he said, "but he was the only one I could find who'd take the job. He never done a lick of work around here, but at least he filled up *space* when I had to be gone."

The cords in the liveryman's neck stood out like cable. His face was brick red. I nodded to show I was listening and sympathetic, and set down on a hay bale.

"I take that back," he said, "som'bitch *did* put in *one* day's work—I believe it was the twenty-third of May—it was such a shock to his system he was out sick for a week!"

I could see he was pretty near done. He sort of quivered as he stood scowling at the stable floor, but his face was beginning to lose some of its flush. He frowned, then blowed up again. "Find *gold!*" he snorted, "Fool kid couldn't find a black cat in a *cream* can!"

All of which, strange as it may seem, helped give me the notion to stay on awhile in Maiden. Even though I'd found nobody yet who claimed to know of Fontayne and Gossert, I believed them boys had ties to the town. I figured if I was patient I'd find someone who'd help me learn their whereabouts.

The trouble was, I had no idea where they might be. They surely wouldn't have gone anywheres near Fort Maginnis; the army was out scouring the country for horse thieves right then. Besides that, there was supposed to be a deputy sheriff staying at the fort.

They could have gone north, or east, to the rustler dens along the Missouri, or even over the line into Canada. They could be holed up somewhere in the Judith mountains or the Big Snowies. When my Pa and me were hunting wild horses he used to say "There's many a place them mustangs *could* be, but there's only *one* place they're *at.*" I figured the same thing applied to Fontayne and Gossert; I just didn't know where "at" was *at.*

• • •

There was no end of maybes. Maybe them boys would run into one of Stuart's hemp committees. Hell, maybe they already had. Maybe they'd get theirselves snake-bit, or die of the epizootic. Or, at the rate things was going, maybe them hardcases would perish of old age. The fact remained they didn't seem to be in or around Maiden. The trail had gone cold as a gambler's heart.

Still, for no reason I could put a name to, I had the feeling I would either get word as to their whereabouts or some day they'd come back through Maiden. The way I saw it, hunting men was like hunting other critters—when the trail fades and you lose sight of your quarry, it's time to stand still. I figured Maiden was as good a place to bide my time as any.

My other concern was that I was rapidly running through my cash. I still had just over a hundred and fifty dollars, but money went fast in a mining town even if a man was frugal, which I oft-times was not. I was a long way from my home range. I had men to find and a horse to locate, and I had no idea how much time and money them enterprises might require.

I stood up and grinned at the liveryman. "I find I've took a fancy to your town," I said, "How much would that job pay?"

I had seen him mad and cussing; now I seen him surprised and speechless. For a moment he just stared like he wasn't sure he'd heard me right. Then he asked, "*You* want the job?"

"I might. Used to work at a stable down at Dry Creek."

"Well, what would you say to four bits a day and free board for your horse?"

I grinned. "I'd say '*howdy,* four bits a day; I sure druther you was *six.*'"

The liveryman laughed out loud. His smile took ten years off his age. "Six bits it is," he said, "You've got yourself a job, son. My name's Garrett Sinclair. What do you call yourself?"

I gave him my hand. "Merlin Fanshaw," I told him, "When do I start?"

Garrett bent down, picked up the manure fork, and handed it to me. "You've *started,*" he said.

All of which is how I found gainful employment at the Sinclair Livery Stable in Maiden, Montana, during the summer of '84. Them first few days on the job were the hardest; there was plenty that needed doing and a good plenty that had long been left undone. During the next few weeks I cleaned the stalls, put down fresh straw, and fixed what boards and gates were broke or loose. I whitewashed the walls, set out mousetraps in the grain bins, and cleaned and soaped the saddles, harness, and other tack.

Garrett kept a buckboard, two buggies, and the undertaker's hearse in the wagon yard out back, and I washed and polished them all. There was usually four or five saddlehorses to tend each day, including my Morgan, and I took care of them horses as if they was my own, which of course one of them was.

Some of the best advice my pa ever gave me had to do with work. He'd told me, "Whoever you work for, Merlin, make them a good hand," and over the years I've mostly tried to do that. I never gave it much thought, but times I've followed Pa's advice the men I worked for mostly responded in kind—not always, but mostly.

I've thought about it some, and I think the reason they done so is because so many workers tend to do the least they can, not the most. When a boss finds a feller who's a self-starter and will go the extra mile he knows he's found himself a rare bird. At that point he'll generally show his appreciation however he can. At least that's how it's always turned out for me.

It sure worked out that way with Garrett Sinclair. He praised my work, gave me extra time off, and seemed to enjoy my company. By the end of the third week he'd pretty well turned the running of the stable over to me. He still took care of ordering feed, grain, and such, and of course he paid the bills and done the banking, but it seemed like the longer I worked for him the more he trusted me.

Working nights gave me time during the day to take the Morgan out and explore the country. Some days I'd ride up to the diggings and watch the miners work their claims. Other times I'd just ride slow and easy through the timber and out into the grass of some mountain park.

When I first took to the gulches some of the boys were a mite goosey. I believe they thought I might be a claim jumper or a sluice-box thief, but after a time they came to know me by sight and welcome me when I came around. They'd howdy me, take a break from their labors, and we'd pass the time of day. I'd tell them such news as I'd heard from fellers passing through Maiden, and sometimes I'd bring them an old newspaper from town. They'd give me letters to post, or they'd ask me to fetch them back things they were short of when next I came—coffee, flour, tobacco and such—and I did.

Always, wherever I rode and whoever I met, I asked about a blood bay thoroughbred and the men who had stole him. The answer was always the same: no one had seen them.

It was on a sultry Saturday in late July when Garrett asked me to Sunday dinner at his cabin. I was pleased by the invite, but surprised at first. The livery barn never closed. It was a general rule that either him and me had to be there at all times. Garrett said that wasn't a problem; he'd asked the blacksmith next door to keep an eye on the place until Sunday evening.

The barbershop up the street never closed, either, and come Sunday morning I treated myself to the works—shave, haircut, and a good soak in the tub out back of the shop. My hair growed thick, black, and straight as a string in them days, but my whiskers was still few and far between. Once or twice I'd tried to cultivate a mustache, but as the weeks went by and nothing much sprouted but fuzz I'd had to accept my crop failure and abandon the enterprise. To his credit, the barber never turned a hair (so to speak) when I asked him for a shave; he just lathered, stropped, and scraped away as if I really had whiskers.

Afterward, I put on my cleanest shirt, beat the dust out of my hat, brushed it, and blacked my boots. Then, a little before noon, I stepped up onto the Morgan and rode out. Garrett had never talked much about personal things—I didn't know if he was married, widowed, or what—so I was curious as to what I might find at his place that day.

He'd told me his cabin was about a mile east of town in a good-sized aspen grove, and I found it without trouble. Garrett came out as I rode up and welcomed me. We shook hands, and he showed me inside. I couldn't see much right off. It had been bright out in the sunlight and the cabin was dim, but I had no trouble at all picking up the good smells of dinner on the stove. I couldn't recall the last time I'd had a home-cooked meal, and I was sure looking forward to it.

As my eyes growed accustomed to the dimness I could see the cabin was neat and tidy inside, with two fair-sized rooms up front and a sleeping wing in back. Just off the front porch was a keeping room with two easy chairs and a sofa. A bookcase holding maybe two dozen volumes stood against the far wall. There was a good bearskin and two bright-colored Navajo rugs on the puncheon floor, and a coal-oil lamp with hand-painted flowers on it stood atop a desk of solid oak.

Just beyond, through an open door, I spied a sawbuck table set for dinner, a homemade hutch, and a big kitchen range with a warming oven. An elderly Chinese gent tended the cooking pots, and he turned and gave me a wide and mostly toothless grin as Garrett led me into the kitchen.

Garrett put an arm around the old man's shoulders. "This old ruin is my friend Lee Sun Yung," he said, smiling, "He's a sinner and a heathen, but he cooks better'n my sainted mother ever did. Besides, he tolerates my moods. Lee, meet our guest, Merlin Fanshaw."

The old man's hand felt frail-boned as a bird, but the firmness of his grip surprised me. His skin was like parchment and beneath a small skull cap his fine gray hair was pulled back into a long pigtail. A pair of gold-rimmed spectacles with colored lenses hid his eyes, and he wore a loose blouse and trousers of some dark and shiny cloth.

When he spoke his voice was more music than words. "Wel-come," he said.

Then I heard the door between the kitchen and the sleeping wing open, and I turned to see a boy maybe ten years old walk through it. He was smiling, but he held his hands out away from his body in a curious way, touching counter top and sideboard as he came. Then I saw the boy was blind, the pupils of his eyes clouded by a dull, white film. Behind me, Garrett's voice sounded different than I'd ever heard it, more gentle, somehow, and soft. "And this handsome young man is my grandson Winslow. Winslow, say howdy to Mister Fanshaw."

I took the boy's hand, and we shook. "How do you do, sir," he said. I have to confess I was somewhat taken aback at first. I had never been around a blind person before, and I felt uneasy. I suppose I feared I would say or do something wrong, and for a time there I was nervous as a short-tailed bull in fly-time. Except that he couldn't see, Winslow appeared to be no different than any boy his age. He was polite, cheerful, and seemed bright as a new penny. Because of his attitude, and that of Garrett and the old Chinese gent, I soon came near to forgetting the boy was blind.

At half-past twelve we all set around the table while Lee Sun Yung brought out the vittles. There was roast venison, mashed taters and gravy, hot rolls and honey, creamed onions, and green beans, with apple dumplings for dessert. Turned out Garrett kept a cow, so we had our choice of milk, coffee, or cider to drink.

Before we commenced, Lee Sun Yung filled a plate and set it in front of Winslow. Then he leaned over and spoke low in the boy's ear, and I figured out he was telling him whereabouts on the plate the lad would find each item. Garrett said a quick blessing (my favorite kind), and we all fell to chucking it in. Because I was on my best behavior, I kept a check-rein on my gluttony, but the old gent's cooking was prime and I have to tell you it wasn't easy to hold myself back.

After dinner, Winslow took me out to a small barn in the trees behind the cabin to show me his horse. He ran on ahead of me through the dappled sunlight and shadow, sure of his ground as his feet followed the familiar path. At the barn, he quickly unlatched the double doors and stepped inside. Directly, back he came, leading a clear-footed sorrel gelding by the halter.

There was joy in his voice. "Ain't he a dandy, mister Fanshaw? I named him Carson, after Kit Carson. Grandpa gave him to me for my birthday."

Carson was a dandy, all right. He was a small horse, maybe thirteen hands high, just about right for Winslow.

"You bet," I said, "He's a good 'un." I couldn't help noticing the way the boy read the horse with his hands. In smooth, graceful strokes, his fingers slid across the animal's chest and down its strong forelegs, then back up along its neck and down again to its withers. The sorrel nickered its pleasure and nuzzled the boy. Winslow's laughter was the sound of pure delight.

"I wanted you to see him 'specially, Mister Fanshaw," the boy said, "Grandpa says you're a man who savvies horses."

"Well, I growed up with them," I said, "and some of my best friends have been horses. My pa always said there's somethin' about the outside of a horse that's good for the inside of a man. I've found no cause to doubt it."

"That's how I feel, too. Your pa sounds pretty smart."

"He was smart about horses, anyway."

Except about the crazy black stud that killed him, I thought. That one, and a hundred others that stomped and kicked and bit him; horses that threw him and marked him and broke his bones. The truth was, Pa loved horses; nothing they could ever do would change that. Sometimes I think he loved the man-killers best of all, maybe because in their wildness he saw something of his own. Pa had loved me, too, the best he knew how, and he'd passed on his love of horses to me. Looking at blind Winslow and his little sorrel, I was glad the boy had a grand-dad like Garrett, a horse like Carson, and love.

Back inside the cabin, Winslow pulled out a checker-board and asked if I'd play him a game. The board was a real beauty, handcrafted of dark and light wood squares set into a rosewood frame. The checkers were round, of course, made of the same dark and light wood as the board was. The light-colored pieces had been roughed up on their edges as by a file. I figured that had been done so Winslow could tell the difference by touch.

Now I fancied myself a pretty good checkers player in them days, and I have to admit I was feeling a mite smug when I made my opening move. I seen Garrett and old Lee Sun Yung exchange a quick glance, but I didn't know until later what it signified.

I figured I'd go easy on the boy and let him win the first game or two, but Winslow seemed to sense I wasn't playing my best. There was a hint of disappointment in his voice as he said, "You're not really tryin', mister Fanshaw."

I denied going easy on him, of course. "Yes, I am, Winslow. Looks like I'm gonna have to try harder though, don't it?"

I decided to win the next game, but that's not what happened. I lost that game and the one after that—and the one after that. I lost two more after that. The boy would sit perfectly still, his head cocked to one side as if he was listening to some sound only he could hear. Then his fingers would brush lightly over the checkers and board and he'd make his move. He was a good winner, I'll say that for him. I don't know what kind of a loser he was, because he never did.

In our final game that afternoon he drawed me into a trap and wiped me out in a triple jump that was more of a massacre than a plain victory. I throwed in the towel.

"You're too good for me, Winslow," I said, "I guess I'm gonna have to take some lessons."

Garrett's laugh was a hearty one. "Well, don't look at me," he said, "I ain't been able to win a game with the boy for more than a year now."

The sun was setting as I said my thank yous and made ready to go back to work. I shook old Lee Sun Yung's fine-boned hand again and said he was a world-beater of a cook, which he surely was. I thanked young Winslow for showing me his horse and for trouncing me at checkers. I told him it had been good to meet him and said maybe him and me could go riding together sometime. When I thanked Garrett for asking me to dinner and letting me share the afternoon with his family, he put his arm around his grandson's shoulders and grinned his pride.

"Glad you came," he said, "I hope you'll come again sometime when you can't *stay* so long." His smile made a lie of his words.

In Maiden, lamplight already glowed in the windows as I rode the Morgan around back of the livery barn and stepped down. From a saloon up the street came the sound of a fiddler tuning up, and miners were drifting in from the hills like moths to a lamp. Over at the Lucky Dollar I could hear the clattering of the seven-foot wheel of fortune. Like me, the gamblers were making ready to begin their night's work. From somewhere off in the darkness came the knowing laughter of a sporting woman.

I thought of the miners' hard and lonesome life and of how their hunger for the company of their fellow humans led them to spend their hard-earned gold on counterfeit love and friendship. I had been riding a hard and lonesome trail myself. I knew I would stay with that trail until I found the men and the horse I was hunting for, but on that special Sunday in the Judith mountains I'd been drawed inside the circle that was Garrett Sinclair's family and had for awhile been made to feel a part of it. I was more than grateful for the gift.

TWENTY-THREE
In the Good Old Summertime

The first days of August were sweltering and hot, with only a now-and-then breeze in late afternoon for relief. The sun rose early and stayed up late, and men and critters alike slowed down to match the summer's mood.

In the gulches, prospectors struggled in the scorching heat as they labored at their claims. Alone or with a pardner, they swung their picks and plied their hard rock trade, coaxing ore from veins that had rested unmolested and secret since God laid the chunk.

Down below in the valley, the town of Maiden bode its time until evening and the miners' return. Sallow-faced gamblers sipped brandy and played patience in the darkened saloons while barkeeps tapped beer kegs and polished glassware against the coming of night. At Dutch Annie's place, hard-eyed chippies looked down from second-floor windows like wolves above a waterhole, cooling themselves with cardboard fans from the funeral parlor.

At the meat market the butcher's dog passed his days in a shallow hole he'd dug beneath the board-walk. He laid there panting with his eyes half closed, and I wondered what, if anything, that hound was thinking about. With his ears laid back and his great pink tongue lolling almost to the dirt it looked for all the world like he was laughing at some private joke, which maybe he was.

Come late afternoon, high-piled thunderclouds stacked up black and warlike over the mountains, but they seldom brought showers. Oh, they'd grumble and bluster, of course. Every now and then there'd come a gust of wind that scattered the discarded playing cards and swept grit on up the street, but for all their fuss the clouds failed to keep their promise and the rains they threatened never came.

As for me, I did my nightly stint at the livery barn, thankful to be earning my living in the cool of evening. Garrett came in right at five in the morning. We'd generally talk awhile before I went to catch some shut-eye. Then I'd roll out around noon or one o'clock, break the fast over at the New Chicago, and begin my day.

I still made regular rounds of the saloons and gambling halls seeking news of Fontayne and Gossert, but even though a number of folks knew them boys nobody seemed to have laid eyes on them lately. After awhile, it got so I hardly even had to ask a question; most of the bartenders, card-sharps, and girls of the night already knew who I was looking for. I could be wrong, of course, but I believe somebody would have told me if they'd had any knowledge of their whereabouts.

Every now and then I'd give thought to moving on to new towns and ranges in *my* quest, but I never did.

I was loath to leave the town of Maiden unless I got word them hardcases was some definite elsewhere. Besides, my gut told me them boys weren't all that far away, and I wound up drawing cards to my hunch.

As before, it was my habit to ride out on the Morgan of an afternoon, only now I took to bringing Winslow along. The boy would follow me on the sorrel he called Carson, full of questions as boys generally are, and I'd answer every one whether I knew the answer or not. I'd describe the country as we passed through it, and Winslow took it all in, seeing everything by way of my eyes and his ears.

Some things were hard to describe. What the boy knew of his world he knew through taste, touch, smell, and hearing. When we spoke of things them senses wouldn't cover I had to get downright creative. I remember he asked me one time what clouds were like, and I felt all but tongue-tied trying to explain them. I spoke of fluffy things like rabbit tails, goose down pillows, and such, but I could tell he didn't really get my drift. Finally, I seen a clump of dandelions alongside the trail that had gone to seed, picked a few, and let Winslow touch them. He felt of that dandelion fuzz with the tips of his fingers and held the dandelions up to his face.

"Clouds look like that *feels*," I told him, "only they're a whole lot bigger." Then I opened another can of worms. "They're mostly white," I said.

"What's 'white'?" asks Winslow.

Well, if you've never tried to explain colors to a blind person you have no idea how hard it is. It took some time, but over the next few weeks I came to give the boy some idea of the subject, anyway. I recall we were talking one day on the front porch of Garrett's house. Lee Sun Yung had brought out a big pitcher of lemonade and poured Winslow and me each a glass. I'm not sure where I got the idea, but all at once it occurred to me I could maybe explain colors by way of temperature. Folks spoke of warm colors and cool colors, didn't they? Well, I figured, maybe I could give Winslow some kind of idea that way. I fished a chunk of ice out of my glass and ran it up his arm.

"Blue," says I, "the color *blue.*" I led him off the porch and out into the sun. I tilted his face up into the light. "Yellow," I said, "the color *yellow.*" In the kitchen I held his hand over the stove until he commenced to draw back from the heat. "Red," I said, "that's *red*, Winslow."

Well, a big grin came over his face; Winslow looked like a prospector who'd just struck the mother lode. From that day on he came to have some idea, anyway, about colors. Even when I couldn't think of a way to use temperature as a way of showing him, I'd try to explain in other ways. I'd have him feel the leaves of trees, pine needles, and grass.

"Green," I'd say, "they're all the color green, Winslow." I never did know how much he understood, but he sure seemed tickled. I was mighty pleased to have been able to show him what little I did.

I liked the boy a lot. He was a quick learner, and interested in everything. Garrett told me he appreciated the way I spent time with Winslow and his words kind of surprised me. I hadn't done it out of kindness, but because I liked the boy.

The livery stable did a land-office business that summer, which was all right with me, keeping busy made the time pass faster. I enjoyed talking with the riders who came through town, and taking care of their horses was an education in itself. You can tell a lot about a man by the horse he rides and how he cares for it, and I reckon I seen pretty much every kind during those first weeks in August.

From the fellers I spoke with I learned the big rustler roundup had pretty well ended. There'd been a few more hangings and a shoot-out or two up along the Missouri, but Stuart's Stranglers had apparently caused the horse and cattle thieves to repent of their wicked ways. Near as I could tell, most of the rustlers had either perished at the hands of the hemp committees, moved on to healthier climes, or quit the business altogether. As always, I inquired after Fontayne and Gossert but again no one had any word of them, nor of a blood-bay thoroughbred racehorse neither.

I thought often of Pandora. I wondered how she was doing and whether her broke leg had mended. I wondered if she was still in Lewistown or if she'd managed to find her way back home. Maybe Colonel

Charlie had took her in at his ranch on Careless Creek while she done her healing, or maybe—well, I suppose a man could "maybe" forever.

Once or twice I thought of asking Garrett for some time off and going back to find her, but I never did. I figured it would be just my luck to set out for Lewistown on the very day Fontayne and Gossert showed up in Maiden with my horse.

I thought about writing to her. I actually did write a couple of letters, one newsy and casual and the other a kind of mushy one in which I shared my deepest thoughts and fears, but I never mailed either of them. I don't know what good it done to write them anyway. Unmailed letters may be all right for getting a feller's thoughts down, but they're not of much account when it comes to communication.

Sometimes when my night shift ended and after I'd slipped between the soogans I'd lay there and recall the way Pandora had felt in my arms. I'd feel again the softness of her lips when I kissed her and the way she had embraced me with her whole self, nothing held back.

I remembered that morning in the outlaw camp when the night riders hanged Cock-eyed Clarence and me to a cottonwood branch. I recalled how I seemed to be two places at once and how my other self had watched Pandora and Colonel Charlie come riding like the wind to my rescue.

Most of all I remembered Pandora's soft, dark eyes and the way I'd looked into them and saw myself there. At one time or other she had looked at me with admiration, amusement, disappointment, hurt, anger, and what I took to be the beginnings of love. It was the memory of that last look that brought the stirring to my blood and made it hard for me to fall asleep.

On a clear Saturday morning somewhere around mid-August I came sauntering out of the New Chicago and nearly ran into Garrett at the door. I had took on my usual substantial breakfast and had just let my belt out a notch to accommodate the swelling of my paunch. In short, I was full as a tick, happy as a clam, and everything was more or less right with my world.

"Well, howdy, Garrett," says I, "was you lookin' for me?"

He nodded. "Yes," he said, "I reckon I was."

I stood there and prospected my teeth with a toothpick while I waited for him to say more. He was silent for quite a spell, and then he said, "Why don't you throw your saddle on that chesty gelding you're so proud of and come take a ride with me? I need to talk some."

"You bet," says I, "where we goin'?"

"Wherever we take the notion to," he said, "the ride is just to have somethin' to do while we talk."

At the livery, I saddled the Morgan and led him through the barn to the street beyond. The blacksmith from next door was setting at Garrett's desk when I passed the office, and I figured he'd been asked to mind the place while we was away. I traded nods with him as I walked the gelding through. Outside, Garrett was already mounted. He set astride a blue roan gelding and watched as I untracked the Morgan and stepped across him. Then he touched spur to the roan, and we rode up Montana Street and took the trail north to Whiskey Gulch and beyond.

The day was hot and muggy as we started up the steep, rocky trail. The horses were sweated and breathing hard before we'd gone hardly a mile, and Garrett and me reined up at a switchback and let them catch their breath. I said nothing, leaving space for Garrett to speak as we set our saddles and waited on the horses. I glanced at his whiskered face and grinned to show him I was ready to listen, but he neither met my gaze nor spoke. He just looked down at the town below, his expression hard as flint. After a time, we rode on.

I was some curious as to what was on the man's mind. He'd told me he wanted to talk, but so far he hadn't said so much as a single word. I figured there was nothing to do but wait until he did, so I fell in behind him and took to admiring the scenery.

An hour later we came upon a good spring in a spruce grove just twenty yards off the trail. Garrett pulled aside into the shade and stepped down from the sweated roan. The Morgan made it clear he thought I should foller suit and I did so, no doubt to his relief.

It was cool there in the shadows by the spring. Water trickled out of a cleft in the rocks and flowed clear as glass into a deep pool just beyond. I fell to my belly and drank, the water so cold it hurt my teeth. When I had my fill I dried my mouth on my sleeve and set down upon a fallen log. Garrett squatted on his bootheels, cupped his hands, and drank as well. Then he set cross-legged in the grass, filled his pipe and lit it, and looked across at me. He drawed deeply on his briar, let the smoke drift out into the morning sunlight, and commenced to talk.

"I was thirty years old when I joined the Kansas volunteers during the War Between the States. My son Ted was ten that year, the same age Winslow is now, and I left him and my good wife to mind our farm while I rode off to fight the Rebels. A year later I got word my missus had died of diptheria and that Ted had gone to live with the neighbors.

"When the war ended I took up the peace officer trade in Kansas and brought Ted along with me. I worked the cowtowns during the years of the big Texas drives, served as deputy under Hickock at Hays and Abilene, and worked Dodge City with the Mastersons. My son Ted married in '72 and followed his old man into the law and order business. Ted was a good officer, better than I was, and he had the knack of keeping the lid on them wild Texans and making friends of them at the same time.

"In '74 Winslow was born in Dodge City with what the doctors call congenital cataracts. What that means is the boy has been blind from birth, able only to make out light from darkness. Ted took it hard. He seemed to change overnight into a different kind of man, harder and more bitter. He took to drinking and

342

staying away from home nights. His wife, my daughter-in-law, tried to care for Winslow as best she could, but it was a hard thing to do alone.

"I tried to talk to Ted, but each time I did we wound up shouting at each other. I don't guess I saw it at the time, but I've come to know since that his anger wasn't really with me. I tried to help out with Winslow. My daughter-in-law wasn't much more than a girl herself, and she sure didn't know how to deal with the boy's blindness. A doctor at Fort Dodge told me most congenital cataracts are found in children born imbecile or idiotic. Sometimes, he said, the child itself is stunted and poorly developed, but none of that was true of Winslow. He's always been the bright, good natured kid you see today."

Garrett broke off his story then. He puffed, drawing on his pipe, but it had gone dead. Striking a match, he relit it.

"Man who smokes a pipe seems to use more matches than tobacco," he observed.

For a time he smoked in silence, seeming to gather his thoughts. When he spoke again his voice sounded tight as stretched wire, and sorrow had moved over his face like cloud shadow over a hillside.

"It wasn't a Texas drover nor a desperado who killed my boy. It was whiskey and a hurt so deep nobody knew how to reach it. Ted fell drunk under the wheels of a freight wagon and died there on Front Street in the Kansas mud.

"Somethin' seemed to snap in my daughter-in-law

when Ted died. The day after the funeral she brought little Winslow to me at the city marshal's office and vamoosed for parts unknown. Heard later she took up with a fancy man over in Kansas City, but I don't know that for a fact.

"I reckon somethin' snapped inside me, too. It's a helluva thing for a man to outlive his only son. I quit the peace officer trade, left Kansas, and came west. Opened my first livery barn in Deadwood, moved to Colson down on the Yellowstone, and came to Maiden in '82."

Garrett paused, and I stepped into the gap to ask a question. "And Lee Sun Yung?"

"A good friend," Garrett said, "from my first days in Dodge. Sometimes I almost think the old pirate loves Winslow even more than me."

My next question was hard to ask. It ain't real easy talking around a lump in your throat. "Ain't there *anything* can be done about Winslow's eyes?"

Garrett knocked the dottle from his briar and put the cold pipe in his shirt pocket. "I've been told there's a specialist in St. Louis who's had some success at restorin' vision through cataract surgery. Doctor who told me also said the operation is about as difficult as they come, and that only a few surgeons can do it."

"Still, if there's a chance Winslow could be made to see—"

"There's one *more* problem, son. The operation costs better than three thousand dollars. I ain't *ever* had more than four hundred at any one time in my life, and it ain't likely I ever will."

Garrett stood up, stretched, and smiled at me. "But I didn't bring you up here to sing you sad songs. My grandson is a good boy and a happy one. You've done a great deal to help make him so. Only way I could think of to thank you was to let you in on Winslow's history and my own. I've told no other man 'til now what I've told you, but I've oft-times felt the need to. Anyway, I just wanted to say much obliged—until you're *better* paid."

I swallered the lump in my throat and grinned. "Hell, Garrett," I said, "I've already been *over-paid*."

The weather changed that week. Clouds rolled in like wooly sheep drifting onto new range until at last they filled the skies and covered all the blue. The change brought welcome relief from the hot spell we'd been a-suffering, and even though the calendar stubbornly insisted it was still August—and still summertime—the cooler days and nights felt more like early fall.

Winslow and me still rode the mountain trails, drifting farther back into the Judiths on our afternoon rides. I've always been quite the one for searching out new country, and I took pleasure in the way I was able to help the boy see it too. We'd ride up onto some high, windy point and Winslow would draw close and take in my every word. I'd tell him the names of the creeks, canyons and gulches, if I knew them, and try and help him to see the country through my eyes.

"There's a deep canyon just below us yonder," I'd say, "with a long bench of red rock up near the top. Remember the color *red,* Winslow? From there the country drops off steep between thick stands of green fir and pine trees. Down at the bottom, a grove of aspen trees straddles a narrow stream flowin' green-gray in the shadows, trimmed with whitewater like lace as it breaks over its bed."

Or I'd say, "Well, ain't he somethin'! A fast-flyin' bird just darted past you, Winslow—he's bright blue in color, so bright it startles a man. He just sailed out over the canyon and snatched up a bug as he flew."

I'd describe deer, elk, moose, and such when I seen them, and sometimes when I didn't, but it seemed like somehow Winslow could always tell when I was making something up. As soon as I'd start describing some imaginary animal, he'd call me on it. "You don't *really* see a wolf," he'd say, "you're just pretending, Merlin." I never could figure out how the boy knew, but he always seemed to. Maybe it was something about how my voice sounded, I don't know.

It was on the afternoon of August 18 that Winslow and me rode out of the trees below New Year Peak onto a broad and open meadow. Rich grasses, turning now in midsummer from green to tawny gold, carpeted the sunlit park and wildflowers were everywhere. We hobbled the horses and set them to graze while we hunkered cross-legged in the grass to eat the lunch we'd brought. A mile below us lay Ruby Gulch and the thin shining thread that was Boyd Creek, but the day was still and peaceful and I saw no movement in all that broad expanse.

Winslow curled up in the sunshine and fell asleep after we ate, and I sauntered off by my lonesome so as not to disturb his slumbers. I took Pa's old Army field glasses out and commenced scanning the valley for signs of life. Out beyond the dark trees a red-tailed hawk soared above the gulch, drifting easy on the rising air Boyd Creek glistened in the sun. From the silent woods nearby I heard the noisy chittering of a squirrel, and, a little later, the raucous call of a jaybird. A great cloud blocked the sunlight and the afternoon was suddenly cooler as the gulch came beneath its shadow. All at once I felt uneasy and strange. There seemed to be nothing in all that wide country to cause me worry, yet worry I did.

I had never believed much in hunches or premonition. Oh, I'd heard folks talk of sixth sense, second sight, and such, but I hadn't experienced them things myself. I didn't disbelieve, you understand; I just didn't know one way or the other. Mostly, I tried to make do with the five senses I knew I had, but that day, as I looked down upon the silent floor of Ruby Gulch, something came over me I can't explain. There was nothing I could see, hear, smell, taste nor feel to account for it, but all at once the hair on the back of my neck stood up and I felt the cold grip of fear upon my heart.

Far below, I saw five horses come out of the trees, cross Boyd Creek, and line out across a clearing.

347

Behind them, clear and sharp in the lenses of the binoculars, came a rider mounted on a long-legged blood-bay thoroughbred. My hands began to shake. I couldn't hold the glasses steady, but I had seen the rider, and I had seen the horse he rode. Crossing Boyd Creek below me was Turk Fontayne and my horse Quicksilver!

Winslow woke at the sound of my spurs as I strode through the meadow grass toward the horses.

"Stay here, Winslow," I told him, "I've got to ride down to the gulch. Be back in just a little bit."

I figured the five horses I'd seen were stolen and that Fontayne was moving them to a hidden corral someplace nearby. I determined to follow him and find his hideout, then take Winslow back to town and out of danger before I came back. I slipped the hobbles off the Morgan, tightened the cinch, and swung into the saddle. The big gelding was moving even as I mounted, and I reined him downhill through the trees.

The hillside was steep, dropping off into a tangled maze of thick brush, sliderock, and fallen timber a hundred feet below, but there among the tall trees were game trails and I eased the big horse down one of them in a zigzag series of switchbacks. As I broke out into the sunlight that cold hand of fear I'd felt before clutched my heart again. What *was* it? What was the danger?

Suddenly, from someplace above the slope and behind me I heard the snapping of dry branches back in the trees. I turned my head just in time to see the glint of light reflecting off metal, and knew I was too late.

The bullet struck me high in the back like the blow of a sledgehammer and knocked me out of the saddle. At almost the same moment I heard the sound of the shot and fell hard and clattering onto the loose rock and on down the steep slope. Stunned and dazed, I came to a hard and sudden stop amid the fallen timber and thick brush at the bottom, knowing I was hard hit but not hurting greatly yet. I felt like I'd been bored through by a white-hot poker; my breath rushed out of me as from a bellows.

I grabbed my shoulder where the bullet had struck and felt the warm wetness of my blood. My hand came away red (Remember *red,* Winslow?) and my vision commenced to fade and grow dim. Then all the world went black, and I fell away into a darkness so deep it had no light in it at all.

TWENTY-FOUR
Back from the Edge

I was eight years old on that long ago winter morning, waking from sleep in our house at Dry Creek. Outside, a blizzard shrieked like an angry monster, rattling windows and scatter-shooting volleys of dry snow and sleet against the cabin's north wall. Even beneath the goose down comforter I could feel the monster's icy fingers reaching for my vitals. Chilled to the bone, I shuddered. Tiny snow crystals invaded the room through gaps in the chinking, glittering like gold dust in the lamplight. The vapor of my breath clouded white in the cold air. Underneath the covers I hugged myself, closed my eyes, and tried to fall back to sleep. I wondered if I would ever be warm again, and I recall the question that came to my child's mind that morning was, "Is this how it feels to die?"

I was awake again. I lay sprawled in the tangled brush and deadfall above Boyd creek, cold as a carp and hurting. I tried to move, but could not; my brain issued its orders but my body told my brain to go to Hell. "You led us out of the trees back yonder and got us backshot," said my wounded body, "I don't much feel like moving right now, and by damn I ain't a-going to."

At first my eyes joined in the mutiny, too. They refused to open, taking refuge in darkness instead. Tired of fighting, I let them be. I lay still awhile, feeling the pain in my shoulder and yielding to it. Then, after a time, I managed to open my eyes and put them to work. I glanced about, looking for some sign of my horse. I seemed to recall him bolting as I left the saddle, but had no idea whether he'd run off or stayed somewheres nearby. Deep in the tangle of brush and down timber where I lay, I could see only a jumble of branches, loose rock, and undergrowth.

There was no sound. Even the birds had gone quiet in the aftermath of the rifle shot. My brain issued its orders again, trying to get my body up and moving, but it wasn't having much luck. From high up the mountainside came the sound of a horse's hoof scraping rock and the low murmur of voices—was the shooter coming back to finish his work?

My headlong fall down the slope had left me laying facedown in the dense brush, but I had somehow managed to turn onto my right side. My holstered revolver lay beneath me. I'd have to roll over to reach it and I feared the bushwhacker would likely blow out my lamp before ever I could.

The pain in my shoulder was worse. I wanted to cry out—yell, cuss, or groan but knew I must not. My options were to fight, beg for my life, or play possum, and only the last notion seemed to hold any hope at all. A man who'd backshoot a feller wouldn't be much inclined to show mercy. Pulling my pistol, even if I was able to, would only be a shortcut to the boneyard.

So I laid there like a shot deer, hurting so bad I could hardly think. On the slope above me I heard again the sound of horses' hooves and the low murmur of voices. A scatter of loose rock, apparently dislodged by the riders, cascaded down the hillside and into the deadfall where I lay.

The men were close. I could hear the squeak of saddle leather as a rider shifted his weight. Somebody spat. A voice, nasal and high-pitched, sounded clear as a bell in the stillness. "Som'bitch is down there somewheres. That was a helluva shot, if I do say so myself. Must've been anyway two hunnert yards."

The second voice was flat, cold, familiar somehow. "More like a hundred and fifty. I was watchin' through the field glasses as you fired."

Silence. Then, "Did you *know* the feller, Portugee?"

"Yeah, I knew him," said Portugee Gossert, "Turk and me stole that blood-bay thoroughbred off him back in June. Fool kid's been doggin' our trail ever since."

Nasal voice giggled. "Well, I do believe his doggin' days are over," he said.

"I hope so. Kid was gettin' on my nerves."

Again, silence. A wave of pain swept through me like a prairie fire. I closed my eyes and rode it out. Nasal voice spoke again.

"You reckon he's dead?"

"Dead or dyin'. You want to go down and find out?"

"Hell, no. My old lady only raised *one* stupid child, and that was my *brother.* Like you say, the kid is likely dead or dyin'. But if he ain't and I go down in that tangle—"

I heard no more. Hot winds fanned the flames of my torment, and I fell off into darkness once again.

It was full dark when next I came to myself, and the pain in my back and shoulder was grievous indeed. My shed blood had pooled beneath me and had soaked into the black dirt where I lay. My mouth was dry; I felt I could have drunk up the entire Missouri River. I commenced to worry about poor blind Winslow, and I wondered where the bushwhackers had gone.

Crawling a foot at a time, I dragged myself clear of the deadfall and into a clear space. The moon was high, its pale glow casting shadows black as ink among the trees. I lay sprawled and panting amid a litter of pine needles and fallen branches, too weak to move any farther and cold as a snake. My teeth were chattering and I couldn't seem to stop shaking.

I tried to set up but found I wasn't able and fell back onto the earth again. I couldn't seem to make my mind work. My vision had gone blurry again and my tongue felt dry and too big for my mouth. Then I heard something coming toward me through the undergrowth, and I caught my breath. Panic stampeded through my mind as I remembered Gossert's voice and his pardner's. Had they decided I wasn't dead? Were they coming back to kill me after all? Or was something *else* coming—a bear, maybe, or a mountain lion?

Somehow fear got me to my feet but I fell again. Too weak either to fight or flee, I laid there while the sound grew nearer. Then, suddenly, it was upon me. I looked up to see Garrett Sinclair leading his blue roan through the moon-shadowed timber. When he caught sight of me he dropped his bridle reins and rushed to my side.

"It's all right, Merlin," he said, "Everything's gonna be all right, son." I'm not sure why, but somehow I believed him.

I awoke to pain and the smell of coffee. The pain in my shoulder throbbed in rhythm with my heartbeat, but I was relieved I still had a heartbeat. It was daylight, and I was on my back in bed, my head and shoulders propped up on pillows. With my right hand I touched my wound and found it swathed in bandages. My eyes didn't focus well at first, but when they did I saw Garrett Sinclair's weathered face. He sat in a chair at my bedside, a cup of coffee in his hand, and his grin touched off a riot of wrinkles when he saw me looking at him.

"With your luck you ought to take up card-playing," he said, "the bullet put a hole in your shoulder blade and busted a couple of ribs, but it passed straight through you like crap through a goose. You've lost a great plenty of blood, but the slug didn't hit anything vital. Barring complications, you ought to be good as new in two or three weeks."

"If I'm so dang lucky," I said, "how come I got shot in the first place?"

I closed my eyes again. Recollection came in bits and pieces, like colored glass in a kaleidoscope. Riding out of the trees. Wink of sunlight off gunmetal. The bullet's hammer blow. Falling down the mountain and into darkness. Waking to pain. Sound of horses. The voices and the fear. Then blackness again, and waking to Garrett and his roan.

"How—how did you find me?"

"You can thank Winslow for that. The boy stayed there in the meadow like you told him to, but he worried. Said there was something in your voice that made him afraid for you. Later, he heard the rifle shot and waited some more, an hour maybe.

"Finally figured you weren't coming back, maybe because you couldn't. Proud of the boy; he didn't lose his head. He caught up his horse, gave the animal its head, and the little sorrel brought him all the way back to the barn. Winslow said he just slipped the bridle off, took hold of the saddlehorn, and let Carson carry him home. He told me what you'd told him—that you were at Ruby Gulch, above Boyd Creek. That's where I found you. Seen your horse first—that chesty Morgan had run halfway up the mountain. Reckon he'd be runnin' yet if his bridle reins hadn't caught in some deadfall."

"I shouldn't have left the boy that way, Garrett. I'm sorry—"

"I figure you had your reasons. We can talk about that later."

"Who—who patched me up?"

Garrett took a sip of his coffee and smiled. "The town of Maiden has one doctor, but he was visiting his lady friend over in Lewistown when I brought you in. Thanks to the war and the cowtowns of Kansas I probably know more about bullet wounds than he does, so I took on the job myself."

Just then the door opened and Lee Sun Yung came in. The old man carried a brass tray which held a teapot, cup, spoon, and couple of dark-colored medicine bottles. Garrett stood up.

"Lee Sun Yung is a pretty fair healer himself. Take whatever heathen nostrum he gives you and try to get

355

some sleep. I'll let Winslow know you're still among the living."

I started to protest. I wanted to tell Garrett I'd found the men I'd been hunting and that I'd seen my horse Quicksilver, but he was already on his way out. He stepped around the bed, squeezed my good arm as he passed, and left the room.

I don't know exactly what kind of "heathen nostrum" Lee Sun Yung gave me, but whatever it was caused me to fall into a deep and restful sleep. I woke up refreshed and hungry as a January bear. I later learned I had slept through that first day and well into the following night but at the time I had no idea I'd been asleep that long. The lamp beside my bed had either been blowed out or had went out on its own, and the room was dark as a tomb.

Because I found my mind more agile and less confused, I recalled more quickly than previously the events of the past few days. At first I just laid back and enjoyed the peaceful, easy feeling, but after a bit I commenced to grow restless. Something was different, something was missing, somehow, but what? Then all at once I realized—the pain in my shoulder had almost completely disappeared. I changed positions and the hurt came back, but nowhere near as bad as before. Whatever medicine the old gent had gave me sure had done its job, and I was grateful.

As I growed more used to the dark I sensed, then saw, someone in the chair beside my bed. "Who's there?" I asked, "How come you're a-settin' there in the dark?"

Winslow's bright laughter answered my question. "Dark and light are pretty much the same to me," the boy said, "How are you, Merlin?"

Well, of course I felt like a dang fool, but I tried not to show it. "Fine as frog hair, Winslow," I said, "Lee Sun Yung's medicine and my snooze done me a world of good."

Winslow was quiet for a time. Then he said, "I was scared when you didn't come back. I stayed in the meadow like you said to for a long time."

"I know you did, pardner. I sure am glad you stepped across old Carson and rode for help. I'd be a gone gosling if your grandpa hadn't found me."

"What happened, Merlin? Who shot you?"

"A bad man, Winslow—a horse thief. I believe there's at least three such evil-doers up yonder in the Judiths. I figure they shot me because they feared I would find their hideout."

Again, Winslow fell silent. He got up from the chair and stood facing me in the darkened room. "Merlin?" he said.

"Yeah?"

Winslow's voice was tight with feeling. "You are gonna be all right, aren't you?"

"You bet! I'm too tough to let a dry-gulchin' stop me."

As he passed my bedside Winslow surprised me. He suddenly bent and hugged me hard around my neck. I felt a wetness on my cheek and realized the boy had been crying. The thought passed through my mind that one thing both blind and seeing eyes have in common is tears. A moment later Winslow was out the door and gone.

"Tough" is the very *last* thing I felt like.

For the rest of the week I mostly set around healing up and growing stronger. Lee Sun Yung kept his eagle eye upon me, cooking my meals and doctoring me with his mystery medicines. The old gent pretty much had the Injun sign on the entire household, and I have to admit I was no exception. I never have been much of a tea drinker, but I swallered his brew by the potful rather than risk putting him on the fight.

Winslow and me must have played a hundred games of checkers. I even managed to beat him a time or two, although to this day I'm not certain he didn't let me win out of kindness. We read together some, too, by which I mean he would get me to read his favorite stories to him. I recall I read him most of a book by Nathaniel Hawthorne called *Grandfather's Chair,* and we both laughed ourselves silly over *Roughing It,* by Mark Twain.

By the following week I felt pert enough to help out with the chores, carrying water and splitting kindling for the stove one-handed. I helped Lee Sun Yung in the kitchen some, too, although I tend to be better at wolfing down grub than cooking it. I fetched and carried, set the table, and washed up the dishes.

Since I'd been laid up, Garrett spent most of his time over in town at the livery stable. He'd leave home at daybreak, come back at suppertime, then go back for awhile in the evening. There was much I wanted to tell him, but what I had to say was for his ears alone. Somehow it was hard to find the right time.

Garrett had never asked, but I'd made up my mind to tell him the whole story about losing my horse to Fontayne, Gossert, and poor old Clarence, and of all I'd been through trying to track them hardcases down. I particularly wanted to tell him about seeing Fontayne and Quicksilver the day I'd been shot. I wanted to let him know why I'd left Winslow alone in the meadow, and I figured I surely owed him the courtesy of letting him in on my plans, such as they were.

When I was able, I took to walking outdoors. At first it was hard even to reach the little barn out back of the house, but each day I'd go a little farther until I finally made it all the way uptown. My shoulder wound was on the mend, although my left arm was still weak and all but useless to me. I carried the limb in a sling made from my black silk bandanna and even though I worked arm and hand all I could, full healing seemed slow in coming.

On Friday of the second week since my ambush I walked to Maiden and stopped in to see Garrett at the livery stable. I could tell by the way his face lit up when I walked into the barn that he was glad to see me. His blue eyes sparkled and he grinned like a kid eating a watermelon.

"About time you came back to work," he said, "I was about to go out and hire a *good* man."

He led me into the office and produced a quart bottle

of Tennessee whiskey from a desk drawer. Pouring three fingers each in two enamel cups, he handed one to me and raised the other in salute.

"To your recovery," he said, "and to your health." We drank then, and the whiskey went down smooth as silk and glowed warm when it hit the belly.

For a long moment I was silent. Garrett Sinclair had paid my wages; he had taken me into his house as if I was a member of his own family. He'd shared his past with me. Alone, he'd rode into the mountains by moonlight to find me. He had doctored me, fed me, and seen me cared for. Garrett had been a true friend; he had saved my life. All of which made it hard for me to tell him what I had to—that the time had come for me to leave Maiden, and why. I sat there by the cold stove and stared down at the amber fluid in the cup, trying to find a way to break the silence between us. As it turned out, Garrett did that for me, too.

"Rest easy, son," he said, "I've known you'd be movin' on since the day you rode into Maiden. I've had your horse grained and trail-ready for a week now."

"I—I'm obliged to you, Garrett. I'd like you to know the why of it."

"There's no need. A man does what he has to."

"I'd like to tell you."

Garrett came around from behind the desk and poured another two fingers of the good Tennessee into my cup. "In that case," he said, "I'm all ears."

Getting started was like opening the spillway of a

dam. My words began in a trickle, slow and halting as I reached back in memory to Dry Creek, to old Walt, and a horse named Quicksilver. I told how Fontayne and his boys had stole the thoroughbred, and of the way Orville had gone down before Gossert's gun on the street in Shenanigan.

I told Garrett about Pandora and our trail together, of hailstorm and hoosegow, and of the killing near Merino. I recounted how I'd trailed the horse thieves to the outlaw camp where vigilantes had hung Cock-eyed Clarence and me to a tree. I told of my rescue by Pandora and Colonel Charlie and how we'd jumped Fontayne and Gossert at Lewistown on Independence Day. I related the events at the creek where Pandora broke her leg and where my Little Buck horse died of Gossert's bullet and my own.

I spoke of my ride to Maiden. I recalled how Garrett had bade me come in out of the rain. Finally, I told him about the day above Ruby Gulch when I watched Fontayne and Quicksilver cross Boyd Creek with the loose horses. I told him how I'd asked Winslow to wait for me in the meadow and how I'd hoped to locate the outlaws' hideout. I told him about the shooting, playing dead while Gossert and the third man set their horses on the hillside above me, and the miracle of looking up out of my pain and seeing Garrett coming through the trees by moonlight.

Finally, I slowed down and stopped. All the water had run out of the dam. I had said it all, or nearly so.

"I don't know where or how it will end," I said, "I

just know I have to keep a-goin.' It's a thing I have to finish."

Garrett had said nothing as I related my story. He'd just lit up his pipe, set back in his chair, and sipped his whiskey as he listened. Now he straightened, tapped the ashes from his cold briar, and smiled.

"Then," he said, "I reckon all that's left is for me to help you get ready"

TWENTY-FIVE
Into the Mist

Garrett Sinclair was as good as his word. First thing next morning he led me down to the gunsmith's shop at the end of the street and introduced me to the proprietor. "Shake hands with Wolfgang Klein-schmidt, Merlin," he said, "He ain't much for social-izin,' but what the man don't know about firearms ain't worth knowin'. Wolf—meet my friend, Merlin Fanshaw."

The gunsmith was a short, tidy man of about forty, with thinning gray hair plastered across his pate as though he'd arranged each hair one at a time. Behind thick spectacles his faded blue eyes were alert and alive. He smiled a tight smile as he reached across the counter to shake my hand.

"How do you do, Herr Fanshaw," he said, "Welcome to my shop."

I looked around. The shop was dark, but neat as a

pin. Revolvers and derringers lay in gleaming rows within a glass-topped display case. Along the wall, rifles, carbines, and shotguns stood in ranks, secured in their places by a brass padlock and a thin steel chain. Through an open door at the rear of the shop I saw a lathe, vise, and a variety of hand tools laid out atop a sturdy workbench. The smell of gun oil, black powder, and solvent hung heavy in the air.

"Merlin here has need of a good second weapon," Garrett told the gunsmith, "something in a .44-40. He's already got him one revolver and a carbine in that caliber."

The gunsmith looked thoughtful as he considered the weapons inside the display case. Making his decision, he slid open the back of the case, carefully selected two revolvers and laid them side by side atop the counter.

Picking up one of the weapons, he said, "We have here der Schmidt und Wesson Russian Model. Single-action, top-breaking, with a six-shot cylinder und seven-inch barrel. Cartridges contain 23 grains powder und 246 grains lead."

He broke the piece open and handed it to me butt-first for my inspection. I had seen such revolvers before, though I'd never owned one. They were handsome weapons, but my eye had already caught the second revolver he'd taken from the case—a Single Action Colt Frontier with one-piece ivory grips, similar to the one I already carried. Like the Smith and Wesson, it sported a seven-inch barrel. I picked it up and spun the cylinder.

"I'm partial to the Colt's," I said, "growed up with my Pa's old Dragoon. I like the balance, and the way the grip fits the hand."

"A good choice," said Kleinschmidt, "und a powerful weapon. It shoots a 255-grain bullet, propelled by forty grains of black powder."

"I like a Colt's myself," Garrett said, "though they do tend to be a mite delicate in their innards. But they're reliable weapons all the same, and a man can generally find a way to fire them no matter what happens."

He took the revolver from my hand, cocked the hammer and let it down easy under his thumb with a soft squeeze of the trigger. "Smooth as oil," he said, turning to the gunsmith, "I see you've done your usual job of fine-tunin' this piece." Garrett handed the weapon back to me. "My friend will take it," he told Kleinschmidt, "he'll need four boxes of cartridges, too.

"Wait a minute," I said, "how much is that gonna set me back?"

"Thirty-five dollars," said Kleinschmidt, "und I throw in the belt und holster."

"Done," said Garrett, ignoring me. He glanced at the long arms displayed along the wall, "He'll also require a shotgun—that short-barreled Greener ten-gauge oughter do. And two boxes of shells."

"You figure I really *need* this arsenal?" I asked.

"I only hope it'll be *enough,*" Garrett said.

By the time we'd walked back uptown to the Livery Barn my shoulder was hurting again and I found myself sweating and short of breath. I wasn't near as well healed as I'd have liked to be, but with both Colts belted about my waist and the scattergun in hand I surely was "well heeled" in another sense. Garrett didn't seem to notice my condition, but throwed a saddle on his blue roan as I gritted my teeth and done likewise with my Morgan. Just before we stepped up onto the horses I saw Garrett pick up a gunny sack full of empty bottles and tin cans and tie it on behind the cantle of his saddle.

"Let's ride, son," he said, "School's in session."

About a mile from town Garrett reined up in a sunlit clearing that faced a deep cut in the hillside. A red dirt bank ran maybe a hundred feet along the base of the hill, and a fallen pine tree, nearly three feet thick and white with age, lay rotting in the high grass. Garrett got down off the roan and set bottles and cans along the tree about three feet apart.

"Now, son," he said, "before I commence with Garrett Sinclair's short course on the art of deadly force, I feel duty bound to point out one or two alternatives to your plans. Maybe you've already thought about 'em and throwed 'em in the discards, but I figure I need to mention 'em just in case. When a feller takes on a man-huntin' job he needs to have a clear picture of the task at hand.

"Now the fact is this county does have a sheriff, of sorts. You could let him go after them horse-thieves. You've already been shot once; next time could turn out to be permanent."

"Uh-huh. You figure this lawman would get the job done?"

"No. To be honest, I don't. First off, this is a big county. The man's got too much ground to cover. Besides that, he's inclined to be a mite over-prudent. He don't figure he's paid enough to take serious risks."

"He could be right. Anyway, it's my horse that got stole."

"Which leads us to a second possibility. Instead of ridin' out all by your lonesome, like Sir Galahad a-huntin' the Grail, you could take along some help—sort of even the odds."

"Like who? You?"

"No, son, not me. I think you know I would go. Truth is, it's more my kind of play than yours, or anyway used to be. But I've got my grandson to care for now, which means my risk-takin' days are over. There are men in this town, though, who'd rent their guns out for the price of a bottle of whiskey."

"Worth every penny of it, too, I'll bet."

"Point well taken. Which pretty much makes it Sir Galahad time."

Garrett studied me for a long moment. Then turning away, he reached into his saddlebags and brought out a gunbelt and holster containing a short-barreled

Colt's revolver. The leather was worn and shiny, and Garrett's hands buckled the belt about his hips with a smooth and practiced motion.

"Haven't worn this rig in years," he said, "but there was a time when it was more a part of me than my hat."

The revolver seemed to jump from the leather into his hand. I had never been all that good with a short gun but I'd known a few men who were. Garrett Sinclair was as good as most any I'd seen. The six-gun came alive in his hand, spinning, flashing, dancing in the sunlight. I watched as he did forward rolls, reverse rolls, border shifts, holster flip draws, and road agent spins.

Garrett stood, his feet wide apart in the grass of the clearing, his face a mask that told me nothing. Abruptly, he dropped into a crouch and fired once, twice, three times, each shot breaking a bottle or spinning a can off the log. He holstered the revolver, turned, spun back, drew and shattered another bottle. Then he turned, firing a fifth shot behind his back and sending a tomato tin spinning high into the air.

Garrett relaxed, shucking the empties from the smoking revolver and reloading. "From what you've told me about the men you're huntin'," he said, "that's what you're liable to be up against."

He grinned, holstering the Colt's with a flourish. "But don't let it trouble you, son. The practice of deadly force has a heap more to do with determination than speed. The race don't always go to the swift, and oft-times a tortoise has managed to gun down a hare, so to speak."

Garrett paused. He seemed to be remembering, maybe thinking back to the cowtowns of Kansas, to a time and place where each day could bring the danger of death by gunfire and a man's life could end sudden and hard because of a moment's carelessness or a lapse in concentration.

Garrett shook his head and turned back to me. "Oh, speed is all right, as far as it goes," he said, "and it's generally a good idea to get your shot off before the other feller does—but only if it hits the mark. First and foremost, I want you to set your mind on hittin' the target dead center. Do it as fast as you can, but never shave accuracy for speed. It ain't generally the *slows* that puts a man in the bone orchard, it's the *misses*. Get steady and calm in your mind, determine that you will hit the target, and go to work."

In the hour that followed I ran through the better part of two boxes of cartridges, but I came to where I could hit whatever I fired at with reason-able speed at up to maybe thirty yards. Getting used to the light trigger pull and smooth, quick action of the new Colt's wasn't easy at first, but by hour's end the weapon had become almost a part of me.

Through it all, Garrett was at my side, offering advice, correcting my thinking, and guiding my hand. "Get the idea of 'fair play' out of your mind altogether," he said, "killin' ain't a game. When you go up against a man who's tryin' to snuff your candle only one thing matters—that you live and he don't.

"Go into the fight with every advantage you can muster. Go in with your gun already drawn, with the sun at your back and in the other man's eyes, charge him from on horseback, ambush him from behind a tree, shoot him in the back, belly, or wherever, shoot him 'til he's down, then keep a-shootin' him 'til he's dead. Never forget: he'll be tryin' his damnedest to do it to you.

"Most of all, be single-minded and sure. There's no room for doubt in a gun battle. If you ain't plum' rock-solid certain, you'd best stay to home and let them hardcases keep your racehorse."

I holstered the Colt's with a flourish that almost equaled Garrett's. "I've come too far to turn back now," I told him, "besides, I figure it ain't how *long* a man lives, but *how.*"

I spent my last evening in Maiden with Garrett and the family at his little cabin in the trees. Lee Sun Yung had cooked up a fine supper of roast venison, spuds, and all the trimmings, and we four set up to the table together the way we'd done a dozen times before. We joked and laughed as we always did, and if a stranger had looked in on us he'd have thought we hadn't a worry in the world.

But that evening was different, and we all knew it. Garrett had told Lee Sun Yung of my plans, but the three of us made every effort to keep the truth from Winslow.

It was all to no avail, of course; Winslow seemed able to sense things more than other people, and the boy could read more in a silence too long than most folks could learn from a two-hour lecture. Winslow knew, all right, but like the rest of us he pretended everything was the same as usual, that all was well.

I couldn't help it; there was little enough to lighten my spirits that evening, but somehow the situation struck me funny. There we were—all four of us aware of the dangerous course I was set upon, yet acting as though we weren't.

After supper, I helped Lee Sun Yung with the dishes, then walked outside with Garrett while he smoked his pipe. A cold wind had come up, and it swept down the valley, bending the grass before it and rattling the nervous leaves of the aspen trees. Fast moving clouds lay ragged against the mountains like torn and dirty cotton, and the sky had took on the color of lead. I could smell the coming rain.

Garrett and me stood close together on the porch, each of us thinking our own thoughts, but sharing them not at all. There was no need for talk between us; we had pretty much said it all. So we shared the silence.

I heard the screen door open and close softly behind me. Overhead, thunder boomed and rumbled, and as if on order the rain commenced to march across the valley floor. Turning, I watched Winslow come outside and walk toward his grand-dad and me. His expression was troubled, and he held his head high and turned into the freshening wind.

"Merlin?" he said.

I reached out and took his hand. "You bet, Winslow. I'm right here."

For a moment he was silent. Then he said, "I know you're goin' away tomorrow. I think maybe I even know why. It has somethin' to do with the men who shot you, don't it?"

So much for keeping the truth from Winslow. "Yeah, it does," I said, "They've got somethin' that belongs to me—my horse. I aim to get it back."

"Will—will you come back and see us again—after?"

"Sure, I will. We're pardners, ain't we?"

"You bet. Merlin?"

"Yeah?"

"I'm gonna pray for you, okay?"

While I was still trying to swaller the lump in my throat Winslow gave me a quick hug and dashed back inside. My face was wet, and it wasn't all rain.

I slept that night, or anyway tried to, in the hayloft above the livery barn. I laid there in my blankets and stared into the darkness as the rain pattered on the roof and thunder rolled above the mountains.

Fear came upon me there in that darkened loft and covered me like a wet and moldy shroud. My mouth went dry as dust and there was a hollow, empty feeling deep inside my gut. I saw again in memory the cold, leering face of Portugee Gossert. I remembered the quickness of his hand and his six-gun spitting fire. I saw again my friend Orville, lung-shot and dying in the street. I recalled the blood lust I'd seen behind the killer's crazy yellow eyes. I felt again the hammer blow of the rifle shot that day in the Judiths as it took me high in the back and throwed me off my horse and down the mountain. I looked down once more into the bottomless pit where death lives and felt panic roll over me like a wave.

It seemed like I was two people one a man with a job to do and the other a child, scared of the dark and wanting its Ma. Just as a man might hold his ground and slowly calm a bronc he was breaking, I stood firm against my fear. After a time, the fright growed less and commenced to fade. The tightness in my muscles eased. My mind gave up its alarms and settled into a peaceful, easy place. As the rain drummed a rhythm on the barn roof, I let go of dread and drifted into a slumber too deep even for dreams.

It was 4:22 by Pa's silver watch when I awoke. The rain had slackened, but the morning was cold and gray as ashes in the thin predawn light. Water dripped from board awnings and stood puddled all along the muddy street. Across the valley, fog snaked among the dark pines and lay low upon the meadowlands like clouds that had fell to earth.

I fired up the stove and put the coffee on while I curried and saddled the Morgan. I traded my bright yellow slicker for an old black one Garrett kept in the office. I wanted to be dry where I was going, but I had no particular wish to draw attention to myself. Standing in the wide doorway of the livery barn, I breakfasted on beef jerky and coffee while I looked out onto the rain-soaked street. Then I slipped my Winchester into its boot ahead of my right stirrup, hung the ten-gauge by a thong from the saddlehorn, stepped up onto the Morgan, and rode out into the cold morning.

With the coming of daybreak the rain tapered off to a drizzle, but the trail that led to Ruby Gulch was slick as grease, and the big gelding chose his footing with care as we climbed. The trail rose steadily up the mountain in a series of switchbacks, and by the time I reined the Morgan up for a breather he was wet to the hide and steaming in the cold morning air.

Even at the mountain's crest the air was still. Only the deep breathing of the big horse and the sound of his footfall on the muddy trail broke the quiet. Gray as a shroud, fog drifted slow and mysterious, now settling, now lifting, as it swirled among the trees. Scenes and views took shape out of the mist, then faded and disappeared as the fog closed in again. My hearing seemed unnatural in its sharpness; I could hear the creak of saddle, the rustle of oilskin, even the scratch of whiskers against my collar. Now and then I'd catch the scolding chitter of a squirrel or a fragment of birdsong, but mostly the fog smothered sound and left damp silence in its place.

• • •

It was nearly nine o'clock when I topped out on the long ridge over-looking Ruby Gulch. The fog had growed thicker, if anything, but even so I took care not to show myself in the open, holding instead to the cover of the trees. I pulled the Morgan up, straining my eyes to study the valley below, and listened. Fingers of mist crept through the dark pines, reaching and drifting. Water gathered on the dark branches overhead, falling upon my hat and slicker with a pattering sound. Somewhere back in the trees a pine cone fell skittering to the forest floor. I heard the deep, steady breathing of the gelding, the soft rattle of the roller on the bit in his mouth, but nothing else. A blanket of silence seemed to cover all of creation.

I checked my weapons. Slipping the Winchester from its scabbard, I levered a cartridge into the chamber. With my finger on the trigger I eased the hammer down from full to half-cock position and slid the rifle back into its boot. I broke open the Greener and checked its loads. The twin shells, each loaded with nearly 4 drams of black powder and a full charge of double-ought buckshot, nestled ready beneath the hammers. I closed the gun and looped its lanyard back around the saddlehorn.

Finally, I drew the two Colt's, opened their loading gates, and rotated the cylinders. As usual, I'd loaded only five chambers in both revolvers, letting the hammers down on the sixth for safety. Now I loaded those, too, and eased the weapons back into their holsters. I touched the big horse with my spurs and started him down through the trees to the valley below.

At the bottom, nearly at the place I'd been bush-whacked, I held again to the trees as I scanned the open land beyond with the field glasses. The fog kept moving in and lifting, and while I cussed its contrariness I was grateful, too—maybe I couldn't see as well as I'd like to, but neither could I be seen. After a time I rode the gelding out of the trees and crossed Boyd Creek.

If the horse-thieves were still in the area, I figured they'd be holed up somewheres near a hidden pasture or horse-trap where they could hold their stolen stock. Riding slow across the open space, I studied the lay of the land. Mist still clung to the peaks, but it seemed to be breaking up and lifting below.

Ahead, a narrow trail skirted the trees beyond the creek and wound through a willow thicket that led across a rock slide and into a narrow canyon. I had many times played the fool in my young life, but even at my most careless I'd not have crossed that slide while in enemy country for a thousand-dollar bank note. Taking a horse across that loose shale would make enough noise to wake the dead. I reined the Morgan off the trail and started him up the forested slope to the ridge top.

Thirty minutes later, I found the robbers' roost. I'd worked my way up to the top of the steep slope that overlooked the valley. Fog still shrouded the bottoms, so I'd tied my horse to a young spruce tree and found myself a vantage point where I could glass the country. Beneath me, the mist eddied and swirled as before, hiding the canyon floor from view. Then, like a curtain going up on a stage play, the haze lifted. Sunlight broke through bright and clear, and the outlaws' hideout jumped into sharp focus.

A low cabin hugged a bend in the narrow creek that meandered across the valley's floor. Smoke billowed from a stovepipe, and a saddle horse grazed in its hobbles alongside the creek. Beyond the cabin, partly hidden among a grove of aspen trees, a dozen horses stood inside a small pasture. One of them I'd have recognized even without the glasses—the handsome, blood-bay thoroughbred that had brought me so many miles, the horse known as Quicksilver.

I stared at the scene below for what seemed a long time, but I know it could only have been a minute or two. I was surprised how calm I felt. The fears of the previous night had faded like dew under the morning sun, and in their place was a kind of bold sureness I can't explain, even now. I had come to the end of a long, hard trail, and I felt ready—I *was* ready—for whatever the showdown would bring.

Below, at the cabin, something moved. As I steadied the glasses I saw the cabin door had opened and that a man stood in the doorway. He leaned against the doorsill, hat on the back of his head and his thumbs hooked in the belts that held his two pistols. Through the field glasses the hard, pinched face seemed to be staring straight at me. It was Portugee Gossert, and no mistake.

He spat, turned, and went back inside, closing the door behind him. As quickly as it had lifted, the fog closed in again. The cabin, the horses, the small creek all seemed to fade and disappear in the mist, but I had seen what I needed to see. Gossert was in the cabin, and probably Fontayne, too. But who else was there? What about the nasal-voiced man who shot me? Was he down there? And how many others might there be?

I turned and started the climb back up through the trees to where I'd left the Morgan. I moved through the mist at a steady pace, pausing now and then to listen before moving uphill again. The curtain of the mist parted once more. There, not thirty yards away, a slim, bearded man sat cross-legged beneath a towering pine.

He held a rifle cradled in the crook of his arm, and he was looking off down toward the valley floor, just as I had only moments before. He wore a shapeless black hat and a tattered army overcoat, and it came to me he must be a lookout, on guard against unwanted visitors. The man heard me coming. His head jerked around and the rifle followed, but he was a day late and a dollar short. His eyes bugged out and his jaw dropped as he seen me; my new Colt's was cocked and pointed square between his eyes!

"Drop the rifle and show me your armpits," I told him, "or you won't have a head to put that hat on."

He must have believed me, for he dropped the rifle like it was hot. His hands shot straight up. "Lordy!" he choked, "where—where did *you* come from?"

I'd heard that voice before. It was the voice of the man who'd shot me in the back, then boasted to Gossert of his marksmanship. "I came from your worst damn nightmare, bushwhacker," I said, "and you've got less than a second to live unless you get real helpful."

"Lordy! Don't shoot me, kid—I'll do whatever you say!"

"Who's down below in the cabin?"

"Why, uh—nobody," he said, which is when I laid all seven inches of the Colt's barrel hard across his jaw. He set down like a dropped grain sack, real fear in his eyes now.

"Lordy! They's—they's *two* fellers down there—Portugee Gossert and Turk Fontayne. Who the hell *are* you, kid?"

I struck him hard behind his ear with the long-barreled Colt's and the backshooter collapsed in a heap.

"Well," I told him, "I ain't a *kid* no more, for one thing."

TWENTY-SIX
Valley of the Shadow

The bushwhacker lay on his belly with his face in the dirt. Bright blood and spit trickled from his open mouth and mixed with the earth beneath him, but I felt no pity. Only weeks before he had shot me in the back from ambush with no more thought than a man might give to swatting a fly. Had I been of a vengeful nature

I would no doubt have took the feller's life then and there. Instead, I merely left him with a short snooze, which would be followed by a headache. I figured it was less by far than he had a-coming.

I pulled his ragged overcoat off and hog-tied him with the catch-rope from my saddle. Then, using his own bandanna, I gagged him. Up the slope a ways I found his horse tied short and high to a green branch, and I loosed the animal and led it down to where I'd left its rider. The horse was a mouse-gray gelding which seemed a mite skittish at being handled by a stranger, but I soon made it known I was in no mood to tolerate his foolishness. Doffing my oilskin and hat, I put on the man's battered sombrero and slipped into his overcoat. The backshooter was a lanky bird, longer of arm and leg than me, but a few turns to the sleeves brought my hands back into view. I hung my shotgun by its lanyard inside the coat and swung up onto the gelding's back. With a touch of my spurs we were off and headed down the mountainside.

The fog was lifting, but the air was cold and dank as I rode out of the trees and onto the valley's floor. Steam rose off the narrow creek I'd seen earlier. Sunshine played tag with shadows and mist. When the light did break through, everything seemed to come into clear focus—every leaf, rock, and grass blade sharp-edged and shining. There was no wind at all. Except for the rippling water of the creek, nothing moved. The valley seemed absolutely still and calm. As I turned the gelding upstream toward the outlaws' hideout, I was surprised how calm I was myself.

I have oft-times wondered whether the sights and sounds of that afternoon were truly as sharp and detailed as I recall them now, or whether the clarity of the day is but a peculiar condition of my memory. All my senses seemed razor keen—magnified, somehow. My ear caught sounds I seldom noticed—the buzzing of a bee amid a patch of daisies, a chipmunk's chitter somewhere far back in the trees, the soft swish-thud of the gelding's hooves on the sod beside the creek.

I watched a yellow butterfly do its jerky dance across the meadow. From the corner of my eye I spied a fast-flying tree swallow as it suddenly changed course to catch a bug in midair, then swooped to its nest in a hollow tree. I smelled the yeasty odor of the earth, the clean scent of pine and spruce, and the smell of woodsmoke as, just ahead, the outlaws' hideout came into view.

The cabin hunkered four-square and squat in a brushy patch along a bend of the creek. The saddled horse I'd seen earlier stood as before, grazing in its hobbles. Hearing my approach, it turned its head and whinnied a shrill greeting to the gray. After the manner of horses, the gelding answered.

Inside my head, a roaring like the distant thunder of a waterfall commenced to grow as I drew near the cabin. The very air seemed to tingle, the way it does before summer lightning. I felt fine-honed and keen as a barber's razor, but calm and steady deep inside at my center. I reined in the gelding with my left hand.

Inside the overcoat, my right found the hammers of the shotgun and eared them back.

Portugee Gossert stepped out of the cabin, a coffee cup in his hand. He took a sip, then glanced up, watching my approach.

"What the hell brings you down so early, Slim?" he said, "It ain't time to go off guard yet."

Beneath the brim of the bushwhacker's floppy hat, I fixed my gaze on Gossert. As always, he wore a pistol on each hip, low and tied down. It wouldn't have surprised me to learn he wore them while he slept. I made no reply, but continued to ride toward him. When I reached a point maybe thirty yards distant it suddenly dawned on him I wasn't who he'd thought I was. He stiffened. He thrust his head forward, the better to see me. His eyes widened, then narrowed to slits.

"*Sonofabitch!* It's *you*—the kid from Shenanigan!" he said.

"I've come for my horse," I said, "I've come a damn long *way* for my horse."

Gossert's laugh was short and ugly. "You're crazy as a shit-house mouse, comin' here," he said, "but I'm glad you did, by god! I've had a bellyfull of you doggin' my trail!"

Gossert moved slowly away from the cabin, but his eyes never left me. He stopped at a chopping block near the woodpile, bent his knees, and carefully set his cup on the block.

At the cabin, Turk Fontayne appeared in the doorway. He stepped outside and stood watching me, arms crossed in front of him and his hand near his holstered six-gun. He looked the same as the first day I saw him, in checkered vest and black frock coat, his shoulder-length hair lank and greasy beneath his wide-brimmed, dirty-white hat. Over by the woodpile, Gossert eased farther to the right, and I saw their plan was to catch me in a cross-fire.

I made my move. I slacked my rein and spurred the gelding hard in the belly! With a startled squeal, the horse jumped out, running straight toward the gunman. Gossert had already started his draw. Eyes wide with surprise, he took a step backward, stumbled, and dodged to one side as the gelding bore down on him like a runaway train. Swinging the shotgun out and up, I fired one-handed as I came abreast of him. The charge caught Gossert hard in the right breast and spun him off his feet and into the low, tangled brush.

Behind me, Fontayne pulled his Colt's and fired point-blank from the cabin door. I felt the wind of the bullet's passing as I turned the gray around and drove back toward the cabin. There was fear on Fontayne's face as I rode down on him. He tried to retreat back inside, but too late; the charge from the scattergun's second barrel took him full in the chest and threw him shattered and dying back through the open door.

The frightened gelding fell to bucking then, and I dropped the shotgun and stepped off just beyond the cabin. My revolver was cocked and in my hand as I ran back to where I'd seen Gossert fall. The brush was thick and high as a man's waist along the creek. I knew that somewhere in its tangle the gunman lay, wounded and waiting.

I stood stock-still, staring at the thicket, watching for movement, alert for some sign of Gossert. Bright blood on the green leaves marked the place where he'd fell, but the gunman himself was nowhere in sight. I held my breath, straining to hear, listening for a rustle in the underbrush or the clatter of gravel. Inside my head, the distant roar of a waterfall began again. Beyond the brush, the creek gurgled, lapping softly over its rocky bed. I heard the muted drone of the bee. Heavy in my hand, the long-barreled Colt's watched the silence before me with its blind, dark eye.

Thirty feet away, Gossert exploded out of the brush like a grizzly from a berry patch. Hatless, his right side soaked with blood and his face twisted with hate, he swept his left-hand pistol up and fired. I felt a sharp tug as the slug tore through my coat sleeve, brought the Colt's to bear with both hands, and touched its trigger. The roar was loud in my ears; my bullet struck Gossert just above his belt buckle with a sound like a struck pumpkin. The gunman grunted; he stared at me, yellow eyes glowing like coals. He tried to raise his pistol but dropped it instead, fell heavily to his knees, and sprawled headlong into the thicket.

I drug him out of the brush and up onto the creek bank, but he was fading fast. He took three long, rasping breaths and died hard. There was a great plenty of blood, more than a person would think.

All at once I felt light-headed and queasy. My hand

commenced to tremble and I could scarcely holster my Colt's. It seemed like my shirt collar was choking me; I was having trouble catching my breath. The waterfall sound inside my head had become a roar. Blindly, I stumbled up the creek a piece, dropped to my knees, and throwed up everything my belly held.

I'd like to believe Quicksilver recognized me when I walked up to him in the horse pasture, but the truth is I don't know if he did or not. I do know I was mighty glad to see him. I ran my hands over the thoroughbred from poll to hoof but could find neither wound nor blemish. Giving the devil his due, I had to admit the horse-thieves had fed and groomed him pretty well. In the late afternoon light his rich, blood-bay color shone just the way I remembered it. As I stroked his sleek neck I told the big horse how fine and handsome he was. He rubbed his soft, velvet nose against my cheek and agreed with me.

By the time I made my way back up the mountainside the slim jasper I'd left gagged and hog-tied seemed plumb overjoyed to see me. Before I turned him loose, though, I told him what had occurred down at the cabin and brought him up to date on the status of Turk Fontayne and Portugee Gossert. I said I was a fortune teller of sorts, and while I maybe couldn't tell him much about his past I had his present and future pretty well figured out.

I predicted he would help me load the bodies of his

pardners in crime on a couple of horses, after which we'd take our cold cargo down to Maiden and find us a peace officer. I said he didn't have to help me if he didn't want to, and that I could probably load *three* dead outlaws all by myself if I had to. His face turned fish belly white and his eyes bugged out something pitiful as he pondered my words. When I seen that my prophecy had took effect I loosed his gag and untied him.

An hour later we took the trail back down to Maiden. The bush-whacker led the way astride his mouse-gray gelding, followed by the corpses of Fontayne and Gossert, belly down across their saddles. I brought up the rear of our grisly caravan, riding the Morgan and leading Quicksilver. I carried my Winchester at the ready, but it wasn't needful. Mister bush-whacker had turned meek as a lamb. He seemed to have lost his spirit of adventure altogether.

Now if you've looked into local history for the year 1884 you may have read that in early September of that year horse-thieves Turk Fontayne and Portugee Gossert were killed resisting arrest by the intrepid county sheriff. According to the newspaper account, the killings occurred during a daring raid by the sheriff on the outlaws' hideout in the Judiths, at which time the sheriff also recovered eleven stolen horses. The truth, as I've told you, is considerably otherwise, but the good sheriff had an election coming up that year and was badly in need of a boost at the polls.

Darkness had fell on Maiden by the time bushwhacker Slim and me rode in, and it was Garrett Sinclair at the livery barn who first laid eyes on our grim procession. It was also Garrett who notified the sheriff. The aforementioned peace officer kept an office in Maiden, but that wasn't where he was found. When Garrett finally located him he was electioneering in his underwear upstairs at Dutch Annie's place—and enforcing the law, no doubt. Anyway, the sheriff was so excited by the news of our arrival that he showed up at the livery barn with his boots on the wrong feet and his shirttail hanging out.

As for bushwhacker Slim, the sheriff took that worthy into custody on a charge of horse theft. I suppose I could have made a fuss about Slim ambushing me, but I'd gunned down the only witness to that unhappy event, which weakened my case against him somewhat. Besides, old Slim seemed to be one of them hard-luck types, and I'd come to feel about half sorry for the poor devil. Last I heard, he'd served his time for horse stealing and had took a job as swamper at a Fort Benton saloon.

Garrett seemed plumb tickled I'd come back in one piece, and of course that made me feel good. He throwed a feast for me at his house with Winslow and Lee Sun Yung that was half reunion and half festival, and we all laughed a good deal and ate about twice what we should have. The only cloud on my triumphal return was that Garrett also seemed about half surprised I'd come back. That troubled me somewhat. I'd set forth on my chancy quest believing he had confidence in me. If I'd thought he hadn't I ain't sure I'd have fared so well. Anyway, I didn't brood for long. I was too happy to be among the living and to have my horse back.

Knowing my feelings for Pandora Pretty Hawk, you might think the very next thing I done was ride over to Lewistown and inquire as to her whereabouts, but I didn't. Instead, I saddled the Morgan, put Quicksilver on a lead rope, and took a ride over to Colonel Charlie's ranch on Careless Creek.

The day was sunny and hot as I rode down off a broad sagebrush flat and through the wide gate that led to the Bannerman ranch house. As it turned out, Colonel Charlie Bannerman himself was outside on the long verandah when I came up the lane, and he looked at me like he couldn't believe his eyes. He stared, took a step off the gallery, and stared again. Then his face lit up and he broke into a toothy smile.

"Young Fanshaw?" he said, "Is that you?"

I grinned. "If it ain't, I've even got myself fooled," I said, "How are you, Colonel?"

"By Jove, it is you!" he said, striding out to meet me, "and you've got Quicksilver! Strord'nary! Bloody marv'lous!"

The colonel took my hand in a grip that could have crushed a pool ball and we pounded each other on the back awhile, grinning like fools. In less time than it takes to tell it, Colonel Charlie helped me turn my horses out and swept me on into the house. "Can't tell you how delighted I am to see you, young Fanshaw,"

he said, "Strord'nary! Must tell me all that's transpired—did you encounter Fontayne and Gossert?
How did you regain possession of Quicksilver? Dash
it all, tell me everything!"

I laughed. "I'm fixin' to, Colonel," I said, "I just
didn't want to interrupt."

His grin got wider and his face turned red. "*Touché*,
as the French say—I'm *not* giving you much chance,
am I?"

He took hold of my elbow and steered me through
the house to a good-sized room that held a big oak
desk, two leather chairs, and what seemed like more
books than a man could read in a lifetime. "My
office," he said, "have a chair while I pour us a drink."

The colonel poured us each four fingers of that
smoky booze from Scotland and over the next hour I
told him all that had transpired since we parted company back in Lewistown. I told him about Garrett Sinclair and his family, how I'd got myself ambushed at
Ruby Gulch, and how a blind boy had saved my bacon.
I told him about my showdown with the outlaws at
their hideout in the Judiths and of finding Quicksilver
in their horse trap. Finally, when I'd told it all, I just set
there for a spell while I considered my next words.
Colonel Charlie seemed to know I was trying to round
up my thoughts. He just set there behind his desk, fingers laced across his paunch, and waited.

It was hard at first to ask the question, but I'd made
my decision. I looked the colonel in his honest blue
eyes, cleared my throat, and spoke my piece. Colonel

Charlie didn't hesitate. He grinned his toothy smile, nodded, and we shook hands. A minute later, he poured us each another drink and our deal was done.

Colonel Charlie said Pandora's broken leg—excuse me again, *limb*—had nearly mended by the time she left Lewistown. He'd brought her out to the ranch as his guest while she completed her healing, and she'd stayed there nearly a month. The colonel said she'd fretted and fussed about me considerable, wondering whether I was still in Maiden or if I'd moved on, and whether I was all right or otherwise. Finally, she'd made her mind up to go back home to Dry Creek. "If Merlin comes back—when he comes back—that's where he'll go," she told him.

She was right. I took one short trip back to Maiden where I said my good-byes, loaded my plunder on the glass-eyed packhorse, and made a beeline for my home town.

Dry Creek hadn't changed a lick. I don't know why I thought it would. It never had, as far back as I could remember. Oh, folks came and went, babies got born, old folks passed away, and the general population spent their days practicing all the sins and virtues, but the town itself never changed. Like the preacher in the good book remarked about the earth, Dry Creek just "abideth forever," or anyway seemeth to.

I turned my horses onto the town's dusty main street an hour past sun-up on the twenty-third day of September in the year of '84. It was good to be back. I'd spent the previous evening camped on a high ridge east of town. I'd rolled out my bed and had laid looking up at the star-studded sky until I began to feel overwhelmed by the bigness of it all. I had traveled a far piece since I left, both in miles and experiences, and I was coming back a different man than the one who'd left. One thing about me hadn't changed, though; as usual, just as I commenced to ponder the big questions like The Meaning of Life, I dropped off to sleep like a milk-fed pup.

I left the horses at old Walt's livery barn and made my way up the street to Ignacio's cafe. The place was nearly full when I walked in. A steady rumble of voices filled the room, together with tobacco smoke and the clatter and clink of eating tools on china. The good smells drifting out of the kitchen told me Ignacio's place hadn't changed all that much either.

My appetite seemed the same as ever, too. I ordered a breakfast of hotcakes, ham and eggs, a side order of biscuits and gravy, and half a pot of coffee. By the time Ignacio brought it out the morning rush had slowed somewhat, and he set down across from me and grinned his big-tooth grin.

"¡Hola, amigo!" says he, "I ain't saw you for a few days, kid—where you been?"

I gave his grin back. "Oh, here and there," I said, "you know."

I took a big swig of coffee, swallered it, and tried to sound casual. "Uh—say, pardner," I said, "you ain't

390

seen that girl—what's her name—Pandora Pretty Hawk, have you? I heard she's back in town."

Ignacio raised an eyebrow. His grin got even wider. "Pandora? *Si, amigo*—she comes in sometimes. Always she asks about you. I think she's sweet on you maybe."

I ignored his droopy-eyed leer. "Uh—you don't know where she's stayin,' do you?"

"*¿Si, como no?* Pandora, she works for Senora Blair, at the boarding house. You gon' to marry with her, kid?"

"Bring me the damn bill," I told him.

Pandora was coming down the back stairs of Blair's boarding house with a load of wet wash when I rode up the alley and drawed rein at the gate. The back yard clothesline already had a couple loads of laundry pinned to it; bedsheets, towels, and tablecloths snapped like flags in the fresh morning breeze. Pandora let the screen door bang shut, picked up the laundry basket, and had just started down the steps when she seen me. She tried to speak, but no words came; instead, a kind of bright squeal like a happy puppy escaped her lips. She dropped her basket, rushed into my arms, and found her voice. "Merlin," she said, "oh, Merlin."

For what seemed a long time I just held her close, dizzied by the feel of her strong, firm body and the sunshine scent of her silky hair. At length, I tried to break away but Pandora drew me back and nestled her head close upon my chest. "I'm not *ready* to stop hugging you yet," she said.

391

Later, as we sat together in the widow Blair's parlor, I told her of my adventures in Maiden. I told her how I'd been backshot by bushwhacker Slim. I described the showdown in the Judiths and how I'd finally got Quicksilver back. Then I told her the rest. "I sold Quicksilver," I said, "to Colonel Charlie. He paid me $3,500."

"*Sold* Quicksilver? Old Walt's *gift?* But—*why?*"

"Couldn't pass up the colonel's offer. Besides, I ain't cut out to be no racehorse man."

"I suppose not. It's true—thirty-five hundred dollars is a great deal of money. I'd say that makes you a wealthy man."

"It would, if I still had it. I sort of *invested* it."

Pandora frowned. Her dark eyes searched my face. "Invested it? In what?"

I didn't meet her gaze. Instead, I took to studying the faded Persian carpet at my feet. "Well," I said, "I guess you could say I put the money into futures— Winslow futures, over in St. Louis. Supposed to be a venture with *vision.*"

Pandora reared back on the settee and looked at me as though she was certain I'd lost my mind.

"Merlin Fanshaw!" she scolded, "After all we went through! You were beat up, jailed three times, nearly killed in a hailstorm, hanged by the neck, and *shot* trying to get Quicksilver back! How *could* you just *sell* that beautiful horse and put the money into some risky scheme?"

I drawed her into my arms again and kissed her puzzled brow. "You know me, darlin'," I said, "easy come, easy go."

About the Author

STAN LYNDE is a fourth-generation native Montanan, born and reared on the range lands of the Crow Indian Reservation in southeastern Montana. He is the creator, author, and artist of two highly acclaimed syndicated cartoon strips, *Rick O'Shay* and *Latigo*, and is the author of *The Bodacious Kid*, *Vigilante Moon*, and *Saving Miss Julie*. Stan is a recipient of the *Inkpot Award* for achievement in the comic arts, and the *Montana Governor's Award for the Arts*.

Center Point Publishing
600 Brooks Road • PO Box 1
Thorndike ME 04986-0001 USA

(207) 568-3717

US & Canada:
1 800 929-9108